Vamps and Vendettas

A SPICY SLOW BURN PARANORMAL ROMANCE

AK NEVERMORE

Copyright © 2026 by AK Nevermore

All rights reserved.

This is a work of fiction. Any resemblance to actual persons, living or dead, business establishments, events or locales, is entirely coincidental. No part of this book may be reproduced in any form or by any electronic or mechanical means, including information storage and retrieval systems, without express written permission from the author.

NO AI TRAINING: Without in any way limiting the author's [and publisher's] exclusive rights under copyright, any use of this publication to "train" generative artificial intelligence (AI) technologies to generate text is expressly prohibited. The author reserves all rights to license uses of this work for generative AI training and development of machine learning language models.

Cover design by BookMojo

Paperback ISBN: 978-1-964466-56-9

Digital ISBN: 978-1-964466-25-5

Dedication

Real life sometimes bleeds into my characters, and there's a certain Scorpio out there Ophelia shares a trait or two with. Keep being a bad bitch, my friend. I can't wait to hear all about it over sushi.

CONTENTS

A Heads Up on Content	ix
Before	1
Chapter 1	13
Chapter 2	25
Chapter 3	39
Chapter 4	48
Chapter 5	60
Chapter 6	70
Chapter 7	79
Chapter 8	88
Chapter 9	96
Chapter 10	110
Chapter 11	122
Chapter 12	135
Chapter 13	150
Chapter 14	162
Chapter 15	173
Chapter 16	184
Chapter 17	195
Chapter 18	206
Chapter 19	219
Chapter 20	228
Chapter 21	238
Chapter 22	248
Chapter 23	259
Chapter 24	269
Chapter 25	280
Chapter 26	288
After	298
Acknowledgments	303
Books by AK Nevermore	307
About the Author	309

This book explores themes which some readers may find uncomfortable and/or offensive to include:

- **Spice -** Open door sex.
- **Violence -** Blood, guts, and nasty rotting things. No lie, it gets pretty gory—oh, and there's bugs.
- **Language -** Some variation of the "F" word is used 149 times and other salty language abounds.
- **Mention of Sexual Assault / Imprisonment / Trafficking -** Nothing is on the page, but the resulting trauma is explored and it's intense.
- **Generally unsavory behavior -** My bad guys / girls aren't good people. They do bad things and aren't sorry, but I promise they get what they deserve.

If any of the above are triggers for you, please put this novel down and back away slowly.

Still here? Awesome. Just remember, it's a fantasy, people. Don't try this stuff at home.

Greenthorn Indoctrination Center, Vampire Tribal Lands

OPHELIA SAT on a hard plastic chair, clenching a mangled pamphlet between her sweaty palms. The silence in the stark, cream and beige waiting room was beyond oppressive. She'd been there since six that morning, and the hour hand on the clock above the frosted glass door had made almost a full circuit.

She riffled her hair. The wait was fucking ridiculous. What the hell was going on back there? All her forms had been completed, every legal requirement satisfied. She'd even taken the intro course to their bullshit religious instruction and been blessed by one of their preoti. This part should've gone faster, especially after her more-than-generous donation to the cause.

Fucking bloodsuckers.

God, she just wanted to burst through that stupid door and get this over with. *Damn it. No. Breathe.* She struggled to bite back her temper. *Be contrite, Phe. Try to channel fucking worthiness.* She snorted. Like that was hard. She was a hell of a lot farther up the food chain than the rest of the losers that'd shown up to volunteer.

Throughout the day, seats filled with indigents and the

dying had slowly emptied to the right and left of her until only herself and two other people were in the room.

One of them was laid out on a hospital gurney. Bags of saline and Lord knew what else hung from an IV stand beside him. The other, a woman and presumably the infirm man's caregiver, slowly flicked through her tablet. By the way she was chewing her lower lip and shifting in her seat, whatever she was reading was juicy.

Ophelia scowled, hooking the long, jagged bangs of her pixie cut behind an ear. What the woman should be doing was reading up on how to properly care for the soon-to-be-corpse's colostomy. Even across the room, the stench of shit was eye-watering.

What a cunty little campfire scout, all prepared for the wait. Ophelia flicked her nails and picked at the black gel tips, begrudgingly admitting that she'd been too confident she'd be one of the first volunteers called and hadn't thought about how to pass the time. Normys looking to join the vampiric tribes and subscribe to their fucked-up religion were usually either vagrants, on death's door, or some special kind of desperate.

Ophelia was a very healthy twenty-nine, a rising star in the litigation world, and fell squarely into the last category.

She was also positive that her soon-to-be-husband would completely lose his shit if he knew she was here, and every second that ticked past increased the probability of him figuring out where she was. Ophelia wiped her sweaty palms against her thighs, all too clearly imagining him bursting through the door, full-on gargoyle.

Her eyes flicked to the clock. These assholes needed to hurry the fuck up.

The bullshit work conference she'd invented wasn't going to hold up to close scrutiny, but it was the best she could do on short notice. The approval for her to join the tribes had come through almost immediately, and she needed that goddamned virus.

She slowly exhaled and flipped open the mangled pamphlet for the umpteenth time, smoothing it over her bespoke, tailored slacks. Glad her phone had died after the first few hours, nixing any temptation to call Deo and come clean about what she was doing.

Fuck around and find out never went over well with him, but that—and his abs—were one of the many reasons she was head over heels for the guy. No one else had ever cared enough to call her on her shit. She chewed a nail, knowing exactly what he would say about all this, but screw him. He wouldn't understand. How could he? He was a supe and she wasn't. This needed to happen. She could feel it in her bones. It was the next step.

She couldn't lose him, couldn't think about him with someone else after the fact, and her mortality guaranteed that was gonna happen.

Yeah, over her undead body.

Her gaze dropped to the pamphlet. Rereading it was stupid. At this point, she could recite it verbatim.

"Vampirism is a sacred gift."

Ophelia didn't quite snort, but damn, that line got her every time. Bit of a stretch there. Though, she had to admit, the tribes had a killer marketing team. She did snort at that, running a hand over her face. God, she'd been here too long, but Vampiric Syndrome wasn't a gift, sacred or otherwise. It was caused by a virus carried by gravers, a rare species of centipede from the eastern continent that fed on dead bodies.

Gotta love nature, right? Gross, but nothing special. Well, unless they chowed down on someone that hadn't quite passed into the hereafter. That was unfortunate, and probably unpleasant if said undead were a supe, but if one had the questionable honor of being born a normy like her?

Hello, vampire.

Ophelia put a hand to her churning stomach. She wasn't particularly looking forward to ingesting one of the fucking things, but if the Victorians could down tapeworms to drop a pound or seventeen, how bad could this be? Granted, tapeworms didn't have twelve rows of razor-sharp teeth, but…

Fucking A. Who was she trying to kid? It was gonna be horrible.

God, stop being such a pussy. To be with Deo forever, she'd chase the fucking thing with a shot of broken glass if that's what it took.

Ophelia blew out her cheeks and slumped, her tailbone throbbing from the hard plastic. It was a serious bummer she'd been inoculated for Vampiric Syndrome as a kid. Before the Purge, all you had to do was bang someone already infected to contract VS.

Which was what had kicked off the Purge, the development of the vaccine, was the reason all corpses were now cremated, and a whole host of other shit.

Including the tribes' need for volunteers to maintain their population.

A shadow moved behind the frosted glass. Ophelia sat up as a brunette vamp with a severe bun and a nurse's uniform straight out of the 1940s pushed through with a clipboard. A name tag at her breast read "Crake," and the tatuaj around her eyes radiated to her temples like a spider's web. The markings looked like a tattoo but weren't. It was how the virus presented itself and was the basis for their fucked-up caste system.

"Ms. Diamondé?

It was about goddamn time. "Here," Ophelia said, raising a finger before she stood. She wiped her palms on her slacks and grabbed her purse.

Nurse Crake tongued her cheek, her unnaturally red lips pressed together. She looked Ophelia up and down before checking off something on her clipboard and gesturing for her to follow.

The hallway beyond was as stark as the waiting room had been. White walls, sanitary molding, doors with stainless steel kickplates. All of those had bars dropped across them, moans and thumps coming from within. One of the long fluorescent bulbs flickered above.

"Birthdate?" the nurse asked, her dark eyes on the clipboard.

Something hit one of the doors as they passed, and Ophelia adjusted her purse higher onto her shoulder. "Uh, November third, 2015."

"And you're here because…?" The nurse flicked through a bunch of papers, and Ophelia caught a flash of her signature at the bottom of one of the many consent forms she'd signed.

She wet her lips. "Vampirism speaks to me," she bullshitted, though it wasn't totally a lie. The part where it extended one's existence indefinitely was absolutely calling her name. The rest of it could fuck off, but if she had to eat a bug then drink blood to make that happen, so be it.

Nurse Crake glanced at her askance like she knew Ophelia was full of shit. Well, at least she wasn't stupid. She stopped at a door and pushed it open, gesturing for Ophelia to go in.

The room beyond looked like every other doctor's office she'd ever been in. Padded, papered table, crappy cream and blue wallpaper, a wheeled, stainless steel table, and a little laminate counter area with a tiny sink and canisters of swabs and cotton balls.

"Remove your clothes and put them and the rest of your belongings in here," Nurse Crake said, handing over a clear plastic drawstring bag with Ophelia's name scrawled on it. "There's a gown on the table, ties in the back. The doctor will be with you shortly."

The door clicked shut behind her, and Ophelia took a deep breath before beginning to undress. Her hands shook as she unbuttoned her slacks and wriggled out of them. *Deo. Think about Deo.* A visual of the mountainous, gruff blond man flashed across her mind's eye. The way his stubble glinted on his square jaw, his intense turquoise eyes…

"It doesn't matter how much time we have together, Phe. We'll make the most of what we have, and I'll love you until the end…"

But it did matter. She flicked a hand across her cheek. The thought of growing old while he stayed eternally young—there wasn't a fucking chance she was going to subject him to mashing up her food and changing her diapers. And he would, damn him. No. This would take all of that off the table. It was the only way they could be together without her fucking mortality hanging over them like a shroud.

She tied the gown and sat on the table, paper crinkling beneath her. Her pulse raced. He was going to be so angry with her, but he'd get over it…right? He always did. And then they could be together forever. With her credentials, whatever tribe she was assigned to would give her a dispensation to work outside the tribal lands.

The mandatory tithe her position at the firm would provide all but guaranteed that. She'd done the research. Save for two she couldn't track down, every volunteer since the Purge with a high-paying career had returned to their normy lives. Tithing was how the tribes were funded, and her salary was three times what the majority of them made.

Then why are you sweating so much?

Fuck. She raked a hand through her hair. Did it matter? Introspection was pointless and not her jam to begin with. For better or worse, this was happening.

A soft knock sounded at the door, and a moment later it was pushed open. A thin, dark-haired vamp in a lab coat came into the room with another, younger male and Nurse Crake behind them. She carried a stainless steel tray. A crimson velvet cloth covered whatever was on it. She set it by the padded table, then busied herself by the counter.

The dark-haired vamp flipped through her chart, pursing his lips, and pushed up his glasses. The tatuaj beneath them were the same webbed design as Nurse Crake's and the other vampire's. Guess there was a tribe of medics.

"Ms. Diamondé," the dark-haired vamp said. "I'm Doctor Wong, and this is my intern, Louis. He'll be observing today, unless you have any objection?"

"Nope." As long as they made her into a vampire, Ophelia didn't care if they did it on stage and sold tickets.

"Wonderful." He smiled, the tips of his pointed incisors gleaming. "I apologize for the wait, but in cases such as yours, we like to give the applicants time to fully consider their commitment to our cause."

Seriously? That'd been some kind of test? Ophelia bit back a snarky retort, the paper drape crinkling beneath her. "Of course." She smiled back, hoping it looked more genuine than it was. "Completely understandable. However, I am fully committed."

The doctor nodded, and Nurse Crake took Ophelia's arm, swabbing it to install a port for an IV. Ophelia winced at the pinch. The woman might not be particularly pleasant, but she was efficient.

"Well, then everything appears to be in order," the doctor said, flipping through pages as the nurse sent a burst of frigid saline through the IV. Louis scanned the chart over the doctor's shoulder, reading along with him and taking notes. "I see you've completed the first course of religious instruction as well. Highly commendable. Are we ready to proceed?" he asked Crake. At her nod, his eyes flicked to Ophelia.

She swallowed roughly, her mouth dry. "Please."

Doctor Wong and Nurse Crake exchanged a glance.

"Then lie back to be secured," the doctor said, reaching for a box of blue gloves on the counter. "The process doesn't take very long, and as soon as we've finished here, you'll be transported to the applicable tribe's sect for recovery. That usually takes two to three days, and your reintroduction will be evaluated based on how well you adapt to reanimation."

Ophelia nodded, fighting a sudden burst of anxiety. The wedding was in a week, and there wasn't a chance in hell she was missing it. *You can do this, Phe.*

She lay back, and Nurse Crake moved to her side, pulling thick leather straps from the sides of the table. She buckled them around Ophelia's torso and forehead, then pulled out others for her arms and wrists.

"For your safety." Crake smiled, her grin much more predatory than the good doctor's and about as legitimate as Ophelia's had been. The nurse filled a hypodermic, then plinked it.

"Ah, what is your preferred orifice?" the doctor asked.

Ophelia started, her gaze fixed on the needle. "What is that?"

"A lethal injection," he murmured, pushing up his glasses and still scanning her chart. "Where would you prefer the vessel to make entry? It's not listed here."

"I-I thought I had to eat it?" Ophelia stammered.

"Any hole will do," the nurse murmured with a smirk, setting the needle aside to transition the end of the table flat and secure Ophelia's legs. A slot opened beneath her rear and Crake yanked up the drape leaving Ophelia's bare ass to dangle.

Her nether regions clenched. She hadn't— "Mouth. Mouth is fine."

The doctor grunted and reverently folded back the crimson cloth. He murmured something and made a solemn gesture before lifting a low jar that'd been nestled on a cushion.

Ophelia's breath sped at the writhing contents, reconsidering all of her life choices. No. She could do this for Deo. For them, for their future.

The doctor shook the jar, sending the churning mass to the bottom before setting it back on the cushion and opening the lid. Decay laced the air. He picked up a pair of long, silver tweezers and plucked out a flailing insect. Its fanged maw gaped as it struggled, twisting and curling up on itself.

"Injection please."

Nurse Crake jammed the needle into the IV's port, and a horrible, searing burn sped up Ophelia's arm. She whimpered at the rush of heat cresting over her, her heart stuttering. Its fluttering beat a mantra: *For Deo, for Deo…for Deo…*

The doctor held the irate centipede above her. "Waiting for pupil dilation…and open."

Her lips refused to cooperate.

The doctor frowned and gripped her jaw—

The centipede fell from his grasp and hit Ophelia's face with a cold, chitinous slap. She recoiled as it flipped, its tiny legs scrabbling to grip her skin. Its length conformed to the contour of her cheek and then skittered sinuously to her nostril. Her arms jerked against her restraints, her head unable to thrash, and a terrible lethargy stealing over her. Heart slowing, her vision grayed, fingers twitching, mind screaming: *get it off, get it off, GET IT OFF!*

It wriggled into her nasal cavity, clawing into her sinuses, and a garbled moan slipped from her lips. Blinding agony seared across her vision, and she screamed, sharp teeth feasting inside her skull. Her eyes watered. No, it was too hot for tears, the scent of copper thick, cloying the back of her throat. Her pores wept, her skin coated with a slick, sticky film, and the air redolent with the scent of blood.

Nurse Crake licked her lips.

An unnatural numbness bloomed from the bridge of Ophelia's nose, radiating from her eye sockets, and the rest of her body seized. Foam flecked her lips, her eyes rolling back into her head. A bright, white light shone down for a moment and was ripped away, along with any sense of peace she'd ever felt. Nothing was left but searing, burning, unrelenting pain.

Emotion dissolved beneath it, thoughts a murky haze, her body unresponsive. She was hollow, her mind a void. Empty.

"Very good. It's taking well. Note the patient has entered rigor. Her sudden pallor coinciding with the sheen of bloodfever and the emergence of the tatuaj around her eyes, there and there…" the doctor said, pointing with his pen, his voice distant and tinny. A godawful cramp went through her body, and a horrific, spattering stench filled the air. "Bowels voided…" He frowned. "Someone didn't fast as instructed."

The urge to laugh burbled up Ophelia's throat, spittle foaming from her mouth. Agony morphed into a bizarre euphoria, her limbs leaden and the feeling of an immense weight crushing down on her. Her heart, still.

Dead.

A wrenching shudder wracked her body as her heart spasmed, once, twice, then sluggishly began to beat again. She strained against the straps pinning her to the table, her chest heaving with the effort.

"Very good," the doctor murmured.

The room came back into focus, sounds sharper than they should be. The flow of ink from the doctor's pen as he wrote. Loose strands of Crake's hair rubbing against one another. The slow scrape of Louis's blink.

"What the fuck?" Ophelia gasped, her tongue thick and her eyes darting, colors far more vivid than they had been. Bright, everything was too damned bright.

"Welcome back, Ms. Diamondé. Disorientation is a normal side effect of transitioning," the doctor said absently, busy making notes. "Rest assured, any increased sensitivities you may be experiencing will lessen over the next thirty-six to forty-eight hours as the virus continues the reanimation process." He stabbed the pen against the clipboard, finished with whatever he was writing, and set it aside with a wide smile. "Now, let's see where we'll be sending you, shall we?"

Crake wheeled over a tray. The doctor snugged his gloves before taking a pair of hemostats from the nurse and dipping a wad of gauze into a yellow solution. He dragged it across Ophelia's brow, then discarded it almost immediately for another, the tiny pad thick with gore.

Ophelia winced at the rough drag of it across her skin. *Jesus Chri—*

Agony flared through her skull, and she cried out. The doctor hummed above her and swapped out the gauze again. "You need to put a call in to Vesper," he murmured.

"Vesper?" the nurse spat out behind him, incredulous. "Are you sure?"

"Mmm" he hummed again, swabbing. "The tatuaj are gifted as the Great One wills, and whom are we to judge which tribe she's been deemed worthy of?"

"But—" Crake pushed forward, her eyes narrowing above pinched lips. "I'll alert the Court." She scowled and left the room. Louis raced after her, his face white.

"What—what's happening?" Ophelia lisped, her tongue fumbling against sharp incisors. A terrible thirst had overcome her, making it hard to think. She licked her parched lips, the acrid taste of her own sweat roiling her stomach. Vesper? She couldn't remember a tribe called Vesper.

"Your transition may have very well just signed the death warrants of everyone who witnessed it," the doctor said, snapping off his gloves. "Prince Kremlyn suffers no rivals for his concubine's attentions."

What? Ophelia's mind raced. No. She couldn't be a—Deo. The wedding. She'd left her engagement ring by the sink. That last fight they'd had. He'd think she abandoned him, that she'd run. "No, no. I-I'm not a concubine, I'm an attorney—"

"You are whatever the tatuaj has decreed," the doctor said

firmly, moving to the door. "Someone will be in to take you to seclusion. Whatever call to vampirism you felt, I very much hope it keeps you warm at the Citadel. You won't be leaving it."

The door shut behind him with an ominous click, and Ophelia's breath stuttered. The Citadel? No, that was impossible. What had she done, what had she done? *Oh, God—*

Agony bloomed through her skull at the word, and she whimpered, tears tracking from the corners of her eyes. The awful reality of her actions crashed down around her, and an insatiable thirst gnawed at her hollowed insides.

The names of the women she couldn't track down—the two who had disappeared—flitted through her mind, along with a very bad feeling that she'd be joining them.

Chapter One

Twelve Years Later

OPHELIA SAT at a conference table in the mayor's office, a pencil to her lips. Across from her, Chase Montgomery rested his forearms on the table. His massive shoulders rounded and his biceps bulged, reminding her far too much of an entirely different man.

Ghandi, she'd fucked that up.

"I've got no idea where Patrick could've disappeared to," Chase said, shaking his head, then reaching up to muss his messy caramel waves from his eyes. "We weren't close."

"Mmm," Ophelia hummed, totally engrossed in her memories, yet well aware of his very pregnant wife, Jena, glaring daggers at her from Chase's side. Back to reality. "What about his friends?"

"Patrick didn't have any friends, and if you keep eye-fucking my husband, I'm staking your trashy vamp ass," Jena growled, the karma at her fingertips sparking purple.

Ophelia smiled at her. "Trashy? Really? Was it the top that put it over the edge?" she asked, running a hand over the low neckline of the bandeau beneath her cropped hoodie. And here, she'd thought it would've been the Daisy Dukes that raised brows. Not that she gave a shit after a decade plus of being swathed in heavy wool robes. She'd be here in pasties and a thong if she thought she could get away with it.

"Oh, no, it's the whole package," Jena growled, a hand on her belly. Chase took the other, kissing her knuckles. He was disgustingly devoted.

"Aww," Ophelia moued. "You always say the sweetest things."

Felix, Havers's current mayor, snorted from the head of the table. "Yes, Jena has a real way with words, but can we stay on topic?" he asked, glancing at his phone. "Liam just pulled in to drop off the urchins. We've got a plane to catch, and we're already cutting it close."

Ophelia rolled her eyes, glad spawn weren't on her bucket list. Aside from the occasional freak mutation, vampires were sterile and thank Ghandi for that. She winced at a door banging on the other side of the building and the pitter-patter of obnoxious little feet speeding closer.

"Last chance to bail," Felix said to Jena and Chase. "In five, four, three—"

The door flew open and a redheaded blur streaked into the room, making a beeline for the closet. "I get to feed him! Uncle Felix said so!" Swan? Swish? Ophelia couldn't remember. It was something stupid.

"You got to feed him last time," an older boy grumbled, slouching in after her with his hands in his pockets. The two eldest girls stopped in the hall behind him, heads together and giggling at their phones.

No, the kid was called Sway, and if memory served, all but one of their names were equally as dumb. Apparently, Felix wasn't to blame for that, but if anyone ever needed evidence that their mother was an unfit parent, hello exhibits A through D.

"So? He doesn't like you," Sway shot back, sticking out her tongue and hauling a bag of kibble over to the ferret cage in the far corner of the office. The previous mayor chittered inside, throwing up a clump of wood shavings as he searched for someplace to hide.

The boy snorted. "Yeah, well, he doesn't like you either."

"Chambers doesn't like anyone," Felix said, pinching the bridge of his nose. "And if you're going to fight about it, I'll feed him."

The two narrowed their eyes at each other and continued to the cage, momentarily at détente.

"Right, so was there anything else before Liam and I take off?" Felix asked, running a pale, freckled hand through his ridiculously red curls and standing as his husband came into the room holding their youngest. Liam was tall, dark, and swoony, if you were into angsty gay men.

Ophelia wasn't. Her eyes drifted back to Chase, not particularly into him either, though big blond alphas used to be her favorite flavor. Well, one big blond in particular, and damn Chase for making her think about Deo every time he entered the fucking room.

Jena glowered at her, and Ophelia batted her lashes, more than happy to take out her frustrations by baiting the curvy little witch.

"Yes, there is something else," Ophelia said, sitting back in her chair and running a hand over her very flat stomach just to fuck with her. The way Jena's eyes narrowed, she got what Ophelia was throwing down. "Have you heard from that bounty hunter? The subpoena for Patrick was issued weeks ago, but it's not gonna do us any good if your guy can't serve it."

"Ryland will get it done," Liam said. The chubby toddler in his arms popped its thumb from its mouth and started to fuss. He set the squirming kid down, and it shambled over to the other brats by the ferret cage with all the speed and grace of a drunk spotting a taco truck at two a.m.

Liam huffed out a breath. "We really appreciate you guys doing this. My parents would've taken them, but with all the shit going on with Kelsey and that emergency Shifter Council meeting—"

"Don't worry about it," Jena said, cutting him off. "You guys deserve an early Valentine's getaway, and the urchins can't possibly be as awful as Aggie's been lately."

"Still?" Felix asked, his brows furrowing.

Jena nodded. "Yeah, and it's really starting to worry me. She never used to be like this. I'm sure she's had another vision, but…" She chewed her lip, then shook her head. "Anyway, it'll be a nice break for all of us."

Chase kissed her knuckles again. "And it'll be good practice," he said, his face alight as he watched Felix's brood.

Ophelia rolled her eyes. Oh, absolutely. It was super important to test out any given torture device before bringing it home. Ghandi, with that level of anticipation, Chase was obviously suffering from some kind of psychosis. Being shackled to all that baggage had to be beyond miserable. It was no wonder Felix and Liam were dumping the lot of them for the week, but to willingly offer yourself up for the interim? Suckers.

Right, enough with the stupid kids. "So, does Ryland have any leads?" Ophelia asked.

"I dunno." Liam shrugged, his hands in his pockets. "But him going dark isn't unusual. Wherever Patrick is, Ryland'll dig him out and haul him in. It's just a matter of time before he pops up."

"Time we don't have," Ophelia muttered, her eyes flicking to the kids at the ferret cage. They were dropping the kibble through the bars piece by piece, and the weasel wasn't impressed.

She shook her head, right there with him. For whatever reason, the witch responsible for transmogrifying the sack of shit was being a pain in the ass about reversing the curse. That was an issue, especially if they couldn't track down Patrick. They needed someone to pin criminal charges on to clear Havers of this lawsuit, and right now, Chambers was it. "How long until we can switch him back?"

"No clue." Jena frowned. "Matilda says the planetary alignment's not right."

"Not that she'll give us the heads up when it is," Felix muttered, pulling on a massive white parka over a paisley jacket that looked more like a carpet sample than couture.

"Well, she better make something work, because if Ryland falls through and I can't get a deposition out of Chambers, this case is lost before I step into that courtroom," Ophelia snapped. And if that happened and Fayet took over the town, her oath to Havers's node would be null and void. Without a covenant with the stupid thing, she'd be back at the Citadel before she could blink. She shivered, rubbing her arms. Ghandi, she'd stake herself before that happened.

"Cold?" Jena asked sweetly. "Maybe you should try wearing actual clothes. You know, something seasonally appropriate for February?"

Ophelia smiled back at her. "Oh, honey. Your concern is warmth enough—"

A hellacious screech came from by the cage and everyone spun at the sound.

The toddler's chubby little arm was through the cage's bars—and the weasel was gone.

"Fuck!" Chase was on his feet, lunging for the office door. He hit it just as the weasel cleared the jamb. The girls on the other side screamed. He ripped it back open and disappeared into the hall.

"Are you fucking kidding me?" Ophelia yelled, wide-eyed and on her feet. The little shit screamed louder. No. Nope. Not happening. The cage's door was still closed. How could it be empty? "Tell me we didn't just lose our only witness."

Jena's face was white. "Chase will get him," she said like she was trying to convince herself.

Liam picked up the screamer, shushing her, his face

equally void of color, and the boy clamped around his leg. The redheaded terror glommed onto Felix, sobbing.

"It was Poe!" she wailed. "She did that thing again, Uncle Felix, I swear it wasn't us!"

"What thing?" Ophelia gritted out through clenched teeth. Fucked. They were fucked.

Felix ran a hand over his face. "It has to do with her powers. We've been calling it 'reaching.'"

"'Reaching?'" Ophelia glowered at him. "Like, through solid fucking matter?"

"Yeah, and that son of a bitch bit her," Liam growled, consoling the whimpering little shit.

Served the kid right. Ophelia scowled, hoping Chambers had taken off a finger, then looked over at voices in the hallway. Chase came back in.

The big were shook his head. "Lorraine was coming back from lunch, and the side door was wide open. I lost him down a sewer grate."

"Well, you better un-lose him," Ophelia spat, pushing away from the table. Her stomach lurched. She wouldn't go back to the Citadel, she wouldn't! "I've got to be in judge's chambers in two hours to meet with the prosecution and go over the case. Which just happens to be entirely built around this being a criminal matter, not civil. There's not a chance in hell I can argue based solely on arcane precedent."

"No." Liam exchanged a pained glance with Felix. "But I can, at least for long enough to find Chambers or Patrick." He frowned, shaking his head. "I'm sorry, baby, Calabro's gonna have to wait."

"Of course it is." Felix's eyelids fluttered, and he sighed into Sway's curls. "Fine, but you owe me so many margaritas after this."

"You're not the only one who needs a drink. Three more months and we're renting out Snaps," Jena grumbled, wincing as she stood and retrieved her messenger bag. "In the meantime, I'll head over to Matilda's and get her to scry for Chambers and Patrick. Maybe this time she'll find something. Can you talk to Sal?" she asked Chase.

He nodded chewing his lip. "Yeah."

Ophelia looked between them, lost. Sal? Wasn't he the troll that owned the grocery store on Main Street? "What the hell does he have to do with any of this?"

"Sal's kind of like the unofficial spokesman for Below Havers," Chase clarified, mussing his hair. "It's where most of the lesser fae in town live."

They made the lesser fae live in the sewer? What the hell was wrong with these people? "Sounds delightful."

"It's not what you think," Felix said, smoothing Sway's curls as she continued to bury her snotty little nose against his neck. "The Below is supposed to put the rest of the town to shame. A century or two ago, an earthquake dropped everything on the north side of town into a chasm. Entire neighborhoods are down there. It's below sea level, and the town abandoned it, declaring it a loss. When they built over it, the lesser fae moved in, bougie-fied it, then evicted all the 'thumps,' still hanging around," he finger quoted.

Ophelia cocked a brow. "'Thumps?'"

"Big people," Jena murmured, chewing a nail. "Weres, witches—supes and normys in general. It was a whole thing."

"And they're really particular about who visits," Chase said. "I don't know anyone who's been down there, which is why there aren't any updated town schematics. I doubt Sal will be able to get us in, but he can put the word out, and maybe if we offered a reward…?"

Felix buzzed his lips, detaching himself from the kid. "Do it. There's still plenty of the dragon's horde to make it worth someone's while, though you'd think the threat of Fayet taking over the town would be incentive enough."

"Oh, I have no doubt they'll agree to catch the prick," Jena said, grabbing her jacket and heading for the door. "But if we want him back in one piece, it's gonna take a more than a sense of civic duty. Unless you can do something useful like turn into a legion of rats and root him out real quick?" She batted her lashes at Ophelia and took Chase's arm.

Ophelia's mood turned blacker. "Wow. Why didn't I think of that?" She pinched across her temples, a migraine imminent. "Oh, I know. Maybe because it doesn't fucking work that way."

At least not for her tribe, and even if it did, you needed to be a vamp for a hell of lot longer than she had before the virus gave you any bennies. Not that rupturing flesh was something she was keen to make a practice of. Didn't matter. She wasn't about to get into that with any of them.

Ophelia rolled her eyes. "Look, you work on finding him, and Liam and I'll work on stalling the case. You ready, champ?" she asked Liam. He was still consoling the little shit that'd gotten them into this mess.

"Yeah. I just need to change." His face was drawn, but he seemed resolute.

Ophelia didn't care. His baggage had put them here, so he damned well better pony up to get them out of it. "Then I'll meet you in the library in an hour, and you," she purred at Chase, taking perverse pleasure in making Jena lose her shit, "I'll meet wherever and whenever you want."

The witch sputtered and Ophelia grinned. She looked him up and down one more time, then sashayed past him and his fuming wife, wondering exactly how long it would take for Jena to snap and make good on that threat to stake her.

Ophelia couldn't wait.

∼

GIDEON STOOD on the rooftop of the apartment he'd leased in Klineville, unimpressed. It was a pathetic excuse for a city; any one of the arrondissements on the continent across the ocean would easily bury its meager population. The complacency that had once charmed him now rankled. He'd been here for too long. No influx of new ideas, few opportunities for meaningful conversation, negligible intellectual stimulation—all of it was sadly stagnant. His knuckles whitened at his side, reminding himself that he hadn't come here for discourse or companionship, though there was plenty of the latter if he'd wanted it.

He didn't, which begged the question why that needy little sidepiece, Monica, was still downstairs. Gideon ran a hand over his face, excuses pinging through his brain. Habit. Expectation. The high he got from ending it. Twisted, yes, but he didn't particularly care, and evicting her from his presence was long overdue. Her belongings had begun to appear beside his own. That wasn't acceptable. She'd grown far too comfortable.

And he felt nothing, his heart long since consumed by another.

Heart. He didn't have a heart. Not anymore. *Stone. I am stone.* He closed his eyes, the frigid wind teasing his tousled blond hair, grounding him in solitude.

The cell phone in his pocket chirped, and he sighed, scratching his stubbled jaw before he glanced at the screen. A bevy of emails had come in since the last time he'd looked, and he was due in chambers in another hour.

Gideon shoved the annoying device into the pocket of his sweats and lumbered across the icy rooftop to the stairway leading down. He reached his door all too soon. His apartment was on the top floor, a conglomeration of glass and steel, so different from the granite and limestone of his beginnings.

The manmade materials grated, but his options were limited. The apartment's one saving grace was that it looked out over the gothic church across the snow-covered green. His jaw tightened as he let himself in. "Saving grace." All the little carved grotesques lining its frosty roofline only served to make him even more homesick.

After this case, he was done. There was nothing here for him.

He'd tried making a life for himself on this new continent, but all that had gone up in flames. His family had been right about him leaving, and he was only prolonging his inevitable return. His place was beside his brethren protecting the node at the center of the City of Light, not finding legal loopholes for the Vampire Court to exploit.

And by the Gods, he was so damned sick of the gray. He longed for black and white. For a purpose.

This case would be the last in a very long line only serving to highlight that. Yes, he'd make enemies by leaving, but that wasn't anything new, and honestly, it was quite satisfying to be hated.

He went over to his desk and flipped through the folio that had been delivered earlier that morning. His phone chirped again, and he tossed it beside the stack of papers, sick and tired of dealing with emails. If it was just Fayet's mayor yapping at him it would've been one thing, but Gideon's leash was held by those with considerably more clout.

And in retaining his services, Fayet's Mayor Jeffries had climbed into bed with the wrong people, though the greedy idiot was too stupid to know it. Gideon got that Fayet and Havers-by-the-Sea had some bizarre feud going on since time immemorable, but no matter how badly Jeffries wanted to sink the neighboring town, garnering aid from the Vampire Court was not the way to do it.

Especially when one took into account how eager they'd been to help.

That should've been the first of many red flags, but the bloated tick only had his eye on the prize: Havers's node. Gideon snorted. But then again, who didn't want the node? The power it represented was immense, and having been left unguarded for so long, the magical wellspring made a tempting prize. He had zero doubt that the court had somehow manipulated events to put the two towns exactly in the situation they were in right now.

Well, not quite.

His gaze lingered on the name of the attorney representing Havers, his finger sweeping over her looping signature. Bold. Reckless. Taking up too much space.

Ophelia.

Gideon's hand tightened to a fist, his knuckles popping. He still didn't believe it and had kept the opposing counsel's name from the Vampire Court until he verified it really was her. It had to be a fluke. How could she completely disappear off the face of the earth for twelve goddamned years only to reappear now?

The fates weren't so cruel. She, however, was another matter entirely. If it really was her, she had to be doing this just to torment him.

Gideon would be damned before he let her. He'd moved on, and the cloud of chaos surrounding Ophelia Diamondé was not a part of that, nor was it going to be. He was going to bury her, along with Havers-by-the-Sea.

"There you are." Hands slid around his torso, long, fuchsia nails trailing from his sternum to his abs. Monica pressed her lips to his shoulder blade, slicking herself to him. "I missed you. Come back to bed?"

"No," he said, pushing her hands away. "I have to be in court, and it's time you leave."

She paused, then stepped away from him, her short, silken robe gaping. Gideon's gaze roamed over her. She was a beautiful little viper. Spawned from old money, tall and lean with sharp cheek bones accentuated by her blunt bob, and a keen intellect.

If he'd met her first, they might've been happy, but as it stood, she, and all the rest of his dalliances, were poor simulacrums of the goddess he'd once worshipped. They were always beautiful, always poisonous, and always wanted more than he could give.

Ophelia hadn't wanted any of it.

"Why should I leave?" Monica asked, coming close again to run her hands over his chest. "It's only an initial status conference. That'll take, what? An hour? Two? We can get a late lunch after. I wanted to try that new Japanese place on Fifth."

"Then go by yourself. I'm not interested. Now, gather up your things, and leave," he deadpanned. His lips twitched as understanding bloomed across her countenance. At the pain and disbelief. At her anger sparking. Gods, that never got old. Something almost stirred in his breast, then died.

"But—" She stared at him for a breath longer before her face contorted. "This is it? Jesus, Gideon, they warned me about you, but I thought after a year… You really are a cold bastard, you know that?"

He hummed, turning away to scroll through his emails. "Don't forget your crêpe pan."

"Go to hell," she spat, storming away.

He glanced at her retreating from. Too late. He was already there.

Chapter Two

OPHELIA STOOD at the bathroom sink of Thaddeus's lair finishing her makeup. It was not an ideal setup. Everything was balanced on or in the stupid console sink, and the lighting sucked. She was positive once she went topside, she was gonna look like a freak.

She tossed her mascara into the basin and frowned. Screw it. As long as her fucking tatuaj were covered, she'd deal. Even out in this armpit of the country, advertising she was part of the Vampire Court didn't strike her as wise. She misted her face with setting spray, then waved a hand, coughing, and huffed out a breath.

Ready or not, here I come.

Yeah. Keep telling yourself that, Phe. After losing that Ghandi-damned weasel, she was light-years away from ready. She pushed through the narrow, paneled door and out into the dimly lit hallway, her day skipping its usual slow slide into crap-itude and diving right into the deep end of shitty.

Ophelia hated Havers-by-the-fucking-Sea.

She huffed a lock of hair from her eyes and headed toward her room, buzzing her lips at all the wasted opportunities making up her current existence. Case in point? Being sprung from prison by the coven and landing in some exiled vampire king's lap had dark romance written all over it. *Excuse me? A shadow daddy?* Um, yes, please.

Except.

The reality of the situation was that even after escaping the Inchisoare, the thought of anyone touching her was enough to induce a panic attack, and Thaddeus…Thaddeus was more like a shadow uncle who kept forgetting to take his meds. Like, yes, super creepy, and definitely intimidating, but half the time there was a geriatric hamster at the controls working with a broken joystick.

And the lair? It wasn't anything special. She'd have thought that after being in this miserable little town for close to five hundred years, Thaddeus would've done something with the crumbling stone building above that served as Havers's library, but nope. Aside from his study on the main level, the rest of the living areas were cobbled from the library's basement, or at least what she'd seen of them were. She had a sneaking suspicion that his chambers were more than the little room crammed with oddities she'd caught a glimpse of past his shoulder.

Stupid men. Ophelia supposed she should be grateful Soku came in twice a week to tidy up, do the laundry, and cheat at Uno. If it wasn't for the brownie, Ophelia probably would've offed herself already, and her unremarked corpse would be rotting beneath Thaddeus's dirty socks and empty ramen noodle packages.

Her stomach growled, reminding her she hadn't eaten today, but she wasn't desperate enough for that. Maybe she'd grab something after the initial court conference. Klineville was supposed to be a decent sized town with more than pizza, Tex-Mex, and a smattering of bars. She'd kill for some decent sushi or a wedge salad right about now—anything that wasn't fried.

The concept of eating was weird since she was technically dead, but Bram Stoker must've been smoking crack, because

Dracula was about as far from the truth as you could get. Being a vampire wasn't much different than being a normy.

Yeah, so, okay. She had to drink blood to make sure the virus keeping her corpse animated didn't run rampant and turn her into a mindless revenant hell-bent on destruction. Sunlight was okay, but hanging out at the beach wasn't advisable unless she wanted third-degree burns, and the whole stake-through-the-heart thing was legit, but the rest of it was bullshit.

Ophelia snorted. If only she was comatose during daylight hours. Maybe then she wouldn't be bored out of her skull in this podunk town. She flicked her nails. At least the salon was on point. The rest of it sucked as much as the lighting in the bathroom.

Whatever. She supposed she should be lucky they'd installed basement plumbing when they tacked on the ugly brick addition to the main building. By all the squealing and scampering, that was currently infested with rugrats. Ophelia scowled, eyeing the rafters at a particularly loud bang. Her tolerance for the little shits was seriously lacking after the weasel debacle. She paused for a breath, weighing the pros and cons of going up there and threatening to eat one of them.

Her gaze flicked to Thaddeus's door. Unfortunately, not intimidating townsfolk had been explicitly mentioned in his list of how she was to comport herself. And, after having pissed off the entire Vampire Court and being thrown in the Inchisoare and subjected to their tender mercies for far longer than she cared to remember, she had zero intention of bucking the system in Havers. She wasn't gonna screw this up like she had everything else.

But Ghandi, it was tempting, and her personality didn't exactly lend itself to compliance.

She frowned again and stepped over the extension cord leading into a tiny, previously unused storage space. A thick rug covered the concrete slab, and Soku had hung blankets over two of the rough stone walls. A janky dresser was pushed against the warped studs of a third, and across from it, a bare twin mattress sat on milk crates. Christmas lights were strung along the rafters.

It wasn't the Ritz, but after the Inchisoare, it was a palace, and she was stupidly grateful for it—not that she was about to say thank you.

Ophelia went over to the rolling rack of clothes and flipped through them. Black suit, black suit, gray suit…and slut wear. She eyed a micro-mini. Probably not the look she was going for, though the thought of being encased in fabric made her skin crawl. Black suit it was. If Fayet's attorney turned out to be as much of a dick as she'd heard, she needed to come out of the gate swinging.

She gritted her teeth and pulled on a pair of sheer black nylons, making sure the seams were straight, then wriggled into a pencil skirt. High-necked, jade green shell, fitted blazer —Ghandi, she missed her closet before everything went to shit—and black, six-inch designer heels. The suit might not be bespoke, but she'd be damned before she slummed it with her footwear.

Well, more damned than she already was.

Ophelia ran a hand through her dark pixie cut, willing herself not to sweat. *You can fucking deal with clothes touching you, Phe. At least it's not a corseted robe.* She took another deep breath and swept up the diamond studs Thaddeus had given her from the top of the dresser.

Okay. Pop these babies in, and all she had left to do was grab her purse and go. Everything for this meeting should've already been delivered to the courthouse. *Now to just show up and do what you do best.*

Which was essentially be a litigious bitch.

Still, her fingers shook as she fastened the studs through her lobes. She hadn't been in a courthouse in over a decade, never mind dealing with the public. Seclusion at the Citadel had messed with her, and her already shitty people skills were seriously out of practice. Here in Havers it was one thing—everyone pretty much left her alone—but this was going to be the first time she'd left the town since the coven's spell had summoned her here.

Ophelia closed her eyes. She could do this. She knew she could. She just needed to channel the Ophelia from before she'd set her life ablaze.

The Ophelia she'd been before Kremlyn.

The vampire prince's name opened a churning pit in her stomach, and bile seared the back of her throat, her clothes abruptly suffocating. She staggered, catching herself against the dresser. What that monster was capable of…if he knew where she was, he'd come for her. He wouldn't let her go. She knew he wouldn't.

A sheen of sweat broke out on her brow, anxiety cresting over her in a wave. She forced herself to breathe through it. No. He had no claim on her as long as she served the node, and for what it was worth, Thaddeus had sworn he'd stay close and watch over her while she was in Klineville—at least while he was lucid, no matter who might come for her.

And they both knew Kremlyn would, any covenants she'd made be damned. It was just a matter of time.

No. She'd stake herself before he touched her again. Well, unless Jena did it first. Fingers crossed there. Though why Thaddeus had so eagerly become her protector…Ghandi, Ophelia didn't care. Having to constantly question everyone's motive, to be on her guard twenty-four seven. She was sick of the mind games and backbiting of Court. Tired of being dissected and manipulated. Exhausted by the struggle just to survive.

And thanks to the virus she'd so gleefully infected herself with, that was never going to end.

Ophelia pinched across her temples. How something so

logical at the time could be so fucking stupid in retrospect... She laughed, blinking away the tears threatening to fuck up her mascara, and a knock sounded at her door.

"Are you ready, child? Mr. Montgomery is here."

Nope, but she was doing this anyway. "I am," she said, smoothing her blazer with a trembling hand and grabbed her purse. She left her room and met Thaddeus and Liam in the hallway.

Her brow rose at the angsty were in a business suit and heavy wool trench, carrying a briefcase at his side. "Well, don't you clean up nice," she snarked, trying to ignore the urge to rip off everything she was wearing.

Liam frowned, running a finger under his collar. "Thanks, I guess. Let's just get this over with." He was obviously nervous, and with good reason.

The commute to Klineville was supposed to take roughly an hour and a half. She could've driven, but until her status with the Vampire Court was settled, Thaddeus insisted on shadow walking her there, which meant Liam was coming along for the ride.

Overprotective? Not in the slightest, and short of nuking the Court, Ophelia didn't see anything ever being settled. Thaddeus, however, seemed confident. That probably should've been concerning, but she didn't have the bandwidth for it, and if he wanted to play taxi, she wasn't gonna complain.

Like about anything to him, ever. To say his person was threatening would be grossly misleading. She'd never been considered short, but Thaddeus was close to seven feet tall. Even stooped in the hallway and with her in heels, she barely came up to his shoulder. He was wrapped in a dark, fur-lined cloak that made her anxiety roil just looking at it, and his fine, snow white hair brushed its collar.

Whatever his tatuaj had originally been, the virus had advanced to the point where they were now indistinguishable, blackening his eye sockets and dripping down his cheeks. Ophelia had never seen anything like them. Not even Vesper's were that muddled, and the vampire queen was *old*. Ophelia had no idea what tribe he'd been part of before coming here and wasn't about to ask. She'd definitely never read about him in the Citadel's hall of records, and she'd read a lot.

But there had been whispers about an ancient, deposed king, and he sure as fuck fit the brief. Including the part about him being crazy. Ophelia hadn't figured out if that was like a fox or certifiable, though she suspected in his case neither was mutually exclusive.

She stepped close to him and Liam, her palms clammy. Thaddaeus threw his cloak around them, and she bit back a scream, panic clawing at her throat. Her stomach lurched as she tried to focus on reality wavering and not the sudden, suffocating press of textiles around her.

Shoes, look at your shoes. There was light. There was air. The concrete hallway beneath her pumps dissolved, and the nasty asphalt of an alley strewn with rock salt formed in its place.

Thaddeus dropped his cloak to his sides, and she slapped a hand over her mouth, her nostrils flaring with breath as she staggered. A hand settled on her lower back, and she jumped.

"Easy," Liam murmured, his eyes full of concern. "Breathe in through your mouth. Flex and release, stomach, fingertips, toes, then breathe out through your nose."

"Don't fucking touch me," she snapped, stepping away. Like she needed his fucking sympathy. Ophelia looked around, avoiding his gaze. Yep. They were in an alley. The one beside the courthouse, if those columns were any indication.

"I'll be near," Thaddeus chuckled, inclining his head at them as he dissolved back into the shadows, his irises much paler than they'd been a moment before.

And if that chuckle was any indication, he was slipping

into batshit mode. Great. Ophelia rubbed her arms, pretty positive he'd need to top off with somebody before then to rectify the situation. Man, shadow walking might be a hell of a lot quicker than the commute, but it was a creepy way to travel. She glanced over at Liam, still staring at her through that stupid fall of hair always in his eyes.

"You ready?" she snapped, pulling out her flask for a quick swig of coagulating courage.

He shrugged. "I was waiting on you."

"Don't." Ophelia pushed past him and marched toward what'd better fucking be the front of the building. The early afternoon sky was overcast, but thankfully, the frozen hell scheduled to descend wasn't due to start until this evening. Fingers crossed she'd be long gone by then with a poke bowl for later.

She hurried up the wide granite steps and through security, collecting the badge waiting for her at reception and signing Liam in. More than one person looked like they were about to come over and say hi to him, but she hadn't perfected her resting bitch face for nothing.

"I take it you've been here before?" she asked him as they got into the elevator and the doors closed on the vaulted, marble lobby.

He pressed the button for the fifth floor, then fiddled with his collar. "Yeah, I interned here beneath Judge Carey."

Ophelia's brow quirked. "Isn't he presiding over this case?"

"He is, but my history's not going to give you an edge, and don't let him lull you into getting too comfortable before we begin. Man is sharp, and he won't let anything slide. Fingers crossed he's too busy trying to figure out what Sperry's trying to pull to focus on us."

"He dirty?" Ophelia hadn't been able to find much on the opposing counsel, aside from his court filings being immaculate. Records had him actively practicing law for a little over a decade, but the quality of his arguments suggested he'd been doing it for far longer.

"No, he's just really fucking good."

Sweat beaded her upper lip. Ghandi help her if he was a vamp. Though, that would explain why she hadn't been able to track down a photo of him. No. Not this close to Havers. Thaddeus had claimed the entire county as his territory, and she was the only other vampire inside its borders.

The elevator's doors slid open, and they exited into the dark-paneled hall. She kept pace with Liam, following him to Judge Carey's chambers. He blew out a breath before he knocked on the heavy oak door, then went in.

They were the first people there, which was exactly how Ophelia liked it. She dropped her purse on a chair facing the door and opened the box waiting for her on the polished mahogany conference table. She rooted around until she found a copy of Havers's response to the lawsuit and tossed it in front of Liam. If he hadn't read it yet, now was the time.

"Trust me, I've been following along." He frowned, pushing it to the side.

"Happy fucking day," she muttered, glad they weren't totally on the back foot.

The door opened, and she glanced up. A rotund balding man in a baby blue sweater vest came in with a large folio and a mousy woman with a laptop. That had to be Judge Carey and the court reporter. She scurried to the end of the table and set herself up.

"Well, I'll be. Liam Montgomery, it is you. I heard the chatter downstairs, but didn't believe it." He rounded the table with a wide grin to shake Liam's hand. "Especially not after that turn of events out west. Nasty business."

Ophelia's brow cocked as she flicked through the case particulars. That certainly sounded like a juicy morsel, and given Liam's abruptly high color, not one he wanted to discuss.

"Ah, yeah. Thankfully, that's all behind me."

The judge hummed sagely. "Good, because if you pull the same stunt here, I'll have you disbarred." He turned to her as Liam blanched. "And you must be Ms. Diamond?"

"Diamondé, Your Honor," she said, pausing before she shook the man's proffered hand. Her mouth went dry at the innocent touch, and she fought the urge to wipe her palm against her skirt.

"Diamondé. How very continental. You've Frankish ancestry?"

"Jewish, actually, but yes, that's the area they settled in," she said, trying to recover her equilibrium.

"Ah. You'll have to forgive me, I'm what my wife calls a 'genealogy geek.' It drives her crazy, but I find it fascinating." He took a seat and set his folio to one side.

"Of course." Ophelia smiled at him, taking a seat as well. *Note to self, play up Jena's hereditary role as the node's guardian.*

"I'll also admit I'm intrigued as to what brought you to our neck of the woods. Hale and Davis isn't a law firm many leave to set out on their own. That must've been quite the pay cut."

"Money isn't everything," she said, praying the trite expression would suffice.

"Indeed, but why did you decide to practice law again? Twelve years is quite a hiatus."

Shit. Thaddeus had done his best to bury her association with the tribes, but she hadn't settled on anything to fill in the gap and regale anyone with some bullshit life story. Ophelia forced a smile. "This case called to me."

Judge Carey grunted like he was open to the possibility, but didn't totally buy it. "I'm sure Liam's given you the inside scoop, but even with him on board, you're not in for an easy time of it. Sperry's one of the best prosecuting attorneys in the county. I'd suggest you bring your A game."

Ophelia forced her smile wider. "That's the only one I play."

He chuckled. "Well, then I'm looking forward to seeing the match up. Ah." He turned as the doorknob rattled. "Time for round one. Here he is."

GIDEON FROWNED down at his phone, the barrage of texts from Monica beyond the pale. He flicked a thumb across the screen, blocking her. If she'd just left when he'd asked her to instead of acting like a child, all of this could've been avoided.

"Mr. Sperry, so nice of you to join us," Judge Carey said, the man's perpetual good mood grating on Gideon more than usual.

He tucked his phone into his pocket with a shake of his head and looked up. "My apologies, I was detained by a personal—"

Phe.

Gideon froze. She sat at the far side of the table. Her makeup was heavier than he remembered, but she was still stunning, exactly the same as the morning she'd walked out on him. And by her sudden pallor, he was the last person she'd expected to see.

So why did it feel like she had the upper hand?

Judge Carey looked between them and cleared his throat.

"Ah, a personal matter. It won't happen again," Gideon recovered, his mind racing with his pulse as she looked away. He unbuttoned his suit jacket and ripped back a chair to sit, running a hand over his face. His jaw tensed, beyond irritated she was still able to affect him like this. The fact that she was sitting next to Liam Montgomery only served to further incense him. Were they together?

Gideon blew out a breath, resisting the urge to fly across the table and throttle the little prick. He was stone, damn it.

"Um, are you all right, Gideon?" Judge Carey asked.

"Of course." He glared at Ophelia, willing her to meet his gaze. She wouldn't. No smirk. No saucy glance from beneath her lashes. What kind of game was she playing?

"All right then. If you're ready, Louise?" Judge Carey asked the mousey woman. At her nod, he continued. "Then let's proceed. This is the case of *Fayet v. Havers-by-the-Sea*, Case Number 2056-CV-8906. I'm Judge Carey, and we're here for the initial status conference. Counsel, please state your names and who you represent."

"Gideon Sperry for the Plaintiff, the town of Fayet, no representative is present."

"Your Honor. Ophelia Diamondé for the Respondent the town of Havers-by-the-Sea, no representative present."

"Liam Montgomery, co-counsel for the Respondent, the town of Havers-by-the-Sea, no representative present."

"Thank you," Judge Carey said, still eyeing Gideon. "Mr. Sperry, if you would, please outline the nature of the case and the relief sought?"

"It would be my pleasure, Your Honor," Gideon said, leaning forward. "My client alleges gross neglect and willful appropriation of magical resources on the part of Havers-by-the-Sea. The Plaintiff is seeking monetary damages totaling eighteen point two million dollars, plus interest and legal fees, dissolution of the township, and to be granted oversight of the node."

"Ms. Diamondé, your response to the allegations?"

She wet her lips, still not looking at him, damn her. Wait, was she trembling?

"Ah, Your Honor," Liam jumped in, "the Defendant denies the allegations, arguing in the alternative that the events impacting the leyline's flow of magic were the result of specific, rogue individuals and should be tried as a criminal case. Additionally, as per arcane law..."

Gideon stared at her, his blood pressure steadily rising with every word that fell from Montgomery's lips. All the emotion he'd thought he'd been past, all the anger, the hurt, it burbled to the surface, threatening to consume him. His skin coarsened, graying and numbing him to it. The physical response was infuriating.

And she just sat there, listening to Liam present their damn case like she didn't have a care in the world. Like nothing that'd happened between them mattered. What a manipulative little strumpet. His fingers twitched, the need to lay his hands on her overwhelming.

"Understood," Judge Carey said, glancing at Gideon again. "Let's discuss discovery, shall we? What's been completed? What remains?"

"An explanation," Gideon growled.

Across the table, Ophelia flinched.

"I'm sorry?" the judge asked, his brows furrowed. "Can you be more specific?"

Shit. Come on, keep it together, Gideon. He cleared his throat. "This criminal case the Defense is alleging. There's no associated testimony with their quote unquote, 'rogue individuals.'"

"That is correct," Ophelia said, her face still turned away.

Gods, he wanted to wring her slender little throat.

"The former mayor," she continued, "Daniel Chambers, is currently in weasel form, and his accomplice, the former town attorney, Patrick Montgomery, has fled. A subpoena has been issued, but has not yet been served."

"And the weasel? Can his, er, condition be reversed?" the judge asked.

"Yes," she said, her voice gaining strength, "but apparently we need to wait for the correct phase of the moon, and the witch responsible for the transformation has been hesitant to attempt it prior to."

"Let me guess, Matilda Hanson?" Judge Carey grunted at Ophelia's slight nod. "Well, that's not surprising after the frog debacle, but I'll need a date. Now, I'm pretty sure I know the answer, but I'll ask the question anyway. What's the potential for settlement?"

"Zero," Gideon said, cutting Carey off before the word had fully left his lips.

The judge sighed and flipped his folio open to a calendar. "Well, given that, I'm inclined to expedite this. Barring the miracle of a settlement being reached sooner through mediation, the parties are to file a joint status report no later than next Wednesday. I'm scheduling a case management conference for the eighteenth of next month to review discovery completion and set a date for the trial. Very good? Very good. This meeting is adjourned. Ah, Mr. Sperry, if you have a moment?" he asked as Gideon stood, popping his knuckles at Ophelia grabbing her purse and skittering from the room. Liam shot him a glance and followed in her wake.

"I get the impression that you two know each other?" Judge Carey asked.

"We did." Or Gideon had thought he'd known her. Whatever she was playing at now, wasn't it.

The judge pursed his lips. "Is it going to affect this case?"

"No," Gideon said, tugging his lapels and re-buttoning his jacket. He'd planned on winning it regardless.

Chapter Three

OPHELIA FORCED herself to walk from the judge's chambers, anxiety tunneling her vision. Deo—no, *Gideon Sperry*. When she'd known the gargoyle, he'd been Deo Spallou, but it was the same man, just so much harder. God—pain shot through her temples at the appellation, and she winced—that was on her. She knew it was all her fault, and now she'd reap the whirlwind.

Liam called out after her, and she ducked into the bathroom, shutting herself into a stall, knock-kneed and shaking as she sat.

Deo was here, and he hated her.

The way his eyes had been turquoise ice… She couldn't look at him. Couldn't deal with the hatred behind them. Not after what he'd meant to her, what they'd meant to each other. Everything she'd gone through, everything that she'd suffered, had been for him. For them.

And now she had nothing. Not even the memory of him to keep her warm.

She lifted her gaze, blinking back tears and smoothed a trembling hand over her cheeks. Not here. She couldn't fall apart here. Couldn't let anyone know how much seeing him had upset her.

An explanation. He wanted an explanation. A sad laugh slipped past her lips. She didn't even know where to begin.

Or rather, she did, and it began and ended with her being a fucking idiot. Somehow, she didn't think that would suffice.

Ghandi, she couldn't lose this case. Couldn't be sent back to the Citadel.

Back to Kremlyn.

Her stomach lurched. He wouldn't kill her. Oh no, it would be much, much worse. The repercussions for inciting dissent had been horrific enough, but to defy him by escaping her punishment? It didn't matter that it'd been the coven's spell that had ripped her from that prison cell. All of his rage would fall on her.

Ophelia took a deep breath, completely dissociating from that possibility, her insides hollow. It wasn't going to happen. He didn't know where she was, and she would win. It didn't matter if Gideon was the opposing counsel. Didn't matter if he hated her. She'd suffered worse. Been punished for her shitty bright ideas. Nothing he could do could hurt her as much as Kremlyn had, or would, if she lost. Not even the hatred in Deo's—no, in *Gideon's* eyes. She wouldn't let it.

She wouldn't lose.

She left the stall and paused to touch up her makeup in the mirror above the sink, scowling as her hands shook. *Stop it.* "You are a bad bitch, Ophelia Diamondé," she murmured, reapplying her lipstick, then wiping it off to do it again. "And bad bitches don't slink home; they go eat fucking sushi." She popped her lips and snapped her purse shut on her way out the door.

Liam was waiting for her, his phone to his ear. She strode past him to the elevator, ignoring his furrowed brow as he ended the call and hurried after her. His hand shot out, stopping the doors from closing, and got in with her.

"You want to tell me what that was about?" he asked, running a hand through his hair.

"Nope."

He snorted, ducking his head as the elevator descended.

"Look, obviously you and Sperry have some kind of history, and it was enough to put you off your game."

"My game was fine, thank you, and my past is none of your business," she said, briskly walking away from him as soon as the elevator doors opened. *Keep it together, Phe.*

"Damn it..." He caught up with her, smart enough to keep his mouth shut as they exited the building. Ophelia turned left, heading away from the courthouse. "Where are you going?"

"I'm hungry," she said, flicking her jagged locks from her eyes. The wind had picked up, the pending storm imminent. "Feel free to wait in the alley for me."

"I'd rather not leave you alone," he said, pulling on a pair of gloves as he kept pace through the sad excuse for a downtown. It might be bigger than Havers, but after living on the West Coast, it was barely a blip on the map.

"Aww, thanks, champ, but I'm a big girl. Pretty sure I can take care of myself." It wasn't like anyone else was going to. She pressed the button for the crosswalk, cursing the steady flow of traffic trapping her there with him.

He jammed his hands into his pockets, his breath spiraling away. "I'm not doubting your competence, but as one headcase to another, I get it. You can pretend I'm not here, but I'm going with you."

Ophelia blinked rapidly, her eyes misting up. "Fuck you."

She crossed the street, hating herself for feeling better at his footsteps echoing hers. Damn it, she didn't need this shit. Didn't need him or anyone else. She pulled her phone, trying to figure out where the hell she was going. Two more blocks, then another left.

Several minutes later, she pushed through the restaurant's double doors. Inside was narrow and dark, with booths separated by rice paper screens and a smattering of tables. A bar was at the far end of the room. Ophelia nodded to the

Asian man behind it, then took a seat at the end, plopping her purse on the seat beside her.

Liam took off his big coat and jacket, then dropped them both over the back. Asshole.

A skinny blonde handed them each a menu, twirling her high ponytail around a finger as she left. Ophelia ran her gaze over the selection, then placed her order with the chef in flawless Japanese. The corners of his eyes crinkled. They went back and forth for a few moments before he dipped his head and got started, yelling her drink order at the back.

"I'll have the same," Liam said to him, putting aside his menu and loosening his tie.

Ophelia shook her head. "Do you have any idea what I just ordered?"

"Nope." He stretched out his arms. "But it sounds like you know what you're talking about. I'm sure it'll be good."

"Suit yourself," she muttered, watching him roll up his sleeves out of the corner of her eye. Felix had certainly hit the jackpot with him, but why Liam was into the scrawny redhead was a fucking mystery. It sure as hell wasn't for his fashion sense.

The blonde came back with two hot sakes and proceeded to drool over Liam. Ophelia's brow rose as the little bitch poured his drink for him and then left without glancing in her direction. Guess someone wasn't interested in a tip.

The bell over the door rang, and an anemic woman in a full-length faux fur and pink business suit came in. She did a double take at Liam, her severe bob whipping around her overly-contoured cheeks.

"Liam? Holy shit, it is you," she said, a broad grin across her face.

He turned reluctantly. "Oh, hey, Monica."

"'Oh, hey, Monica?'" She marched over and put her hands on her slim hips. Ophelia smirked, more than ready for some entertainment at someone else's expense. "Is that all you've got to say after how many years? I heard you moved back to Havers and finally divorced that shrew. You need to tell me everything! Monica Freznoi," said, holding out a hand to Ophelia as an afterthought. "Liam and I interned together."

Whoop-de-fucking-doo. "Ophelia Diamondé. Charmed," she said, lying through her teeth and ignoring the woman's hand.

She held it out for a moment longer before forcing another smile and taking the seat beside Liam, practically in his lap. He scooched his chair closer to Ophelia's purse, obviously uncomfortable with the lack of personal boundaries. Monica didn't seem to notice, or care if she did.

The chef delivered Ophelia's meal, and she thanked him. Liam did the same, the woman nattering in his ear about people and places Ophelia had zero interest in. Monica hadn't been kidding about practicing law the way she was firing off questions, but Liam was better. She got out maybe a handful before her martini was delivered, then he was the one running the interrogation.

Monica was just tickled to fill him in. Ghandi, Ophelia had not missed small talk. She concentrated on her fish, enjoying it despite the shitty conversation beside her. The chef definitely knew what he was doing.

"Am *I* seeing anyone? Hah, funny you should ask." Monica laughed bitterly, flicking her hair from her face and throwing back the majority of her drink. "Not as of three hours ago. Up until then, I had been seeing Gideon. God. I know, I know. He's such a fucking asshole. I hope you two eviscerate him in the courtroom."

"That's the plan," Liam said, smearing wasabi over a roll. He popped it into his mouth and chewed slowly. "I was surprised to see he's still working for Fayet. I would've thought he'd have moved on by now. He's not exactly what I'd call a small town prosecutor."

Monica cocked a brow. "Oh, you have been gone forever.

Yes, he's on Fayet's retainer, but he spends most of his time shilling for the Vampire Court."

Ophelia grabbed her napkin, coughing into it, and Liam shot her a glance. She waved him away, throwing back her sake. It landed in her stomach like a rock. *Gideon was working with the Court?!*

"Oh yeah?" Liam asked.

"Mmm." Monica finished her martini and spun the glass. "Apparently, they recruited him when he was still with some big firm out west and Fayet was part of the deal. Not surprising when you think about it. Damn the man, but he's good, and sure as hell doesn't have any compunctions. He represented the vamp that went on a rampage a couple of months ago up north, and got the monster off on a technicality."

"No shit," Liam murmured. "Didn't close to two dozen people die in that?"

"Yep, and he earned one hell of a bonus." Monica pursed her lips, her gaze flicking to her to-go bag as it was delivered. "I still can't believe he just kicked me out. A *year* of my life wasted. You hear that, honey?" she called over to Ophelia. "Stay far away. You're just his type and fresh meat to boot. If Gideon Sperry so much as smirks at you, run in the other direction. His abs and that chiseled jaw of his aren't worth it, trust me. Guaranteed, the sack of shit'll break your heart, then forget you existed, along with everyone else he's left in his wake."

Oh, Deo… Ophelia set her chopsticks aside, her appetite gone. That wasn't anything like the man she remembered. What the hell had she done?

"Can we get the rest to go?" Liam asked the chef. "I have to get back for the kids."

Ophelia swallowed her scowl, equal parts grateful and irritated at him giving her an out.

"Oh my God, of course. I'm sorry to dump all that on you,

but it's been forever, and I missed you!" Monica wrapped her arms around him, and Ophelia felt him stiffen two seats over. He woodenly patted Monica's shoulder, and she stood, beaming. "I won't keep you any longer. Now that I know you're back, we are so doing this again!"

"Yeah, sure." He raised a hand in farewell and puffed out his cheeks as she minced from the restaurant with her takeout.

"Bet you're sorry you came now, aren't 'cha?" Ophelia asked from behind the rim of her cup, her brow cocked, and trying to play off everything the woman had just word vomited.

Liam shrugged, dipping his napkin in water to scrub at the lipstick on his cheek. "I knew I'd run into people, but yeah, Monica's always been a lot. You okay?"

Ophelia poured the rest of her sake, shaking out the last few drops. "Why wouldn't I be?" And fuck him for asking.

He shook his head. "Just checking in."

"What's that? You're paying the check? Thanks, champ. Grab my bags, too. I'll meet you outside in ten after I powder my nose." She downed her drink and swept up her purse, heading to the little girl's room.

The door clicked shut behind her, and she leaned against it, her emotions running riot. Ophelia closed her eyes, raising a trembling hand to her lips. If Gideon was working for the Court, they'd know exactly where to find her. She wasn't safe here.

Ghandi, she wasn't safe anywhere.

GIDEON RAGED THROUGH HIS APARTMENT, upsetting tables and sending a chair through his eighty-six inch flatscreen. His wings unfurled as he roared his fury, fangs descending, and tail thrashing, his suit in tattered ribbons across the floor.

His mind churned over the past hour in chambers, dissecting it and splaying out for interpretation. Nothing about Ophelia's demeanor sat right. It had been years, yes, but a cheetah couldn't change its spots. Not to that degree. The blasted woman had seemed almost contrite. There was none of the haughty disdain, not even a shadow of the sly brat he'd taken such pleasure in disciplining.

He closed his eyes and stood panting.

Gods, Ophelia.

Gideon raked a hand through his hair. What had happened to her? He couldn't let this go. He needed to see her again. To figure out what game she was playing.

Why she was there.

The way she'd paled when he'd entered the room. She'd had no idea he was involved with the case. But if she hadn't come to turn his life upside down, then why? Why represent Havers-by-the-blighted-Sea?

His phone chirped from the other room, and he ran a granite hand over his face, getting control of himself. Ever so slowly, mottled gray stone became pink flesh, his wings folding against his back and disappearing. He ripped a pair of sweats and a tee from the splintered remains of his dresser and pulled them on.

His phone chirped again. Goddamn it. There was only one person on the planet ballsy enough to be that persistent with him, and she was the last person he wanted to talk to right now.

Unfortunately, his wants counted for very little where the vampire queen was concerned.

He stormed into the living room and tossed aside the ruin of his couch to find the damned device. "Sperry," he growled, answering it.

"You were supposed to report in after the initial status

conference," a velvety female voice purred at him. "Do I need to remind of our extreme interest in this case?"

The small hairs rose on Gideon's nape. It wasn't often that Vesper called, and when she did, it never boded well. "No. I'm well aware, and it went fine. There was a small complication, but I'm handling it." Poorly, but she didn't need to know that.

"A complication?"

He raked a hand over his jaw before settling on a half-truth. "The defense added Liam Montgomery to their team. It sounds like they're going to lean into the arcane aspect of the case. It's nothing I can't handle."

"Mmm. Unsurprising, given his connection to the town. And the lead for the defense?"

Gideon frowned, his gaze drifting to the destruction surrounding him. Their lead? She was pure chaos, and he was being drawn right back into it. "Ophelia Diamondé."

The silence on the other end of the line was so complete, he thought he'd lost the connection.

"Hello?"

A pause. "We'll be in touch."

The line went dead.

What was that about? Gideon jammed the phone into his pocket. It didn't matter. He couldn't stay here, he'd go mad. He kicked through the splintered remains of his coffee table. Christ, he'd already gone mad. He laughed at the rapid thud of his heart, his pulse pounding in his ears, the dam on his emotions well and truly broken for the first time in over a decade.

He breathed in his rage, savoring it as he grabbed his keys.

Ophelia would be on her way back to Havers, and once he cornered her on that squalid little peninsula, there would be nowhere for her to run.

Chapter Four

OPHELIA STARED at the Witchery from the shadows across the street, trembling in the icy drizzle. *Hold it together just a little bit longer, Phe. You can do this.* Hah, she said that, but making it back to the alley to meet Thaddeus with Liam up her ass had about tapped any reserve of bad bitch she had left.

She took a shaky drag of her cigarette and washed it down with a mouthful from her nipper. The unctuous coppery tang of semi-coagulated blood coated her tongue, and she grimaced as it buzzed through her veins. Seeing Gideon and then finding out he was working for the Court had fucked with her hardcore. Everything in her was screaming to run, and if it wasn't for her Ghandi-damned oath to the node, she would've.

Which left her with no option but to talk to Jena.

Ophelia didn't like the little witch, but she was hella powerful and the guardian of the node. If there was anyone on the planet that could help her, it was Jena Seymore.

The Witchery lights were still on, but it was getting late. If Ophelia was going in, she had to do it now before they closed or she totally chickened out. She took one more drag from her cigarette, then flicked it into the gutter, glancing down the street as she hurried across. *There's no one out there; rein it in, Phe.*

But there would be, and time was running out.

An uncomfortable buzz of magic went over her skin at the shop's stoop. The hair on her nape rose, remembering how badly asking for help had burned her before. Damn it, she knew it had, but as much as she didn't want to, she was desperate.

Whether Jena would give it was a different story.

Fuck it. It was this or a stake, and she hadn't survived the Citadel to end it here.

The bell above the door tinged, and Jena looked up from a book splayed over the back counter as Ophelia entered the shop. After standing in the freezing rain for so long, the heat of the room hurt.

A frown immediately darkened the witch's face. "Don't I have to invite you in?" she snapped, cocking her head with her arms crossed over her chest.

Bitch. "Technically, this isn't a private residence, so no," Ophelia said, wandering further into the shop and picking up a heavy crystal. Ghandi, there was all kinds of weird, hippie-dippie-om shit in here.

"Don't touch anything unless you're buying it. I don't have the time to scrape your shitty aura off my merchandise," Jena snapped. "And I thought Felix said he had to invite you into town hall."

"My bad, and yes, but no. I was just trying to keep up the mystique. It's a vampire thing." Ophelia set the crystal back where she'd found it, resisting the urge to trail her fingers over everything else she passed. She wiped her palms on her damp skirt. *Shit. Be nice, Phe.*

"Great, so you're a liar, too," Jena muttered.

"More like conditioned. Any luck finding Chambers?" Ophelia asked, pausing to peruse a bookshelf full of bird skulls and ratty tomes. She couldn't even begin to pronounce half their titles.

"No," Jena answered, suspicion all over her face. "But Sal

put the word out to the Below. Right about now they're supposed to be having a meeting about letting us down there. I'll be shocked if that actually happens, but all Matilda can tell us is that Chambers is underground. She can't get a good read on him with the lesser faes' magic clouding everything up."

"And Patrick?" Ophelia asked, chewing a nail to keep from touching stuff. *See? You can do this.*

"He's on the move, so she can't get a good read on him, either." Jena eyed Ophelia, her expression sour. "What about you? How did that court thing go?"

Shitty. "It went, and we have a whopping week and a half to get all our ducks in a row—well, weasels, I guess." Ophelia shrugged, working her way toward the counter.

Piles of weeds were scattered over the top, and it looked like Jena was braiding them into rough figures. The shop was cuter than Ophelia had expected, in a moldering, antique-y kind of way. It was obvious it'd been a sitting room at one point, and the dark woodwork and arsenic green wallpaper looked old enough to be original. The gas fireplace was newer, but didn't look out of place. It was…nice. Homey, even. She could do without all the incense though. Shit was so thick she could taste it.

Jena narrowed her intense green eyes. "What do you want?"

Ophelia bit back a quip about Chase. Ghandi, that was painful. "I-I need your help."

The curvy little witch just looked at her.

"Ah…I mean, with like a spell or—or something." Ophelia vaguely gestured over her shoulder at the room behind her. Ugh, why was this so frickin' difficult? *Maybe because the last time you asked for help it landed you in the Inchisoare.*

Jena's brow quirked. "Or something."

"Look, this is hard enough, just—" Ophelia closed her eyes and took a deep breath, willing herself not to tear up.

Just tell her what you want. "I need something to ward off vampires."

Jena opened her mouth and then closed it again. "Um... you do realize that—"

"Yes," Ophelia snapped, dashing a hand over her eyes. "I know, I am one, but I mean the rest of them. Fun fact: Fayet's prosecutor works for the Vampire Court, which means it's only a matter of time until they know I'm here, if they don't already, and not for nothing, but Thaddeus is Thaddeus."

The witch's brow furrowed. "You're not going to get any argument out of me that Mr. Brock isn't exactly reliable, but the node's claimed you. As long as you're in Havers—"

"And if I'm not?" Ophelia shot back. "Once this trial starts, I'm screwed, and considering there was a fucking dragon camped out on your doorstep, the node's idea of what constitutes a threat doesn't exactly set my mind at ease."

"Okay, point taken." Jena drummed her fingers on the counter. "But a vamp-b-gone charm's not gonna work without affecting you too. Though maybe..." she stared off into the distance for a long moment. "I might be able to do something, but I wanna know why."

Ophelia's throat bobbed. "Why?"

"Yeah." Jena's eyes were hard. "Why were you in that prison of theirs?"

Fuck. Ophelia blew out her cheeks. "For inciting dissent."

"I'm gonna need more than that. If helping you fucks up my karma—"

Ghandi damn it. "All right, CliffsNotes. Vampires have a caste system. You don't get to pick that, how the tatuaj around your eyes develops determines where you end up. When I volunteered, I figured I'd land in some shit tribe, and they'd spit me back to the outside world to bank my tithe. Instead, I ended up in seclusion at the Citadel as Kremlyn's fuckdoll. I hated it, hate him, and might've started a minor rebellion hoping he'd get staked in the process. He won, I lost, and he's not done making me sorry for it." Her eyes misted up, and she gritted her teeth, looking away. Damn it.

"Oh." Jena blinked at her. "Okay then." Her brow furrowed, and Ophelia sniffled, steeling herself for the next barrage of questions. "You seriously volunteered? Don't they make you eat a bug?"

That's what she was gonna fixate on? Not that Ophelia was complaining, but— An image of that bitch, Crake flashed across her mind's eye. "More like it eats you. It's a centipede and any hole will do," she muttered. "It went up my nose."

Jena slapped a hand over her mouth. "Oh, gross. Is it still there?"

"What? No. They extract it after thirty-six hours along with any eggs it might've laid. Otherwise, it keeps eating, and you turn into a revenant." And wouldn't that have just solved all of her problems?

Jena looked ill. "Good to know."

Ophelia shrugged, dragging a finger under her eye. Ghandi, she was pathetic. "It's not for everybody."

"Clearly." The witch eyed Ophelia with a look she couldn't quite decipher, but it better not be fucking pity. "How long were you there with—at the Citadel?"

"Eleven years, three hundred forty-six days, and nine hours."

Jena winced, offering her a box of tissues. "I am so sorry. I had no idea. That had to have been awful." Oh yeah, that was definitely fucking pity. Ghandi damn it.

"Enough to make me desperate enough to take this job pro-bono," Ophelia snarked, snatching a tissue and dabbing at her eyes like her makeup wasn't already a mess. "Now, do you have something for me, or do we have to braid each other's hair first?"

Jena snorted, then chewed her lip. "I'm pretty sure the best I can do is an ill-intent charm, but it'll be a one-hit wonder. Like, it'll stop a speeding bullet, but you better hope they don't fire twice. Unless…" She cocked her head like she was listening to something.

"Unless?" Ophelia prompted.

"Unless I link it to the node, but like you said, that's got defined boundaries. Once you're out of Havers, it'll be back to one and done."

That was better than anything else she had. "Sold. How much?"

That fucking look crossed Jena's face again, and she shook her head. "No charge."

"What? Fuck you."

The bitch scowled. "Look, I don't want your money, I want you to stop hitting on my husband and being such a miserable cunt."

"How's it feel to want?" Ophelia snorted, then winced at the knee-jerk retort. Damn it. "You know I don't really give a shit about him, right?" she backpedaled.

Jena rolled her eyes. "Oh, please."

"Trust me, after the Citadel, I'm not big on physical contact. He just…reminds me of someone." Or did. After the way Gideon had looked at her that afternoon, the thought of hitting on Chase even to piss Jena off turned Ophelia's stomach. Leaving him alone wasn't going to be a problem. "Whatever. Fine," she muttered. "I'll stop hitting on Chase."

"Thank you, and a free tip? The sin on you is stupid thick. You're a proverbial feather away from the universe doing something to balance your scales and fucking the consequences. I don't recommend adding to the karmic load. If you're stuck here, you might, I dunno, try to be nicer and make some friends?"

Ophelia looked at her blankly. "Are you serious?"

"Yeah, granted, there are a lot of jerks in this town, but we're not all bad, and 'tis the season."

Ophelia looked at her blankly. "What season?"

"Imbolic," Jena huffed. "It's when you examine and

discard the things holding you back. You know, like your shitty attitude? You might actually try being nice to people and see what happens."

"Oh, no," Ophelia laughed. "I don't—peopling isn't one of my things. I meant are you serious about the sin stuff. You can see it?"

Jena pinched the bridge of her nose. "Yeah, kind of, it's—whatever. It's my line's bent. All witches have one, and your karma's filthy, which is why I don't need you fondling my merchandise."

"Huh. Good to know. So, when can you do whatever you're gonna do?"

Jena cocked a brow. "Are you agreeing to my terms?"

Ophelia buzzed her lips. It wasn't like she had any other recourse. "Fine. No hitting on Chase, and I'll try to be less of a bitch."

"Thank you," Jena muttered, walking over to the charms dangling from a velvet-backed display. "Is silver a problem, or is that more of the mystique?"

"Mystique." Jena shot her a look, and Ophelia shrugged. "What? I don't make the rules, I just had to follow them, and FYI, the garlic thing is bullshit, too."

Jena sighed, shaking her head, and chose an elongated oval charm on a fine chain. Runes ran around its edge, but the center was a plain with a slight burnish. She closed her eyes, chanting, and purple sparked at her fingertips, traveling along the necklace and flaring around the pendant.

"Mazel tov," Jena said, handing it over.

Ophelia took it from her. "That's it?"

The witch cocked a brow. "What were you expecting?"

"I have absolutely no idea," Ophelia answered truthfully. Witches weren't anything she'd been exposed to growing up at the group home, so what their magic could and couldn't do was pretty much a mystery. That hadn't changed since she'd gotten VS. Vampires didn't use magic and didn't particularly trust anyone who did.

Which she supposed evened things out, since vampires kept their abilities on the DL, too.

"You should be good as long as you wear it," Jena said, going back behind the counter. "If something triggers it, bring it back. The node should re-prime it once you're in Havers, but if it makes you feel better, I can check."

Ophelia's eyes narrowed as she slipped it around her neck. "What do you mean 'if something triggers it?'"

"It's an ill-intent ward, and you haven't exactly endeared yourself to anyone. Trust me, the way most of the women in town look at you, it'll be activated before you get halfway down the block."

Ophelia frowned, but the witch wasn't wrong. "Thanks," she said, surprising herself with her own sincerity after having parroted the vile word so many times at the Citadel.

"Aww. You're welcome," Jena said all saccharine, batting her lashes. "See? Now, was that so hard?"

Ophelia glowered at her. "You have no idea."

GIDEON CROUCHED over the steering wheel of his long black sedan, gritting his teeth as he passed through the town of Fayet. Gods, he hadn't been back to this blighted hamlet since he'd first accepted their retainer, and as hard as it was to believe, it was even worse than he remembered.

Not that there was much of it, and what there was certainly wasn't anything to write home about. Main Street was ruinously pitted and, aside from a questionable liquor store on the corner, laundromat, and some new age headshop, it was rife with boarded up storefronts. The government complex was all of two buildings, one of which doubled as the local soup kitchen. The icy, rain-slicked streets were empty, and the canted lights lining the way buzzed and flickered intermittently. He swore, swerving into the oncoming lane to avoid a pothole that would've swallowed his front end.

Havers interrupting the leyline running through Fayet had hit the town harder than he'd thought. It was no wonder they were looking to get eighteen million with this lawsuit. Quite frankly, he should've asked for more if they wanted any chance of reviving the dump. At this point, they were probably better off bulldozing it and starting from scratch.

Gideon swept a finger over his lip, sitting back as he merged onto the blessedly well-paved county road leading to Havers. Wondering for the umpteenth time in the past hour how any of this had become his problem. The chain of events after Ophelia had disappeared was murky at best, but some salient points he remembered with crystalline clarity.

The Vampire Court had approached him a scant week after she'd left him at the altar, and he'd signed their proffered contract without thinking twice. Getting away from the West Coast had been a godsend at the time, and the amount they offered him to do so was obscene. He frowned, thinking about his retainer. It'd always niggled why they'd made babysitting Fayet a term of the contract, but not enough for him to stop taking their money.

Especially since he'd only been called to represent the town in a handful of low profile complaints. The Vampire Court's interests had kept him occupied elsewhere, and Fayet had been relegated to an afterthought.

Until now.

He was positive that was entirely due to the node being in play. Gideon ran a hand over his jaw, more than familiar with the magical repositories. The cathedral his family had watched over for centuries was situated over one. He and the rest of his kind, grotesques—gargoyles, on this side of the ocean—had been created for the sole purpose of protecting the arcane hotspots where leylines crossed.

At least, in the old country they had. Over here, covens had assumed the role, supporting one of their members as guardian. From what he could gather, that was passed down through the maternal line, and in Havers, the family charged with the task had almost been snuffed out, then the position abandoned for decades.

It was a situation ripe for exploitation, though he didn't understand all of the implications of the Vampire Court gaining access. Grotesques were born of the node's magic and immune to it in all forms, save the node itself. They couldn't use it, but then again, neither could vampires, which begged the question, why did they want it so badly?

His frown deepened. A better question was, why did he care? Delving into the motives of his employer or the ethics of his cases wasn't something he'd bothered himself with for a very long time, and at this point, to no purpose.

Still, the last of his conversation with Vesper bothered him.

He passed a sign for Havers. Twelve more miles. His knuckles whitened on the steering wheel, almost there, and then he'd finally get closure.

Ophelia.

Gods, why did she have to show up now? Gideon riffled his hair, his jaw set and fully aware how asinine hunting her down like this was. He didn't care. He'd find her if he had to rip the goddamned town apart. He was getting an explanation, damn it.

Gideon shook his head, forcing himself to focus on navigating the narrow, curving road clinging to the cliff face, instead of the unwelcome ache in his chest. The freezing rain had begun to come down harder, and the waves crashing against the cliffs below were ominous.

He rounded a corner, and an odd violet shimmer lit the

horizon. Gideon frowned. That had to be the ward he'd read about. Interesting. If that was real, was the bit about the dragon real as well? The photos splashed over every front page nationwide had to have been sensationalized. An abnormally large wyvern, perhaps. There was no way Havers had been home to a dragon, and that they'd manage to slay the beast was farcical.

Gideon slowed as he approached the opalescent curtain, trying to gauge how far it went up. He should be able to pass through without issue, but if the node beneath the cathedral was any measure, Havers's would test him.

Or rather the spirits residing inside of it would, if there were enough of them to have gained a collective sentience.

Gideon doubted that was the case, the network of nodes and leylines on this side of the ocean was far too young. But, if its guardian was skilled enough, she could direct it to deny him entry. In that eventuality, he supposed he could attempt to fly over it, though he didn't relish leaving his car here. His jaw tightened. Supposition was futile, and it would be what it would be. He kept driving.

As anticipated, the car slowed as it hit the boundary, moving as if through jelly. Gideon gritted his teeth at the tingle of the node's regard lingering upon his person, plucking at him.

That had nothing to do with its guardian.

Good Gods, it was strong. He'd never felt anything like it, not even in the old country. How was that possible? His breath quickened, his skin turning to stone as it slowly let him pass.

A distinct sense of the node's amused anticipation rolled over Gideon, along with its welcome, as if it'd been expecting him.

Sweat beaded across his forehead. That couldn't be good.

He stopped the car on the other side of the ward, his pulse thudding in his ears. He retracted his earlier summation. The node was definitely sentient, and with that amount of power to call on, slaying a dragon was firmly within the realm of possibilities.

Gideon's stomach churned, positive that no matter how persuasive his arguments in the courtroom were, Fayet wasn't getting its hands on Havers or its node. Not without the node's consent. He'd discounted the rumors of the magical repository rejecting other candidates as guardian, but those abruptly tracked.

It clearly had its own agenda, and crossing its will struck him as being exceedingly unwise. Gideon ran a hand over his face and continued on, driving down into the light-speckled valley below, and more than a little discomforted at the firm impression that he had a part to play in whatever was coming.

Chapter Five

OPHELIA HUGGED herself as she walked through the freezing rain, back toward the library. After visiting the Witchery, her anxiety had waned, but hello, pity party, table for one. She kept her head down, trying not to think about what Jena had said. Damn the bitch, but her bullshit words had hit a nerve Ophelia didn't think she had.

… *"Imbolic is all about examining and discard the things holding you back. You know, like your shitty attitude?"*…

Fuck her. Ophelia liked her shitty attitude. Besides, she was pretty sure that whatever phase of the moon or made up high holy hoopla Imbolic was, it boiled down to some witchy excuse to dance around a cauldron naked or whatever it was they did. Stupid witches.

Ophelia's footsteps slowed in front of Fynbender's Jewelry Store. She fondled the charm around her neck as her eyes roamed over window display. They had some decent stuff. Most of it was granny-chic, cameos and scroll-y antique silver, but there were a few nice modern pieces. Her gaze drifted to a set of platinum wedding bands, not so different from the ones she'd picked out a lifetime ago.

She wiped a hand across her cheek and scowled, catching her reflection in the glass. Ghandi, she was pathetic. She looked like a drowned rat, her makeup all but gone. Streaks of mascara bled into the feathering swirls of her tatuaj. They radiated around her eye sockets like a Venetian lace mask, curling down her cheeks and above her temples.

Or they had. Ophelia frowned, flicking her hair in front of her eyes. Stupid marks had gotten a lot darker since she'd been here, and the thinner, spidery lines had thickened, running together. Pretty soon she was going to have to shellac on pancake makeup to cover them.

She turned away, thankful there wasn't anyone out here to see her. The lousy weather had chased people off the streets, and all of Cups's patrons were inside. A thick coating of ice glistened over the little wrought iron tables and chairs in the glow from the streetlights. Inside the café, people laughed. Gossiped. Did all the shit she used to and had zero idea how fucking good they had it.

She sure as hell hadn't.

A gust of wind sent a spray of frigid sleet over her, and she shivered, reveling in the way it pinged against her flesh, numbing it. Wishing it could do the same to her insides. Her relief at escaping the Citadel was slowly being chipped away by the hard truth that there was nothing waiting for her outside of it.

No family. No friends. And—after this case—no purpose.

… *"If you're stuck here, you might, I dunno, try and make some friends?"*…

She stumbled and caught herself against a lamppost. Did she miss having someone to talk to? Yes, but like it was just that easy. First of all, who in their right mind made friends with a vampire, and second, she'd been dumb enough to try that back at the Citadel.

Okay, yeah, that didn't say much about her, but whatever. She'd figured she and the rest of the concubines were in it together, right? Wrong. Each of them was just waiting for the others to show a hint of weakness they could exploit to buy themselves favor. It hadn't taken long for Ophelia to do the same, and she'd been way better at it than the rest of those bitches.

Too good. Which is why they'd banded together to get rid of her instead of Kremlyn when push came to shove. Fucking idiots. Ghandi, she didn't want to think about that.

She stumbled again, her toes totally numb, and laughed. More of that fucking mystique. Vampires could feel cold. In fact, it hurt more now than it had when she'd been alive, but that was the way it should be. She deserved to be punished after all the shit she'd done.

Sin? Yeah, she was lousy with it all right, and redemption wasn't a thing.

Neither was making friends.

Ophelia staggered across the street, not giving a shit if the headlights slowly rolling down Main stopped for her or not. She ducked into one of those stupid bus stop booths to light another cigarette, checking out the long black sedan with dark tinted windows as it passed. Plates were local, not that it meant whoever was driving it was.

She fondled the charm at her breast, wondering if Jena had been bullshitting her about the node protecting her. The car parked across the street from Cups, and whoever was driving it cut the engine. Fuck that shit. Ophelia wasn't hanging around to find out.

GIDEON PULLED into a spot on the side of the road, unable to believe his luck. What were the odds of Ophelia darting out directly in front of his car in this mess? He cut the engine and checked his rearview, but she was already gone. No matter, he had her general direction, and she would've left a trail through the slop coming down.

He got out of his car and hit the sidewalk to avoid the plow coming through. The temperature was steadily dropping, and the freezing rain turning to snow. The drive home would be treacherous, and dallying here any longer than he needed to, unwise.

Though, it was certainly more pleasant than Fayet. He rolled his shoulders, looking around. True, Main Street was touristy, but clean and well lit. It was also very obviously thriving, if the cultivated displays in the shop windows were any indication—though, he hadn't a clue what the "wanted" posters featuring a pair of redacted butt cheeks was about. He shook his head, looking across the street. The café appeared to be doing brisk business despite the inclement weather, and everything was in good repair.

It was no wonder Fayet was so desperate to absorb the municipality. Gideon frowned, seeing that eventuality playing out poorly, node or no node. Given even half a chance, Jeffries would run Havers into the ground as assuredly has he had Fayet. Gideon frowned, returning to his quarry's trail.

Because why did he care again? Oh, right. He didn't.

Ah. As he'd thought, the rambling path of Ophelia's stilettos had left a clear track through the slush coating the sidewalk. Gideon followed them, irked by her less than confident stride. Had she been drinking? He couldn't think of any other reason she'd be out in this storm or darting across the street so carelessly.

Ophelia had been ever a strategist. Every move she made, professionally or personally, was done to elicit an exacting response from her intended target. It was one of the things that had drawn him to her. Her competence and drive, her poise. His footsteps slowed. This…this wasn't like her.

But then, nothing had been since her reemergence.

He scowled, shrugging his heavy coat closer to his ears. He glanced up at the mishmash of her steps dallying before a storefront's window. Mmm. Jewelry. She hadn't been much for it, and Fynbender's wasn't what he'd consider her taste, though it looked like quality. His gaze lingered on a set of wedding bands, and his chest constricted. Was that what she'd been looking at?

Gideon snarled. Or was it what she'd wanted *him* to look at? As irrational as it might seem, he wouldn't put it past her and wasn't about to be led around by the nose. He spun, his long coat furling in his wake as he followed her prints to the street and then picked them up again on the other side.

Here, her steps had become more assured. Purposeful. She was going somewhere—or knew someone was after her. He grinned, hoping it was the latter. *That's it, poppet, I'm right behind you…*

Her trail turned a corner onto a small street lined by quaint residences on one side and a wrought iron fence atop a low stone wall on the other. Tree branches thick with ice hung low, draping over the sidewalk. Beyond stood a gothic stone building, the inset stained glass above its arched doors occluded by thick ropes of hairy ivy. A more modern, brick addition had been tacked to its side, ruining any appeal it might've had.

Gideon's gaze flicked to the sign beside the walkway declaring it the town's library, though the gothic portion was more reminiscent of a chapel. In either event, Ophelia's footprints had eschewed its wide, worn stone steps and taken a smaller path around the edge of the building. His brow furrowed at the scent of tobacco in the wind. What game was she playing?

It didn't matter. He would win.

He clenched his jaw as he continued to follow her trail, amber light leaking from the ice-encrusted windows and spilling onto the narrow path. The scent of tobacco grew stronger. Tree roots and canted pavers slowed his steps. He picked his way across them to a stone-framed opening at ground level, enclosed by a low, latticed fence riddled with ivy. Gideon stood at its perimeter, hidden from whatever lay below.

The gate was open. Steep stairs led downward to a small, darkened courtyard nestled against the foundation of the building and a large, iron-bound door.

Ophelia sat on a bench in the shadows beside it, smoking.

Gideon took a step forward and rested a hand on the open gate, his mouth dry. She leaned forward, her head dangling, forearms upon her knees. For all intents, unaware of him lurking above her.

A lie. She'd lured him to this spot.

Yet... His jaw tensed at her trembling hand, the unwelcome constriction in his chest increasing. She raised the cigarette to her rouged lips, her dripping hair framing the smoldering nub. The cherry flared as she drew upon it, then cast it away, a trail of light streaking through the twilight to die abruptly as it landed in a puddle.

He started forward, and a hand fell on his shoulder.

Gideon spun, behind him the creak of the door opening, and before him a cloaked figure. It loomed above him by a good foot, the top half of the man's face hidden by a drooping hood. Gideon opened his mouth to protest the interruption, and the figure raised a gnarled finger to its bloodless lips.

The door closed behind them, and the figure smiled, his sharp-tipped canines flashing.

Vampire.

"Mr. Sperry, if you'll follow me? We need to talk, and the weather's not conducive to niceties."

Gideon's brow furrowed at the odd invitation. Had the court sent someone out here? The thought of being micromanaged infuriated him. The cloaked figure turned and started away before he could formulate a retort. Gideon took one last look at the door. He had no fear of a single vampire, and Ophelia wasn't going anywhere. Now that he'd tracked her down, it would be easy enough to return.

He followed the cloaked figure to the back of the library and up the steps to the building proper. Gideon filled his lungs as he stepped inside, the air redolent with the vanillin and furfural of moldering tomes. They lined the walls and were stacked throughout the cavernous space, a balcony running the circumference of the room. Heavy tables dotted the floor with volumes spread about their crowded surfaces. His brow rose. It looked more like a madman's private study than a public space.

The vampire wended through the chaos and stopped before a low fire burning in a hearth at the far end of the room. He removed his heavy fur cloak and laid it over the back of a chair, then held out a long-fingered hand, inviting Gideon to sit.

"Welcome to my demesne," the vamp said, his voice heavy with age.

"And you are?" Gideon replied amiably, navigating the jumble to the proffered chair by the fire.

The vampire took the seat across from him, his fine white hair settling to his shoulders in a cloud. His eyes were dark pits within the tatuaj staining his skull. Gideon had never seen their like. Whoever this vampire was, he was ancient enough to make Gideon reassess his lack of fear.

"But a player, as are we all." The vampire smiled and reached over to pour himself a glass of something from a crystal decanter on the table between them. "The town of Havers knows me as Thaddeus Brock. You may call me Thaddeus, and you, Gideon Sperry née Spallou, are not supposed to be here, you naughty boy."

Gideon bristled at his past persona being so carelessly thrown upon the table. As far as him being here, the vampire wasn't mistaken, but… Gideon pursed his lips. "My presence in Havers has nothing to do with the case."

Thaddeus sat back with his glass and crossed his legs. "Doesn't it?"

"It does not."

"Mmm. A personal matter then?"

Gideon blithely stared back at the vampire, and Thaddeus hummed, taking a sip. "The sherry's quite good, if you'd care for some."

Tempting, but— "Thank you, I'm fine."

"Pity. It's so rare I'm able to offer any of my collection to a fellow connoisseur and, as you know, 1942 was an exemplary year." He took another sip, holding it in his mouth before he swallowed.

Gideon's brow rose at the vamp's allusion to his one remaining passion. He'd obviously done his homework and knew entirely too much about him. Best to end this quickly. "Indeed. You said we needed to talk."

"We do. I find your associations problematic." Thaddeus held up a hand at Gideon's snort, his retort cut short as the shadows wavered around him and drew closer. The need for caution tripped up his spine. "Now, pour yourself a glass and allow me to tell you a story, won't you?"

It wasn't a request.

"Very well." Gideon leaned over and filled the waiting tulip-shaped glass, unable to resist holding it aloft to examine the color.

"Like you, I once hailed from the far continent," the vampire said, once Gideon was settled. "My wife and I fled after the first of many purges, seeking someplace where our kind weren't reviled. Not surprisingly, it didn't exist, and with good reason. This virus…changes a person."

Obviously. Gideon grunted, holding the glass to his nose. Almond. Citrus. And the barest hint of toffee. He took a sip. Damn the man, but it was remarkable.

"I'm not just speaking about the reanimation of flesh," Thaddeus clarified. "As the need for fresh blood to sate the virus comes upon us, so do its whispers, and the paler our irises grow, the louder the Great One's voice sounds within our minds. You know this, or should. That last case of yours, the vampire up north that killed two dozen people. You argued that she was schizophrenic."

"I did. What of it?"

"You should've argued that she was possessed. There's a reason vampires can't utter certain *titles* without duress. Believe me when I say, some take far more joy in the creator's absence upon our tongues than others."

Gideon took another sip of his sherry, enjoying it despite the vampire's company. "And it's important for me to know this because…?"

"Because I have worked very hard at keeping this particular hamlet free from Vesper and her deranged cult, and would become quite enraged should some pissant gargoyle ruin that for me. Do you have any idea how long it takes to cultivate a hedge of roses?"

Gideon paused. He didn't, but that hardly seemed relevant. "You're not part of the tribes?"

"No." The vampire shook his head and scowled. "I want nothing to do with any of it or *her*." Gideon had no doubt as to whom the vampire referred to, and his rancor spoke of personal association.

Gideon's brow rose, intrigued despite himself. "You know her, Vesper."

"Once upon a time, I thought I did," Thaddeus muttered, the words too close to the ones Gideon had thought in Judge Carey's chambers. "Have you heard of the 'rakash?'"

Gideon frowned. His last client had used the term, but refused to elucidate. "I have, though I couldn't tell you what it means."

"Mmm. It's the ceremonial practice of depriving oneself of blood and allowing the virus to take over." The vampire leaned in to pour himself another glass. "The lack causes visions, mania. It's said that the Great One speaks, and those who listen bring back his will."

Gideon snorted. "Before or after they murder scores of people whilst 'thinning the herd?'" he asked, his lips pruning with distaste at the vampiric term for the wholesale slaughter of innocents.

"Well, during, of course," the vampire said, either not catching the sarcasm or ignoring it entirely. "A sacrifice is always needed when dealing with dark forces, and the greater the offering, the richer the payout."

"And this…payout…is?" Gideon asked, his gaze roaming over the tomes littering the tables around the room.

"Messages from beyond, my boy," Thaddeus said, resting an ankle over his knee. "Make no mistake, the Great One is very real, and the virus creates a direct pipeline to his realm. Through it, he's been influencing this plane of existence from beyond the veil for centuries."

"As unfortunate as that sounds, what does my case or the Vampire Court gaining access to the node have to do with it?" Gideon asked, leaning forward.

The vampire's eyes glinted in the firelight. "Nothing. The node is only of tangential importance. However, the quality of blood it engenders to the residents of Havers and the effects on those who imbibe of it are a very different story."

Chapter Six

OPHELIA RAISED a toe above the rapidly cooling water of her bath. The blue tinge had faded along with the sensation of burning needles being driven into her flesh. She frowned at their loss, almost missing her daily dose of flagellation and torture. There was something to be said for being punished for your sins, imagined or otherwise. Of course, skin was nice, too.

So was having a soul, but that bird had flown.

The door opened after a perfunctory knock, and Ophelia sank lower into the tepid water as Soku came in. Only the diminutive woman's feet were visible beneath the mound of towels she was carrying, and the top of her neat bun even with the countertop.

"You planning on trying to drown yourself?" The brownie reached up and hefted the fluffy mound onto the corner of the sink, then turned with her arms crossed below her generous breasts.

She looked exactly like one of those girly bleach-blonde dolls Ophelia had made a point of not playing with when she was a kid. Not that she'd ever tell the brownie that. She'd seen Soku deadlift a refrigerator to clean beneath it, and her temperament was uneven at best.

Soku'd been in the middle of vacuuming when Ophelia had returned, and she'd hoped that Soku would be gone when she got out. It wasn't that they didn't get along, she just was way too perceptive, and Ophelia didn't feel like getting into things. Which was the entire reason she was still in the tub. She didn't have the mental capacity to match wits with the brownie after today.

"If only," Ophelia muttered. Unfortunately, she knew for a fact vampires couldn't drown, though it hurt like hell once the reflex to breathe kicked in. Actually, that wasn't a bad way to punish herself, now that she thought about it.

Soku rolled her big blue eyes and jammed up a sleeve. She reached into the tub to pull the stopper, almost going in head first. "Then I suggest you get out before you catch your death a second time."

"Yes, mom," Ophelia grumbled, though they were probably the same age. Well, they would be if Ophelia wasn't technically dead. Ghandi, the way the woman thought she could boss her into things… Whatever. Arguing with her was pointless, and it would only prolong her hanging around. Ophelia stood, and Soku handed her the towel.

"Wow, your day was that shitty, huh?" she asked, raising a meticulously threaded brow and proceeding to climb onto the toilet seat so she could tidy up the sink.

Ophelia scowled at her, drying off and wishing yet again that the brownie wasn't there. "It wasn't great, okay?"

"If it makes you feel any better, mine wasn't all tits and ass either," Soku said, wiping down the backsplash with her ever-present rag. "This weasel thing has got the Below in an uproar. I would've been here earlier, but the meeting they called dragged on for like, four hours."

Oh? Ophelia scrubbed the towel through her hair. "Are they going to let us down there?"

"It was close, but no." The brownie frowned at her in the mirror. "Don't look at me like that. I voted for it, and now half my flat is pissed at me and everyone else who did. I don't see how letting Chambers run around sniffing through everyone's business is any better than you or Jena going in to haul his ass out. No one else can find him, and the last thing we need is that thump tripping over something that puts him back on two legs so he can blab all our secrets. At least you have that attorney-client thing going on, and Jena's, well, Jena."

She leaned over and shook her rag into the garbage. "The pixies are fucking pissed about it, too. The entire Below sounds like it's full of enraged bees, and I've never seen the harems agree on anything. No good's gonna come of any of this. Pixies are nasty little fuckers."

Well, she would know. Ophelia sighed, cringing as she wrapped the towel around herself. Ghandi, she hated how that felt.

The brownie tongued her cheek, not missing the reaction. "But it's not all bad, I managed to get you something from them before all hell broke loose." She jerked her head at the door. "I left it on your bed."

Ophelia raised a brow and crossed the hall. A plain brown bag sat in the middle of the bare mattress. She unrolled the top and reached in, then dumped it out when she didn't feel anything. A hank of…something fell out. It was a weird, opalescent gray. She picked it up, and her brows knit. She could see it, but her fingers didn't register that it was there.

"Go on, shake it out. It's bigger than it looks," the brownie said, following her in. "I had one of the harems make it for you. It's woven gossamer. When they're not high as fuck, they've got a side hustle making clothes for people with sensory issues. There's no seams or anything to rub weird."

It was a tunic. Ophelia held it up to the light, a lump steadily growing in her throat.

"Well, try it on," Soku snapped, rolling her eyes.

Yeah. Easier said than done. Ophelia wet her lips, fighting a wave of anxiety as she slipped it over her head. The sleeves fell to past her wrists and the hem hit mid-thigh.

And she couldn't feel it at all, or the chill in the room.

Soku sniffed, broadcasting "I told you so," and not-so-chalantly flicked her rag at a spider web. "If you like it, I can have them make up some leggings or whatever to go with it. I wanted to make sure you didn't hate it before I went whole hog. The shit's not cheap."

"I... No, I don't hate it," Ophelia sniffled, trying for the same breezy tone and failing miserably. "How much do I owe you?"

Soku rolled her eyes again. "Trust me, not having to see you run around half naked all the time is payment enough. You can spring for anything else, but that's on me. Consider it a late Yule present."

"What? No, I can't—"

"Shut up, you can." The brownie scowled. "It's obvious you struggle with sensory crap, and it's not like I wouldn't have done the same for any of my other friends."

Ophelia ducked her head, running a finger over the fine stitching at the edges of a sleeve with Jena's words ringing in her ears. "Thank you," she rasped. It came out easier that time, damn it.

Soku bustled past her and started wiping down the side of the dresser. "You can thank me by going upstairs and having yourself a pint by the fire. Your irises are paler than I'd like, and Mr. Brock is up there. He said he wanted to talk to you about something. Besides, this room's next on my list, and I'd rather not clean with you here."

Yeah, that hadn't gone well the one and only time Ophelia had tried to stick around. Forget about the pixies, Soku was downright evil when someone stood between her and a dust particle. "You know what he wants?"

"Nope, and I don't care, either," Soku said, giving the mattress behind Ophelia a meaningful look.

Oh yeah, it was time to go. Soku was definitely in cleaning mode. Ophelia grabbed her towel off the bed and returned it to the bathroom on her way past. Her steps slowed as she made her way upstairs to the tiny alcove that served as a kitchen. An outdated fridge was jammed into it beside a rolling cart with a microwave that probably pre-dated tubed television screens.

She grabbed a bag of blood from the fridge and tossed it in the microwave, turning the dial to zap it for fifteen seconds. It powered on with a horrific hum that raised the small hairs on Ophelia's arms. Well, that or the radiation it was throwing off. The nuclear-event-waiting-to-happen dinged, and she poured the pack into a mug, frowning at the ruddy liquid.

Granted, after giving herself frostbite, she needed the boost. The virus would repair any physical damage, but it needed fresh blood to do it, or it would burn through her stores. Get too low on those and hello mindless revenant hell-bent on destruction.

Unfortunately, it wasn't like becoming a vampire had suddenly made blood super delicious. Drinking it was disgusting, but the alternative was worse. Ophelia took a cautious sip, hissing as it burned her tongue, and a weird tingle went through her.

That hadn't started until she'd gotten to Havers, and she had no idea what it meant, but she was pretty sure magic was involved. The same tingle had gone through her crossing the threshold of the Witchery. Maybe that meant a supe was donating. Back at the Citadel, they'd fed exclusively on normys. She didn't think that was all on the vampires. Supes just steered clear of the tribes and vice versa.

With good reason. She wished she had. Ghandi, she was an idiot.

Ophelia took another sip and leaned against the fridge, her eyes on the dark hall leading to Thaddeus's study. She shivered. As cozy as it should've been, given the perpetually roaring hearth and all the books, it wasn't. The place gave her the creeps. She took another sip of blood. Maybe she'd just finish this first. Whatever he had to tell her, she was sure it could wait.

"I DON'T UNDERSTAND," Gideon said, putting down his glass. How was the quality of blood different in Havers?

"No, I can't imagine you would." The vampire pursed his lips. "And I'd be misleading you if I said that I understood all of the particulars. However, the fact remains that when a vampire consumes the blood of one of Havers's residents, it subtly alters the virus, as evidenced by the way it presents itself." He gestured at the weeping dark marks around his eyes.

Gideon sat back in his chair, waiting for the vampire to explain what the hell that meant.

Thaddeus smiled after a long moment. "Suffice to say, my tribal affiliation has been erased. Forgive me if I don't expound further. All you need to know is that this… mutation…is something Vesper would very much like to capitalize on, and it's crucial that she does not."

Gideon frowned, trying to read between the lines. He assumed that whatever the vampire was alluding to equated to Vesper somehow gaining more power.

"Then why hasn't she come here in force?" he asked, playing Devil's advocate. Lord knew she wouldn't hesitate if she thought the risk was worth the reward, federal jurisdiction and anything else be damned.

The vampire clucked his tongue. "Who's to say she hasn't?"

Gideon's eyes flicked back to him, that shiver of caution traveling up his spine again.

Thaddeus laced his fingers over his abdomen. "A very long time ago, we reached a détente. Not that she hasn't seen fit to test it every so often." He smiled, and Gideon repressed a shudder. "This lawsuit is nothing more than an evolution of tactics, and I'm embarrassed to admit that it falls into a rather large loophole in our original agreement."

"May I?" Gideon asked, reaching for the sherry.

"By all means. Delightful, isn't it?"

"Yes, it's exceptional, really." He poured himself another glass and sat back. "But as interesting as this conversation has been, I fail to see why I should care about any of it."

"No. Not yet. But you will." The vampire's eyes glittered as he pulled a folio from beside the chair and tossed it onto the table.

Gideon's brow quirked. "Do you expect me to read that now?"

"Indulge me."

Gideon sighed and leaned forward to pick the folio up. It wasn't particularly thick, but he was tiring of the cloak-and-dagger byplay. He sat back and flipped it open, perusing the pages. Photocopied documents. Emails, surveillance photos.

His fingers tightened at a grainy shot of himself and Ophelia leaving the apartment they'd once shared. "What the hell am I looking at?"

"Mmm." The vampire hummed, holding his glass up to the light. "You know, a great many things have changed for my kind since the Purge, with all of the government regulations. Our numbers are down. Donations falling off beneath the mountain of paperwork required—"

"Forgive me if I don't give a shit," Gideon growled.

"Fair enough," Thaddeus grinned, "but were you aware that all of that oversight has necessitated in the tribes engaging in targeted recruitment campaigns?"

Gideon's gaze fell back to the photo, his stomach roiling. He abruptly had a very bad feeling where this turn in the conversation was going. *Gods, no...*

"The bulk of volunteers are made up of those with limited options. Physical. Financial," the vampire continued.

"However, that's not how the tribes maintain their, ah, lifestyle, for lack of a better term. To do that, they discreetly solicit and groom professionals to join their ranks. Their mandatory tithes fund the tribe's expenses, and/or they fill a need; a friendly ear in government, lenient law enforcement, or say, legal representation. The promise of immortality can be quite tempting to those in high-powered positions. More so when the individual feels they have no other recourse."

Gideon wet his lips, a lump in his throat. "I don't like what you're insinuating."

"Oh, it's not insinuation." The vampire chuckled. "It's a fact. As is that once an individual is marked for indoctrination, they become the target of an elaborate grooming program playing into their fears." Thaddeus picked up his glass, rolling the sherry to examine its legs in the firelight. "I'm very sorry to inform you that Ms. Diamondé fell prey to their tactics."

"That's preposterous, Ophelia would never..." Gideon trailed off, his hand shaking as he turned the page. But wouldn't she? A closeup of her stared back at him. That last argument they'd had... She'd always been so insecure about her mortality.

... *"I can't, Deo! The thought of growing old while you—no. I won't do it!"*...

He ran a hand over his face. Is that where she'd gone? What had happened? That ruse of a conference, her engagement ring left at the side of the sink. He'd been so sure she'd abandoned him.

Dear Gods, what if he'd been wrong?

"Is it?" Thaddeus asked softly. "Despite my imbroglio with Vesper, I have associates at the Citadel. As you can see from Ophelia's recruitment file, they'd been grooming her for quite sometime before she capitulated."

Gideon paled. And he'd left her in their clutches.

No. He threw the folder back onto the table, trying to

convince himself it was impossible. Goddamn it, he couldn't. Whether he trusted Thaddeus or not was irrelevant. As much as he hated to admit it, this was exactly the kind of reckless move Ophelia would've made, and with all of the surveillance photos, the details of their lives, her signature on the volunteer's application, for Christ's sake!

His stomach dropped. Vesper knew. That pause. The line going dead. She knew what Ophelia had meant to him and had known when to strike him—them both—at their weakest to further the Court's machinations.

And recruited or no, they'd both signed on willingly, but why hadn't Ophelia returned? Thaddeus had just said that was how the tribes were funded, and she'd been making money hand over fist as a litigator.

"Then why isn't she prosecuting this case?" he growled. "Why defend Havers?"

"I'm afraid that part of the story isn't mine to tell," Thaddeus said, his gaze intent on something past Gideon's shoulder. "But someone's here who can."

Chapter Seven

OPHELIA STOOD FROZEN in the doorway to Thaddeus's study. From across the room, the vampire's gaze held her trapped, but every ounce of her being was focused on the big man in her peripheral vision, silhouetted by the fire. Her heart pounded against her ribs. No. It couldn't be. Chase. It had to be Chase.

The man stood, and she quailed, her mouth dry as Gideon's massive frame filled the space. He slowly turned toward her. Ophelia's thighs clenched, the urge to piss herself intense. Of course it was him. He'd said he'd wanted an explanation, and Gideon had never been one to take no for an answer.

Behind him, Thaddeus rose. "Talk to him, child. He needs to know." The vampire stepped into the shadows beside the hearth and disappeared, leaving them alone, and Ophelia free to move again.

She bolted.

"Phe!"

No, no, no, no, no…not like this. Gideon couldn't see her like this. She fled down the stairs and into the bathroom, slamming the door behind her and locking it.

"Ophelia!"

Gideon's heavy tread followed her, and a moment later, the door jumped at her back as he hit it. She sprang forward like she'd been burned, her pulse pounding. What should she do, what should she do? Ophelia wrung her hands, pacing, and caught her panicked reflection in the mirror over the sink. She stumbled, and her stomach dropped.

Her tatuaj. Fuck. She lunged for her makeup bag. He couldn't see them. Couldn't know what she'd done.

"Ophelia! Goddamn it, open the door!" It shook in its frame, and the knob rattled. "Ophelia!"

The hell she would. She spun off the cap to her concealer and fumbled with the fucking thing, dropping it at another blow to the door. The little bottle spattered its contents over the sink. She bit back a sob and swept up what she could, slathering it around her eyes.

Wood cracked, and the door flew open. Ophelia screamed, throwing her hands over her head and cowering between the sink and the toilet. She squeezed her eyes shut, retreating into herself.

This wasn't happening. It wasn't. She trembled, trying to steady her jagged breath, her past melding with the now, throwing her back into the Citadel, feeling *him* come closer. The air currents changing. The heat of his body. Sand crunching beneath the soles of his shoes as he stepped inside the little room and crouched before her, a rumble in his chest. She was prey, and he— The scent of sherry and a metallic citrus musk enveloped her.

Her brows furrowed. Wait, that, that wasn't right…

"Phe."

No. It was a trick. She bit her lips, shoulders rounding, curling further in on herself, hiding behind her knees, palms pressed to her eye sockets, and memories muddling. No. A trick. It was a trick. She wasn't there. If she wasn't there, he would go away. Soon. Soon. Everything would be okay soon, because she wasn't—

"Ophelia! Please. Look at me."

His voice—the wrong voice?—was soft, kind. It wouldn't

stay that way. She knew it wouldn't. As soon as she dropped her guard, it would change, and then he'd—no. She shook her head, rocking. She wasn't there. Wasn't there...

Broad fingers brushed over her temple to her ear, softly tracing to her jaw. She flinched from him, bracing herself for the blow.

"Damn it..." His voice cracked. "I'm not going to hurt you, poppet, but I swear to every God, I am going to kill whoever did this to you."

She whimpered, stilling as his hand cupped her cheek. Poppet. Only Gideon called her that. She'd never told... This was Gideon, it wasn't—oh God—pain lanced through her head at the appellation, and she fisted the hair at her temples. Fucked up, she was so fucked up. A sob burst from her lips. She dropped her head to her knees, broken.

"Phe?" He swept her hair aside and raised her face to his with a finger beneath her chin.

Ophelia flinched from his touch, but didn't resist, her eyes downcast.

"Oh, poppet..." he murmured, sweeping a thumb over the marks beneath her eye.

Her breath hitched, face crumpling with another sob. Her lower lip trembled. "D-don't look at me. Please..."

His gaze was the azure of a clear Caribbean Sea. Kind. Understanding. Too understanding. Ghandi, she didn't deserve it.

"Tell me what happened. Who hurt you?"

She shook her head, tears rolling down her cheeks. "Me. I did. It was my fault," she whispered raggedly, wishing he would just go away, yet desperately needing him to stay.

"No." A growl rumbled through his chest, and she cowered back. He scrubbed a hand over his face. "No. I don't believe that. Not with what Thaddeus just showed me, and every last one of them will pay for what they've done."

Her stomach clenched, hearing the promise for what it was.

Suicide.

Gideon reached up and wet a cloth in the sink, pausing as he brought it close. "May I?" She didn't answer, and he frowned, then gently began to wash her face.

Her head fell back, retreating into herself again, nausea roiling with every sweep of the cloth exposing the monster she'd become. Tears tracked from the corners of her eyes, but what was the point of fighting? Somehow, he already knew. Let him see the entirety of her shame.

At least he didn't have to live with it.

GIDEON SWABBED the makeup from Ophelia's too-pale skin, banking his rage. This wasn't the time for it. She needed him, and his vengeance would wait. The opportunity would come, and when it did, he would wipe every last one of those bloodsuckers from the face of the earth.

Gods, Ophelia. What's happened to you?

Her silence just reinforced what he'd learned tonight. Those pieces fit far too neatly with that last fight they'd had. Damn him for being too stubborn to hear her. He'd brushed her fears aside as pre-wedding jitters. A product of her youth. If he'd just listened, had just taken them more seriously...

"Chase Montgomery! What the hell do you think you're doing? I just cleaned—"

Gideon's attention snapped to the tiny, irate woman standing in the doorway, and she gasped, her back hitting the cracked doorframe. Her hands rose, clutching a cloth to her breast, and her eyes wide in her pretty, china-doll face.

"You're not—Jesus. Who the fuck are you?" she swore.

"I—"

The woman's gaze snapped to Ophelia's crumpled frame,

her features reddening and growing darker. "What the hell did you do to her?" Her mass increased, bulking up and morphing into something decidedly threatening.

"Nothing."

"Try again, asshole," she growled. "And you better step away from her while you do."

Damn it. Whoever this woman was, she was a brownie and about to go full boggart. He wasn't worried about himself, but the damage those creatures could cause wasn't something he needed Ophelia in the midst of. Especially not in her current state.

Gideon slowly stood, putting himself between her and Ophelia. He held out a hand in supplication. "My name is Gideon Sperry, and the last thing I want to do is hurt Ophelia. She's my fiancée." At least, she had been, and come hell or high water, he'd make this right and her his again.

The brownie's eyes narrowed. "She's never said anything about a fiancé."

"No." Gideon frowned, not surprised. Even before she'd disappeared, Ophelia rarely offered insight into her past. "I can't imagine she would've, but I can assure you, I mean her no harm."

The brownie glanced at the damage to the door and snorted. "Is that a fact?"

Gideon's cheeks grew warm. "She may've had an adverse reaction to discovering my presence in Thaddeus's study."

Her shoulders relaxed a fraction. "*You* were what he wanted to talk to her about?"

"I...believe so?" It had certainly seemed like a setup the way the vampire had left them. Gideon retracted his proffered hand and ran it through his tangled hair with a sigh. "Is there someplace more appropriate I can take her to rest whilst we finish this conversation?"

"I don't know if that's best." The little woman chewed her lip, her aggression fading to suspicion. "She doesn't like to be touched, and when she's like this…" she shook her head, her face clouded with worry. "It's not a good idea."

Gideon's rage flared anew at what Ophelia must've gone through to make it so. He pushed the emotion aside for later. There wasn't any point in berating himself about it now. She'd already taken the brunt of both their poor choices, and Vesper and her ilk would pay for preying on her fears.

"I'm not leaving her here to languish against the commode," he growled.

The brownie sniffed, not intimidated in the slightest. "If it makes you feel any better, I just cleaned it."

Gideon scowled. "It does not."

She stared at him for a long moment. "Fine, but if you make her worse, that's on you. Follow me," she muttered as she passed through the broken doorway and stood in the hall, her arms crossed over her chest, glaring at him.

Gideon crouched before Ophelia again, the woman's gaze hot on his back as he tossed the cloth he'd been clutching into the sink. He reached out and cupped Ophelia's cheek, his thumb sweeping over the edge of the delicate lacework around her eyes. It reminded him of the masked fêtes of his youth. As much as he hated what the dark markings meant, they were fetching.

The emptiness of her eyes was not. His jaw tightened. "Come, poppet," he murmured, as if coaxing a wild thing. "Let's get you out of here." Gideon swallowed his scowl at her lack of response, then leaned forward and pulled her lax form into his arms. She whimpered as he held her against him, and a fist constricted around his heart.

Gods, had she always been this slight? He stood, her head lolling against his chest, and shouldered out of the bathroom, past the broken door to follow the brownie down the hall.

She led him to a closed door and pointedly looked at him. "See? This is how they're supposed to work." She turned the knob and it swung open. "And if it doesn't do that, it generally means you should stay the fuck out."

"I'm aware," he retorted dryly.

"Huh." She cocked her head and stepped to the side so he could enter. "And here I was, thinking that what you did to the one in pieces suggested otherwise."

Gideon glowered at her. "Listen, Tinkerbell, as much as I'm enjoying your wit, now's not the time for it." He pushed past her into the little room, his brows furrowing at the bare mattress and stark environ. "This is where she's staying?" he asked, the question rendered rhetorical by the precise line of designer shoes beneath a rolling clothes rack.

The brownie's gazed narrowed at him again, that menacing bulk returning to her form. "The name's Soku, and you got a problem with the accommodations?"

"Yes," he gritted out, glowering at the poor excuse for a bed. Where were the mounds of fluffy duvets and blankets? A pillow, for Christ's sake.

"Look," she spat, her hands on her hips. "I don't know what your *fiancée* was like before she got here, but all this is her choice. She turned down the room at the bed and breakfast, and I tried bringing her blankets, but they sat in a pile on the floor." Soku scowled and shook her head at his look of incredulity.

"I told you, she doesn't like anything touching her, and she doesn't people. Not well, at least. She has some serious sensory issues. Fabric, blankets, clothes, anything against her skin freaks her out. After the coven summoned her from whatever hole she'd been left to rot in, she slept on the concrete floor without a stitch on for weeks. That," she nodded at the mattress, "is a vast improvement."

Gideon closed his eyes, his Adam's apple bobbing. He held Ophelia closer, his nose in her hair. *Gods, Phe, what did I leave you to suffer?*

It was immaterial. He was here now. Still, guilt churned in

his stomach. He had to make this right. "Thank you. I'll take it from here," he said, forcing the words past the growing lump of self-recrimination in his throat.

The brownie put her hands on her curvaceous hips. "And exactly what do you think you'll be taking?"

"Care of her. If she finds comfort in stone, I'm more than able to accommodate." His skin grayed, coarsening, and Ophelia murmured softly against him, her arm rising to tighten around his neck.

Soku's eyes widened at the movement. "Gargoyle," she hissed.

"And do you have a problem with *that*?"

"Not yet, but there's still time," she huffed, attempting to compose herself, but by the tremor in her hands, obviously still shaken. Understandably so. His kind were an anomaly on this side of the ocean, and their reputation for violence well deserved.

"Fine," she said after a tense moment. "But don't think I won't be watching, and you owe me a door, Quasimodo."

He inclined his head, not about to get into the inaccuracies of her intended insult. His hadn't been particularly veracious either. "I do, and my apologies for the inconvenience."

"Call me Tinkerbell again or fuck her up any more than she already is, and you're gonna find yourself with a hell of a lot more 'inconvenience' to deal with than that." The little woman sniffed again and left the room with once last glower.

He was oddly comforted by the brownie's words. At least Ophelia had one staunch ally, and brownies weren't to be trifled with. Gideon blew out a slow breath and set Ophelia on the mattress. She curled into a ball, her back to him. He sighed and closed the door. Watching the subtle rise and fall of her shoulders and thinking about what Soku had said. He slowly began to remove his coat and t-shirt, his great stone wings shimmering into existence.

If Ophelia took succor in stone, he would give it to her.

He climbed onto the narrow bed and nestled her against his chest, one wing beneath her and draping the other over them both, cocooning her against him. The heat from his body —his rage—quickly warmed the space. Minutes ticked by, and she incrementally relaxed, leaving whatever manic state she'd been in and falling into a true sleep.

Gideon was not as fortunate, his mind churning with all he'd learned. All he still had left to discover. Plans of vengeance. This goddamned case.

Somewhere, a clock struck one, then two, and three. His eyes grew heavy, his mind still racing, nothing and everything settled.

He would make this up to her. Ophelia was his, and the Court would pay. The only question was where and when they would bleed out beneath his hands.

Chapter Eight

OPHELIA WOKE with a solid weight across her waist, pinning her down. Only habit keeping her from reacting. She didn't move, her breath even and her eyes shut. Her thoughts swirled. The last thing she clearly remembered was Gideon cornering her in the bathroom, seeing her for what she'd become. Bile rose to her throat and she ignored it, her thoughts far away from the acidic burn.

What'd happened after?

Instead of the expected chill of tile, she was deliciously warm. The air had the close stillness of an enclosed space. Her heart rate ticked up, thinking of the sarcophagi in the Citadel's catacombs, except those were frigid. *Ugh. Stop it and think, Phe.* She forced herself to remain calm and take in the small sensory details around her. The almost imperceptible rub of stone beneath and behind her. Its gentle rise and fall at her back. The subtle scent of citrus.

Ophelia's eyes flew open. Gideon.

Her gaze fixed on his lax hand dangling off the edge of the mattress, her head pillowed upon his stoney bicep. His other arm accounted for the weight across her waist, and the gargoyle's wing draped over her, explaining the stillness and heat.

Yeah, that didn't do anything to calm her anxiety. Her breath hitched. Why was he here? Why had he stayed?

He stirred, pulling her closer to him, the rasp of his granite fingers over her body a strange comfort that just unsettled her more. "You're awake," he said, groggy with sleep.

She chewed her lip, praying he couldn't feel the rapid beat of her heart. Shit. This was it. She was going to have to explain. "Y-you're still here," she whispered.

"I am. I couldn't leave you like—like that."

The silence thickened around them, heavy with everything said and unsaid, and all that was still waiting to be spoken.

Finally, "Thaddeus showed me a file from the Citadel last night," he continued. She stiffened, and Gideon hushed her. "I know you joined the tribes, and I think I understand why. I'm so sorry, Phe."

The regret in his voice broke her anew, and she swallowed a sob. His arms tightened around her. So solid. So unshakable. How could she have ever let her stupid ego get between them?

It didn't matter. It had, and there was no coming back from it.

"I should've taken your fears more seriously," he went on. "If I'd known, I would've burned their filthy enclave to the ground before I let you remain inside of it…but, what's done is done. I'm not upset at you, Phe. I just…I need to know. Why didn't you come back?"

Ghandi, he sounded wrecked over all of it, and telling him wasn't going to do anything to make that better. But she also knew damned well he wasn't going to let it go. Fuck it. Maybe it was better this way. Once he knew, he'd leave, and that would be that. Ophelia sniffled, trying to find the words. He could hate her. Ghandi, he *would* hate her, but— No. She didn't care.

Keep telling yourself that, Phe.

"I couldn't. My tatuaj…" She closed her eyes, fighting the anxious nausea rising to drown her. "They mark me as

Damă." Her mouth curdled as she rasped out the word, hating everything about the fucked up tribe the stupid marks around her eyes had assigned her to.

Gideon frowned against the crown of her head, lacing his fingers with hers. Ophelia's eyes misted up again at the simple gesture of intimacy. How long had it been since someone had touched her like that? Him, it'd been him, that last night before everything went to hell. Ghandi, she missed it but… She bit back a whimper. It wasn't going to last.

"I don't understand," he rumbled.

Ophelia was silent, not wanting him to.

"Phe, please. Tell me."

She blinked away the tears weighing down her lashes. "They took me to the Citadel right after my reanimation. I wasn't allowed to leave. None of the Damă were."

"That word. What does it mean?"

"I-it's my tribe," she gritted out bitterly, her insides heavy with dread. "I-it loosely translates to wife, but it's— When I was first put into seclusion, there were only a handful of us. Five. Six. S-seclusion isn't—" She broke off, trying to calm herself and not think about that awful place and failing miserably.

Gideon was silent, presumably waiting for her to go on. Then, when it was clear she wasn't going to: "Wife?"

A sob burst past her lips, and she cursed herself. What the fuck was the point in dragging this out? He wasn't going to leave it alone until he knew all the dirty details. She ripped her fingers from his and dashed a hand across her eyes, pushing up from the bed. "More like unwitting whore."

Gideon rolled onto his back, the initial shock on his face morphing into lividity. "They prosti—trafficked you?" he amended, his nostrils flaring.

Yeah, to a clientele of one and a dozen of his closest friends. Ophelia laughed, throwing up her hands. "Sure. If that's what you wanna call it."

He sat up and caught her wrist as she paced, pulling her between his granite thighs. "I wish I didn't have to call it anything. Ophelia, if I'd known—"

He'd already be dead.

"It doesn't matter." She stared at the door, the wall, anywhere but at him.

He reached up to tip her face to his. "It does, and none of it's your fault. The tribes recruited you. Thaddeus showed me the evidence last night."

She froze, her gaze flicking to his. "Evidence?"

He exhaled heavily and ran a hand over his stubbled jaw. "The file from the Citadel I mentioned. It has surveillance photos of us at the old apartment. They were stalking you, Phe. Intentionally grooming you to volunteer."

She put a hand to her throat. "No, that's…" Entirely possible. Her shoulders slumped, and she swallowed hard. Ghandi, how pathetic was she to fall for something like that? She'd willingly signed up for a fucking cult. Her knees gave out, and Gideon pulled her onto his lap, her skin crawling at the rub of his sweatpants beneath her thighs.

He brushed her hair from her face. "Thaddeus thinks their interest had to do with your position and your potential tithe. They wanted you to litigate for them, but given what you've said, I think I understand why they ended up recruiting me after the fact. Their offer came through a week after you disappeared. I can't believe that's unrelated."

"During the initial interview, they were really interested in my record," she admitted, chewing a nail. "That's why I thought—" She shook her head. It didn't matter what she'd thought. It hadn't happened. "Everyone was shocked as shit when this appeared," she murmured hollowly, vaguely gesturing at her tatuaj.

His brow furrowed, and she sighed.

"Historically, Damă aren't common. Like, one-in-thousands not common…and w-we aren't treated well." She looked away at the admission, and he tipped her face back toward his with a finger.

"I have to believe the universe brought you back to me for a reason, and I plan on rectifying that. You're mine, poppet, and I'm never letting you out of my sight again."

∼

GIDEON BREATHED through his rage as Ophelia slumped against him. That she'd been abused in such a way, it was little wonder she couldn't bear to be touched. He fingered the odd garment covering her slight form, wondering if he had the brownie to thank for that. His esteem for the little woman grew. It was gossamer, if he wasn't mistaken, and cost a pretty penny.

The price didn't matter. If that's what Ophelia needed, he'd beggar himself to swath her in it. The thought of using the small fortune he'd accrued working for the tribes to help mitigate the trauma they'd caused her was far more satisfying than purchasing another villa he'd never visit.

His temper rose at his increasing certainty of the trap they'd both fallen into. Gods, Vesper had to have known he was desperate to find Phe and had never said a word. The police, all those private detectives he'd hired—how many of them had been on the Vampire Court's payroll?

"I looked for you. For years."

A small smile ghosted across her lips. "I never doubted you would, if only to wring my neck."

"My prior motive was based on false information, and is no longer relevant," he said with a small smile of his own at her eye roll. "What is, is that I have you back now."

She froze, the pulse at her throat quickening. "Gideon, I'm not the person you remember. I can't ask you to—"

He grasped her hand and held it to his heart, desperate to make her understand. "You're not asking, I'm offering. Yes, things change, even stone, but this, this has ever beaten for you. A gargoyle's heart— You're mine, unless you don't want this, and even then, I don't think I could let you go. Not again, and not knowing what I do."

Her brow furrowed and her gaze dropped to her lap, tears falling to stain her tunic. "I—but you don't know everything," she whispered hoarsely.

He pulled her close and kissed the top of her head, frowning at her slight recoil. Damn it, all he wanted to do was touch her. No. He could wait. However long it took. After all, they had an eternity to make this work.

If she wanted it to.

Gideon sighed. "I know enough. What's important. You never left; you were stolen from me. Tell me you want this. Another chance at us?"

She was silent long enough for him to begin to sweat. "I-I do, but I don't think I can be what you want anymore." The smallness of her voice stoked his temper. Damn it, this wasn't her.

"I'd say given your track record of deciding what's best for us, how about you let me be the judge of that?" he asked, far too tempted to put his fist through something.

Annoyance flashed across her countenance at the jab, and he fought a grin. There she was.

"What about the case?" she snapped back, moving away from him, her posture straightening.

He fought the urge to chuckle. Oh, how easily they fell back into their old routine. Gideon was painfully aware of his hot temperament, but Ophelia had ever been his match. If he had to antagonize her into remembering who she was, he'd do so with aplomb.

"Mmm. Yes. The case." He pursed his lips, and a grin sliced across his face at her narrowed eyes. "Leave that to me. There's several…inconsistencies…I've willfully overlooked. Perhaps it's time to explore them."

Ophelia nodded, the glimmer of the goddess she'd been fading. Damn it. She looked at the floor like she wanted it to swallow her.

His wet his lips at her tell. "What else, Ophelia?"

She shook her head, then sighed. "The coven. When they summoned me here, I-I was in the Inchisoare."

Gideon's guts churned. Dear Gods, they'd thrown her into that hellhole? "For?"

She chewed her lip and shrugged. "Inciting dissent."

"Against?" he prompted, feeling like he was deposing a reluctant witness.

"Kremlyn," she said in a very small voice.

"Kremlyn," he repeated, her flinch at the name telling him everything he needed to know. His knuckles popped as he tightened a fist. "He'll come for you."

Her gaze shot to his. "How do you—"

"I've met the prince. Numerous times." And all the while that pompous son of a bitch had to have known Gideon was looking for Ophelia whilst he'd had her at his mercy. A muscle in Gideon's jaw ticked, not fond of being the butt of anyone's joke. "And I'm quite looking forward to seeing him again."

He was going to eviscerate the bastard.

"Gideon, you don't understand," Ophelia said, wrought. "K-Kremlyn's not what's important right now. I mean, he is, but when the coven summoned me, I pledged myself to the node. Jena says it will protect me, but I have to win this case. If I don't, my covenant with it is broken, and the tribes can take me back."

He stared at her in shock. "You pledged your service to the node?"

She nodded, sending his mind racing. If that was true, then it would indeed protect her, as long as she stayed within its bounds. But outside of it…

Its welcome abruptly made sense, and damn every last

one of those blighted spirits to hell for trapping him as neatly as the Vampire Court. He shook his head. It didn't matter. Ophelia's safety was paramount. "Then until this is settled, you're not leaving Havers unless I'm by your side."

Ophelia scowled, and his heart leapt to see a glimmer of her fire. "And how will that look, the defense shacking up with the prosecution? I'm not even sure he knows where I am."

"Oh, he knows," Gideon muttered, the ringing silence of the line going dead echoing through his mind. "Earlier, I had to disclose who the opposing council was."

Her face ghosted white.

"But I vow to you now, Ophelia, they'll not have you," he said, grasping her shoulders.

Her gaze searched his. "You really believe that, don't you?"

"I do. I failed you once, and I won't fail you again." He leaned forward to kiss her forehead, and this time, she softened against him. Gideon smiled at the increment of progress. She would come around, he just needed to be patient. "Now, we've work to do. Hand me my shirt? I think we both need to speak to Thaddeus."

Chapter Nine

OPHELIA SHIVERED, her hand brushing against Gideon's as they stepped into Thaddeus's study. The gargoyle had reabsorbed his wings, but his skin remained reminiscent of stone. She reached out, running a finger over its rough texture. It was so weird how that didn't set her off like everything else did. He smiled down at her like he knew what she was thinking. Ghandi, she couldn't believe he was really here, with her.

She sniffled, turning away and wiping a hand beneath her eye, waiting for it all to crash down. It would. She knew it would. The things she'd done... *Enjoy it while you can, Phe.*

Yeah, right. What she should be doing is figuring out how to make Gideon see her for the lost cause she was, but the thought of him looking at her again with the malice he had in judge's chambers made her want to puke.

"Your benefactor appears to be out," Gideon said, leading her to a chair by the fire. "Is he usually, ah, indisposed, at this time of day?"

Ophelia sat, grimacing at the rub of upholstery as she drew her legs beneath her, and Gideon handed her a file. "I'm pretty sure Thaddeus keeps a schedule the same way he keeps his marbles—loosely at best."

Gideon grunted. "Well, read that while we wait," he

muttered, moving to the window. The sun was just pinking the horizon. The storm had passed, and the sky above a vivid, cloudless blue. "If he's not back by the time you finish, is there some place we can get coffee this early? Breakfast perhaps? You're far too thin."

She blinked back tears again at his concern. "Cups," she said before she'd thought better of it. But she supposed it was the lesser of two evils. She didn't particularly relish the thought of taking Gideon there, but was even less eager to offer him ramen or leftover sushi.

He grunted and turned back to the window, his tousled, golden hair wheaten in the subdued morning light. He raised a hand to scratch the stubble over his square jaw and frowned at its rasp. A smile ghosted across her lips. Not being able to clean himself up must be driving him crazy. He hated looking anything but put together, and being in a t-shirt and sweats outside of the house wasn't anything he'd usually be caught dead in.

Which was probably why she'd always preferred him like this.

Ophelia looked away as she opened the file, and her breath caught. Gideon hadn't been understating things. Her entire life, professional and personal, had been distilled onto the pages. Ophelia's knuckles whitened at a handwritten note scrawled across the bottom of one of them:

TARGET IS DESPERATE FOR LOVE.

Fuck them.

"I've seen enough," she said, snapping it closed as she stood. "Breakfast?"

Gideon turned, an errant lock over his cocked brow. "Already? Are you sure?"

"Positive." She frowned, tempted to throw the stupid file

into the fire. "Just let me fix my face." The looks they were going to get at the café would be annoying enough without everyone staring at her stupid tatuaj.

"I hope you don't feel you need to do so on my account." His lips quirked as he came to her side and tucked a strand of hair behind her ear. "However, as enjoyable as the rest of the visual is, you putting on pants would be appreciated. I'd hate to start off the day with murder."

Ophelia scowled, and the asshole had the nerve to grin at her.

Damn it, he'd do it too, but pants weren't happening, and neither was leaving the lair without makeup. She stomped back across Thaddeus's clustered study, trying to ignore Gideon's chuckle at her back. He trailed after her, smart enough to disappear into her room while she continued down the hall to the bathroom.

The concealer she'd spilled over the sink had been cleaned up, but the door was missing. Ophelia vaguely remembered Gideon being responsible for its demise, and the damage to the frame certainly backed it up. She buzzed her lips and rummaged around in her makeup bag, her fingers stilling, then pulling out a new bottle of concealer.

Soku.

Ophelia's eyes welled up for the zillionth time in the past few hours, and she swore, pulling off the packaging. Ghandi, she was pathetic and, thanks to vampirism, she couldn't even blame it on her stupid period. What the hell was wrong with her?

So, so many things.

She dashed the back of her hand across her eyes, sniffling, and started sponging the thick concealer over her tatuaj. Damn it. Either Soku had gotten her a defective bottle or the frickin' things had gotten darker again. Ugh. This was pointless. She was gonna need to get a compact of pancake.

Ophelia threw her sponge at the sink and grabbed her toothbrush. But really, what was the big deal? It wasn't like everyone in town didn't already know she was a vampire, and if anyone said shit, Gideon would pummel them.

Her lips tipped up around her toothbrush as she scrubbed, having missed his temper more than she'd thought. He'd always been her champion, ready to beat the hell out of anyone who even thought about looking at her the wrong way.

Damn it. Her mirth quickly faded. Gideon never made idle threats, and he was serious about going after the Vampire Court. She didn't doubt his abilities, but not even a gargoyle could compete against the entirety of the Crimson Guard. The elite force was made up of the most powerful vampires in each tribe, and every last one of them was rabidly loyal to the cause.

And to their general, Prince fucking Kremlyn.

Sweat stippled her body as she spat into the sink, her head hanging. What the hell had she been thinking instigating that uprising? Memories of blood washed over her. Ghandi, so much blood. Flesh rupturing from paralyzed victims, assassins stepping from the writhing shadows, their victims being overrun by hordes of rats…

No. She locked it all away, struggling for calm. That was then and this was now. She'd enjoy this while she could. Ophelia ran a hand over her face. As long as she stayed in Havers, they were safe. She had a little over a week before she had to submit all her evidence to the court and go back to Klineville.

Plenty of time for Gideon to write her off.

She puffed out her cheeks and dabbed on some mascara, because why not draw more attention to her eyes? Whatever, it would have to do. She zipped her case closed and tossed it back onto the sink as she left the room. At least the stupid marks were muted. She'd stop at Sal's and grab whatever the grocer had in his depressing selection of cosmetics on her way back.

Ophelia stopped short in the doorway of her room. Gideon sat at the edge of her bed, staring at her shoes. Visions of him doing the same a lifetime ago rose with an unexpected warmth in her breast. Ghandi, she wanted that again. Him. He looked up as her shadow darkened the room, and she shook the sudden longing away, bustling over to her clothes rack.

"Is there a problem?" she asked.

"No," he said slowly. "I was just thinking about all your things in storage. I could have them couriered here, if you'd like."

Her fingers stilled on a blouse. "Y-you kept them?"

Out of the corner of her eye, he nodded, looking away, his blunt fingers laced together in his lap. "When the vampires' offer came in, I hired someone to box up the entire apartment. Getting rid of everything…I suppose it was too much like losing you twice."

Ophelia kept her back to him. *Damn these fucking tears.* She sniffed. "Not the cat, I hope."

"No. Mrs. Johnson down the hall took Octavius."

"She was always nice," Ophelia managed, pulling a micro-mini from the rack. She closed her eyes, breathing deeply to steel herself before pulling it on.

"Why do clothes bother you?"

Her eyes flew open at his innocuous question. "What?"

"Clothes, fabric. Last night, that brownie, ah, Soku, said you couldn't stand how they felt. I can understand your aversion to being touched by someone, but…" He shrugged.

A bitter laugh slipped past her lips. Well, she wanted him to know what a headcase she was, right? No time like the present. "They make the Damă wear heavy robes. We were sewn into them, then corseted. They cover you head to toe and are lined with crushed glass."

Gideon looked up at that, his turquoise eyes flashing.

She forced herself to continue. "One of the older Damă said it was so they could keep track of us by the trail of bloody footprints we left in our wake."

Ophelia turned from him to the rack. The heated rage coming off Gideon hit her back like a furnace, his silence deafening. She flicked through her clothes, the click of hangers against the bar the only sound in the little room.

A long moment passed, then— "I suspect that explains why shoes aren't a problem?" His tone was light, but that was bullshit. His knuckles had gone white, and that muscle in his jaw ticked. Ophelia wet her lips, the air stifling with his repressed rage.

"You would be correct," she rasped. Ghandi, this was going to backfire. He wasn't disgusted with her; it was just further fixating his anger on the Vampire Court. She swallowed the lump in her throat, desperate for a way to backpedal and knowing it was pointless. Gideon was worse than a terrier with a bone. "Pick out a pair of heels for me?"

He met her gaze, his expression softening at the callback to their life together. He'd loved choosing what she wore. Ophelia looked away, and he cleared his throat. "The gray snakeskin."

She nodded and bent to slip on her skirt beneath the tunic Soku had given her, praying he couldn't see her revulsion as it slid over her hips.

"I'm going to kill them, Phe."

"After breakfast." She wiped her sweaty palms against her thighs and grabbed her purse.

He grunted and stood, offering his hand as she stepped into her heels. "No jacket?"

"No."

Gideon grunted again, gesturing for her to lead the way.

She shivered as they climbed to crooked stone steps to ground level. The day was clear, but frigid. Thank Ghandi there wasn't any wind, but there was humming. Was that Thaddeus?

Ophelia exchanged a glance with Gideon, and they headed behind the library. The ancient vampire had his back to them, busy at one corner of walled garden. Thorny hedges lined the waist-high stacked fieldstones, and a crumbling fountain stood at the center of the space.

"Mustn't let the cold in," he muttered to himself, wrapping thick black paper around a tower of stacked boxes. "Winter is coming," he giggled.

Great, he was in batshit mode. Ophelia turned to leave and Gideon stopped her. "Ah, Thaddeus? Pardon the intrusion, but if you have a moment?"

"Moments are all we ever have, my dear boy," he said, fastening the paper with a bungee. "Life is ever fleeting." He turned to them and smoothed the tower's top with a gnarled hand. "Honeybees, for instance, only live four to six weeks. Less if you've been unlucky enough to be born a drone. Then they chew off your wings and evict you from the hive to die when the queen's finished with you...or so they hope." His smile was gruesome.

Gideon's brow furrowed. "Ah, yes, that's fascinating, but—"

"Did you know that each worker has a specialty? Some make up her retinue, others are nurses, guards, foragers, or scouts. Thousands of them teeming within a single hive, bound to a single queen via the pheromones she emits, influencing the entire populace's behavior." Gideon drew a breath to speak, and Thaddeus raised a finger, cutting him short. "However, those same pheromones also signal when a queen is past her prime. Any idea as to what happens then, child?" he asked Ophelia.

She shook her head, not caring, but she'd been down this road before, and they were in it now. "Nope."

"The workers secretly create new queens. Several at a time, in hopes she won't be able to sniff them all out and kill them before they mature."

Gideon's lips pursed, and he looked thoughtful. "And if they do?"

"Well, then if all goes well, they swarm, leaving with a portion of the populace and start a new hive somewhere else." Thaddeus shrugged. "Others follow suit. Eventually, the old queen is left with nothing, and the original hive dies out."

"And if it doesn't go well?"

"Ah. One might call that something akin to a failed coup." His eyes lingered on Ophelia, and the overwhelming desire to run came over her.

"Wow, great, thanks for the *National Geographic* short. Boy, I am starving. Breakfast?" she asked, tugging on Gideon's sleeve. He grunted, something passing between the two men before he followed her from the frost-riddled garden.

Ophelia rummaged around in her purse. She had no idea what the fuck all that was about, but she didn't like it. Whatever. Thaddeus was off his rocker. Why else would he wax poetic about frickin' honeybees in the middle of February? The stupid things were probably all dead.

Somehow that didn't make her feel any better.

At this time of the morning, the streets were still, only the odd car passing them. Gideon kept his head down, shoulders rounded and pensive as they walked toward Main Street side by side. Ophelia lit a cigarette, and he glanced over with a frown, never a fan of the habit.

Oh fucking well. It wasn't like it was gonna kill her. She blew out a stream of smoke with a little shimmy in his direction. He didn't quite smile, but the edges of his eyes crinkled like he wanted to.

"Brat," he murmured, his hungry gaze skating over her. A whisper of desire coiled in her belly at what that endearment had always been prelude to.

What the— Ophelia stumbled as she took another drag, shocked at her body's response to him flirting. She hadn't felt that in over a decade. Ghandi, she'd been pretty positive she was totally dead from the waist down. *Okay, poor choice of words, Phe.*

She swallowed heavily, her steps slowing at the implications and her limbs trembling. Could she...? Her eyes flicked to him, and he coughed into a fist, forcing a smile before he looked away.

"Gideon, I—"

"You said Damă were rare and cloistered because of their tribal affiliation," he interrupted. "Why put any of you through that torture? If your tribe was so reviled, why not just kill you as you come into being?"

"I-I'm not sure." Ophelia frowned, grateful for the reprieve on the chat about her bedroom issues, but not wanting to examine anything Citadel related too closely. "And I really don't want to talk about it or bees anymore."

Gideon's lips pursed. "Fair enough. That's it up ahead, isn't it?" He waved a hand at Cups's pink-stuccoed brick face.

Shit, it looked busier than she would've thought for a Tuesday morning, but they were up far earlier than she usually was. "Yeah." Her voice wavered, wishing she had offered him ramen.

Too fucking late now.

Gideon stepped in front of her and the bell above the door tinged as he held it, his big black trench billowing with the movement.

She paused, taking one more drag before she ground out the butt beneath her stiletto. Ghandi, she didn't want to do this. The scant makeup on her face left her feeling far too exposed. Her pulse ticked up. Gideon raised a mocking brow, like he was daring her to go inside, and she scowled, anger replacing anxiety. She pushed past him and went into Cups.

∼

GIDEON ATTEMPTED to shake off his black mood as he followed Ophelia into the café. The implications of the little nature special they'd just been privy to were enough to drive him to distraction. His gut said that Thaddeus was quite mad, but Gideon was also positive it'd been a message. Unfortunately, that meant that Ophelia's escape was more than an insult to the Vampire Court, it was a threat.

Kremlyn would be incensed by the loss of his "property," but Vesper…Vesper would seek to make an example of Ophelia, lest risk more dissent.

Gideon shook his head, the look of shocked terror in her eyes at his flirtatious banter hitting harder after the fact. He wanted to destroy this entire town and flee with her across the ocean. Gods, if only she wasn't pledged to the blasted node. Vengeful spirits weren't anything to trifle with, and should she break her covenant, the node's ire would follow them wherever they might go.

It didn't help that she was parading around so scantily clothed, and he itched to take her over his knee for smoking, but now wasn't the time to press the issue.

Not yet anyway.

A yokel standing by the door gave a low whistle as she passed, and Gideon growled. His knuckles whitened as he fought not to jack the man up by his throat and evict him from the premises to beat him bloody.

Given the yokel's hasty retreat, he was smart enough to clearly read Gideon's intent.

The door swung shut behind the uncouth delinquent, and Gideon rolled his shoulders beneath his coat. So much for shaking off his black mood. He breathed through his fury as he took in the establishment. Like the rest of what he'd seen of the town, it was touristy but clean, and apparently as popular in the morning as it had been last night. Why, Gideon couldn't imagine. The decor looked like a cupcake had vomited, yet the kitschy little tables were full, and the line to the counter exceedingly long.

He joined Ophelia at the end of it, his bulk definitely not an asset moving between the clientele. More than one of the tables' jostled occupants glanced up at him only to look away just as quickly. The hum of conversation dropped, and the feel of eyes on him prickled the back of his neck.

"Is it always this welcoming?" he murmured into Ophelia's hair as he positioned himself behind her, a hand at her slim waist.

"Oh, this is nothing," she replied dryly, slightly recoiling at his touch before easing against it. "You should see what it's like when you're not here glowering."

His mood darkened.

The door tinged again as someone else entered. "Chase!" an unfamiliar voice said a moment later at his shoulder.

Gideon turned, and a slim redheaded man in a ridiculously puffy jacket recoiled. "Oh! I'm sorry, I thought —" His eyes fell on Ophelia. "Never mind, even better. Excuse me." He went to push past, and Gideon thrust out an arm, blocking the man's progress.

"And you are?" Gideon growled, annoyed at being mistaken for whomever this Chase person was for a second time.

"Gideon, this is Felix Simms, Havers's mayor," Ophelia said, a hand on Gideon's forearm. "And technically, my boss."

Ah. The warlock who'd reportedly slayed the dragon. Gideon frowned, eyeing the man. Even given how powerful the node was, he found that highly unlikely. "How unfortunate."

"And here I was about to say the same." Felix flicked an unruly curl from his eyes, karma sparking in their depths. Perhaps he wasn't as effete as he seemed.

Ophelia snorted. "Felix, this is Gideon Sperry, Fayet's prosecutor."

Felix paled. "You're here already?"

"Excuse me?" Gideon's gaze narrowed at the warlock.

"I, uh, can I speak with you for a moment, Ophelia?" Felix asked, his throat bobbing.

"I don't believe she's on the clock until after eight a.m., and her eating takes precedence over whatever task you have in mind," Gideon growled.

Ophelia glanced between them. "Um, can it wait until after breakfast?"

"No. No, I don't think it will." Felix sucked in his cheeks. "Ryland showed up about an hour ago with…cargo in tow."

They both looked at Gideon, the tables around them suspiciously quiet. He had the sudden urge to create a scene.

"Oh." Ophelia's hand tightened on his forearm and she wet her lips. "I'm assuming said cargo wants a lawyer?"

"Mmm. You would be right." Felix said, the spry man's body language all but telling Gideon to fuck off.

Ophelia's eyes flicked to his, and Gideon's knuckles whitened at her unspoken request for him to give them a moment. Fine. He stepped around them to the tchotchke-laden counter, beyond irritated at the man's gall. Work should not cut into Ophelia's personal time.

"A bottle of water, two black coffees, a breakfast special, and garlic bagel with cream cheese, smoked salmon, and extra capers," he said to the frumpy woman at the register, handing her his platinum card. "Actually, add a cheese danish to that." Ophelia needed the calories.

The cashier did a double take at him, then shook her head before she swiped it.

That was getting old, fast. So was the franticly whispered

conversation between Felix and Ophelia. The muscle in Gideon's jaw jumped and he breathed through his temper.

"For here or to go?" the cashier asked, handing his card back.

"To go," Ophelia said, joining him. "Have you checked your phone?"

"No. I'm not on the clock yet, nor are you." He shot a pointed look at Felix putting in his order, and the man blatantly ignored him.

Ophelia gave a long suffering sigh. "Gideon, please."

He frowned and pulled the annoying device from his jacket pocket. He'd silenced the blasted thing after that last call with Vesper. There was a single alert from the Justice Detainee Information System. He frowned, the lack of anything else gnawing at him. He scrolled through the alert, his brow rising.

It appeared that the "cargo" Felix had mentioned was one Patrick Montgomery. He'd been taken into custody and booked at the Havers County Jail roughly an hour ago. Gideon was certain the Vampire Court would've gotten the same alert and arranged for someone to run point. Patrick Montgomery was too important to the case to do otherwise. That they hadn't pinged Gideon to do so spoke volumes.

They knew he was turning on them and were cutting ties.

He re-pocketed his phone, his mind churning.

"Anything?" Ophelia asked, turning from the counter with a drink tray and a to-go bag.

He caught the eye of a woman eavesdropping, and she quickly looked away. "No, which is worrisome. Shall we? My car's right outside, and I'm assuming we'll need to drive."

Ophelia wet her lips. "Drive?"

"Mmm," he hummed, taking his coffee and the bag from her, then ushering her toward the door. "I believe it would be wise to take a detour to Havers County Jail."

"Actually, it's more of glorified drunk tank," Felix piped

from right behind them as they left the café. "You mind if I tag along?"

"Yes," Gideon said, pulling Ophelia to his side as he took a sip of his coffee. It was far better than he'd expected.

She shot him a look, and his temper mellowed at her annoyance. "But don't let that stop you," she said sweetly to Felix.

The warlock glanced between them. "Okay, so, how long have you two been fucking?"

Chapter Ten

OPHELIA DREW in a sharp breath as Gideon spat his coffee onto the sidewalk, coughing. Felix inspected his nails, looking way too satisfied with himself, and Ophelia wanted to strangle him. Gideon was prickly enough, and his temper had been simmering all morning without Felix egging him on. If he kept it up, someone was going to get hurt.

"I mean, he's obviously the guy you told Jena about. No wonder you're always drooling all over Chase," Felix continued with a huff, openly appraising Gideon. "The two of them could stunt double for each other."

Ophelia's burst of fury over Jena blabbing died at the gargoyle's furious expression.

"Who is Chase?" he growled staccato, his skin graying with his temper.

Felix's brow rose, and he took a step back. Smart man. Ophelia moved between them. Gideon glanced at her and flicked coffee from his hand, still glowering at the warlock.

"Jena's husband. I wouldn't worry about it. They're extremely devoted to one another, though not for someone's lack of try-ing," Felix said all singsong, eyeing Ophelia.

Gideon's growl deepened, and his features coarsened.

"Will you shut the fuck up?" she snapped at Felix, grabbing Gideon by his lapels and jerking hard. "Hey, stop it."

His eyes dropped to hers, and she squirmed beneath the intensity of his turquoise gaze. Ophelia wet her lips, and he focused on them. Her breath quickened, that whisper of desire back from earlier. "H-he reminded me of you, but I only flirted with him to piss Jena off. It's done."

"Is it though?" Felix asked.

She whipped around to face him. "Do you seriously have a death wish?" Because if Gideon didn't kill him, she might.

Felix buzzed his lips. "That depends. At the moment, no, but I'll take a rain check. Rehearsals for *Cats* starts in two weeks, and Sway got a part, presumably because her singing actually sounds like a very, very sick feline." He pinched the bridge of his nose, then looked at Gideon. "Did you say you were driving?"

The gargoyle sucked in his cheeks and strode past them both without a word to the long black car she'd seen last night. The door slammed behind him, and the engine roared to life.

"So, is sleeping with Fayet's lawyer part of our defense or just a side benny?" Felix asked, brow raised as he sipped his coffee.

"We're not sleeping together." Ophelia gritted out, waiting for a line of cars to pass so they could cross the street.

"Mmm hmm…" Felix tongued his cheek. "Which is obviously why he's here before sunrise on a Tuesday in sweats, taking you to breakfast and hulking over you like a cave man."

She scowled at him. "We knew each other before I was a vampire, okay? Now stop pissing him off."

"No promises, that seems like a pretty tall order. He's even less pleasant than you are. And I'm totally taking you 'knowing him' in the biblical sense, by the way. The man is obviously smitten, though lord knows why. I mean you're cute, but…" Felix made a face, letting the rest of what he was going to say to her imagination.

"Fuck you."

"See? That right there. You know, Jake Overbeck has been trying to get up the nerve to ask you out for weeks."

"Who?" Ophelia's brow furrowed, tempted to dart out into traffic. It was way too fucking early for this.

"Tall, glasses, wears flannel."

She snorted. "You've just literally described half the town."

"Okay, you have a point," Felix said, flicking a curl, "but mine is that I figured he finally had, and you'd turned him down—unkindly, as expected. He came out of Cups looking like he was about to piss himself."

"I didn't notice." And didn't care. Besides, who the hell was stupid enough to ask a vampire out on a date? She started across the street.

Felix followed, still running his mouth. "Exactly, which means someone else put the fear of God into him. I wonder who it could've been…perhaps another jealous suitor?"

"You need to drop it," she hissed, waiting at the passenger door for Felix to get in the back. She was pretty sure Gideon would drive off and leave him there if given half a chance. Though why she didn't just let him…

Felix smirked as he climbed in.

Fuck my life. Ophelia closed her eyes for a breath and got into the car. The look on Gideon's face when she slid into the posh leather seat confirmed her earlier theory. A muscle in his jaw ticked as he waited for her to buckle up, then pulled into traffic, following his GPS.

"So, where did you two meet?" Felix drawled from the back.

A low growl started in Gideon's chest, and she put a hand on his thigh, struggling with her own temper. "We worked at the same firm, got engaged, and then I left him at the altar to become a vampire," she said, turning around to bat her lashes at Felix.

He blanched, throwing his freckles into stark relief. "Oh."

Gideon turned a corner, glancing at her askance as she sat back. The rest of the car ride was awkward but blissfully silent, save for Felix's rapid texting in the back. Ophelia gritted her teeth, sure what she'd just spilled would be all over town in the next few minutes.

Ghandi, she fucking hated Havers.

They pulled into an unpaved parking lot in front of a low, brick building about a mile away from the main drag. Gideon killed the engine and grabbed his briefcase and their breakfast from the back. Habit took over, and she stayed where she was until he rounded the car to open her door. His lips twitched as he offered her his free hand.

"Ophelia."

"Gideon." She smiled as she took it, then scowled at Felix's raised brow, striding past him with Gideon's palm at the small of her back. This time she didn't flinch. Instead, she felt almost…safe. He held the door for her, and she entered the Sheriff's Department. Why these places were always in shades of baby-shit brown…

Felix waved at the unkempt, uniformed woman behind the glass, and she nodded, buzzing them through into a room partitioned into low cubicles. A deputy was working at one of the desks, his head bobbing to what was playing on his earbuds. Liam Montgomery sat at another, laughing with an unfamiliar man. Whoever he was, Ophelia hadn't seen him around Havers before.

Liam looked up as they entered, his smile faltering. "Sperry. That was fast."

"I was in the area," he said, frowning at the lackluster facility. "Has the witness given a statement yet?"

"No. He's waiting for his lawyer."

Gideon grunted. "Well, then I suspect you should let him know I'm here."

What? Ophelia shot him a glance. He couldn't represent Patrick and prosecute the case.

"Yeah…" Liam drawled. "I'm pretty sure that would be a raging conflict of interest—"

"And I'm positive that ship has long since sailed," Gideon said, cutting him off. "Recent events have made it impossible for me to objectively represent Fayet, so I'll be recusing myself from the case shortly, if I haven't already been removed. However, at this juncture, you have two options: you can either let me into that room to find out what I can before the Vampire Court has him killed, or I can bludgeon you to death and then do it anyway."

They all stared at him.

"What do the vampires have to do with this?" Felix asked.

"He works for them," Liam answered.

Felix pinched the bridge of his nose. "Okay, I think I'm gonna need a minute."

"And I think I'm gonna get going," the other man said, standing up and clasping Liam on the shoulder. "Call me if you need me again."

"Yeah, thanks."

The man waved a hand over his shoulder as he left. He was ridiculously tall, with feathers braided into his wavy auburn hair and a massive knife riding at his hip. That had to have be Ryland, the bounty hunter they'd hired.

Ophelia shook off her shock as the door closed behind him. "Y-you're going to recuse yourself from the case?" she stuttered, agape. What was Gideon thinking? The Vampire Court was going to go mental.

He turned to her. "There's a reason the court didn't call me as soon as they knew he'd been taken in, Phe. And even if they had, do you honestly think I can continue working for them, knowing what I know? You're right, this is more than a civil case, but it's also more than criminal. Those inconsistencies I mentioned, my gut is telling me this is a full-blown conspiracy, and I'm willing to bet that Patrick Montgomery's the lynchpin."

Felix laughed. "A conspiracy. Great. I need more caffeine for this." He headed past them to a makeshift coffee bar set up against the far wall.

"Whatever you found out wouldn't be admissible," Ophelia said, still fixated on Gideon.

Liam clicked his tongue. "Maybe not, but I don't know that it needs to be. If we can get enough information to follow a trail ourselves…" He shook his head. "Look, Patrick is an asshole, but he's a smart asshole. If the Vampire Court is involved, he would've kept something to hold over their heads. Records, transcripts of phone calls, bank statements. If we can get access to what he's got squirreled away, we wouldn't technically need his testimony. A witch could summon a specter from their auric residue if the court needed context. It's standard practice in arcane cases."

Ophelia frowned. "I still don't like it. Gideon could get disbarred for misrepresenting himself to a potential client."

"I don't care," Gideon growled. "You're not losing this case."

Liam looked between them. "What the fuck is going on?"

"Oh, they're a thing," Felix said from the other side of the room, then mouthed "fill you in later" at Gideon's glower and pulled out his phone, texting again.

"Now," Gideon rolled his shoulders, "I'm assuming whomever the Vampire Court has tapped for Montgomery's defense is on their way. We've limited time."

"What about that thing you do," Ophelia said, turning to Felix and grasping at straws. "You know, your bent or whatever it is, where you disappear. The whole town was talking about it after the dragon. You could slip in with whoever's going to represent him."

"Distortion?" The spry warlock stirred his coffee and

raised a brow. "Oh no, honey, this has bad karma written all over it. You're not getting me into that room."

Behind them, the door banged open, and Chase strode in, murderous, with Jena on his heels. "Where the fuck is he?"

Gideon straightened at Ophelia's side. "Ah. You must be Chase Montgomery."

The big blond man stopped short. "Do I know you?"

"Holy shit." Jena looked between them, then her gaze found Ophelia's. "Are you fucking kidding me?"

Ophelia went to say something and shrugged instead. What was the point?

"Jena, Chase, this is Gideon Sperry, Fayet's prosecutor and Ophelia's ex-fiancé," Felix said into the silence. "I mean, kind of. All of that," he swirled a finger at them, "is just... complicated."

"And it's about to get more so," Gideon muttered looking at his phone as it pinged with another alert. "Brendan Thackett has been assigned to Mr. Montgomery defense. I'm assuming he's already on his way."

Liam swore from behind the desk.

"Who's Brendan Thackett?" Felix asked before Ophelia could.

"More like what," Liam muttered. "He's a defense attorney, but the elf is shady as fuck. You can't pin anything on the guy, but let's just say not all his clients make it to trial."

Ophelia looked over at Gideon re-pocketing his phone. Based on his expression, he agreed with Liam's assessment.

"So, let me restate my earlier question," Gideon said, clasping his hands over his briefcase's handle. "Are you going to let me into that room, or am I going to make you let me into that room?"

∽

GIDEON WAITED as the door to the drunk tank was opened for him. Apparently, Havers was too small for a multi-cell facility, and the long, concrete-block room partitioned with silver bars was the extent of their penal capabilities. Several bunks lined one end of the far wall, and Patrick Montgomery sat at the edge of one of the lower ones, looking far less smug than the last time Gideon had seen him.

Patrick had never been a large man, but the were had become rangy, the scraggly beard covering the lower portion of his face doing nothing to improve his visage. His eyes followed Gideon as he pulled a folding chair away from the wall and set it in front of the bars.

"Since when are you a public defender?" Patrick grumbled.

"Oh, I'm not, but I assumed you'd want to speak with me first. PD Thackett is on his way. Do you mind if I record this?" Gideon asked, sitting as the realization of the stakes bloomed over Patrick's face.

"You can do whatever you want."

Gideon took out his phone and thumbed on the app. "Then I'll proceed. What follows is the sworn statement of Patrick Montgomery regarding the case Fayet v. Havers-by-the Sea…" he rattled off the date and the rest of the jargon needed to make it admissible, then turned back to Patrick. "I'm glad to see your little sojourn into the wild hasn't dulled your delightful personality. As much as I do enjoy it, why don't you tell me why the Vampire Court is so invested in you."

"You really want that on file?" Patrick laughed, then licked his cracked lips. "Whatever, it's your neck in the noose. I don't know, and if they're sending Thackett, they obviously want me dead."

"Perhaps, but from what I understand, so does the majority of this town. Why is that?" Patrick's lips tightened, and Gideon sighed. "Come on, you know how this works, help me to help you." He slid a folio from his briefcase and flipped it open. "Fine. Let's have a refresher, shall we? It's being argued that you knowingly procured the grants for three wind turbines, and then filed the necessary permits to situate them across the leyline. The defense is arguing that during the process, you altered the scope of work…" Gideon flipped through a few pages.

"Ah, yes, here it is, 'by substituting carbon steel in lieu of the originally approved composite fiber,' making you ultimately responsible for disrupting the flow of magic between Havers and Fayet and causing irreparable damage to the neighboring town. Now, this is where you need to tell me whether you'd like to plead guilty or not guilty."

Patrick stared at the floor between his feet. "Guilty."

"And are there any defenses that could mitigate your guilt? Duress, perhaps?"

"No," Patrick snorted.

Gideon leaned forward, trying to keep the surprise from his face. "Are you sure? You do know that *if* that's your plea and *if* evidence or a statement corroborating it is filed, the current case against Havers will get thrown out. And *if* that were to happen, a new one will be filed in its place that, in all likelihood, would result in Fayet's inability to collect redress."

"Good." Patrick glared up at him through his ragged hair, his eyes telling Gideon that he knew full well they weren't talking about Fayet and that his plea would seal his death warrant.

Gideon sighed, sitting back as he pursed his lips. "If I might ask, what did the Vampire Court promise you?"

"Why, you worried about them turning on you?" Patrick laughed. "It's only a matter of time. Don't think I don't know my days are numbered. Shit, if Thackett's coming, more like hours."

"Yes, I'm well aware of the Court's duplicitous nature,"

Gideon said, more bitterness bleeding into his tone than he'd intended.

Patrick's brow knit, and he sat back, his eyes calculating. He glanced at Gideon's phone still recording. "Fine. You want the details? They didn't promise me anything, and I never spoke with them directly. Whatever happened with them in the back room was between Malcom and Chambers. When they brought me on to secure the grant, Malcom looped me into it with the promise of supporting my bid for Alpha. Honestly, I didn't care about anything else."

"But you knew about the vampires' involvement."

Patrick looked at him like he was an idiot. "Who do you think was behind the grant in the first place?" He scowled. "Yeah, I knew, but I didn't know about the composite fiber being switched out until after the witches started losing their shit over it. I'm pretty sure that was all Malcom. Chambers said he'd handle it, and not long after, the funding was pulled."

Gideon frowned. "Do you have anything to corroborate that?"

"No. Like I said, I never spoke with the tribes directly, and Malcom…" He shook his head, his face tight. "He was more of a father to me than my own dad. I trusted that son of a bitch, and he was old school. Everything was face to face."

"What about Chambers?"

"He was just straight up paranoid. Nothing was written down, and I couldn't even bring my phone into our meetings. Why the hell do you think I ran? If I had anything on them, I sure as fuck would've used it by now." Patrick shook his head, then laughed. "And if you're planning on burying Chambers, you're gonna have to dig deep my friend, because there's no way the tribes were the only ones pulling his strings."

Gideon's brow quirked. "Who else—"

The door banged open and Gideon quickly pocketed his

phone. Brendan Thackett strode into the room in a cloud of cheap cologne. Patrick's eyes deadened as Gideon stood.

Thackett stopped short. "Gideon. I didn't expect you here."

"I don't know why I wouldn't be," he said, as if nothing were amiss. "I'll anticipate a copy of his statement in my email before noon. Mr. Montgomery has already informed me of his intent to plead 'not guilty.' I'll let the powers that be know that the case will be continuing as expected. Mr. Montgomery," he said, nodding to Patrick. "Try to stay comfortable. I anticipate resolving this lawsuit outside of court."

Patrick swallowed heavily and looked away.

"But I thought..." Thackett's brow furrowed, more than a little confused. "Wait, you think they'll settle?"

Gideon leaned down to grab his briefcase. "I think there will be very little recourse once all the facts are in, and that it would be foolish to proceed, especially after hearing what Mr. Montgomery had to say."

The odious man chuckled. "Well, that is why they pay you the big bucks. I don't know why I thought..." He shook his head. "Give me an hour, and I'll have everything sent over."

Gideon grunted and left the room, hoping Patrick was wise enough to take the out he'd just given him. Best case, his plea of 'guilty' would've only kicked the proverbial can down the road. Worst case, he'd be dead before he saw another sunrise, and they'd be right back where they'd started.

Several sets of eyes landed on him as he stepped back into the sheriff's department's sad excuse for a bullpen.

"Well?" Chase growled, standing with his arms crossed over his chest.

Gideon tongued his cheek, not liking the man on principle. "Might I suggest we go somewhere more private before discussing sensitive information?" he asked, eyeing a deputy across the room.

"Yeah," Jena said, stroking her gravid abdomen. "We can go back to the Witchery. I don't think Aggie's back from her trip with Gorman, so we'll have the place to ourselves."

"We'll have to get the replay," Felix said, glancing at Jena. "Liam and I have that thing."

She gave a subtle nod. "I'll text you."

"I'm sure you will," Ophelia muttered, scrunching up the wrapper from her bagel and tossing it into a bin. Jena's cheeks flushed, and Chase put his arm around her.

Gideon didn't know what all that was about, but aside from Ophelia having eaten, he really didn't care, and the less time spent with Havers's mayor, the better.

"Well then," he said, forcing a smile. "Shall we?"

Chapter Eleven

OPHELIA STOOD in the doorway of the drafty kitchen in the apartment above the Witchery. It was in the midst of renovation, and everything behind her draped in plastic, save for the stove Jena had uncovered when they'd arrived. Ophelia sniffed, running a hand under her nose at the weird chemical tang in the air.

"Sorry, that's the paint stripper," Jena said, handing her a cup of tea as she joined her and gestured at the convex tin ceiling above them. "Chase did the tiles this weekend, and we all had to clear out. I had no idea how thick the crap on them was. He had to remove the windows to air the place out. We've been staying at Felix's. You know, because of the fumes."

"Oh, yeah." Ophelia turned to look, not having a clue what Jena was talking about, but she'd promised to be less bitchy, right? Still, it was a ceiling. She raised her mug and took a sip. "Neat."

Jena rolled her eyes. "I'm assuming renovation's not your thing?"

"No. Shoe shopping is my thing." Her eyes flicked to Jena's All Stars. "But like, good shoe shopping."

The little witch fell back with a hand over her heart. "Wow. I really don't like you."

Ophelia batted her lashes. "I'm glad, especially since you blabbed all my business to the entire town."

"It wasn't the *entire* town," Jena said, her face red. "It was just to Chase. Okay, and to Felix…and he probably told Liam, but they're not going to say anything to anyone else."

"Oh. Cool." Ophelia nodded, plastering a smile on her face. "That's so much better. Remind me to tell you more things in confidence." She scowled.

The curvy little woman fidgeted. "Look, I'm sorry. I shouldn't have done that, it's just…no one knows anything about you, and here you are, responsible for saving the entire town. Can you really blame any of us for wanting to know what your deal is?"

"Yes."

Jena sighed. "Yeah, all right, I'd be pissed too. It won't happen again." She made a weird gesture with her hand. "Witches' honor."

Ophelia frowned, shooting her a side-eye and wondering if whatever that had been was the equivalent of a pinky promise or closer to a gang sign.

"So, what's with the Chase clone?" Jena asked, recovering enough to jerk her head in Gideon's direction. He sat in one of the overstuffed chairs in the other room, stroking his lip and lost in thought. He hadn't said anything on the drive over to the Witchery, which meant whatever he'd found out from Patrick, something about it bothered him, and he'd be insufferable until he figured it out.

"What about him?" Ophelia raised her mug again, sorely tempted to do something to annoy him. On second thought, better take a rain check. Present company was bound to do that soon enough. She paused before she took a sip. "And technically, Gideon's way older than Chase, so that would make him the original."

Jena's brows furrowed. "Um, okay…well, Felix said you'd been engaged but you left Gideon at the altar? I'm assuming that's because of what you said about not being able to leave the Citadel?"

Ophelia glanced at the little witch, she was seriously pushing her luck, but—Ghandi. It wasn't like she didn't already know most of it. "Yeah. The whole thing was an accident, and I sure as fuck didn't have any idea he was working out here."

"You know…" Jena hummed, tapping her teeth. "One of the coven members who was at your summoning said something about your manifesting here balancing karma."

Yeah, right. Ophelia rolled her eyes and took another sip of tea. "Why does everything with you turn metaphysical?"

"Um, witch, hello? And I wouldn't discount it. Sweets thought it had to do with evening out Mr. Brock's scales, and then I thought maybe it had to do with Liam getting Kremlyn's brother locked up, but maybe…maybe the universe was trying to right a wrong and brought you and Gideon back together."

And that was entirely too close to what Gideon had said earlier. Ophelia cocked her head, her tea mug clasped to her chest. "Aww. That's so sweet. Should I throw up now, or do you think there will be time to do it later?"

"God, you're miserable." Jena snorted. "Whatever, maybe it's a three-fer. And as for you hitting on Chase, I get it now. For the record, my ex was a knock-off too," she said, eyeing the big man as he came up from downstairs. "Chase and I didn't exactly part on amicable terms before I left for college, but second chances are legit. Things between you and Gideon could still work out if you want them to. I mean, it seems like he does."

He did, and she did too, but— Damn it, she wasn't doing this. "I'm gonna bet that no matter how bad the dorm rooms were, the Citadel had them beat," Ophelia muttered.

"No arguments there," Jena said, still eyeing her man. "We should get started. Grab a seat."

She slipped by Ophelia and sat on the big corduroy couch amidst the jumble of mismatched furniture around the living room. A seat? Yeah, that wasn't happening. Ophelia glanced at an overstuffed chair beside one of the long floor-to-ceiling windows, her skin crawling, and went to sit on a bare scrap of linoleum by Gideon's feet.

"Right, so what did the prick have to say?" Chase asked, dropping down onto the couch beside Jena.

Gideon's eyes flicked up, and as anticipated, was obviously annoyed by the interruption. "It wasn't him," he said curtly.

"Bullshit," Chase spat.

"Perhaps," Gideon sighed, "but in Patrick's rendition of events, he was brought on after the fact with the promise of support for Alpha. He seems to think that Malcom was responsible for the materials being swapped out, but said that Chambers was the main contact with the Vampire Court, which, incidentally, was responsible for the grant becoming available in the first place. He also insinuated that they weren't to only ones Chambers was beholden to."

"There's no way," Chase laughed. "Chambers is a fucking idiot—"

"That said, Patrick was going to plead guilty," Gideon interrupted. "If I may…" He pulled out his phone and played the recording he'd taken in back at the station.

Ophelia perked up when it'd concluded. "They'll have to dismiss this case and open a new one."

"Perhaps. When Thackett came in, I said Patrick was pleading 'not guilty.' Whether or not he took the out remains to be seen."

Everyone in the room stared at him, and Gideon shrugged. "I highly doubt the statement will be admissible, and if Patrick maintains the same guilty plea to Thackett, the odds of him living long enough to have it put in the record are nil. Despite my defection, a plea of not guilty will ensure the Vampire Court thinks everything else with the case is status quo. That should buy us time for that witch to change Chambers back."

"Um, yeah, small problem," Jena said. "We kind of lost him."

"Excuse me?" Gideon sat forward, his eyes narrowed.

Ophelia sighed. "Chambers escaped. He's somewhere in the sewers below Havers, and the lesser fae aren't letting us down there."

"How do you know that?" Jena asked.

"Oh, I dunno," Ophelia moued. "Maybe someone texted me."

The witch scowled at her.

"This information would've been more helpful about an hour ago," Gideon growled, running a hand over his face.

"Noted, but what I wanna know is what the hell the vampires have to do with any of it," Chase said. "I thought it was Fayet who's suing us."

"They're being bankrolled by the Vampire Court and given that they provided the grant, I'm positive that they've orchestrated your current position," Gideon muttered, his finger stroking his lips again.

"And you would know this because…?"

"Because I'm currently on their retainer," Gideon growled at Chase. "Do try and keep up."

"Then why—"

"I'll explain later," Jena murmured, a hand against the big were's chest. Huh. Guess she didn't tell him everything. "Okay, so what do we do now? If they won't let us into the Below, we're screwed."

"Yeah, and apparently the pixies are really pissed about it," Ophelia muttered.

Chase's eyes flicked to her. "Are they?"

"I guess." Ophelia shrugged. "The brownie that cleans Thaddeus's lair said it was like the only thing she's seen the harems agree on ever, and the entire Below sounds like it's full of pissed off bees."

"You need to talk to them," Chase said to Jena. "Dangle enough coconuts, and I bet they'd sneak us in."

Gideon pinched across his temples. "Dear God, please tell me that's not a euphemism."

"What? No, they've got a thing for them," Jena murmured. She turned to Chase. "You think that would work?"

He nodded and got to his feet, heading for the door. "I think it's worth trying. Give me a couple minutes and we'll find out. I'm pretty sure I saw a harem hanging around the dumpster when we came in."

"Coconuts?" Ophelia asked as the door closed behind him.

"Yeah. We've got no idea what they do with them, but for whatever reason, pixies go crazy when you offer one up." Jena sighed, running a hand over her stomach, then laughed. "God, even if they do agree to sneak us in, I have no idea how I'm gonna be much help. I can't even touch my toes, never mind catch a weasel."

"I still can't believe you lost him," Gideon muttered. "Wasn't he in a cage?"

"Right up until the moment one of Felix's kids let him out," Ophelia said. "Apparently, whatever kind of supe she is, she can 'reach' through solid matter."

"Poe's two," Jena tsked. "She didn't understand what she was doing."

"Oh, well then, no harm no foul," Ophelia said, rolling her eyes.

Gideon scowled. He stared at Jena for a long moment, pensive again. "So, you're the node's guardian."

She gave a little wave. "Yep, that's me."

"How long has it been sentient?"

She stared at him blankly. "Umm…"

He took a breath. "How long has it spoken to your line?" he asked slowly, as if to a child.

"Oh, I dunno. I know my mom heard it, but the rest of my family's records were destroyed with the manor house when I was a kid." Her eyes narrowed. "Why?"

Gideon templed his fingers. "Because it takes a great deal of time for a node to gather the required density of souls before it's able to engage in the way I experienced when I crossed into your fair hamlet," he said, his voice dripping with sarcasm. "Impossible, really, considering there are still dormant nodes on the far continent several hundred years older than anything over here."

"Well, Havers is a tourist town," Jena snarked back. "Guess all those souls want to get in on the action, too. Now, you wanna tell me how the hell you know all that?"

Ophelia glanced up at Gideon. He sucked in his cheeks and pursed his lips, the two of them staring at each other. The fact that he was a gargoyle wasn't something he advertised. They didn't exactly have a stellar reputation. People usually equated them to big, dumb constructs akin to golems, but with worse tempers and a propensity for violence when awoken.

Granted, the last part of that was spot on, but the first couldn't be further from the truth. Gideon was brilliant, and Ophelia knew for a fact he wrestled with public perception.

"I'm a grotesque," he finally admitted, shocking the shit out of Ophelia. "One of a handful created to protect the node at the center of the City of Light."

"And if you tell anyone else, I will end you," Ophelia snarled, putting a hand on Gideon's knee. He covered it with his own, his expression reinforcing the threat.

"I—of course not." Jena's throat bobbed, protectively sliding her hands across her abdomen. She shook her head and blinked. "A grotesque, you mean l-like a gargoyle? Then what are you doing over here? Did something happen to your node?"

"No. Unfortunately for my kind, there's less call for our service now than in the old days," he said, uncharacteristically candid. "Quite frankly, I was bored and received a dispensation to come to the new continent. However, given your node's rather anticipatory welcome when I crossed into Havers and the fact that my intended has pledged her service to it, I can't help but feel as if I've been played."

Ophelia's eyes widened. "What are you saying?"

"What I'm saying is, I'll be damned if the blasted thing didn't know I was coming. When we're done here, we're taking a room at the bed and breakfast Soku mentioned and finding a realtor, because in pledging your service to Havers's node, it's gained mine in tandem."

GIDEON STARED into Ophelia's wide eyes.

"Y-you're staying?" she gasped, the repressed hope on her face filing his heart.

"I am." He glanced up at Jena's sharp intake of breath, her presence ruining the moment.

The witch put a hand to her head. Little wonder, the way the node's power was currently thrumming through the room and plucking at them both. It reminded him of a willful child, and given its age, the metaphor was probably more accurate than he'd like.

"Um. Okay. Wow." Jena blew out a slow breath. "No. This is actually good—really good—because I have no idea what I'm doing, and I know the node's only telling me what it wants me to know." She reached for her phone, then dropped it like she'd been burned. "Damn it. I seriously can't tell anyone?"

"I would advise against it until things with the Vampire Court are resolved," Gideon chided. "Their resources are vast."

"Oh, right, yeah. Good thinking." She drummed her fingers against her abdomen, her eyes still on her phone. "And when do you think that'll be?"

Apparently, the node wasn't the only willful child in the room. Gideon ran a palm over his face. Gods, what the hell was he committing himself to?

Ophelia rolled her eyes. "You're like an addict."

"I'm not good with keeping secrets from Chase and Felix, okay?" Jena said, throwing up her hands. "Besides, don't you think the mayor of Havers should know we've got a gargoyle to go to bat for us? I mean, if even half the shit I've heard you guys can do is true—"

"And what exactly might that be?" Gideon asked, intrigued in spite of himself. Most of the lore about his kind had been grossly distorted over time.

"Well, for one, you can fly."

He gave a noncommittal shrug, and the witch started ticking off fingers.

"You're basically immortal, magic can't touch you, your skin's impervious, you can manipulate stone, and—" she tipped her head like she was listening to something. "And you can act like a conduit for the node's power."

Well, that was a remarkably more well-informed answer than he was expecting. Perhaps there was hope for the situation. "A fair assessment," he said, neither confirming nor denying her assumptions. "But unless I directly pledge my service to the node, I'm unable to act as a channel."

The blasted thing's presence around him increased, and he ignored it, not willing to give it the satisfaction. He'd already been neatly trapped by the circumstances and wasn't about to run out there and offer his throat up before getting the lay of the land.

"Just for clarification, are you staying here for me, or to spite the Vampire Court?" Ophelia asked, turning to narrow her eyes at him.

Oh, that fire... Gideon smirked back, raising a brow. "I don't see how either goal needs to be exclusive," he said, settling back in his chair. Ophelia looked like she was ready to pummel him, and he grinned. "There's my girl," he murmured, desire coiling in his belly. She was radiant when riled.

Her cheeks flushed, turning away as the door opened, and Chase came back into the room. A cloud of small creatures zipped in around him, yammering in high falsetto voices.

"Jena-Jena-Jena-Jena!" they cried, crazing around the room and trailing dust. Gideon hunched down, resisting the urge to swat the tiny annoyances from the air.

"Stupid-fae!" one said, landing on the cushion by Jena's head. *"Dumb-dumb-dumb!"*

Another perched on the windowsill. *"We-hate-their-vote-hate-hate-hate-it!"*

Several made exceedingly rude gestures, and Ophelia put a hand to her lips, her eyes conveying her amusement as they descended upon the witch, tugging at her hair and clothes.

"You'll-give-us-coconuts?"

"Coconuts-yes-yes-yes!

"I-want-this-many!" a female shrilled holding up all ten fingers

Another hovered in midair and spread both her fingers and toes. *"No-this-many!"*

The harem dissolved into laughter and took flight again. Gideon put a hand to his brow, his confidence sorely lacking that these creatures could sneak anyone, anywhere.

"Okay, settle down!" Jena yelled over the ruckus and the tiny, winged people alit around the room, focusing on her with a feral intensity that was more than a little disconcerting.

She cleared her throat. "We need to get down into the Below to find Chambers—"

"Who?" one interrupted.

"Weasel-man," another answered, wiggling his fingers like fangs.

"Yes, the weasel man. We need to catch him. If you help us get down there, I promise each of you ten coconuts," Jena said, setting the pixies off again.

"Ten?" Ophelia asked, ducking as one of the little beasts buzzed by her.

Chase shrugged. "It's the going rate."

The harem convened high overhead, their piercing little voices too rapid to follow, then a single pixie with an acorn cap on her head flew down to hover in front of Jena.

"Ten-coconuts-good-but-we're-gonna-need-bribes," she shrilled.

Jena's dark brows knit. "Bribes?"

The harem above all nodded their heads, except for one who shook his, then quickly corrected himself.

"Blackfinger-Grimley-Sweetpea-and-Hops."

"Is that what they need or who they have to bribe?" Gideon asked, totally lost.

Chase scratched his jaw. "Those are the names of some other harems."

"No, that sounds like a shit ton of coconuts," Ophelia snorted. "Hope you guys have a good supplier."

"Okay," Jena said, more calmly than Gideon would've been able to manage. "Any pixie who helps will also get ten coconuts, but one of you has to vouch for them."

"No-slackers!" one of them screamed, scattering the harem again.

Jena ducked. "Right. Ten coconuts each for getting me, Chase, Gideon, and Ophelia into the Below and helping us find Chambers."

Ophelia's spine straightened. "What? Wait a minute—"

"No-no-no-no-no!"

"Too-big."

"Thump-thump-thump."

"Not-them!"

Jena threw up her hands. "I can't go alone!"

"No, you can't," Chase growled.

The pixie still hovering in front of Jena put a hand to her lips and spun around, narrowing her eyes at the three of them. *"Her!"* she screamed, pointing at Ophelia.

"Hey! I never signed up for this!" she protested. "Take Chase, he's the one who wants to go."

"And Ophelia isn't leaving my sight," Gideon gritted out, his hand on her shoulder.

"No-no-no." The pixie raised her pointed little nose. *"Too-big-just-her-soku-say-she's-nice."*

"Soku lied," Ophelia growled, shaking off Gideon's hand. "And I can take care of myself."

He chuckled, and Ophelia whipped around to glower at him, poised like she was about to crawl into his lap and strangle him. Gideon wet his lips, wanting nothing more.

"Fine," she spat, turning away, much to his disappointment. "When do we leave?"

His heart about stopped.

"What? No." Chase shook his head, his biceps tensing as he crossed his arms over his chest. "There's no way the two of you are going down there alone."

"We won't be alone, we'll have each other—" Jena started.

"She's a fucking vampire!" Chase spat, his eyes flicking to Ophelia and Gideon at his growl.

Jena glared at him. "And we'll have the node." She looked at the pixie. "Do we have a deal? You sneak Ophelia and me into the Below and help us find Chambers for ten coconuts each, bribes included, but you have to vouch for any other pixie that comes to collect."

"Deal!" the pixie screamed, the harem darting toward the door. *"Come-on-come-on-come-on!"*

"I don't like this," Gideon growled, a pit opening in his stomach.

Chase echoed it. "Agreed."

"Aww, too bad," Ophelia said, batting her lashes at Gideon. "But I'm sure you two boys can find something to occupy your time. Maybe look up that realtor?"

Jena snickered, then huffed as she got to her feet. "Let me just get my spell bag and coat. I'll meet you downstairs." She left the room, and Chase stalked after her, still protesting.

"Ophelia, you don't know what's down there," Gideon said, rising to stand behind her. If he wasn't there to accompany her and something were to happen—

She shrugged, far too nonchalant. "Can't be anything worse than what I've already seen."

That was entirely not the point. His brows furrowed, and he gripped her shoulders, then sighed, recognizing that spark of determination in her gaze. She wasn't going to relent, and the last thing he wanted to do was snuff the fire from her eyes, but— "Just…come back to me," he said, his voice cracking.

Her expression softened, and she put a hand to his cheek. "That was always my intention."

He nodded, turning his face to kiss her palm. Electricity bloomed between them. "I love you, Phe. However long it takes and wherever you might go, I'll be waiting."

Ophelia's breath caught, her pupils expanding to swallow her irises. He tipped her chin up and kissed her gently. She trembled as he pulled away, resting her forehead against his chest for a breath.

Then walked out the door without another word, taking his heart with her.

Chapter Twelve

OPHELIA TROMPED after the stupid cloud of pixies, her fingers lingering on her lips and cursing herself. Gideon had said he loved her, and she hadn't said it back. Nope. She'd just left. Ghandi. What the hell was wrong with her?

Okay, so that was a rhetorical question. She mentally added what'd happened between them upstairs to the list. Ophelia scrubbed a hand over her face, not caring about her stupid makeup. Ugh, she was a mess. She took a swig from her flask, frowning. Shit. Probably should've topped that off.

The door above opened, interrupting her pity party, and Jena thumped down after her, shrugging on a heavy parka. Ophelia stopped at the bottom of the steps and pivoted, her brow furrowing. Where the hell... Instead of going outside like she figured, the harem had disappeared into the back of Jena's shop.

"Where are they going?"

The witch shrugged, looping her messenger bag over her head and looking just as confused. "I have absolutely no idea."

They followed the trail of sparkling dust into a storage room filled with crap, and to a door leading to the basement. Jena shook her head at Ophelia's look and headed down. Ophelia sighed, following her. Great. The little idiots were taking them on a tour before getting down to business.

Considering the amount of junk upstairs, the basement was surprisingly empty of anything save cobwebs and the packed dirt floor. The pixies were hovering in the corner of the fieldstone foundation nattering.

"Here-here-it's-here!" the one with the acorn top on her head screamed, pointing.

"What's here?" Jena asked, bewildered.

"Stupid-thump," one of them muttered, and another punched them.

"Door-it's-a-door," a third pipped.

The one beside her nodded. *"Goes-down."*

"Below-below-below!"

Ophelia and Jena exchanged a look. "Um, okay. Can you show me how it works?" the witch asked.

The one with the cap rolled her eyes and disappeared into a crack between the stones.

Jena sighed, running a hand over her face. "Okay, yeah, they've done this to me before. Guys, that's not gonna—"

Something clicked, and a section of the wall groaned, swinging inward and leaving a ragged hole about a foot off the ground. A low, dark tunnel lay beyond.

"—work," Jena finished lamely.

"I'm assuming you didn't know this was here?" Ophelia said, slipping off her heels and setting them to the side. It looked like a tight fit, and six extra inches wasn't going to do her any favors.

The witch shook her head. "Nope."

"Oh fun, so this will be an adventure for us both," Ophelia said, clasping her hands beneath her chin.

Jena glared at her, huffing as she clambered through the hole. "At least it's not a coal chute," she muttered.

"Do I want to know?"

"Nope."

"Oh, perfect. Definitely tell me about it then." Ophelia

stepped over the threshold, ducking her head and cringing when the door slammed shut behind them, leaving them in total darkness.

Jena sucked in a breath. "Okay, so this is a problem. I can't see a thing."

"Trust me, you're not missing much," Ophelia snorted, crouched over with a hand against the low ceiling above. No way would Gideon and Chase have been able to squeeze through here.

"You can see?"

"Enough to know you're lucky you're a pygmy." Jena flipped her off and Ophelia grinned. "Fuck you too, babe."

"Fine, then you go first, just give me something to hold on to."

"You're really needy, you know that?" Ophelia grumbled, not about to take her hand. "Here, it's the back of my tunic. Trust me, it's there."

Jena fumbled at the gossamer, frowning. "Does that mean your bare ass is hanging out?"

"You'll never know, and if I were you, I'd crouch down a little more."

"Great."

"*Come-on-come-on-come-on!*" one of the pixies stage-whispered, zipping back.

"Ready?" Ophelia asked.

"Just fucking go."

Ophelia started after the pixie, cringing at the sensation of pulling around her midsection from the gossamer. Whatever, she could deal. It was only temporary, unlike her miserable existence.

The packed dirt and stone tunnel teed. A pixie gestured for them to go right, dumping them out into another tunnel riddled with roots. They poked out from the walls and sloping floor, tripping them as their bristly filaments caught in their hair. She batted at the dangling things and squeezed by a taproot as wide as her thigh, swearing as Jena contorted herself to do the same.

Shit. Maybe Chase was right, and she should've stayed at the Witchery. Whatever. Even without the witch lugging around that huge gut of hers, it would've been slow going. Ophelia sneezed, whacking her head against the ceiling. Ghandi, the must down here was thick enough to taste; no way had anyone come this way in a very long time.

"I think we're following Cross Street, headed toward Main," Jena whispered at another juncture. They pushed through a rusted gate hanging on squealing hinges into the next tunnel lined with stone, a slick of ice running down the center of the floor. Shafts of light hit the far wall, and another set did the same a couple hundred feet away.

"This must be the sewers," Ophelia said, her breath coming out in a cloud as she straightened up, her hands at the small of her back.

"Close-we're-close!" a pixie whispered, appearing beside Jena with an exaggerated shush. She took off, heading away from the center of town. They followed her for about a block, Ophelia's toes totally numb by the time they came to another gated tunnel. This one was in much better repair. It swept to the side, well-oiled.

"Was that silver?" Ophelia murmured.

Jena nodded, the light fading again. She reached down and grabbed Ophelia's tunic. "Where did you manage to score gossamer?"

"It was a late Yule present from a friend," Ophelia said after a moment.

The witch snorted. "You have one of those?"

"Right? Shocked the shit out of me, too."

The tunnel slowly dissolved into a pitch blackness even she was having trouble seeing in. Their too-loud breaths and the tug of Ophelia's tunic barely keeping her grounded enough to go on. Then, something in the distance. Clumps of weird glowing algae began to appear on the walls. The air grew warmer, and the gooey clumps grew larger, their light becoming strong enough to illuminate the tunnel.

Jena dropped Ophelia's tunic. "Okay, I'm good," she said, frowning at the slime covered walls. "Relatively speaking."

A pixie flew back making an exaggerated shushing motion, then mimed creeping along. They slowed, a brighter light source just up ahead, and an angry buzzing reaching their ears. Shit. That must be all the pissed off pixies Soku was talking about. Jena and Ophelia held their collective breaths as they peeked out from the tunnel.

"Holy shit," Ophelia murmured, Jena's eyes as wide as her own must be. Chase and Felix hadn't been kidding: the Below was about as far from a sewer as you could get.

The street running past them was cobbled with polished stones and pristine houses reminding her of a German village lined its sides. Bold geometrics were stenciled on the doors and shutters, and weird plants bloomed in flower boxes and pots below the windows and lined balconies. Huge urns of them dotted the sidewalk beneath tall gas lampposts. Their amber light flickered off the ceiling of crystals above, refracting rainbows over everything.

Ophelia had never seen anything so idyllic. Well, it would've been if an irate cloud of pixies weren't hovering over the buildings like a storm about to break.

"I had no idea there were so many of them," Jena whispered, her eyes huge.

"So, when's that eighteen-wheeler of coconuts coming?" Ophelia asked.

The witch put a hand to her mouth and shook her head.

A gnome with a handcart turned a corner and trundled down the opposite side of the street, muttering. Shit. Ophelia pulled Jena back into the shadowed tunnel. Okay, they were here, but how were they supposed to get any further without being seen?

Two pixies appeared at the mouth of the tunnel. One held up a hand for them to wait, then glanced over her shoulder, giggling. The other held his stomach, full-on belly laughing.

Yeah. No good could come of that

A terrific crash sounded from beyond the tunnel, followed by a smattering of others like bombs going off. A man started yelling, and doors crashed open, footsteps pounding away from them. More angry voices raised to join his, and the pixie frantically gestured for them to follow.

Ophelia and Jena darted after her to an alley across the way, several houses down from where they'd been. The cloud of pixies was at the far end of the street bombarding the irate crowd with flowerpots, gleefully smashing them over the cobblestones. Others were viciously attacking howling residents, their tiny mouths stained with blood. Ophelia snickered as they made it through, glancing at their guide with new respect. Pixies really were evil little bastards.

Thankfully, they didn't have to worry about the ceiling here being low, but it looked like they were coming up on another street. Ophelia held her breath as the pixies hurried them across it into a cultivated space of greenery. A collective shout of dismay went up behind them and something big shattered with a burst of light. Ghandi, Ophelia didn't even want to know what mayhem the little beasts were up to now.

Their guide motioned for them to crawl into a cluster of evergreen bushes, giggling and clapped her hands together. *"Stupid-stupid-stupids!"*

Jena put a hand to her abdomen and cracked a grin, huffing. "You have to admit, that was pretty effective."

Ophelia felt her own lips quirk. "Yeah, but what now? Sneaking around is one thing, but how are we going to hunt down Chambers? We could've already passed him and we'd never know."

Jena rolled her eyes and flipped up the flap of her bag, rooting around. She pulled out a compass, and Ophelia's brow quirked.

"You just carry one of those around?"

The witch looked at her like she was an idiot. "Um, yeah. It's my spell bag. Now shut up and give me a minute." She closed her eyes, and her lips moved, chanting under her breath. Purple mist swirled over the compass resting on her palm and absorbed into the tarnished brass. The needle snapped to their right, and Jena's eyes flicked open. "Okay, I think I got him."

"You couldn't do that above ground?"

"No, and I'm pretty sure the reason no one could get a lock on Chambers wasn't because of the lesser fae's magic, it's because of all those crystals." Jena chewed her lip like something about that really bothered her.

"What is it?"

She shook her head. "I'm just wondering if my mom knew about the door leading here. Some of the stuff in her grimoire makes a lot more sense after seeing this place."

"Figure it out later, he's moving," Ophelia said, watching the needle drift further right.

Jena puffed out her cheeks and nodded. She turned to the pixie perched on a branch, swinging her feet. Three others had joined her, giggling and poking each other. "Can you take us that way?"

The tiny woman frowned and the others went still. *"Not-nice."*

"Why am I not surprised?" Ophelia muttered.

"It doesn't matter," Jena said. "That's the way we have to go."

The pixie shrugged, holding her hands up for them to wait before she zipped off.

"Do you really think they can do this?" Ophelia asked.

Jena looked at her deadpan. "With coconuts all things are possible."

The pixie exploded back through the greenery. *"Come-come-come-come!"* she shrilled too loud. The others burst into the air around her and flew off, Jena and Ophelia scrabbling from the bushes to follow. Jena stumbled, and Ophelia grabbed her arm, pulling her along until she found her footing.

"Thanks," the witch huffed across an expanse of green.

They thudded across a moss-covered bridge, crystal clear water beneath it running over sparkling stones. A nixie glanced up at them and gasped. One of the pixies circled back and shook her fist at the creature. The nixie threw her hands up like she didn't want to deal with it and sank beneath the surface.

Shit. Ophelia swore, not taking much stock in the pixie's threat or the nixie's silence. Sooner or later, they were going to get caught, and she didn't relish the thought of being in the custody of a bunch of pissed off lesser fae. Especially not after all the damage the pixies had caused sneaking them in here.

Ahead, the cultivated green space they'd been in faded into something more wild. Jena's pace slowed, and she unzipped her heavy parka, her face flushed. She pressed a hand to the side of her abdomen, grimacing as she looked around at the twisted trees. Ophelia agreed with the sentiment. By all rights, they shouldn't be growing underground. It was creepy, and more of that luminescent algae dripping from their gnarled branches didn't help.

"You okay?" Ophelia asked, searching the spaces between their trunks, certain she'd seen something back there moving. It sure as hell felt like something was watching them. Place was sketchy as fuck, and the pixies had vanished.

"Just hot. Crampy." The witch nodded, then shook her head. "And not gonna be able to do that again. Shit." She bit her lips and grimaced. "Yeah. No sprinting."

"So, we walk," Ophelia said, feeling like a target was on her back, though she wasn't gonna complain about the temperature. Mud squished between her toes, and it was downright balmy. "Wasn't the pixies helping us track down Chambers part of the deal?"

"Yeah." Jena shrugged. "But they're not great at staying focused." She glanced askance at Ophelia as they continued down the narrow path snaking deeper into the weird woods. "You know, I could just give you the compass and wait here."

"Okay, so first of all, is here really where you want to wait? And second, umm, no," Ophelia said, catching movement out of the corner of her eye again. "I don't care if I have to carry your stupid pregnant ass, you're not getting out of this after roping me into it."

The witch sighed. "Okay, fair." She grimaced, hiking up her bag. "God, I hate this."

"Aww, thanks. I love spending time with you, too."

Jena rolled her eyes. "I meant being pregnant."

"You know they make a pill for that."

"That's not happening." The witch snorted. "Chase wants a big family." She shrugged. "And it's only temporary, right?"

"Way to take one for the team." Shit, there it was again. Something was definitely shadowing them, and the way Jena was ambling along, outrunning whatever it was wasn't an option.

"Okay, that didn't come out the way I meant it to," Jena said, oblivious. "I want a big family, too. It sucked having no one after my mom died. I mean, I had Aggie, but I'd never want any of my kids to go through that. If something happened to me and Chase, at least they'll have each other."

Ophelia chewed her lip. "Don't be so sure," she muttered, the hair on the nape of her neck prickling. Jena shot her another glance, and Ophelia frowned. "This isn't gonna end up in the Havers Herald is it?"

"Dude, I said I was sorry."

Yeah, she knew, but— Ophelia frowned, pretty sure she remembered something about keeping pregnant women calm. Damn it. Clueing her in on whatever was out there was gonna do the opposite of that, and Ophelia didn't like the way the witch kept rubbing her midsection.

"I was a surprise baby born two decades later than my siblings. My parents didn't die, they were just assholes. Long story short, they lost custody, and I ended up in the system. I had three older brothers that could've taken me in and didn't. None of them gave two shits about me, then or now. I can't remember the last time I saw them, and the last time I saw my parents was when CPS picked me up. They didn't even come to the hearing."

Jena sucked in a breath. "That sucks."

Ophelia shrugged. "It is what it is. I'm just saying don't bet the farm on blood."

"Well, hopefully Chase and I aren't assholes."

"Oh, you're definitely assholes," she said as the wood abruptly ended and they came to a tunnel at the end of the cavern. A much smaller path branched off, running beside the craggy wall.

"Thanks for that."

"No problem. What's the compass say?"

Jena glanced at it and then their choices. "Path."

Of course it was the fucking path. Ophelia sighed. "Let me go first."

"No arguments here."

Ophelia glowered over her shoulder and ducked under a slimy branch. "So how far along are you?" she asked, pretty sure that was a valid question. Ghandi, she hated small talk.

"Twenty-eight weeks. God, I don't understand how any of this is down here. It's like the lesser fae created a mini-mound beneath Havers. It's no wonder they don't want anyone down here. People would freak."

"Huh." Nope, didn't have any idea what any of that

meant, aside from it being weird as fuck any of this was underground. Ophelia stepped over a pool of green slime, and it bubbled up, spattering goo down her legs. Ugh, that was foul enough to make her rethink her stance on wearing pants.

"You know what you're having?" she asked. The splotches that'd hit her burned, slowly searing down her legs, and she scraped at them with her bare foot. Yeah, that wasn't any better.

"A girl, and no, we haven't picked a name yet," Jena muttered, skirting around the pool with a hand to her nose. It stunk like rotten eggs.

Ophelia scanned the trees, everything too still. "Trouble in paradise?"

"No, trouble with Aggie," Jena huffed, coming to her side as the path widened. "She's determined that we name the baby after her, and I'm sorry, but Agatha is a horrible name period, never mind for a baby. Why the hell would I do that to my kid?"

"I mean, it's better than Sway." Jena shot her a side-eye, and Ophelia shrugged. Whatever. She knew she was right. "Who's Aggie again?" Ophelia glanced up at a weird harrumphing in the distance.

Jena had heard it, too. "What the hell is that?"

"Not a clue, but we probably don't want to find out," Ophelia said, taking the witch's arm without really thinking about it. "Come on. It probably doesn't even know we're here. You were telling me about Aggie?"

"Um, yeah," Jena said, slowly turning away to keep walking. "She's my godmother and raised me after my mom died. I came back to Havers because she was really sick. And yeah, okay, she gets these premonitions, so there's got to be a reason for it, but she never fucking tells me anything, and it drives me crazy!" Jena shook her head. "Ugh. Sorry. Sore subject."

Ophelia's brow quirked. "Apparently. What's Chase have to say about it?" A branch snapped. Shit, was it getting closer?

"He's fine with whatever I decide," she grumbled.

Ophelia snorted. "What a fucking cop-out."

"I know, right?" she said, flicking a lock of hair from her face. "Like, there's such a thing as too much support. You ever try wearing Spanx for a couple days straight? Don't get me wrong, I love him, but that's Chase lately. Ever since the dragon thing, he just hovers, and I feel like I can't breathe."

Ophelia frowned, not wanting to delve any further into the subject of controlling men. She'd had enough of that at the Citadel, thank you very little. "Was that really legit? I mean, I saw the story in the papers, but come on—Felix?"

Jena chewed her lip. "I was pretty messed up, but there wasn't anyone else but us and Chase out there. The dragon's a lump of stone, so read into that however you want to."

"You know I'm a lawyer, right?" Ophelia snorted. "You totally didn't answer the question, but props for dancing around it."

Jena glanced at her but didn't say anything. Nice to know she was capable of keeping her mouth shut when it suited her. Something crashed out in the swamp, far too close for comfort. They both froze for a split second before picking up the pace.

Whatever was out there definitely knew they were there, and it was heading their way.

They hurried down the path, Jena's arm still looped through hers. Branches broke behind them, and that harrumphing got louder, thrumming through the ground beneath them. The little witch began panting, her hand at the side of her abdomen again.

"Are we still going the right way?" Ophelia asked.

Jena nodded. "Yeah, and I think I see something up ahead."

She wasn't wrong, but it didn't make Ophelia feel any better. A dilapidated stone cottage listed amongst the stunted trees, its roof covered with moss and vines.

"There's definitely a witch in there," Ophelia huffed.

Jena choked out a laugh. "God, I hope so, and if there's not, there's gonna be."

The front door hung open, but it was surprisingly sturdy, the thick oaken beams banded by iron. Ophelia shouldered it open the rest of the way, and the two of them fell inside, then slammed it behind them. She dropped a bar through two heavy brackets on either side, and they put their backs to it, panting.

The cottage was one big open room. Heavy wood beams crossed the ceiling above them, and the floor was made up of wide, filthy wood planks scattered with leaves and rotting detritus. A bunch of unidentifiable crap was in one corner, and what could've been a bed was disintegrating in the other. Directly across from them, a partially collapsed stone hearth stood. The only two windows were on either side of the door behind them.

"Fan-fucking-tastic. We're trapped," Ophelia spat as the floor vibrated with whatever was thumping toward them. The harrumph came again and the building shook.

"No." Jena shook her head. She licked her lips. "We're not trapped."

Ophelia exhaled, steeling herself to look out the grimy window. "I don't know what else you'd call it."

"Um, how about a secure place to regroup?"

Ophelia rolled her eyes, and the window beside her shattered in a cloud of glass as she turned toward it. She screamed, throwing her hands over her head, whatever had come through hitting the remains of the bed and dragging it across the room. She peeked through her blood-speckled fingers at the long gooey rope dripping slime across the floorboards. It smoked where it landed, a horrific stench filling the air.

Jena looked out the other window and gasped, then crouched down at Ophelia's side. "It's a frog."

She laughed. "What?"

"A frog." The witch nodded at Ophelia's incredulity, her eyes wide. "But it's like the size of a VW bus with horns and *a lot* of teeth."

Ophelia laughed again. A frog. What in the ever-loving fuck had her life come to—

She dove to the side, taking Jena with her as the bed careened toward them and slammed against the wall. The cottage shuddered, and the second window above them blew out, peppering them with glass. The frog's tongue hit the far wall. It caught on a moldering sheet, dragging it away.

"Isn't this supposed to be doing something right about now?" Ophelia snarled, yanking on the chain around her neck.

Jena scowled back, wiping blood from her brow. "It's an ill-intent charm, not a no-bodily-harm charm. It won't work if that thing's just hungry. It's just a big dumb animal."

The sheet at the end of the frog's tongue ignited, and the floor beneath it smoldered, leaves and the remains of the cottage's contents going up like straw.

Ophelia put her back to the door. "You sure about that?"

Jena didn't answer, squinting at the far wall. "Come on, I think there's a mirror over there."

"So? Pretty sure I don't wanna see how I look while I burn to death." Fire would absolutely kill her, but it was definitely not the death she'd have chosen.

"Not that kind, you idiot. There's symbols on the frame. If I'm right, that's our way out, and if that thing hits it, we're screwed." She glanced at the compass and then darted around the flames and disappeared into the mirrored surface.

"Jesus fucking—" Ophelia winced at the lance of pain

through her head and staggered to her feet, the room already thick with smoke. Flames glinted off the shards of glass littering the floor. She shuddered, way too familiar with what that stuff could do to flesh. Damn it, her feet were gonna be shredded, but wherever it led had to be better than down a demonic frog's gullet. Ophelia sprinted around the rapidly growing conflagration, agony slicing through her feet. She cried out and stumbled, a shard spearing through her foot, and fell head-first into the mirror.

Chapter Thirteen

OPHELIA LANDED on her face in a snowbank. She spat the icy crystals from her mouth and wiped them from her eyes, blinking. The soles of her feet throbbed in time with her pulse, the left one blinding her with agony. She shook her head to clear her vision, trying to get her bearings. Tall conifers and leafless trees stood around her, and the mid-day sun shone down from above. Where the fuck…

"See? I told you we weren't trapped." Jena grimaced, a hand on her abdomen as she panted, leaning against a boulder not far away. Damn, she looked like she'd been through the wringer. Her matted hair sparkled with glass shards, and her jacket was partially melted. She tried to zip it and gave up, wrapping it around herself. Soot streaked over her from head to toe, and her face was speckled with blood.

Ophelia rolled onto her rear, wincing at the trail of gore from her foot and glanced behind her. Nothing but scrubby brush and snow-filled woods. She picked out pieces of glass embedded in her soles, taking a deep breath before yanking out the long, jagged sliver. It slid free with a wash of blood. Ophelia tossed it aside, frowning at the gash. That was gonna be a problem.

"How did we get here?" she asked, trying to ignore the dread creeping up her spine.

Jena ignored her. The way the witch was staring at the

wound, she thought it was gonna be an issue, too. "Are you okay?"

"Hmm? Oh yeah, it'll be fine in a minute. Now answer the question."

"You better not be bullshitting me with more of that mystique."

Ophelia held up a hand, trying not to tremble. "Scout's honor."

Jena didn't look like she believed her, but let it go. "That mirror was a one-way portal. I'm more curious why it dumped us out on my family's property. The node's about a mile and a half in that direction," she said, lifting her chin to the west. "My mom had to have known about that tunnel," she murmured to herself, shivering as she rubbed her arms.

Ophelia didn't care. She pressed a handful of snow over her sluggishly knitting flesh, the virus rapidly depleting her reserves. "Is Chambers out here?"

Jena nodded, then grimaced as she got to her feet. "The compass seems to think so, and I'm pretty sure those are his tracks. They look fresh." She pointed to a trail of something.

If she said so. Ophelia had no idea what weasel tracks looked like, never mind fresh ones.

"Something must've tipped him off that we're after him," Jena murmured. "If he'd been up here, Matilda would've been able to get a lock on him." She sucked in a breath as Ophelia stood, hobbling. "Wow, you really look like shit. Are you sure you're okay?"

She waved the witch's concern away. "Yeah, I'm fine, and pot, meet kettle. Chase is gonna freak when he sees you."

"Well, at least I'm not turning blue and bleeding to death." Jena frowned, picking glass out of her hair.

"Pretty sure there's still time for that," Ophelia muttered. Even if they got to the ruins, it was one hell of a walk back to town. "You have your phone, right? You should call someone to come get us."

"Don't you have yours?"

"Nope. Just cigarettes and a flask in this baby," Ophelia said, patting her purse. "You know, the essentials. Besides, who the hell am I gonna call?"

Jena looked at her like she was an idiot. "How can you not have a phone? Don't you need to make work calls or something? Answer emails?"

"Town hall has a computer and a land line." Ophelia shrugged.

"You are so weird." Jena scowled. "I'm not calling Chase until we find Chambers. After going through all that, the last thing I wanna hear is 'I told you so,' and if you're fine to walk —" Ophelia rolled her eyes and Jena's narrowed. "What? I told Chase we can do this, and we can."

"I don't doubt that, but figured you might want to avoid frostbite."

"Wait, *I* might want to avoid frostbite?" the witch scoffed. "At least I have a coat and shoes. You're practically naked out here. Do you really not feel the cold, or is that more stupid vampire mystique?"

"Mystique," Ophelia admitted, her teeth chattering. "I feel it, but it's not like I'm gonna die from it." That box had been long since checked.

"Could've fooled me." Jena's brows furrowed. Ugh, there was that fucking pity again. Then— "What can kill a vampire?"

"Why, you thinking of gift ideas?" Ophelia snapped. "My birthday's not until November, but if you must know, the stake thing is legit and so is fire. Technically, bleeding out will do it too, but it takes a good week, week and a half, for the virus to die off completely—don't ask me how I know. Oh! And beheading."

"Lovely," Jena murmured. She flipped up the hood on her jacket and started walking in the direction she said Chambers was in.

Ophelia limped after her, the ankle-deep snow absolute torture after the warm muck they'd been walking through. No. She wouldn't die from the cold, but between that and the slice on her foot, things were getting dicey. The virus was burning through her reserves of blood faster than was advisable to keep her corpse upright. She eyed Jena. Probably best not to mention it. Ophelia pulled her flask from her purse, downing the scant mouthful that was left.

It just made her hungrier.

Great. So much for that. She wrapped her arms around herself and trudged after the witch. The woods here were silent, but not in a creepy way. Just peaceful. Calm. The crunching of Jena's boots. A light breeze rattling the icy tree branches. Ophelia shivered and looked down, watching where she was walking since she couldn't feel her feet anymore. Silver lining there. She focused on staying in the path Jena had rucked up and not the scent of blood drifting in the witch's wake.

"So, you did it for him?" she asked, pushing back the side of her hood to glance over her shoulder at Ophelia.

"Did what?"

"Became a vampire. To stay with Gideon."

"Yeah." Ophelia frowned, not wanting to talk about it. Especially after that kiss. Her insides warmed. She'd been too busy to process it when they'd been in the Below, but out here, there was nothing to do but think. "Why?"

Jena shrugged. "It's really romantic."

"Um, no, it was really stupid," Ophelia snorted. "Vampirism is zero stars, would not recommend." And walking through the woods alone with a hungry one was a close second. *Stop it, Phe. It's just a mental thing. As long as you don't start hearing shit, you're fine.*

"Well, yeah, I can see how that part sucks," Jena said, looking over her shoulder again, "but the fact that you gave up your mortality for him…you must really love him."

"I did. I do, I just…" Ophelia chewed her lips. "I'm not the same person."

"I'm gonna guess he isn't either. The man's obviously devoted to you. It must've killed him when you— Shit." Jena grabbed Ophelia's arm and crouched down behind an outcropping of stone with a finger to her lips. She closed her eyes and took a deep breath before peeking around the rock and slapping a hand over her mouth.

Ophelia wriggled beside her, *not* focusing on how appetizing the witch smelled. Down in the hollow below them was small pond. On the bank closest to them, a dark-haired man crouched inside a circle of bone white trees. Atop the rock in front of him was a weasel, and Ophelia would be damned if it didn't look like they were talking. Shit, that had to be Chambers.

The man threw his head back and laughed, then his hand snaked out, and he grasped the creature as it tried to bolt. It frantically thrashed in his grasp—

A sharp crack echoed through the icy woods.

The man tossed the weasel's body to the side. He stood, then looked directly at them, and smiled before he disappeared.

"Are you fucking kidding me?" No way had she just spent the last few hours tracking down that piece of shit just to see him killed. "Who the fuck was that?" Ophelia asked, her gaze fixed on their key witness's lifeless body and her stomach roiling. "For real. Tell me I didn't just see Chambers get murdered."

"Oh, it happened." Jena swallowed heavily, her eyes wide. "And the guy who killed him was my father."

GIDEON THUMPED down the steps of the bed and breakfast scowling. Not only was it entirely too close to the ocean, but he refused to occupy a space that smelled like last week's catch. It was little wonder Ophelia had declined the lodgings. He scrubbed a hand over his face and climbed back into Chase's truck, regretting not driving himself.

It wasn't that the man was unpleasant, he was actually far more palatable than the town's scrawny mayor. Gideon largely attributed that to the scant amount of verbiage that left the hulking were's lips. However, what had issued from them Gideon wasn't overly impressed with, and there was something about Chase Montgomery and his bride that niggled.

"No go?" Chase asked, throwing his truck into reverse.

"No." Gideon grunted, drumming his fingers on the armrest. "It was far too…provincial."

The big man snorted. "You know, there is one other place you could try. Havers's church isn't doing so hot after Father Pearson passed, and the trustees are looking to sell the vicarage. I don't think it's hit the market yet, but I just finished up a job there, and it's a solid place." He glanced at Gideon. "I mean, if living next door to a cemetery doesn't creep you out."

Gideon snorted. "Considering my intended is technically dead, I wouldn't say that's an issue. The effluvia of rotting fish, however, is."

"You should smell it at low tide," Chase laughed.

"I'll pass, thank you."

"Do you want to check it out? The vicarage, I mean?"

Gideon grunted his assent. If nothing else, it would distract him from Ophelia doing Gods knew what in the Below. He swept a finger over his lips, still feeling her upon them. Damn him, but he shouldn't have rushed her like that. He just couldn't bear her going off into the unknown without telling her how he felt.

That she was unable to reciprocate… He sighed. Emotions outside of anger and disdain had never been her strong suit.

Or his, truth be told. She would've had to take time with his declaration of love under the best of circumstances, and these, admittedly, were not.

Unfortunately, time abruptly didn't feel like a resource they had an abundance of.

Chase drove past the docks and back up into the town proper to an old, weathered church that probably wouldn't have been able to house a fraction of the population. The vicarage itself was set back from the parking lot, off to one side of the church grounds, beneath a pair of large, barren oak trees. An iron fence surrounded what Gideon assumed was a cottage garden on either side of a path leading to the front door.

They parked and got out of the truck. Chase fumbled with a ring of keys. "You're in luck. I haven't had a chance to give these back to the trustees, so you get the private tour."

Gideon listened to the man with half an ear as they entered, running a hand over the small grotesques carved into the door's pointed archway. The architecture was similar to that of the library, without the stain of modernization upon it. What repairs and additions had been made to the exterior had been done so tastefully, blending with the overall feel of the original building. He pursed his lips, not uninterested in seeing more.

Chase flicked on the lights. There was a mid-sized entryway and then another door leading to a long hall that went to the back of the house. A stairway ascended midway on the right and a doorway to a parlor stood on the left. It was modest, but charming with a coal fireplace he could see himself reading in front of and enough room for a small sitting area and a desk.

A decent-sized salon was at the other side of the house, the large, arched windows facing the south allowed for a panoramic view of the graveyard and the town beyond. The half bath in the hall was small, as was the kitchen, but neither he nor Ophelia were particularly domestic.

Upstairs was more appealing. At some point, the tiny bedrooms he'd anticipated had been combined, and the master suite was quite large with dormer windows looking to the east.

"We had to take down some walls a couple of years ago to get all of Father Pearson's medical equipment up here," Chase said, almost apologetically. "The house doesn't have a lot of storage, but it wouldn't be too difficult to put a pair of walk-in closets over there, or we passed a smaller room at the top of the stairs you could use as a dressing room."

Gideon nodded, poking his head into a very disappointing bath. The size was adequate, but the style was not. Well, one couldn't have everything. Not immediately, at any rate. "Very good. I believe this will suffice. Offer them whatever they're looking for, plus ten percent to secure it, should there be any other takers. Then quote me on putting in a decent bathroom. I'm assuming that work wasn't done by you."

Chase took a step back. "Uh…no. I think they had some big box store out of Klineville come in… Are you sure?"

"I wouldn't have made an offer if I wasn't," Gideon said, looking out over the town, past the hill by the bay, and into the distance. The node was out there, calling to him. He breathed in the tendrils of its power, tasting its agitation. Something was amiss.

Behind him, Chase's phone rang. "Sec. It's Jena," he said, answering it. "What? Wait, slow down… You— What?!… Yeah, I'm on my way." He hung up, already making for the door. "They're in the woods behind the ruins. We need to go —now."

"The ruins?" Gideon asked, following Chase as he jogged down the steps and hit the lights.

"Yeah, what's left of the manor house above the node. She

said something about a portal spitting them out there and her father killing Chambers," Chase growled, looking murderous.

Gideon sucked in a breath, the former mayor's demise a bit too timely for his liking, and Patrick's comment about Chambers being beholden to another player surfacing in his mind.

Chase locked up, and they hurried into the truck, Gideon's door barely closed before the man gunned the engine, peeling out of the parking lot and down the street.

"By your eagerness to get there, I'm assuming you've more cause for concern than the disaster this makes of your town's case?"

Chase laughed, squealing around a corner. "If that asshole's back in town? Yeah. It'd say so."

"Care to enlighten me?" Gideon asked, grasping the stability handle above the door. He had no fear of his own safety, but the man's driving was erratic to the extreme. Chase wove in and out of traffic, then floored it once they reached the town limits.

"Jena's dad is unseelie. He killed her mother and fucked over the town hardcore. Before she died, her mom trapped him, then a couple months back, during the turbine thing, he got out and tried to take Jena through the veil. We thought Jena banished him, but I guess we were wrong." He hit a bump and the truck was momentarily airborne, the backend fish tailing as they landed.

Unseelie...which would make her a half-breed and certainly explain the reason Jena Seymore had been niggling at him. Gideon fought the urge to spit at the bad taste the mention of dark sidhe perpetually left in his mouth. The creatures were the vermin his kind had been designed to exterminate. It was little wonder the node had been calling to him if one of their ilk was lurking about. And if he'd been involved with the events leading up to this case, Judge Carey needed to be notified immediately, and charges of a conspiracy filed.

However, it did not explain the similar sense of unease he got around Chase, nor what the hell the node had been thinking conscripting Jena as its guardian.

"She mentioned a portal?" Gideon asked.

"Yeah, a mirror or something."

"No, that wouldn't be the point of egress." Glass was far too fragile to travel through the veil. The miscreant would've needed something grounded by stones or trees. Gideon pursed his lips. "There has to be another one."

Chase glanced over at him, then shook his head and kept driving down the desolate county road. He abruptly made a hard left, turning down a drive between a break in a low stone wall. Gideon gasped at the wash of power coursing through him. Whoever had set that ward knew what they were doing. Six more successive wards followed, and then they were at the base of a windswept tor topped with ruins. Chase paused to throw his truck into four-wheel drive, and gunned it again, skirting around the hill to its backside, then killed the engine. He grabbed a blanket from the back.

"They're in the woods." He raised his head to sniff, then swore. "Wherever they are, it's downwind.

Gideon hummed, his attention focused on the node. Its power whispered around him, seductive, like a lover.

… *"Our service for yours…"*

He frowned, the repository's self-serving manipulation typical. It wouldn't allow those who'd pledge to it to perish, at least not without good reason, and certainly not its guardian if it could be helped. Ophelia however…

Damn it. He couldn't take that chance, and the blasted thing knew it.

"Fine, yes," he growled, knowing when he'd been beaten and not liking it one bit. "My service for yours. Get on with it."

Chase's gaze snapped to Gideon's at the words, his eyes widening. The power of the node coursed through Gideon. He inhaled, drawing it deep into his lungs. His skin grayed, and his fangs descended. Long curling horns spouted from his temples, their tips following the line of his jaw then curving outward, and his brow thickened. The seams of his shirt began to strain, and he fought against the rest of the transformation, not inclined to travel around Havers with nary a stitch. The node giggled within his mind and withdrew, the women's location burning like a beacon within his mind.

"Jesus fuck," Chase whispered hoarsely, falling back. "What the hell are you?"

"Exceedingly annoyed," Gideon said, rolling his shoulders as his musculature resettled. "And they're this way." He set off into the woods, not liking what he was sensing from Ophelia. Her reserves were dangerously low, and Jena was flagging.

"Yeah, I'm gonna need more than that," Chase growled, catching up to him.

Gideon's jaw tensed, but better the man knew the truth of it than suppositions flapping from his gums. "I'm a gargoyle."

"No shit?"

"No shit," Gideon rejoined succinctly, setting off without another word, the node urging him to hurry.

Chase scrambled after him. Gideon ignored the man's blathering questions, intent on his search. About a half mile in, he spied the two women clinging together as they stumbled through the snow.

Dear Gods. Ophelia was blue from the cold, splotches of her flesh gray and blackened.

He tore off his great coat as he rushed to her side, wrapping it around her, and sweeping her into his arms. Her irises were entirely too pale. She opened her mouth as if to protest, and her fangs descended.

"Don't. I'm carrying you whether you like it or not," he growled, trekking back through the woods.

"N-no, l-leave me h-here," she chattered. "S'n-not s-safe."

He didn't doubt that, but leaving her wasn't an option. "Don't you have you anything with you?"

She wet her cracked lips, her gaze straying to Gideon's throat. "M-my f-flask is e-empty."

"Then we'll do what we must." He scowled. Damn him, but he should've made sure she was properly outfitted instead of making grand declarations like some lovestruck school boy. The oversight was shockingly negligent on his part. He wouldn't let it happen again. And if that required he open a vein, so be it.

Her face crumpled, and she burrowed against his chest, weeping. Gideon held her closer, the show of emotion threatening to unman him. Never again. If she needed to go somewhere, it would be with him at her side. Just behind him, Chase had seemed to come to a similar decision as he carried Jena, his eyes burning with the same furious self-recrimination keeping Gideon warm.

Chapter Fourteen

OPHELIA PRESSED herself to Gideon's chest, close enough to hear the steady thud of his heart while her own broke. He didn't understand what he was saying. He couldn't.

… He will…

She flinched, raking a hand over her ear, and Gideon held her tighter, the dark voice in her head chuckling. *Shut up! I won't. Not him,* never *him!*

The voice didn't reply, its crouching anticipation at the edge of her consciousness somehow worse. Her teeth chattered, fangs scoring the inside of her lip. Mineral copper teased her tongue, and she suckled at it, whimpering. Retreating into herself as the virus began to target her nerves, lines of agony searing through her limbs, inducing a haze of mania.

She fought to stay in the now, cruel visions flitting across her mind's eye. No. No. She didn't want to see. *Please, please, no!* The voice laughed again, and she went rigid as images rolled over her. The massacre at the Citadel. The chamber behind the iron door in the bowels of the Inchisoare.

And Kremlyn standing amidst it all.

The voice's laugh cut off, one door in her mind closing and another opening.

A room resolved, details fuzzy, as if she was seeing it from a great distance. The impression of cold marble walls lined with tapestries and thick furs upon the floor. Books, broken glass, and torn fabric strewn across it. A painting lay shredded. Heavy, dark furniture the color of old blood overturned, their edges bleeding into the shadows, dust and eiderdown settling like snow.

"Do you feel better now?" Kremlyn asked. The vampire prince sat at a table oddly untouched by the destruction, his grizzled head cocked, honing a blade. A ropey scar bisected his right eye, the flesh at either side milky and dead. He scratched his closely shorn beard, grit-caked boots propped upon the table's edge and a curling map weighed down with a curved knife at one side. Numbered markers scattered across its indistinct surface, hedging around a central point.

"No," Vesper spat. She paced before the hearth across from him, fists clenched at her sides. Her corseted breast heaved, and a scowl contorted her thin, scarlet-stained lips. She paused to glower at him and straightened the diamond encrusted diadem at her brow, pinning back her long, silvered locks. "And I won't until I drive a stake through that bitch's heart myself!"

Kremlyn blew lightly upon his blade's razored edge. "The means of her death are not for you to decide," he tutted, his voice coming to Ophelia as if through water, its laziness belying the feral gleam in his remaining eye. "And I told you that recruiting the gargoyle in her stead was a mistake. Tempting fate is never wise. Better he had never heard of Havers or its accursed node."

Vesper huffed out a long-suffering breath. "What's done is done. What to do is the question now, and I've little doubt your father will take great joy in muddying the waters further." She spun in a rage, sweeping oddities from the mantle and sending them crashing to the floor. "Thaddeus Brock," she spat. "Oh! I hate him!"

"I'm aware," Kremlyn murmured, busy with his

whetstone. "I'll give you that the lawsuit was clever, but at this point it's dicey at best. Gideon isn't stupid. Perhaps he didn't have reason to ask questions before, but my sweet bride being there changes things. I'm sure Father gleefully sought him out to tell him of our involvement. You know he has eyes in the Citadel."

"And whose fault is that?" Vesper snapped. "Eyes aside, you should've ended that insufferable bitch after her pathetic coup attempt. Your father is enough of a wildcard."

"His nostalgia will be his undoing," Kremlyn tongued a gleaming fang. "And don't worry, Mother. I have plans for my darling little bird, and killing her isn't one of them. She's far too fun to play with."

"Perhaps, but gargoyles are not," a tall man said, stepping from the shadows. He flicked a lock of raven hair from his emerald green eyes. "And I'll wager he's becoming quite perturbed."

"Do we know for certain that they've reconciled?" Vesper asked. "Thackett seemed to think Gideon was still amiable to our cause."

"Thackett is an idiot easily swayed by competence." The man pursed his lips. "The stench of stone upon her was too thick for it to be otherwise. Whether he's sworn to the node is a different matter." He plucked a bottle of something from behind an overturned cabinet and uncorked it, sniffing. "If that's the case, your job has just become eminently harder."

"Regardless, he is one, and the Crimson Guard is legion," Kremlyn said, testing his blade's edge. "Open the way. It's time I collected what is mine, and by moonrise tomorrow, I shall have it." He leaned forward and drove it into the center of the map.

The vehemence of his strike reverberated through the room, and Ophelia gasped, thrust back into the now. She scrabbled against the arms holding her, the virus overriding her reflexes, limbs spasming, and her body screaming for blood.

Foam spattered from her lips. "Coming! H-he's coming!"

"Damn it," Gideon swore, fumbling at her as she thrashed. He took a knee, struggling to hold her. "Go! Quickly, leave us!" he shouted.

Ophelia hissed, her eyes rolling back in their sockets and everything abruptly too loud. His heart a bass drum, and two others nearby. Their beats increased, and a vehicle's door slammed. An engine roared to life and tires spun, ice crunching close and then distant. One of the arms banding her let go. Her back arched, limbs flailing to get free.

Blood perfumed the air and her awareness shrank. She went still. Warm flecks fell against her cheek and rent flesh pressed against her lips.

Ophelia bit down reflexively, quick as an asp, a strangled grunt vaguely registering as she fed. Unctuous, coppery brine filled her mouth and slid down her gullet. Her body tingled. Warmth blossomed within her chest, her gut cramping as it hit, then mellowing with every suck and pull as she glutted herself.

The tingle slowly morphed into a thrumming energy, purple light dancing behind her lids. Voices, pleading and cajoling, called to her, and a strange power flooded her being, beating back the darkness.

And with it came light.

~

GIDEON'S GRIP on Ophelia weakened, her hands fastened around his wrist as she fed. Around them, the node's power thrummed, encasing them in a bubble of purple mist. He breathed deeply, drawing it into his lungs and watching the delicate marks around her eyes darken and smear to resemble Thaddeus's. Gideon's brow furrowed. What had the vampire said? The node's power mutated the virus, changing how it presented itself. Had pledging himself to the magical repository altered his blood the same way Havers's residents' blood had been changed?

Time passed. His thoughts muddled, light-headed with how much Ophelia was taking from him, but unable to deny her hunger. Ghostly fingers plucked at him, and his skin hardened in response. Her fangs were forced from his flesh, and she mewled, lapping at his stony wrist and then falling into a deep slumber.

Gideon's throat bobbed, and he shook his head, dizzy. The bubble of power they'd been in faded, and a chill wind whipped across the base of the tor, hitting them like a fist. Ophelia whimpered in her sleep, burrowing closer. He slumped over her, the seriousness of their predicament slowly registering. He needed to get her somewhere warm. If they stayed out here, she would freeze, and there was no way he could revive her a second time. Frustration raged through him, burning away some of the dross clouding his mind. Fly. He could fly them back to town. Gideon gave a sad laugh. Yes, and if wishes were horses, beggars would ride. In his weakened state, he couldn't even remain upright.

A distant crunching of ice beneath tires reached his ears, and he turned to the sound. Was that a vehicle approaching? Damn the man, Chase had no business leaving his wife's side to come back here given her present condition.

Lights bumped up the rise toward them. Not a truck, but a gray Jeep. Gideon frowned, not recognizing the vehicle. His scowl deepened as it came closer, Liam Montgomery at the wheel, and a stocky, bald man in the passenger seat. The Jeep stopped several yards away, idling, and a window rolled down.

"We good to approach?" the bald man yelled across the distance.

"Yes," Gideon rasped, his relief warring with anger at his own ineffectuality.

The Jeep pulled up beside them, and the man and Liam got out. "Damn, you look even grayer than usual."

"Blood loss will do that," the bald man murmured, digging through a medic's kit. The number of bad tattoos covering him was appalling. "You know your type?"

"No." Gideon fought not to snarl. "And you are?"

"Tom. I'm an EMT. When Chase showed up at the compound, it sounded like you might need medical assistance, so I tagged along." He eyed Ophelia's gore-coated chin and throat, his own bobbing. Gideon had the worst urge to punch the judgmental scab. "She looks better than expected. You on the other hand... I'm guessing we need to get a couple pints into you, back someplace warm."

"I can assure you I'm fine," Gideon growled, his breath shallow.

"Tell me that when you're standing." Tom reached for Gideon's wrist despite his protest and checked his pulse above the rapidly knitting gash his fangs had made. "Yeah. Your pulse is for shit. Let Liam take her, and I'll help you up."

Gideon paused, then begrudgingly let Liam lift Ophelia from his arms, ignoring Tom's outstretched hand until she was safely stowed in the back of the Jeep. The medic grunted as Gideon slapped his palm against his, unable to heft all of his weight.

"Damn, you made of rock or something? Hey, Liam!" he called over his shoulder, missing Gideon's glower. "Little help?" The two of them fought to get Gideon to his feet, an arm over each of their shoulders, his legs not cooperating.

"You have got to be the heaviest son of a bitch I've ever triaged," Tom muttered after they had finally stumbled to the Jeep and hoisted Gideon in. The vehicle was ridiculously small, made more so by Tom's bulk blocking the view out the windshield. Gideon put a hand on Ophelia, lacking the strength to pull her into his lap, and keenly understanding what a canned sardine must feel like.

"We're taking you to the compound. Jena and Chase are there, and we've got plenty of room," Liam said, glancing in the rearview once they'd hit the main road.

"It's also where I left the ambulance," Tom added, exchanging a look with Montgomery. "And you my friend, just might need it."

"I'll be fine," Gideon said again, groggy but certain he'd survived far worse than this. Unfortunately, that had been contingent upon him reverting to his stone form beside the node's well at the center of the City of Light. His strength was rapidly fading the further they got from Havers's node. His connection to it would have to be enough. He refused to be parted from Ophelia, and the offer of alternate lodging was somewhat of a relief. He hadn't been relishing the idea of spending another night on a bare twin mattress. "And thank you for your overture of hospitality."

"'Overture?'" Tom snorted. "Who the hell is this guy?"

Liam ignored him, glancing in the rearview again. "Yeah, man, no problem. It's not like we could just leave you out there."

Gideon frowned, his mind drifting with thoughts of plenty who would. He'd done little to foster relationships outside of his professional network and was certain none of them would lift a finger if there wasn't something tangible in it for them.

It had been a very, very long time since he'd had anything even remotely resembling a friendship, and the potential for finding that in some backwater hamlet shook him. He brushed a lock of matted hair from Ophelia's face, begrudgingly admitting that the prospect was not unwelcome. If they were to build a life here together, coming to a mutual accord with the town's residents would be necessary.

Of course, that didn't mean it would be pleasant. He scowled at the two men in the front seat snickering over an inside joke. But, as long as he and Ophelia weren't the punchline, Gideon suspected he could make do.

Liam pulled off onto a goat path several minutes later, and Gideon's teeth rattled as they bumped down the poor excuse for a road. Tall conifers lined the way, the woods dark and deep. They approached several clusters of snow-bound, dilapidated trailers. Gods help them if this was the compound they'd spoken of. Thankfully, they passed by the sad structures and continued deeper into the forest.

Gideon frowned, his senses tingling as his awareness of the node grew and his strength trickled back. Had they gone in a circle? There was no other explanation as to why he'd feel its presence so keenly. He stared off into the distance to his left, confused.

"What's out there?" he asked, unable to remain silent.

Liam glanced at him in the rearview. "Huh? Oh, um, the hollow, I guess. We're more or less in the middle of the pack's territory. Why?"

Gideon chewed his lip, at odds with himself. "Because the node's presence is much stronger here than it should be," he said, his curiosity overruling caution.

Liam was silent for several breaths. "Ah, that's probably something you should ask Jena," he finally said, running a hand over his jaw.

Indeed. Gideon scowled, his temper rising. If she was leveraging her guardianship to benefit the Unseelie Court— No. The node was young, but it wouldn't risk endangering its existence by allowing a fairy mound to form.

Yet, he couldn't deny the bleed of power. He scrubbed a hand over his face, his thoughts still muddled and nothing fitting together as it should. What the hell was going on in this town? Perceiving power out here didn't make sense. Nodes had defined boundaries and were restrained to the area where leylines crossed. It had absolutely no business popping up in the middle of nowhere.

Jena had some serious explaining to do.

They continued on for several minutes more and came to a large log cabin set in a clearing. Chase's truck, a handful of other vehicles, and an ambulance were pulled beside its long front porch.

"I'll be right back." Liam parked beside them and got out, flipping up his seat to take Ophelia.

"So, you gonna tell me what kind of supe you are?" Tom asked, turning to look at him. "It would be a hell of a lot easier to treat you if I knew."

Gideon glowered at him, remaining silent.

"Then I guess we'll do it the hard way." The man grinned at him. "If it makes it any easier, I'm a were—lynx, specifically. Local pack wasn't too keen on Kelsey and me dating at first, but the Montgomerys, they're good people. FYI, don't fuck with them or I'll bury you."

"You're welcome to try." Gideon fought to keep his eyes open, his breath shallow. "But I'd prefer it if you waited until I'm able-bodied to threaten me."

The man's grin widened. "Nah. I want to give you something to dream about after you pass out. You know, something for your subconscious to marinate on."

The door to the house opened, and Tom got out of the Jeep as Liam jogged down the steps. "Ready?" he asked.

"No, but we're doing it. Jesus, did he get heavier?" He swore, dragging one of Gideon's arms across his shoulder and wrestling him from the vehicle.

Liam grunted, staggering as he took the other. "Sure as hell seems like it." They paused at the base of the stairs. "Fuck. How the hell are we gonna do this?"

"One step at a time, my brother, and if he falls, hope it's forward."

The journey to the front door took entirely too long. Both

men were sweating profusely as a surly teen wearing far too much black opened the door for them.

"Holy crap," she said, her blue, kohl-lined eyes wide. "You do look just like Chase. Well, if he was half dead."

"Not now, Cruze," Liam muttered, huffing past her. "You guys are in the spare room in the back. Kelsey's in there cleaning up Ophelia, and Felix snagged some clothes from my dad's closet that should fit you."

Glorious. Gideon eyed the plaid-on-plaid decor, positive that whatever was delivered would be of a similar aesthetic. The three hobbled across a vaulted great room toward a door at the far end. The windows lining the southern wall looked out over the forest, and a fire crackled in the large fieldstone fireplace at its center.

A woman's soft voice began to register, growing louder as they cleared the doorway. The walls here were a deep green plaster, and a king sized bed dominated the room. Liam and Tom gratefully dropped Gideon onto it. He fell onto his back, long past attempting to maintain his dignity. Gods, why was it so hard to breathe?

"Yeah, that's what I thought." Tom wiped a hand across his brow. "I'm gonna grab my gear. I'll be back."

"That you, Liam?" a woman called from an adjoining room.

He turned his head to the voice, hands on his hips and panting. "Yeah."

"Cool. Help me get her into bed?"

He left the room and returned a moment later with Ophelia in his arms. She was still out cold, and they'd dressed her in a loose t-shirt and pajama pants with pink, fluffy bunnies on them. Gideon gave a weak snort. She was going to hate that.

"Wow, you look awful," a woman said, coming in behind them. Her dark hair was in pigtails and, Gods help him, she was in overalls.

Gideon stared at her, blasé.

She gave a little wave. "Hey. I'm Kelsey, Liam's twin. Tom's my boyfriend." She squirmed beneath his unblinking gaze. "Okay, then. I'm gonna go see what the kids are up to."

And thank the Gods for that. Gideon closed his eyes, drifting off.

Swearing brought him backing into the now.

"Damn it, that's the third fucking needle I've broken. What the hell is this guy?"

"I dunno," Liam murmured. "Chase said something about a gargoyle, but here? I thought they were only on the far continent."

"Yeah, well, big cat shifters aren't supposed to be in this part of the world either, but that sure as hell explains— Sec, looks like he's coming to… Hey, dude, can you quit the stone act? You need fluids."

"No. Allergic to saline," Gideon rasped, his eyes fluttering open. He tried to swallow, his mouth uncomfortably dry.

"Then we'll skip it, but you need blood."

Gideon didn't disagree with Tom's assessment, but reversing his body's reflex to the damage he'd incurred wasn't something as simple as flicking a switch. However, perhaps he could manage a small area.

"Press where you need the needle," he rasped.

The bald man's brows furrowed and then a steady pressure began at the crook of Gideon's right arm. He focused on the dime-sized point, softening his skin—

"Got it." A sharp prick, then a quick burn, followed by a subtle warmth. "Right," Tom said, adjusting a drip. "Let that do its thing, then I've got two more with your name on them. I'll be back to check on you."

Gideon grunted and closed his eyes again, surrendering to exhaustion.

Chapter Fifteen

GIDEON'S EYES fluttered open at the sound of someone moving about outside his room. A single light burned on the bedside table, and Ophelia curled against his flank. Sometime during the night she'd divested herself of her garb. He pulled the sheet up over her milky shoulder. Apparently, his blood supply had been adequately restored. His body was far too appreciative of the bare stretch of flesh given the circumstances.

What time was it? He blew out a breath, that horrendous dryness gone from his mouth. Beside him, an IV on a rolling stand dripped, the liquid in the bag ruddy.

Gods, he felt like shit, and that was a marked improvement from earlier. He pushed up to sit, riffling his hair. Someone had managed to get him into clean clothes, though their condition was questionable. The t-shirt was stained and had a hole by the hem, and the ridiculous mustard and red plaid pajama pants were worn thin from use.

Gideon frowned. He'd have to put a call into the service he used to get his apartment packed up and delivered to Havers. Relying on the castoffs of strangers irked.

He scrubbed at his stubble, attempting to focus his gummy eyes on the small digital clock beneath the lamp. Two-sixteen a.m. When they'd gotten back to the compound, it'd still been light. He fumbled for his phone, frowning at the absence of correspondence. The Vampire Court had definitely cut him out of the loop. He was going to have to send that note to Judge Carey sooner than not, positive they'd already besmirched his reputation, if not ended his career.

Surprisingly, the prospect did little to faze him. The vast majority of the wealth he'd accrued was safe with his brethren in the City of Light, and Gideon had little attachment to his concrete assets. He now had more important concerns, and keeping Ophelia safe was paramount.

His brow rose at the single email from Thackett. Patrick Montgomery had indeed taken the out and pled not guilty, laying all the blame squarely on Havers's coven.

Gideon frowned. Not ideal, but it should keep the man alive, and hopefully he could be persuaded to recant that statement when called to the stand. If it came to that. Given that Gideon had enough evidence to open an inquest into both sidhe and the Vampire Court's involvement in Havers at the federal level, his gut told him they weren't going to allow that to happen. No, this would come to a head long before the government became involved.

Which meant Havers needed to prepare. If the vampires were out for blood, the town was in danger. Hopefully, that was Chase rustling around in the other room, and Gideon could determine where the populace stood defense-wise.

Right, get your ass out of bed, Gideon. Easier said than done. He grimaced, throwing off the comforter and pocketing his phone. He gripped the IV stand, steadying himself as he rose and shuffled to the door with it in tow. In the great room, the fire had burned low, but the lights were on in an adjoining room. He made it as far as a breakfast bar and sat heavily on one of the wooden stools, huffing as he looked into the kitchen. Jena stood with her back to him, rummaging inside of an industrial-sized, stainless steel refrigerator. Ah, even better. He wanted answers about that wash of power he'd felt on the way to the compound earlier.

"Explain to me why I sensed the node so strongly in the center of the pack's territory," he said, his voice raspier than he'd like.

She gasped, spinning around with a plated cake clutched in her hands. "Oh my God, don't do that! What are you even doing out of bed? Tom said you were out cold."

"Tom was mistaken, and one could ask you the same." She was pale, her dark hair hanging lankly to her waist. Small cuts stippled her face, and a blood-spotted bandage was wrapped around one of her hands.

Her cheeks flushed. "I was hungry. You want a piece?"

He eyed the gooey chocolate confection, his stomach roiling. "I'll pass."

"Suit yourself." She shrugged, plopping a generous slice onto a plate. "You felt the node's power out there because it's a reserve nexus. My mom created it to anchor the ward across the pack's territory on this part of the peninsula, and there's another to the east anchoring the ward there."

Gideon pinched the bridge of his nose. "And explain to me why you thought this was a good idea?"

"Um…because it was the only way to power the wards?" she asked, licking frosting off her thumb.

No, that was what his kind were for. He supposed they hadn't had that option, but— His eyelids fluttered. "You really don't have any idea what you're doing, do you? The nodes have a set area of influence for a reason. The grid of leylines needs to remain in balance for it to function properly. By giving more room to the spirits it houses here, you've inadvertently weakened the grid elsewhere."

Jena's jaw dropped. "Oh."

"Oh." Gideon sighed. It would need to be brought into balance, but now wasn't the time, especially with an unseelie lurking about. "Tell me about your father."

The plate she was holding clattered onto the counter, and she rested her hands at either side of it. "He murdered my mother and tried to take me across the veil. I thought I banished him, but I was wrong." Her expression was tight, her green eyes crackling and leaving him zero doubt that there was no love lost there.

A knot in Gideon's shoulders loosened, glad he didn't have a secondary conspiracy to deal with. "Yes, Chase gave me the CliffsNotes. He's unseelie?"

She deflated and stabbed a fork at her cake. "He's… something. Everyone here thought he was a warlock, but he racked up way too much bad karma. I asked him if he was unseelie, and he gave me some line about having enough to qualify and the rest being murkier."

"Well, that's disturbing," Gideon muttered. "You don't happen to know his name or have a picture of him, do you? Any description you can give would be helpful."

Her eyes narrowed as she chewed. "Why?"

Gideon sighed, unable to believe he was offering this up, but he'd pledged to the blasted thing, damn it. He needed to protect the node to the best of his ability—no matter how painful that might become.

And it would.

"In the old country, we have a repository of knowledge. If I have something to go on, I can make a call and attempt to find out exactly what we're dealing with. Those attracted to the nodes' power rarely fade from the radar after they've set their sights on them. Once we have identifying him set in motion, the next order of business is to destroy the portal he's utilizing."

"Everyone here called him William. He's tall, black hair, green eyes and is stupid charming," she frowned at the last bit. "I have a picture back at the Witchery with what's supposed to be his name written on the back."

"You don't remember it?"

"No, every time I try to, it goes fuzzy, but I'm ninety-nine percent sure the portal's in the circle of birch by the pond where he killed Chambers."

Her not being able to recall the fiend's name was concerning, but Gideon's eyebrows shot up at the location of the portal. "It's within the node's boundaries?"

"Yeah." Jena shrugged, chewing. "Is that weird?"

"Everything about this town is weird."

"That's fair." She popped another bite of cake into her mouth.

"I'm more curious as to why you didn't feel him breach the veil," Gideon said, sweeping a finger over his lips. "The node should've given you warning. Even I felt its agitation yesterday."

Jena frowned as she chewed. "There might've been something a few months ago. After the dragon thing, I spent two days in Klineville General. I was pretty out of it."

"If he knew to cross over then, you're being watched." Gideon muttered, a pattern of maleficence emerging. It was not uncommon for unseelie to recruit a handful of useful idiots to push their agenda.

"Lovely." Jena scraped up another forkful of cake. "But I don't get it. If there's a mound, what do the vampires get out of it? Wouldn't it be just as uninhabitable for them as the rest of the supes and normys?"

Gideon scratched his jaw. "One would think, unless the goal was to harvest residents as they were pushed from its confines... Still, that's rather short sighted, and I have a bad feeling they'll be here in force long before that occurs."

She froze. "Why would they want to do that?"

"Because I've enough evidence to initiate a federal inquiry which would put the Vampire Court's existence in jeopardy. According to Thaddeus, their interest lies in the ability of the node to somehow alter the blood of Havers's residents. Imbibing it mutates the virus that causes vampirism, breaking their tribal affiliations. He refused to explain what that actually means, save that it's something the vampire queen has been trying to capitalize on for a very long time. I got the impression he was responsible for rebuffing her efforts, and that this lawsuit was something of a last-ditch effort on her part."

"I'm surprised you got that much out of him. Mr. Brock isn't great at staying on topic."

"Indeed. I went to ask for further clarification and got a dissertation on bees."

Jena snorted. "Well, whatever the vampires are trying to accomplish, I can guarantee you my dad's working a different angle and just using them to get what he wants." She bit her lips, tapping her fork against her plate. "And honestly, I'm not sure if that's creating a mound."

Gideon cocked a brow, skeptical to the extreme. A foothold in this realm was *always* what the unseelie wanted. "And what makes you say that?"

"That night he tried to take me across the veil," she said slowly. "He waited until after I'd pledged myself to the node and became its guardian. Like, it was legit about to go full-on sidhe mound, and he told me to 'take it in hand,' since that's what I was there for."

Gideon's brows furrowed. That was odd. "He did?"

"Yeah." She shook her head, scowling. "And after I'd pledged to become its guardian, he got this huge smile on his stupid face, like he was proud or something."

Well, that left limited options as to Jena's father's pedigree. The odds of him being a sidhe, unseelie or otherwise, had just dramatically fallen, which increased the possibility that they had an extremely large problem on their hands. Gideon pulled out his phone and exhaled heavily, his thumb hovering over a number he hadn't used in far too long. Renard would give him hell for it, but it couldn't be helped.

He shot off a quick text grimacing. Gideon didn't have

what most would consider a family per se, but he and Renard had been created from the same block of granite, which made him as close to a brother as a grotesque could get. It also made him a perpetual thorn in Gideon's side.

The phone rang almost immediately, and he grimaced, holding it at arm's length. *Damn it Ren, I texted you for a reason. A simple yes or no would've sufficed.*

Which Renard absolutely knew and absolutely didn't care.

"You gonna get that?" Jena asked on the third ring.

Not if he had a choice in the matter. Unfortunately, he didn't.

"Gideon," he scowled, glowering at her to leave. She leaned against the stainless steel counter and continued to eat. Fantastic. He was dinner and a show.

"I'm sorry, who's this?" Renard replied in their native tongue. At least the witch wouldn't be privy to everything. "I don't believe I know a Gideon. You must have the wrong number."

"Damn it, Ren. You know very well who I am, and I've little time for your games. I need you to compile a list of entities with—"

"And why, pray tell, would a lawyer need that?" Renard asked, cutting him off.

Gods, Gideon could practically see him sitting there, inspecting his nails with a smug little smile beneath his foppish mustache. The bastard had always bet on him crawling back to the node. That it was Havers's instead of the City of Light's made little difference.

"One wouldn't," Gideon gritted out. "However, my circumstances have changed dramatically within the past forty-eight hours—"

"I knew it!" The glee in Renard's voice was obscene. "Well, well, little brother, look at you coming back to the fold. Granted, you held out longer than any of us expected. I have to ask, did swallowing all that pride hurt?"

"No, but speaking to you does," Gideon grumbled. "Are you going to get me the information or not?"

Renard tsked. "That depends. Are you going to tell me what finally broke you down?"

"No."

His brother sighed. "Well, then I suspect I'm far too busy to—"

Damn it. "Ophelia's here."

"Ah…" Renard chuckled. "I knew I liked her."

"You've never met her."

"No, but any woman that can wrap your dick so neatly around her finger after completely crushing your soul I hold in high esteem. Details, please."

"You're not getting any until I get information on any tall, dark-haired entities with emerald green eyes. He's extremely charming, able to pass as a warlock, and goes by William. His true name slips from people's minds. It also sounds like his interest in the node is tangential."

"Mmm, that's never a good combination."

"Indeed." Gideon pinched the bridge of his nose. He wouldn't have called the damned bastard otherwise.

"Fine, I'll see what I can dig up, but your current location would help. The repository's grown considerably since you were last here. The internet's a marvelous thing. Did you know there's websites where women—"

"Yes, I'm aware," Gideon said, glancing at Jena. "I'm currently in Havers-by-the-Sea. How soon can you have something for me?"

"Give me a few hours. Your email still the same?"

"It is, and thank you."

"Oh no, thank you," he laughed. "This call has just won me a great deal of money. Don't be surprised if some of the others reach out now that we've a foothold on the new continent. You're still the only grotesque that's managed to get a dispensation, and one can't help but wonder why that is…"

Gideon scowled. "I have a theory, but now's not the time to share it."

"Gods, you're such a tease."

"And you're a boorish prick."

"Love you, too, little brother," Renard laughed, ending the call.

Gideon slapped the phone down and raked a hand through his hair.

"Family?" Jena asked.

He glanced up at her. "Pardon?"

"I don't need to speak whatever that was to glean that whoever you were talking to has got to be related to you the way they just got under your skin."

Gideon grunted, not denying the observation. "Regardless, he should have something for me in a couple of hours. Hopefully, we get a hit and can use the information to figure out what your father's after and why he's using the Court to get it."

"Yeah, good luck with that," she said, putting her dish into the sink. "In the meantime, I'm going back to bed."

"I'd like to see those reserve nexuses first thing and then the portal. I'll do what I can there, but the town needs to prepare for what's coming."

"Felix can talk to the coven, and Liam should be able to rally the pack since his dad isn't here. Between the two of them, they'll get the word out to the rest of the town." Jena chewed her lip. "But Chase is going to have to be the one to show you everything." She scowled. "I'm pretty sure I'm under house arrest."

He snorted. Good. She and Ophelia could keep each other company. "Sleep well," Gideon murmured as the witch left, doubting he could do the same. He sat at the counter for a moment longer, responsibility weighing on him.

Jena was right about Renard getting under his skin, but his brother's attitude was the least of it. Their brethren hadn't been pleased when Gideon was released by the node, and it had created a scandal across the continent—especially when he'd braved crossing the ocean and left. Saltwater was the one thing that could destroy their kind, and grotesques steered clear of it. Even traveling over the loathsome stuff by plane had unwholesome repercussions. Without a node to draw on, Gideon had been practically bedridden for nearly a century before returning to full strength. That he'd endured all of that to take up the mantle over here beneath a witch would kick the hornet's nest up all over again.

Gideon shook his head. It couldn't be helped, and what did he care what anyone said about him an ocean away? He didn't care what was said about him beneath this roof. Ophelia, however, was a different matter. Renard had been one of the few who refrained from besmirching her name after their disastrous engagement. Gideon could only imagine how the tongues would wag now.

He stood. It didn't matter, and he'd been away from her side for long enough. Beside him, the IV bag had emptied, and he plucked the needle and its port from his arm before he started back to the room, steadier on his feet than he had been. His thoughts were heavy, churning things, the seriousness of the charge he'd accepted weighing on him.

All of which fled from his mind as he opened the bedroom door. Ophelia had kicked off the covers and lay supine across the sheets in all her glory. His breath caught at her beauty, his pajama bottoms growing tight. *Not the time, Gideon.* He adjusted himself with a slow breath and turned off the light before lying down at her side.

She murmured something in her sleep and rolled over to snuggle against him. He gingerly put his arm beneath her head, and she sighed, a hand over his chest. Her leg rose, knee skimming up his thigh before stopping dangerously close to his arousal. Images of their past life together flitted through his head, all the games they used to play.

None of which decreased the throbbing in his loins.

He watched the slow rise and fall of her breast in the dim light from the moon outside their window. Surely she would be opposed to such advances now. Still…he couldn't help himself from brushing her hair from her face, his fingers tailing down her throat to her collarbone. She was exquisite.

His brow furrowed, it had to be a trick of the light, but the dark markings around her eyes seemed lighter than they had been. The dark smears had faded to gray, their edges indistinct. He mentally added tracking down Thaddeus to his list of objectives for tomorrow, and Gods help the vampire if he mentioned bees.

Gideon closed his eyes, lulled by Ophelia's soft breathing. Her hand had traveled downward, resting across the small slice of bare skin between his t-shirt and the waistband of his pajamas. He pressed his lips to the crown of her head and sighed. Sleep might escape him, but he would gladly forgo it with her at his side.

Chapter Sixteen

OPHELIA LAY against Gideon's chest, pretending to sleep. Ever since she'd woken, that stupid vision had her anxiety on overdrive. After what she'd been privy to in the Inchisoare, she had zero doubt that meeting had been real.

Kremlyn was coming with the Crimson Guard, and Jena's dad was helping them.

Ophelia blinked back tears. She knew it was stupid to lie here and not open her mouth about it, but number one, it was like three in the frickin' morning, and two, she'd been positive that Gideon had abandoned her when he hadn't been at her side earlier. Yeah, so he'd said that he loved her and that he was staying in Havers, but how could anyone love what she'd become?

Especially after what she'd done to him.

Her recollection of what'd happened out in the woods was spotty, but she remembered enough to know that she'd fed on him. The thought made her stomach churn. At the Citadel they reduced the normys that filled that role to livestock, referring to them as cows, chattel far beneath vampires. Gideon was anything but, and to use him like that—Ghandi, what kind of a monster was she?

It would've served her right if he had abandoned her, but he hadn't. He'd come back, and the last thing she wanted to do was anything to screw this up.

Could he really love her?

She snuggled closer, a hum running through her body, her fingers and toes prickling. The sensation wasn't exactly unwelcome, just strange. So was the fact that the sheets weren't making her skin crawl. It wasn't that she liked the feel of them, they were just…tolerable. There was something about that hum… She frowned, realizing that she'd stripped out of the pajamas someone had stuffed her into more out of habit than need.

If she didn't know any better, she'd think whatever that was had short circuited her ick factor, but that wasn't possible, was it? Either way, it was a strange relief and just underscored how badly the Citadel had fucked her up. Not being able to touch and be touched. She trailed her fingers along Gideon's abs, craving the feel of him, starved for skin-on-skin contact.

Fuck it. Whatever this reprieve was, she wasn't gonna waste it.

She held her breath, slowly sliding her hand beneath his waistband. He tensed, then bit back a low groan as her fingers brushed his swollen crown.

"Phe…?" he whispered hoarsely.

She nipped his earlobe trying to channel the Ophelia from before things went to shit. "Were you expecting someone else?" Ugh, she sounded more apologetic than flirty.

"No." Gideon snorted, then groaned as she began to stroke his rigid length. It kicked against her palm, and her thighs clenched. "But I wasn't expecting this either… May I touch you?"

She nodded against his throat, and he ran his hand over the curve of her shoulder to her breast, leaving goosebumps in his wake. Ophelia arched, her nipple hardening against his palm, and he captured her mouth with his. Softly, then more intent, his tongue skimming along her lips, begging for entrance— She pulled away, the intimacy of it throwing her, then tentatively kissed him back.

"We don't have to do this," he murmured, his forehead against hers.

"Shut up." She scowled. "I want to."

"Then I think it best if you take control," he said, pulling off his shirt and settling onto his back with his hands behind his head. The way his muscles bulged wasn't fair.

Her hand on him stilled. "What?"

"I don't know what your limits are anymore, Phe. I need you to show me what you want, because I don't trust myself to not to push them beyond what you're comfortable with. For instance, there's nothing I would love more than bending you over my knee for parading around town in practically nothing and smoking, then teasing you unmercifully until you begged for my cock. I haven't decided if I'd give it to you…though it has been some time and filling every last one of your pretty little holes sounds quite appealing." He scratched his jaw. "Perhaps not here, though. I'd very much enjoy hearing you cry out, and no doubt one of those idiots would burst in here to rescue you."

Ophelia laughed. "They probably would."

"Mmm. So be a good girl for me and take charge."

She chewed her lip. Gideon never gave up control in any aspect of his life; not personally, not professionally, and certainly not in the bedroom. Her eyes narrowed. "Is this a trick?"

His brows knit. "No, poppet, this is about you taking back your pleasure so that the next time I have you in bed, I can worship you as you deserve."

What the hell did she even say to that? Damn it. Nothing, and by the smirk on his face, he knew it. She scowled and busied herself pulling down his ridiculous pajama bottoms so she wouldn't have to look at him.

Well, not his face at least.

Her gaze went to his thick cock as it sprang free and she wet her lips, sweat beading her hairline. She tossed the bottoms to the floor and stared at him for a breath. Ghandi, the moonlight made him look like he was carved in alabaster, a more perfect version of anything the Greeks ever came up with. Ophelia settled beside him and trailed her fingers up his corded thigh, following the dips and valleys of muscle to his hip bone and the sinewy triangle at his lower abdomen.

Her hand hovered above his length, and his hips rose in anticipation. A smile ghosted across her lips. She lightly drew a line from base to tip, pre-cum pulsing from his slit. She swirled it around his fat crown, then brought her thumb to her mouth, glancing at him from below her lashes.

"Brat." He hissed through his gritted teeth, his hands behind him, gripping the headboard's rails. The heat in his eyes stoked the smoldering fire at her core. "You have no idea how badly I'd like to bury myself in your throat right now."

She shivered, straddling him, and pretty sure she'd just discovered one of those limits he was talking about. "Aww. Poor baby. Too bad I'm in charge."

He chuckled darkly. "For now. Enjoy it while you can, poppet, because I'm certainly going to enjoy you later."

"Mmm." Ophelia crept up his body, rising to brush her breasts against his face. He groaned. "How about you enjoy me now instead?"

Gideon's eyes glimmered in the moonlight, and Ophelia's pulse raced as she spread her thighs before him, setting her knees beside his ears. He raised his head to snuff at her, the animalistic instinct catching her breath. His chest rumbled with pleasure, and his eyes flicked up to hers. "May I use my hands?"

Ophelia wet her lips. "Not yet."

"Then let's give you something else to rest upon, shall we?" he said, his horns sprouting from his head and curving down along his jaw, under her thighs. Their flared tips forced her legs wider. "When you start to shake, I want it to be for the right reasons." He ran the flat of his tongue up the seam of her cleft, then delved between her folds to the sensitive pearl at its peak.

Ophelia gasped, pleasure coursing through her, her body softening and opening for him. *Oh God...this is what it's supposed to feel like...* She fisted his hair with one hand, and the other slapping onto the headboard. Gideon drew her flesh into his mouth suckling, then sweeping into her. Her hips began to move against him of their own accord, her nipples drawing into tight, turgid points.

The headboard creaked as he gripped it tighter, groaning and feasting upon her. A tight heat coiled in her core, begging to be released. So long. *It has been so long...* Ophelia's thighs quivered, her breath speeding as her body raced to the finish line. "Deo...oh God...yes..."

He growled, thrusting his tongue into her, his nose rubbing against her clit. That delicious pressure grew, warmth blooming, and her head growing light. She tore at his hair, arching her back as she came, pleasure searing through her, and violet light flaring across her vision. Her thighs spasmed around him, a wash of passion soaking his stubble and dripping from his chin as he grinned.

"Mmm. Good girl," he rumbled, gently lapping up her release.

Holy hell, that hadn't taken long. Ophelia collapsed against the headboard, her breasts heaving. Gideon slowly resorbed his horns, and she tottered to the side, landing on a pillow. She pulled another pillow into her lap as her head tipped back against the wall. What it was supposed to be like. Dear God, what had she just done? Tears pricked at her eyes.

Gideon pushed up to sit. "Are you all right?"

"No." She tightened her lips and shook her head, wiping a hand over her cheeks. Dread churned in her stomach. "I-I shouldn't have done that. Shouldn't have let myself feel how it should be." It would make what was coming that much worse.

He dragged a hand through his hair, confusion and anger etched across his features. "What are you talking about?"

Her throat bobbed as she swallowed. "During my bloodlust I had a vision. Kremlyn will be here with his Crimson Guard tomorrow. They know about us, about you. Jena's dad is going to open the way for them." She turned away from him, her face crumpling.

"Good. Let them come and have done with this," he spat.

She paled. "You can't mean that."

"There's no stopping what's coming, Phe." Gideon sighed, drawing her into his arms. He kissed the crown of her head. "And it's progressed well beyond the point of niceties. Wheels are in motion. We either follow suit or become crushed beneath them."

"There's no time." She shook her head. "Kremlyn—he said he'd have me collected by moonrise."

Gideon's chest rumbled with a low growl. "He's mistaken, and it's long past time he and the rest of to Court suffer the consequences of stealing you away. I'm not without resources, Phe. Especially with a node to draw upon."

He was also not without weaknesses, and Ophelia was positive Vesper knew what they were. "Promise me you'll stay away from the ocean. You know they'll try to draw you out over deep water, and if that happens—" She shook her head, unable to go on at the thought of him trapped as a block of granite at the bottom of the sea.

"There's only one thing that I would take that risk for, and you'll be far from the fray. I want you to stay with Jena. In some respects, she's more competent than I originally gave her credit for, and she and the node will protect you whilst I do what needs to be done."

"I don't want you to leave."

"I don't want to go."

Ophelia turned in his arms to straddle him, burying her face against his neck. "I do love you, Deo. I'm sorry I didn't say it before, I just—"

"Shh. I know," he murmured, stroking her hair. "And since neither one of us is going to be able to sleep, might I suggest we try to relax and enjoy each other's company in the few hours we have before the world wakes up and drags us out to deal with it?"

She sniffled as she nodded, breathing him in. Ghandi, how often had she wished to be exactly where she was right now? He was right, and allowing Kremlyn and the rest of the Court to live rent free in her head was letting them win before they even got here. That was going to be what it was going to be, and if she only had this one night with Deo, she sure as hell wasn't gonna spend it crying.

GIDEON HELD OPHELIA AGAINST HIM, trying to find a balance between his rage and arousal, and failing on both counts. He'd kill every last vermin that dared to step foot on Havers's shores. Ophelia was his, damn it, and the urge to remind both of them what that entailed was fierce. He exhaled slowly, far too aware of her core's proximity to his hardened member.

"Gideon?" she asked, her face rising to his, determination etched across her features.

"Mmm?"

Ophelia chewed her lip and raised her hand, tracing his stubbled jaw. Gods, she was beautiful. His hand slid to the small of her back then came to rest upon her slim hip. He shifted his own, brushing his length against her. Unintentionally, of course.

Ah…the lies we tell ourselves…

A smile teased her countenance. "I was going to apologize

for killing the mood, but that doesn't seem to be the case, now does it, Mr. Sperry?" she asked, a glimmer of the old Phe in her eyes.

His heart leapt to see it. "No, counselor. I'm afraid you're innocent on all counts, and my original motive remains unchanged," he rumbled, playing along. His gaze fixed on her tongue darting over her lips, and he spread his fingers to cup the perfect round of her ass cheek. Gideon's eyes flicked to hers. "But, given that I've a naked goddess on my lap, you'll have to forgive the seriousness of my crimes."

A grin bloomed over her face before she tsked. "I don't know that I can do that. The law is very clear. I'm afraid I'm going to have to recommend an immediate intervention."

He quirked a brow. "Oh? And exactly what would that entail?"

She reached between them, and his head fell back as her fingers wrapped around his cock. Sweet Jesus, the feel of her hand on him.

"Rigorous reeducation, I'm afraid. You obviously have no idea what to do with said goddess."

"Oh, I've several ideas." He groaned as she began to stroke him, his tip sticky with pre-cum. "Why don't we start by—"

She put a finger to his lips. "None of that now, Mr. Sperry. I'm in charge, remember?"

He blinked at her. "You are?" Her hand tightened, and he drew a sharp breath, his pulse jumping with anticipation. "Oh, yes, that's right. You are. Well then, Ms. Diamondé, you have me, now what are you going to do to me?"

"I'm going to fuck you, Mr. Sperry."

His dick became painfully hard, and she gasped as he pulled her against him, nuzzling against her long, white throat. The scent of her arousal tinged the air. Gods, it was divine.

"That doesn't sound like much of a punishment," he

murmured, nipping at her lobe. "What am I supposed to do while you're fucking me?"

"You're going to do whatever I say," she breathed, her free hand tangling in his hair.

"Well, then, I suppose you best get on with it."

"Kiss me, Gideon."

Gladly. He trailed his lips along her jawline and teased her mouth with his. Her breath came faster, and she softened against him, accepting his tongue with a small cry of surrender. He licked into her mouth, her heady musk from earlier still upon his lips.

Her hand left him, arms wrapping around his neck. She moved her hips against him, her slick core stroking over his cock in a hot, wet line. He deepened the kiss, hand raising to fondle her breast, her nipple pearling against his palm.

"Gods, I want you," he murmured, tugging at its hardened peak. "Tell me I can have it."

"Not yet, Mr. Sperry. I need you to touch me."

He growled as she arched back, and he drew her nipple into his mouth, groaning as it contracted against his tongue and drawing it back out against the roof of his mouth. His hand skated between her legs, fingers sliding to her center.

"Don't stop." She rocked against him, urging him on.

Gideon kissed up her chest, fingers circling her nub, still swollen from her previous release and gently tugged. She cried out, and his dick jumped, aching to be inside her. "Shh…quietly now, Ms. Diamondé. We wouldn't want any one to intrude on our little game, now, would we?" he chuckled, loving the way her pupils expanded as his finger breached her tight little hole, pumping. She bit her lip, the flesh turning white beneath her teeth. "Good girl."

Gods, the want playing over her face was exquisite. He added another finger, her brows knitting. Her slick walls softened, blooming for him. He rubbed against that rougher patch of flesh deep inside, and a flush spread up her chest to her cheeks, her core positively dripping for him. "Mmm. That's it, getting so nice and wet for me. Are you ready to sit on my dick?"

She nodded, all pretense of being in charge forgotten. He withdrew his hand, sucking her arousal from his fingers as she grasped him and positioned his fat crown at her entrance.

"Look at me, Ophelia," he said, caging her hips. "I want to your eyes on mine while you're fucking me."

She wet her lips, and her throat bobbed as she lowered herself onto his throbbing cock, eyes widening. His lids fluttered at the sensation of being incrementally encased by her tight, hot flesh.

"Oh, God," she gasped. "I'd forgotten…"

"You can take it, poppet. Up and down. That's it," he murmured, kissing her. "Almost there. Mmm. Good girl, go as slowly as you need. We've all the time in the world."

Her forehead pressed against his as they rocked together. Moving away, then becoming one. Her tight channel rode over his wide length, her passion dripping down his sac. He teased her lips with his, caressing her body, deriving as much pleasure from her small sounds of ecstasy as from what her body was doing to his. Gideon grazed his thumb over her clit, rubbing small circles, a tight heat building in his loins.

"Come with me, Phe," he panted, his gaze locked on hers. "Let me feel you fall apart."

She gasped, her nails raking over his shoulders, the pace of her hips quickening. Her thighs quivered, sweat stippling her body and a low keening coming from her throat. Gideon thrust against her, burying himself in her velvet heat again and again. Her cries became louder, and her body spasmed around him, sucking and pulling at him.

He bellowed, searing ropes of his desire lashing into her, violet light flaring across his vision and the top of his head light. He held her tight against him, twitching, small aftershocks of her release fluttering across his softening member.

"I love you, Deo," she murmured, already half asleep.

"And I you, Phe."

He scooted to lie flat and kissed her neck. She sighed against him, not inclined to move. A sated smile crossed his lips, and he pulled a sheet up over them both. Glad one of them would get some sleep after all.

Chapter Seventeen

OPHELIA OPENED her eyes and looked directly into those of a snot-nosed toddler. The kid wore one of those fleecy zipped onesie things and stared at her like she was a bug. Her dark, curly head slowly cocked to one side, then the kid's tongue poked up, absently licking the slick of boogers dripping onto her lip.

Ew! Ophelia flinched back holding a sheet to her breast. What the hell? She glanced around the room. "Where's Gideon?"

The kid kept licking.

Ophelia fought the urge to hurl and scrubbed a hand over her gummy eyes. Nope. Didn't see that. Ugh. She glanced out the window. The sun was just cresting over the trees. Damn it, she'd slept later than—

"Poe?" a woman's voice called from the next room.

"In here," Ophelia yelled, sitting up. Though how the hell the kid had gotten in with the door closed was a mystery. Ophelia narrowed her eyes. Wait a minute. It was hard to tell without the dumb hat and puffy coat, but that had to be the little shit that'd freed Chambers.

The door cracked open, and a thin woman with pigtails poked her head in. She rolled her eyes with a huff at the kid and came into the room. "There you are," she said sweeping the toddler up, onto her hip and whipping out a tissue to clean the kid up. "Sorry. She's doesn't have a real great grasp of privacy yet."

"Or hygiene," Ophelia muttered, running a hand through her hair. "Do you know where Gideon went?" Damn, was everything in here plaid?

"Yeah, he and Chase left a couple of hours ago. Something about having to file a report and wanting to look at some node stuff. They should be back in a few hours."

Shit. Ophelia had totally forgot about the court filing. She chewed her lip, trying to figure out how in the hell she was gonna get to town hall.

"Anyways, I'm Kelsey, Liam's sister. We met last night. I mean, sort of. You weren't exactly conscious." She hiked the kid higher onto her hip, her brows furrowing. "You look… different."

Ophelia just stared at her, not sure how to read into that.

Kelsey buzzed her lips. "Um, so breakfast is on the table if you're interested, I mean if that's—you eat right? Like food?" She held up a hand. "If not, that's totally cool. Tom's got some IV bags in the ambulance, and I'm pretty sure my mom's got straws somewhere around here."

"Oh, cool, so I can drink it like a juice box?" Ophelia snarked.

"Yeah, no extra dishes, right?" Kelsey laughed, oblivious to the sarcasm. "Hey, is blood type the same as like vintages to vampires?"

"Um. No?" Ophelia blinked at her. Man, this chick was weird.

"Huh. You'd think it would be." Kelsey shrugged. "Anywho, we got you covered." Kelsey flashed her a huge smile and turned to boop the toddler's nose, wiping it again. "But no blood for you, naughty girl. You get nummy nummy blueberry pancakes! Yes, you do!"

Wow. Ophelia puffed out her cheeks as they left the room, unable to believe that just happened or that people still wore overalls. Her gaze flicked around the plaid-on-plaid room again. Okay. Scratch that. Yes, she did. God, what was wrong with this t—

Ophelia froze at the slip, bracing herself for the stabbing agony that always followed even thinking anything remotely related to divinity.

It didn't come.

She wet her lips, pretty certain she'd mentioned the Big Guy's name more than once last night with the same results. What the fuck was that about? No. It had to be a fluke, right? She glanced around like she was being watched. Then—

"God." She slapped her hands over her mouth.

Holy fucking shit—nothing happened.

"Goddamn, Jesus Christ, Holy Moses, and the Trinity."

Nope. Nothing.

She giggled. Okay. No idea why that wasn't a thing anymore, but she'd take it. Swearing had never been as satisfying without being able to blaspheme. God—hah!—the past few days had been fucking wild. It was like she'd cashed in on some kind of vampiric "Get out of Jail Free" card. She pushed off the bed and stumbled into what she really hoped was the adjoining bathroom. Yep, score, and thank *God*, because she was about to burst. She giggled again as she sat on the toilet, way too amused.

Jesus, she cackled, flushing and moving to the sink. *Get a hold of yourself, Phe.*

Her gaze fixed on her reflection in the mirror, abruptly sober. She raised a trembling hand to her cheek. Holy shit. Her tatuaj…they…they were gone. How in the fuck—no wonder Kelsey had said she looked different, but how?

Ophelia craned closer to the glass, her stomach dropping at the paleness of her irises. She blinked at herself. No, they weren't pale… They were normal-ish? Before she'd volunteered, her eyes had been a steel gray. Now they were a smokey lilac. She opened her mouth and tongued a fang. Okay, well, those were still there, so what the hell was up with the rest of it?

… Our service for yours…

She jumped at the reedy whisper threading through her mind, goosebumps raising her skin. Shit. The node was responsible for this? That didn't make any sense, and if it'd killed the virus, she'd be dead. Well, really dead, wouldn't she? Her heart leapt to her throat.

Gideon.

She needed to talk to Jena.

Ophelia ran into the other room and jammed on the stupid pajama pants and t-shirt, only wincing a little bit out of habit as they slid against her skin. She threw open the door and rushed into the other room, following the sounds of people eating through an industrial kitchen and into a dining room behind it.

The long table at its center was surrounded by people. Felix, his six rug rats, Kelsey, some big, tatted bald guy, and Jena all looked up as she rushed in.

"Are you okay?" Felix asked, reaching for the syrup.

Ophelia homed in on Jena. "What the fuck did the node do to me?"

"Umm…"

"Language!" the little redheaded girl screamed.

"Not now, Sway, finish your pancakes," Felix chided, handing the dispenser over. The kid's eyes got huge, and she snatched it, dumping everything in it onto her plate.

"Hey! I wanted some of that!" The swarthy boy across from her growled. Sway stuck her tongue out at him, and he looked like he was about to spring over the wide slab to murder her.

"I'll get more," Jena said, pale as she stood. "Help me?" she asked Ophelia.

Oh, she was gonna help her all right. Ophelia grabbed the syrup dispenser out of Sway's sticky little hands and stomped after Jena into the kitchen. Ophelia thrust the container at her when they were alone. "What the hell? My tatuaj are gone, I can take the Lord's name in vain, and the fucking node's whispering to me about its service for mine."

Jena grimaced as she took the gummy bottle and went to the sink, glancing over her shoulder at her as she rinsed it off. "Yeah, it does that. The whispering, that is. I don't know anything about the other stuff, but considering the color of your eyes, I'd say it's responsible."

"No shit, Sherlock. I want to know what it fucking means!" Ophelia swallowed the lump in her throat. "Am I… am I gonna die, like for real this time?"

Jena left the dispenser by the sink and took Ophelia's hands in hers. "No. The node wouldn't do that, but…" She bit her lip, furrowing her brows.

"But?"

"But apparently Thaddeus thinks drinking the blood of Havers's residents mutates the virus. Something about erasing tribal affiliations—you'd have to ask him about that. Regardless, you fed pretty heavily on Gideon, like four pints heavily. I know he's not technically a resident, but he's bound directly to the node. I'm pretty sure that's gotta be like mainlining whatever the node's doing to the rest of us in Havers."

Ophelia slumped against the refrigerator. That weird tingle that started when she got here, the hum running through her now… Okay, so it tracked that drinking their blood was doing something to her. The question was, what?

"I have to talk to Thaddeus," she said, anxiety pricking at her.

Jena nodded. "Chase and Gideon will be back in a couple of hours. They went out to look at the reserve nexuses."

"What about Felix or you? Can't one of you take me?" Ophelia fidgeted, the need to do something overwhelming.

"No, he's waiting for Liam to get back from talking to the pack. We all agreed to meet back here before nine and figure out what our next steps are, and the coven's meeting at the Witchery right after. Worst case, we can bring you over then."

Ophelia pulled at her collar, a panic attack imminent. That was hours away, she couldn't wait that long. She couldn't!

"Hey, it's gonna be okay," Jena said, squeezing Ophelia's hands. "Here, sit down for a minute and just focus on breathing." She led Ophelia over to a chair in a shadowed corner by an open pantry.

Ophelia balked as she stepped close. "No, you don't understand. I can't stay here. I have to get back to the library—"

Darkness swirled around them, and Ophelia went rigid. What the fuck?

It cleared as quickly as it'd come, and the two of them stood in Thaddeus's study. Jena fell back a step, her eyes wide and her mouth a freaked out "o."

Before either of them could formulate a coherent thought, their attention snapped to a chuckle on the other side of the room.

Thaddeus sat in one of the chairs by the fire, a wide smile across his face. "Well, isn't this a pleasant surprise. Come. Sit. Methinks we need to chat."

GIDEON STARED across the desolate swamp stretching to the horizon to the massive lump of snow-covered stone several hundred feet from the shore. "That's what's left of the dragon?"

Chase nodded, his breath spiraling away. "Yep. That's him."

Gideon supposed he could see a roughly reptilian form if he squinted. Perhaps that there was a wing? It was much larger in person than he'd expected from the pictures he'd seen. Whatever it'd been, it hadn't been a wyvern, and there was no way Felix Simms was solely responsible for its present state.

Gideon shook his head. It was of little import. He had the information he'd come for. Both the reserve nexuses had been directly channeled from the main node and were fixed by outcroppings of granite. Though one was rough stone and the other fashioned into a henge, they served the same purpose, and more importantly, they offered the same potential: the creation of more of his kind.

It wasn't necessarily a boon. Not for him at least. The raw materials were here, yes, but once created, grotesques required a firm hand until they matured. The process was time-consuming and, speaking as a former recruit, not particularly pleasant. Gideon had little desire to act as anyone's general.

Yet, it would return balance to the grid, and further guarantee Havers's safety in the years to come, whatever may happen to its guardian. He turned away from the swamp, pensive, walking back across the hollow to one of the trilithons not toppled by age.

"So, what are you thinking?" Chase asked, trailing after him. He kicked at the frozen, rucked up ground.

Gideon laid a hand on an upright stone. "That I need silence for a moment," he said, dismissing the man. Gideon closed his eyes, seeking the node's regard. It came quickly, as if it'd been lying in wait for his summons. He frowned, not doubting that it had been.

Are there any souls willing? he asked it, positive no clarification would be necessary as to his intent. The collective of spirits knew entirely too much, though how was a mystery. The same wretched properties of saltwater that made it an anathema to his kind also prevented the grid from stretching beyond a landmass's shores. The node's ability to communicate with other constructs on the far continent should've been an impossibility.

Yet, here he was, even more certain that his arrival had been orchestrated between the two.

The node giggled and burbled in his mind as if confirming his suspicions. With it came a strong impression of a child gleefully clapping its hands—and then it left him. He scowled, stepping back, but it would have to do. His message had been received.

"I'm finished here now," he said to Chase.

The big man sighed, jamming his hands into his jacket pockets and rocking back on his heels. "Good. We're running up against the clock if we're gonna make it back on time."

And he was no doubt as eager to return to Jena's side as Gideon was to return to Ophelia's. He'd hated leaving her whilst she slept, but had been loath to wake her, and there was far too much to do.

They started back through the silent woods, snow crunching beneath their feet. Gideon had to admit it was peaceful here, though far wilder than anything he was used to. Grotesques were creatures of the city. He'd enjoyed visiting the gardens dotting the City of Light, but those were refined, cultivated spaces. He preferred their order to the natural chaos surrounding him, yet he could see himself becoming accustomed to this. That was a positive, he suspected, considering he'd committed himself to remaining here in perpetuity.

Especially after issuing his plea to the node just now. Gideon frowned, already hearing the outcry from his brethren, but in blurring the node's boundaries, he'd been left with little recourse. The damage had been done, and he had a responsibility to mitigate it.

"So, what do you think about the nexuses?" Chase asked, breaking the silence.

Gideon pursed his lips. "I think that Jena and her mother have inadvertently created the conditions necessary for birthing more of my kind. The only thing that remains is the node's willingness to sacrifice one of its own."

Chase glanced at him askance, and Gideon frowned. "The balance needs to be restored, and one can't just put the genie back into the bottle. The node will reject any attempt at curbing its sphere of influence, but it may be persuaded to create agents bound to its will."

"You're talking about more gargoyles."

"Just so. However, for that to occur, a soul needs to step forward, eschewing their place on the wheel of recreation, and agree to be bound, dedicating itself to the node's defense." Which was a taller order than one might suspect. Few souls jumped at the prospect of leashing themselves for an eternity, and even less were approved by the node's collective.

Gideon wasn't sure of the exact criteria, but it had resulted in fewer than a hundred of his kind sprinkled across the far continent. Most of the nodes there had a single guardian and never more than three.

Which was largely responsible for the uproar when he'd been released.

"So, you're actually some dead guy?"

Gideon rolled his eyes. The man would fixate on that. "In theory. Though I have no memory of before, just waking as I am with a directive." And a considerable amount of anger.

"Then why haven't the nodes over here just popped out a bunch of you?"

It was a valid question, though one Gideon preferred not to dwell on. "It takes a great deal of time for a soul to acclimate to this form, which is nigh impossible without another of mature status to guide them," he said shortly. And even then, it was not without incident. He was positive that was where their reputation as dumb, violent brutes stemmed from. His own stint as such was not a warm memory.

Chase glanced at him again. "But now you're here."

"That I am," Gideon said with no small amount of acerbity. "Funny how events have aligned themselves, isn't it?"

"Jena would call it karma," Chase shrugged. "That's why she thinks you and Ophelia are here. I dunno, balancing the scales or some shit."

"I'll go with the latter," Gideon muttered.

Chase snorted. "Yeah, that was where my head went." They walked for another few minutes before Chase turned to him again. "Say you do get a soul to bite. Would that make you their dad?"

Gideon swallowed, then cleared his throat. "More like their general, but if it helps you to think of it that way, by all means." He certainly didn't have what he would consider a father-son relationship with his, but mortals went to therapy for a reason. He suspected the comparison was apt.

"Are there female gargoyles?"

"No," Gideon said succinctly. "Our creation predates equality between the sexes."

"But it wouldn't now."

Gideon's brow furrowed, not having considered that possibility. He scrubbed a hand over his face, not wanting to think of the scandal that would cause. His brethren, especially the older ones, would lose their minds, as would those of his generation, albeit for an entirely different reason. "That would be left to the node's discretion." And may the Gods help them all if its other decisions were anything to go by.

"Huh." Thankfully, Chase's phone chirped before he could ask anymore questions. He took it from his pocket and glanced at the screen before he answered. "Hey, babe. What? What do you mean you're at the library? I thought I— WHAT? Yeah. We're almost to the truck. Yeah, we'll meet you there." He hung up and pinched the bridge of his nose, swearing.

"Issues?"

"Yeah, I'd say. Apparently, your girl's learned to shadow walk."

Chapter Eighteen

OPHELIA SAT in the armchair across from Thaddeus, her legs pulled up, watching him warily from behind her knees. She picked at a bit of lint, wishing Jena hadn't left her alone with the vampire to disappear into the newer portion of the building and look for Ms. Pao. The old witch was boring as hell, but Ophelia couldn't blame Jena for bailing on her. She would've done the same given the chance. It was tense in the study, and the atmosphere had thickened to a nail pairing shy of claustrophobic after the witch had left.

The way Thaddeus was staring at Ophelia did not help.

"So…you, um, wanted to talk?" Ophelia asked, fighting the urge to bolt from the room. Then again, she supposed she could just dive into the nearest shadow if things got any weirder. She scowled. Damn it, she couldn't leave, she needed answers.

Thaddeus gave a slow blink and sat back. "I did."

Okay then. *Time to be bold, Ophelia.* "Good. I did too. You wanna tell me what the hell drinking Havers's blood is doing to me? Jena said something about it erasing tribal affiliations? What does that even mean?"

Thaddeus smiled. "Come now, child. I'm sure you have some idea, considering you just shadow walked into my study."

Ophelia gritted her teeth. Yeah, she had some idea all

right, but that wasn't the frickin' point. "I wanna hear you say it."

He chuckled, and the small hairs on her nape rose. "As I said to your swain, I'm not certain of the mechanics behind it, but the fact remains that when one of our kind drinks the blood of a Havers's resident, the virus mutates." He ran his long fingers down the side of his gaunt face, indicating his tatuaj.

"At first, the lines darken, then they become blurred. Once that occurs, it allows one to incrementally access the other tribes' abilities. Shadow walking, for instance, then perhaps exploding into a mischief of rats or the ability to compel. I've only gained access to them all within the last hundred years, but then, I prefer madness to the taste of blood. I can only imagine it would have happened somewhat quicker had I been a connoisseur."

Ophelia shivered, knowing far too many at the Citadel who were. No wonder Vesper was so pissed about the lawsuit falling through. If every member of the Crimson Guard had access to all the tribes' abilities, they'd be unstoppable.

Not that they were anything to sneeze at now.

Thaddeus chuckled again. "I see you've grasped the gravity of the situation. My ability to utilize the totality of the tribes' powers has allowed me to keep the vampire queen and her minions from Havers quite effectively. But, as you can imagine, that's only whetted her appetite, and it's no secret that my mental faculties can be...erratic. After you'd pledged to the node, it was my hope that you would reap similar benefits by imbibing and be able to 'share the load,' as it were. However, the complete disappearance of your tatuaj is fascinating. Humor me, my dear, have you noted any other changes?"

How the hell could he be so nonchalant? And um, hello, what about consent? She glowered at him. She wasn't his goddamned of lab rat or anyone else's. "Why wouldn't you tell me about this?"

"To what purpose?" He shrugged. "The mutation was going to happen regardless. You're bound to the node, and it isn't like you'd be able to airdrop in a steady supply of blood from elsewhere."

Ophelia frowned. Actually, she was pretty sure she could've. "Goddamn you, Thaddeus."

He flinched and then a wondrous smile broke over his face. "Well now, that's new. You've broken free of *Him*." Ophelia shrugged, trying to blow off the abrupt sheen of sweat stippling her brow. The vampire templed his fingers. "Ah…what to do, what to do…"

Fear tripped up her spine at his tone. "What do you mean, 'what to do?'"

"Well, it's obvious, isn't it? Here I've been preventing Vesper from attaining the one thing that could possibly bring her back to me. This could be a cure, a true cure, for vampirism," he mused.

"No." Ophelia shook her head, vehemently disagreeing. "If that was the case, I'd be dead and wouldn't have these," she said, baring her fangs. "And even if it did cure vampirism, Vesper would still be a psycho." Along with every other vampire, as far as Ophelia was concerned.

"Mmm. Well, there is that. Do you know why she wants to kill you, child?" He smiled gruesomely at her silence. "You and the rest of the Damă are all the little queen bees the virus has spawned to fly far, far away and perpetuate our kind. Granted, in this day and age, that's somewhat flawed when modern medical advances such as the VA vaccine are taken into account, but regardless, nature continues to do as it originally intended."

"Then why doesn't she just kill us?" Ophelia asked, trying to keep him on track.

His brows furrowed and his eyes slowly refocused on her.

"Hmm? Oh. Killing the Damă is an exercise in futility. More are just created in their place, and no one knows exactly when and where that will happen." He shook his head. "No, much better to gather them close beneath her watchful eye and grind their wills to dust. Clip their wings before they can fly, hey? How surprised she must've been when you challenged her rule after a decade beneath her boot."

Surprised wasn't what Ophelia would call it, and technically she'd only wanted to kill Kremlyn, but she wasn't going to argue about it. "You know they're coming, Kremlyn and Vesper, tonight. They want to kill you, too."

"Oh, yes. I am aware. 'They have proclaim'd their malefactions; for murder, though it have no tongue, will speak with most miraculous organ.' Act two Scene two, Hamlet." Thaddeus gave a pained sigh. "But what they want and what they'll get remains to be seen. Knowing that it's possible to feel the creator's light upon my face again gives me a certain…incentive to thwart their desires." He looked thoughtful for a moment. "And you, my child, need to be kept out of it. Vesper can't know what's possible. She can't see what you've become."

"What is that?" Ophelia asked plaintively.

"Hope, Ophelia. You are hope." Thaddeus stood, looking to the far end of his study. "Take good care of her, Gideon Sperry née Spallou. I fear if left to chance, the fates will not be kind." The ancient vampire inclined his head, stepped into a shadow, and vanished.

Ophelia sat in shock as Gideon's heavy footsteps approached from behind her. His hand fell upon her shoulder.

"Did you hear all of that?" she rasped.

"Enough. Are you all right?"

She shook her head, chewing her lips. "No." And she wasn't sure if she would be ever again. What had she become?

He sighed and held a hand out to her. "Come. Let's get you someplace safe. Chase seems to think that short of the standing stones at the node, that's the Witchery, and, as sad as it is to say, it's far more comfortable there."

She nodded, and he helped her rise, drawing her into his arms. Ophelia buried her face against his broad chest, the implications of what Thaddeus had said clattering through her mind. Did she really have access to all the tribe's abilities? She didn't even know what half of them were, and the ones she did... She shook her head. It was too much. Too monstrous.

And Thaddeus was right. Vesper could never find out.

Gideon kissed the top of her head and led her out of the library. She blinked at the bright sunlight and paused for a moment to get her bearings. He turned to look at her, his long coat sweeping to the side.

She snickered. "What the hell are you wearing?"

"Hmm? This?" he asked, running a hand down the buttons of a worn flannel shirt with blue and green moose printed all over it. It was tucked into a pair of ill-fitting jeans that had seen way better days. "Why, it's nothing but the very finest in redneck chic."

Ophelia laughed. "Tell me someone took a picture."

"Not if they value their life." He frowned, taking her hand again. "I've arranged for delivery of our belongings from my storage unit, but transport will take several days. Thankfully, the contents of my apartment in Klineville should arrive tomorrow. I left it in a bit of a disarray."

Ophelia swallowed a smile, translating. That really meant that he'd lost his temper and trashed the place. "Aww. And here I was thinking you're kind of cute as a lumberjack."

He snorted. "Then I'd suggest you enjoy it while you can."

Wait a minute. Her steps slowed. Their apartment had been over three thousand square feet, and they'd been planning on moving somewhere larger after the wedding. No way would a room at that crappy little bed and breakfast have enough space to fit half of what had been in his closet, never mind hers. "Where are we going to put everything?"

"Ah. I've procured alternate lodgings, and actually…" He craned his neck. "There. You see that stone building at the top of the hill?"

Ophelia popped up on her tip-toes to look where he was pointing. "The church?"

"No, that. There, the vicarage beside it. I made an offer yesterday, and the acceptance came through late last night."

"You bought a house?" She stared at him in shock, hoping her new ability to speak all things divine carried over to stepping onto hallowed ground. Not that he'd know that. It wasn't something Vampires advertised, but no matter how cute the house looked, the potential of bursting into flames was gonna be a deal-breaker.

"I did." His eyebrows knit and he put his hands on her shoulders. "If you don't like it, we can look for something else, but in the meantime, my preference is not a bare mattress in a library basement or someplace stinking of fish."

Ophelia nodded, and ran her sleeve beneath her nose, sniffling. "No, I know, I just… We're really doing this?" She looked up at him, and he cocked his brow, the heat in his eyes flushing her cheeks.

"If it were warmer and had we not pressing business to attend to, I'd take great pleasure in convincing you of the sincerity of my overture," he rumbled, leaning close to kiss her softly, then offering her his arm. "Alas, it will have to wait. If you'll accompany me, Ms. Diamondé?"

"Anywhere and everywhere, Mr. Sperry," she breathed, her head light.

He led her around the library to a large, forest green truck parked at the curb with a "Caldwick and Sons" logo on its side. Chase sat in the driver's seat and Jena was beside him. Neither one of them looked happy. Great. Ophelia frowned, sure that was somehow her fault. Gideon opened one of the rear passenger doors and helped her up onto the running board, into the back.

Ophelia paused. "Do you think they can drop us off at town hall? I need to file my part of the joint status report."

"That won't be necessary," Gideon said. "I've already been in contact with Judge Carey and filed a motion to dismiss the civil case and recommended criminal conspiracy charges be filed against the Vampire Court."

Ophelia blinked at him. "What? When?"

"Whilst being chauffeured about town earlier." She stared at him and he shrugged. "I dictated most of it on my phone last night while you were sleeping. It was just a matter of polishing the transcription. Now hop in, it's freezing out here," he smirked, helping her in.

Ophelia slid across the bench seat, her mind whirling with a very bad feeling that that wouldn't be the end of it. Gideon climbed in beside her, and she wriggled under his arm, taking comfort while she could. Everything about today was completely overwhelming, and she was positive that it was only going to get worse.

GIDEON SHOULDERED into the apartment above the Witchery balancing a drink tray from Cups and breathed a sigh of relief that Chase's banging from earlier was finally at quits. The man stepped from the kitchen with a hammer in his hand and relieved Gideon of the to-go bag.

"Windows are back it, but it's gonna take a while for the place to heat up." He set the bag on the worn kitchen table, then glanced into the living room with its circle of mismatched chairs and couches. Ophelia stood at one of the long windows, chewing a nail as she stared out into the distance. A smile teased Gideon's lips. As ridiculous as those bunny pajama bottoms were, she looked absolutely adorable in them, and would no doubt be enraged should he say so.

His smile grew wider, so very tempted.

"I haven't gotten in there yet," Chase continued, breaking Gideon from his inappropriate musings, "but restoring that fireplace has definitely moved up the list."

"How about you shoot for finishing the kitchen first?" Jena said from behind him, pulling the last of the plastic sheeting down and rolling it up. The denuded walls behind it weren't an improvement. Strips of tile had been pried from the surface and decidedly unappealing squiggles of yellowed cement scored over what looked like a 1970s conglomeration of wallpaper samples. "Aggie will have a bird if you leave it like this."

"She's gonna have a bird about something anyway, at least that'd be valid," Chase muttered, then glanced at Gideon and grabbed one of the coffees from the tray he'd set next to the bag. "Aggie's Jena's aunt. She's…difficult."

"No, she's a raging bitch," Jena said, then sighed. "Well, at least she has been lately."

"Maybe a couple of days with Gorman mellowed her out."

Jena looked at Chase like he was addled. "You've met him, right?"

"You never know." He shrugged.

"Unfortunately, I do, and that's not happening. Get rid of this for me, will you?" she asked, handing him the wad of sheeting, then claiming a cup from the tray that was more confection than coffee. "I've gotta start getting ready for the coven. They'll be here in an hour. Oh, hey, can you grab that picture of my dad for Gideon? It's in the grimoire." Chase grunted and stuffed the wad under his arm, trundling off to dispose of it. "Ophelia, can you get the tea service out for me?"

"Sure." She turned away from the windows and scooted past Gideon to help. "Where is it?"

"Bottom of the cabinet." Jena pointed, sipping from her cup. "If I bend over that low, I'm not getting back up."

"And what are your plans with the coven?" Gideon asked, taking his own beverage before leaning in the doorway.

Jena huffed a lock of dark hair from her eyes and grabbed a kettle from the stove. "To pick Matilda's brain. If anyone has something nasty up her sleeve, it's her. It's getting the rest of the coven to agree on it that'll be the issue."

"How many of these do you need?" Ophelia asked, setting cups and saucers on the counter behind her.

"All of them, and everything else that's in there." She frowned at one. "Damn it. So much for the sheeting. It's all gonna need to be washed."

"Wasn't Matilda the one who changed Chambers into a weasel?" Gideon asked.

"Among other things. Shit, that reminds me." The little witch left the kettle by the sink and went to the refrigerator. She rooted around for a moment before pulling out a gallon-sized baggie with a furry corpse inside it. "I asked Kelsey to have Tom drop it off on his way back to the fire station. He's going to rally what's left of our local emergency services after the dragon had its way with them," she said, depositing the macabre package onto the butcher block island.

Gideon stared at the baggie. "Dare I ask what you plan to do with the remains?"

Jena shrugged. "I dunno, but I'm pretty sure whatever it is will work best at room temperature. Chambers bit my dad before he died, and there's blood all over his muzzle. I was thinking a tracking spell at the time, but now I'm wondering if maybe we can do one of those auric reconstructions Liam was talking about."

Gideon's brow quirked, intrigued by the possibility. "If you do, record it."

"Yeah, I can do that. Chase gave me the run down on the nexuses. Do you really think the node will be able to create more gargoyles?" she asked, filling up the kettle and then emptying it into a large iron cauldron on the stove.

"Able to, yes; inclined to is a different matter altogether," he muttered, turning at the sound of footsteps coming up the stairs. The door opened and a tall, thin woman in oversized sunglasses and a tapestried, fur-lined cape pushed through it, laden with shopping bags.

"I don't care how romantic your mother thinks the Crabby Cleft is. I'm not eating at some place that sounds like it's gonna have an STD sampler." She swept off her glasses and stopped dead in the doorway, her gaze fixed on Gideon. "Who the hell are you?"

His nose twitched, the scent of sidhe thick in his nostrils as he returned her glower, wondering how she fit into things.

"That's Gideon," Jena yelled from the kitchen. "Be nice."

"That's entirely up to him." Her eyes narrowed at Jena's snort, and she stepped aside, letting an extremely disheveled imp similarly laden with packages into the room after her.

"Where do you want these, Aggie?" he groused.

Ah. Aggie. The difficult aunt.

"Bedroom," she said, tonguing a cheek whilst looking Gideon up and down and making it a point not to come any closer to him. His lip twitched. Oh yes, she'd had dealings with his kind before.

"How was your trip?" Jena asked, oblivious to the potential for violence about to unfold.

"Aside from the company, not bad. Weather was shit, but since *someone*," she called over her shoulder, her eyes still on Gideon, "couldn't be bothered to spring for an all-inclusive resort, that's to be expected."

"Springing for it wasn't the problem, you getting on a plane was," the imp shot back as he returned to retrieve her packages. "You want the wine in the fridge?"

"Of course I want the wine in the fridge. I also wanna know what a grotesque's doing standing in my living room when he should be on his own damned side of the ocean."

The imp froze, his mouth agape.

Gideon couldn't quite swallow his grin. "Is my presence making you uncomfortable?"

"Glencarn, 1498," she spat. "What do you think?"

He winced, all frivolity forgotten. "My apologies."

"Fat lot of good that does now."

"I'm sorry, what's going on?" Ophelia asked, joining him in the doorway.

Aggie did a double take at her, then threw up her hands. "And we've got a vampire in the kitchen. I leave you two alone for three days. Couldn't you have just thrown a house party?"

"Who says this isn't?" Jena asked, batting her lashes at the woman.

"What's Glencarn, 1498?" Ophelia asked again, looking between them.

"It's where the Great Massacre of Feeding Hills occurred," Gideon muttered. "During an unseelie incursion for their node, the grotesque's general was struck down, severing ties to his recruits. Without his influence to stabilize them, they went mad, slaughtering the entire town and several surrounding villages."

"Shit, that can happen?" Chase asked, coming in from the back. "Here you go, man," he said, handing Gideon a photograph as he squeezed past him to get into the kitchen. It was of a smug dark-haired man that looked far too much like Jena not to a blood relation. Gideon pulled his phone and snapped a picture of it and the name scrawled on the back, then texted it to Renard.

"That did happen," Aggie said, shaking a finger. "And him—them—being here is just asking for trouble."

Jena rolled her eyes. "Well, unless you've 'seen' anything

you want to share, you better take that up with karma, because I'm pretty sure it and the node were fishing for him when it brought Ophelia here and bound her."

"Oh!" Ophelia stood up straighter. "You're the one who gets visions. You haven't seen anything about tonight, have you?"

The woman sniffed. "If I had, things would certainly make more sense now," she said, glancing askance at Gideon. "Unfortunately, a grotesque's immunity to magic makes what the sneaky bastards are involved in one of the few things I can't see."

He snorted. "I can assure you that as long as I'm bound to the node's service, I won't be responsible for any harm that might befall you—without being given just cause."

"As far as you know." She scowled, then turned to scowl at the imp still standing by the door. She tugged the bottle of wine from his hand. "Don't you need to go check in with Mommy Dearest?"

"How could I leave without thanking you for such a delightful time?" he simpered, taking her hand and slobbering all over it. Jena made a gagging sound from the kitchen. Gideon wholeheartedly agreed: the display was untoward. He joined Ophelia at the sink, trading the photo for a towel and began to dry as she washed dishes.

"So, will you be joining us for tea?" Ophelia asked, handing him a saucer.

"As much as it pains me to decline, no. I need to get out to the ruins and scout the area where Jena thinks the portal is. If I can close it, I will. If I can't, I need to get the lay of the land, and the sooner that's done the better."

"I can take you out," Chase said around a mouthful of his sandwich. "I have to touch base with Liam and see what he and the pack've come up with. He said something about needing me to handle the Westside weres. Apparently, some of those assholes aren't on board without his dad calling the shots."

Jena shook her head. "I really hate that for him."

"Pack politics suck," Chase sighed. "Anyway, man, whenever you're ready."

Ophelia turned to Gideon, anxiety etched across her face. "You'll be careful?"

He set down the saucer and tipped her face up to his. "There is no future in which I'm not at your side. I won't allow it."

"Shit, even I almost believe that," Aggie muttered, strolling in to grab a wine glass from the cabinet. "Now hop to. I need to get into that drawer."

Gideon frowned at the sidhe witch, then kissed Ophelia. "Stay here."

She puffed out her cheeks and nodded, wringing her hands as she turned back to the sink, and Gideon followed Chase from the room.

Chapter Nineteen

OPHELIA SAT in one of the overstuffed chairs by the boxed-in fireplace wishing she'd picked a seat closer to the door. Around her seven witches and six warlocks filled the rest of the seats, all of them looking dour.

"I knew it was just a matter of time before this bit us," a bitchy little witch with blonde pipe curls groused. "Pun intended," she spat, glowering at Ophelia.

"Matilda Hanson!" A big woman of color in a bright kaftan chided. "We don't need more of your sourness. What we need is a plan, and bitching about what's been done isn't helping."

"Sweets is right," Ms. Pao said, her eyes enormous behind her thick glasses. "Jena had me look into the archives earlier, and I'm afraid the only thing roughly similar to a vampire invasion is when pirates tried to land in 1673. The coven back then warded the town, but the selkies and mers took offense."

"And we all know how cooperative they are," Matilda muttered.

"Pot, meet kettle," Sweets hummed, crossing her arms over her generous breasts. "Warding the town's all well and good, but it's not gonna be enough. You saw how Thaddeus sidestepped the ones at the node with that shadow walking of his. Unless you have any insight?" she asked Ophelia.

Ophelia tensed as every eye landed on her. "Um…maybe?

I know that they have to see where they're going, or have been someplace before to shadow walk, and vampires do need to be invited into a private residence...but some of them are able to compel if they make eye contact. People need to stay away from their windows."

The woman in a pink tracksuit beside her furiously scribbled down notes. "What about holy water and garlic?"

"Garlic doesn't do anything. Holy water, wafers, crosses—anything sacred or blessed is a deterrent, but honestly it just pisses most of them off. They will stay away from hallowed ground." She chewed her lip, thinking about the house Gideon had bought.

"What a fine time to be without a priest," Sweets muttered.

"Agreed, but the church can still suffice as a refuge," a tall, white-haired man said. He'd been paying close attention to everything Ophelia said, like he was weighing the truth of her words.

"Otis, you know we can only get about a hundred people in there," Ms. Pao frowned. "Remember how devastated the Lackland girl was when her cousins from Pelton had to stand outside for her wedding? And in the rain, no less."

"It's still something," Sweets murmured. "And she said ground, not building. That churchyard's been consecrated, right along with the cemetery if memory serves."

Ophelia's gut churned. "Weather aside, you don't want people out in the open. Some of the Crimson Guard can, um, do things."

"Things? Like..." Matilda prompted.

"Control shadow," Ophelia blurted out. "They can make it corporeal. Drag people to where they can get at them. Suffocate. People need to stay behind four walls with the blinds drawn. Even if the vampires can hear their heartbeats, they won't be able to get a good lock on them."

"Hear their heartbeats...?" a big man with a bristly beard asked.

Ophelia nodded. "It's how Cercetaș hunt," she said, naming the tribe.

"Well, isn't that just tits," Matilda spat, throwing her hands up. "So we can't even send Felix out distorted to assassinate the sons of bitches."

"Whoa," he said. "Since when am I an assassin?"

"Well, you killed a dragon, didn't you?"

He sputtered at her, pale. "T-this is a little different!"

The coven muttered like they didn't quite agree with him.

"Okay, calm down," Jena said like she was trying not to laugh. "Ophelia said a stake through the heart, fire, and decapitation will kill a vampire. Let's focus on that. Mr. Sheffield, your family's bent is fire, do you have any ideas?"

A tall warlock with thick gray streaks at his temples pursed his lips. Ophelia squirmed. He'd been staring at her since he'd come in and it was more than a little creepy.

"It would be possible to set up a series of cantrips," he mused, "but once triggered, they're impossible to control. Anything in the vicinity would become engulfed."

"Unless we bolstered them with water and earth," another man with a long, thin nose murmured. "But I don't see it happening. In one location, yes, but we're talking about the entire town, and if it's overrun by a plague of rats, there's no way we can stop all of them."

The coven looked at Ophelia again, and she didn't know what to say.

"Have you seen anything, Aggie?" Ms. Pao asked, scooching forward in her chair.

"Not anything that will help," the crabby witch scowled, "and I'm positive that's because of the gargoyle."

And you could hear a pin drop.

Otis cleared his throat. "I'm sorry, there's a gargoyle?"

"Mmm." Aggie sipped her tea like she hadn't just lobbed

a bomb at them. "What? Don't look at me. Apparently, he came to shack up with little Miss Fang over there and decided to pledge his service to the node while he was at it."

"But that's a good thing, isn't it?" Ms. Pao asked. "Historically, they've been quite effective at defending their nodes. I'm assuming that will carry over to the town?"

Ophelia nodded. "Gideon will do whatever he can to protect Havers."

"Yeah, as long as he doesn't lose his shit and destroy it when something doesn't go his way," Aggie muttered.

Jena rolled her eyes. "As long as Ophelia's safe, that won't happen."

"Then should we be focusing on her?" Sweets asked. "From what I remember, a gargoyle is a hell of a lot more equipped to deal with this kind of thing than we are, but keeping one girl safe? We can do that."

"And the first step is to ward the town," Jena agreed. "It might not keep all of them out, but it should slow them down enough for Gideon and the pack to deal with them easier. I can focus on pulling from the node to power that while the rest of you work on shoring up the Witchery's defenses."

The coven murmured in agreement.

"Okay, then what are we going to tell the town?" the woman with the notepad asked, absently rubbing lipstick off her teeth.

"We tell them the town's warded, but it's not a guarantee of safety. They need to stay inside, lock their doors, draw the shades, and keep away from any windows," Felix said. Surprisingly, he sounded like he knew what he was doing. "Meanwhile, the weres are going to be patrolling the woods and streets, and Gideon will be doing whatever it is that gargoyles do."

Jena pushed up out of her chair with a heavy sigh. "And until then, I'll be in the kitchen making vamp-be-gone charms to go on dog collars. Felix—"

"Yes, yes," he said getting to his feet as well. "I'm already on it. Sal has whatever he had in stock set aside for us, but fair warning, most of them are bedazzled neon pink and are gonna have to be used as anklets. This town has way more Pomeranians than Great Danes. Give me an hour to get town hall situated, and I'll be back with them."

The rest of the coven began milling around, some leaving and others joining Jena in the kitchen. Ophelia chewed her lip, her anxiety rising. Was she just supposed to just sit here?

"Ah, Ophelia, is it?" the tall man with gray streaked hair asked, coming to sit by her. He extended his hand. "Max Sheffield."

"Right, the fire guy."

He chuckled. "Yes, among other things. You probably don't remember me, but I co-own the nail salon on Main with my ex-wife. I've seen you come in quite a few times since we summoned you."

Ophelia stared at him. Dear God, he better not be hitting on her.

Max ducked his head and cleared his throat. "Yes, well, my reason for approaching you is that I couldn't help but notice, ah…" he waggled a finger at his face. "The color of your eyes is quite striking. It reminded of the stories my *babcia* would tell about the *dhampirs* in the old country."

He suddenly had her attention. "*Dhampirs*? I've never heard that word."

"No, not over here at least," he chuckled. "In Eastern folklore, *dhampirs* are the offspring of human mothers and their vampire assailants. Impossible, obviously, but they're said to have all the abilities of vampires without their thirst for blood, possessing violet eyes, and hold a vendetta against the tribes."

"A vendetta?"

"Mmm. In the stories, most became vampire hunters to avenge their mothers' honor. As I said, impossible, but…

interesting." His eyes ran over her face, then he smiled. "At any rate, it's nice to meet you. I should probably try and find Rick to see where he wants me."

"Yeah, thanks…" Ophelia said as he left. Huh. A *dhampir*. It was stupid, but she somehow felt better after talking with him. If there were folktales, maybe she wasn't the only one this had happened to. Well, if that's really what she was. Though you'd think Thaddeus would've said something.

Ophelia snorted. No, he wouldn't.

She got up and went into the kitchen. Sweets, Matilda, and Ms. Pao were all bent over Chambers's bagged corpse with Jena. "Hey, Jena? Can I use your phone?"

"Why, you need to text someone?" she asked, raising a brow.

Ophelia rolled her eyes. "No, I want to google something."

Jena pulled it from her back pocket and tossed it to her. "Just let me know if anything comes through from Chase or Felix."

"Yeah, I will, thanks," Ophelia murmured going back to her nook and opening up the search app. How the hell did you spell "*dhampir*?"

GIDEON CROUCHED on the banks of an ice-glazed pond staring at the copse of birch. He frowned. The woods here were dense, and he'd be hard-pressed to effectively surveil the site from above. Worse, skimming around the conifers and oaks would be an impossibility given the amount of scrub growing beneath them. There were just too many damned places for prey to take cover.

Jena's father had chosen his ingress well, damn him.

That the portal was within the circle of birch was a given, though the copse wasn't what it was anchored by. It hadn't taken Gideon long to see the signs of a former mound scarring the landscape, rather like a pockmark. Which meant that this wasn't a portal, per se, but a scant, and the thin spot between realms that was left behind when a mound was destroyed should've been long since dealt with.

He crouched, thrusting his hand into the snow to settle on the frozen earth. Below the surface, several large outcroppings of shale held the way open. Gideon scowled, but it remaining made a little more sense. Shale was a fickle stone, made up of clay and organic material. It also had the annoying tendency to stratify, making it almost impossible to eradicate from any given area.

And the scant would persist as long as a single sliver remained. Even with Gideon's affinity for stone, there was no way the job could be done in a day, and would undoubtably be beyond a witch's ability, period.

"So…what do you think?" Chase asked.

Gideon sighed, standing. "That we're fucked."

The big man snorted. "Tell me how you really feel."

"It's a larger undertaking than I'd envisioned. Possible, but not within our current time constraints. We'll have to deal with the Crimson Guard as it comes."

"How many vampires are we talking about?"

"I don't know." Gideon sucked in his cheeks. "But, given that Vesper has been planning this for some time, I'd say their numbers will be more than I'd consider ideal."

"Yeah. That's what I was thinking, too. We should get back," Chase said, heading the way they'd come. "Liam's going to have the Eastside pack patrolling the woods around the node. The Westsiders will be back in town. Felix and Tom have people either barricading themselves inside their houses or moving into emergency hurricane shelters. Everyone who's got a boat has already headed out to sea. I dunno which is safer, but the streets will be clear."

Gideon grunted as he followed. That was all well and

good, but his mind drifted to Jena's father. He chewed his lip as they hiked through the woods. What the hell could the fiend be getting out of this? If he was unseelie, Gideon would've bet on this being an elaborate ruse. The problem with that was, in order to gain control of the node, its guardian and now Gideon, would both need to be put down.

He doubted his demise would cause Jena's father to shed a tear, but the fact that he'd encouraged her to take ownership instead of letting events run their course for the node to become a mound niggled.

Why would he allow her to step into that role and create an impediment?

Gideon sighed, checking his phone. Still nothing from Renard. Damn it. He would've bet good money on either the image or the name turning up something.

"Nothing yet, huh?"

Gideon glanced at Chase, his grasp of the obvious profound. "No. Did you ever meet Jena's father?"

He grimaced. "Just the once."

"Any insight to share?"

Chase squinted up towards the sky. "He was kind of a dick. Seemed like he got a kick out of pissing off people just because he could…though, I guess in a way, he kind of saved my ass."

"Oh?" Gideon's brow rose. "How so?"

"I don't know if you know, but Malcom was my father," Chase begrudgingly admitted, pushing a branch from his path.

"Malcom. The one Patrick said was responsible for swapping out the turbine materials?"

Chase nodded. "Yeah. He was some kind of an unseelie prince that got banished here for knocking up my mom." He shook his head. "Long story. Anyways, from what I gathered, the two of them had some kind of a deal. Malcom would get the mound, and Jena's dad would get her. When Malcom released her dad from wherever he was, he made it a point to make a jab at Malcom about his line running true and called me a manifester."

"You're also part sidhe?" Gideon asked, already knowing the answer and eyeing him askance. That would certainly explain the uneasiness he felt around the man.

"Yeah, but I didn't know it until right before then. I'd always thought I was a defective were." He laughed, kicking a stone from the trail. "It's fucked up, but it was that—him saying I was a manifester—that got me thinking. If he hadn't, I don't think I would've been able to put Malcom down."

Interesting. "How so?"

"Malcom was the old alpha's enforcer. He was scary as fuck and could back it up. Physically..." He shook his head. "Yeah. That would've been too close to call. But manifesting's making things happen, right?" Chase licked his lips. "Right then and there, I wanted him dead. I focused my will on that until he started spitting up blood. It weakened him enough that when we got into it, I killed him, then cut off his head."

"That will do it." Apparently, he didn't need to worry about Chase's allegiances either.

Chase grunted. "Yeah. But I think about it sometimes. The way Jena's dad looked at me when he said it. It was like he fucking knew what I'd do with what he said." He shook his head. "I dunno."

"Unfortunately, neither do I." Gideon muttered, though he was certainly intrigued, disturbingly so. "But the more I hear, the less I'm convinced he's a sidhe, unseelie or otherwise."

"What else could he be?" Chase asked as they approached the truck.

Gideon reached for the door. "I hesitate to voice my suspicions. Suffice to say, it's nothing any of us wants to deal with."

Chapter Twenty

OPHELIA STARED out the window and tapped Jena's phone against her chin. Her search hadn't found much more than what Mr. Sheffield had told her, but she supposed that really didn't matter. What did was that last aside he'd made.

The one about vampire hunters.

That had gleaned more interesting results. They weren't so common on this side of the ocean, but on the Eastern continent, an entire society had been built around eradicating any hint of vampirism. True, that wasn't really news. An entire semester back in high school had been dedicated to the Purge and history behind it. Unsurprisingly, she'd been more interested in skipping class than the details of something that'd happened almost a hundred years before she'd been born.

But based on what she'd just read, the Western continent was the only place in the world where vampires had any kind of a foothold. They'd been hunted to extinction everywhere else. Ophelia couldn't imagine they were happy about that. She chewed her lip. No wonder Vesper wanted Havers so badly.

She wasn't going to get it.

Ophelia stood and went back to the kitchen. Jena stood at the stove, dipping a hank of dime-sized charms into a bubbling cauldron on the stove.

"Find what you were looking for?" she asked.

Ophelia shrugged and traded the phone for the takeout bag from Cups on the table. She fished around for her sandwich and sat. "Yes and no. Mr. Sheffield said something about my eyes reminding him of a *dhampir's* from his grandmother's stories. It's like a human-vampire hybrid. There wasn't much more than what he'd said about them, but the vampire hunter bit was interesting."

Jena's brow quirked. "Thinking about a new vocation?"

"No, but it kind of makes sense why Vesper wants Havers so badly. The Citadel is the only place on earth where nobody fucks with them, and I'm pretty sure she's got visions of world domination."

"What?" Jena snorted. "Like 'the South will rise again?'"

"Yeah, something like that. Where did everybody go?" Ophelia asked, taking a bite of ham and cheese goodness.

"You'd think they would've taken the out the feds gave them and laid low after the Purge." The witch shook her head. She hung the charms to dry on a cabinet pull and gathered up another batch. "The rest of the coven went to make sure their families are all safe, and Matilda needs a bunch of supplies to do an auric reconstruction on Chambers. Which, by the way, sounds more like necromancy than the courtroom spell Liam mentioned. Aggie's been in her room." Her eyes narrowed suspiciously, lingering on the doorway before she glanced at the clock on the stove. "They should start trickling back any time now. No messages from Chase?"

"Nope. You think Gideon will be able to do something about the portal?"

"You're probably a better judge of what he can do than me, but I'm gonna go with no. I really wish I knew how it got there in the first place, but it's been there forever, and I'm pretty sure my mom would've closed it if she could've."

"She couldn't because it's a scant, not a portal," Aggie

said, sweeping into the room in a black catsuit. "What do you think?" she asked, giving a spin.

"Oooh baby. Emma Peel's got nothing on you," Jena said, tonguing her cheek.

She looked more like a geriatric version of Catwoman to Ophelia, but whatever. "What's a scant?" she asked.

Aggie grunted, smoothing her zipper. "A scant's what's left where a mound once existed and the veil's at its thinnest. When they originally set up the grid, they put nodes over as many of them as they could, but the fae didn't exactly lay their mounds out in a line. The feds hit most of them out west and up north, but this one and another down south fell into the close-enough-for-government-work category."

"Of course it did," Jena muttered. "But I guess that makes sense, considering we're on the fringe. Better to miss one here than in the center of the country."

"You'd think so, but you'd be wrong. Any witch worth her salt knows picking something apart is easier when you start at the edge. Too bad they've got a bunch of warlocks on the payroll more concerned with their slide rules than doing the job right," Aggie muttered, pulling out a chair and sitting across from Ophelia. The sun streaming through the long windows behind the woman sparkled in her steel gray hair, turning it silver. "That kettle still warm?"

Jena flicked on a burner. "It will be. Hey, do you know anything about *dhampir*?"

"I dunno. You pick a name for that little bundle you're toting around yet?"

"No," Jena drew out the word, visibly refraining from saying something far different. "And technically, it's not me asking, it's Ophelia."

Ophelia nodded, crinkling up the paper from her sandwich as she swallowed. "Mr. Sheffield says my eyes remind him of what he's heard about them."

Aggie waved a dismissive hand. "He was probably hitting

on you. Man couldn't keep his dick in his pants if you paid him. Trust me, I've tried."

The spoon Jena was holding fell the counter. "What? Dear God, please tell me you did not have sex with Max Sheffield."

"I'm not telling you anything until you name that baby Agatha," Aggie muttered, squinting at Ophelia. "Although Max isn't wrong, at least not as far as rumors are concerned, but never in my very long life have I ever met a *dhampir*." She sucked her teeth. "It's not possible. Before the vaccine, shacking up with a bloodsucker would've made you one, too, and even now, they aren't exactly virile."

Ophelia huffed out a breath, having come to the same conclusion.

"Of course, I've also never met a vampire bound to a node." Aggie shrugged. "Who the hell knows? Maybe they are out there. I can't imagine they'd advertise it if they were. People are leery of vamps to begin with. A hybrid would freak them right the fuck out."

They all glanced into the other room at footsteps on the stairs, and a moment later, Chase and Gideon walked in.

"He can't close it by tonight," Chase said without preamble.

Aggie narrowed her eyes at Gideon. "I'm surprised he thinks he can close it, period."

He quirked a brow back at her. "I can do a great many things, madame, and dearly wish that cleaning up after the slipshod use of magic over here didn't have to be one of them, but it appears to be an ongoing theme. One would think, you, of all people, would know better."

"Ouch," Jena chuckled, putting a hand to her breast.

"Leading a horse to water and making it drink are two very different things," Aggie sniffed, looking down her nose at him.

"And why do I suddenly feel attacked?" Jena muttered.

The older witch snorted, patting her close-cropped hair. "Because you're not stupid."

Ophelia glanced from the motion to a flash of movement above Aggie's shoulder outside the window. Ophelia stood and went closer to the glass.

For a split second, a lanky black rat stared at her from the fire escape on the neighboring building, then disappeared. Her heart leapt to her throat.

"They're here," she whispered.

"Come again?" Gideon asked, striding to her side.

"I— There was a rat. On the fire escape, watching us." She turned to him, panic beating through her veins. "It was one of them, Gideon. The vampires are here."

GIDEON SWORE, pulling Ophelia away from the window and into the next room. "Aren't there any shades in this infernal place?" he roared at the row of them overlooking the street.

"Aggie, grab some sheets from the hall closet to tack up," Jena said, wiping her hands on a cloth and grabbing her phone. She began to text furiously. "Damn it, I thought we had more time."

"We should've, Liam's out there with the pack," Chase said, doing the same. "Did you feel anything try to cross the wards?"

"No."

Damn it, Gideon hadn't either. What kind of chthonic sorcery—

"They're not coming from the scant," Ophelia interrupted, back at one of those damned windows. She looked out over the town toward the docks. The sea beyond was covered with a heavy, rolling fog despite the bright afternoon sunlight above. It lapped at the shoreline, as if testing it, and the darker silhouettes of a massive fleet studded the horizon.

A shrill alarm cut through the air. "Felix is on his way," Jena said, hurrying to the hall. "Forget the damned dog collars, Chase, grab those charms and have everyone swallow one of the frickin' things. I need to call corners and draw a circle."

"You better make it fast," he said, "because it doesn't look like they're waiting." At the alarm's cry, the bank of fog had surged forward, engulfing the docks.

Gideon drew Ophelia into his arms and kissed her fiercely. "Stay close to Jena and stay here. I need to get out there."

She nodded, her eyes huge and her lips pressed into a thin, white line.

"How do I get to the rooftop?" he asked Aggie as she gathered things from the kitchen.

"Follow me." She pushed past them, down the hall and through a pair of shoddy doors to a stairway leading up. At the top, it opened to a large empty room, its beleaguered ceiling held up by scaffolding. "Stairs are at the end of the hall, that way, and I'd wouldn't suggest doing any aerobics while you're up there."

Gideon frowned, eyeing the supports and the partially filled buckets of water beneath them. "Indeed."

He sprinted past Jena, who was already chanting at the center of a design laid out in chalk on the floor, sparks of purple flaring from her fingertips. The node's awareness swirled around her, lending its power to her spell and urging him to hurry. A door was at the far end of the hall beyond the main room. He opened it and ascended the short flight, its molding flaking away and water stains blackening the walls.

Gideon threw the bolts on the exterior door and shouldered it open, bursting out onto the roof. It sagged alarmingly beneath his weight, and he leapt to the parapet. He quickly divested himself of his coat as his form tore free.

Great stone wings sprouted from his back and his fingers tapered to claws. His musculature bulked and doubled, skin becoming coarse and grainy. He raised his thickened jaws and roared, birds taking flight as his cry momentarily drowned out that of the siren.

Then he was in flight, soaring over the town. A wave of the node's power coursed through him as a flash of purple light shot out from the witchery and domed over the municipality.

Inhuman screams rent the air and a gruesome smile split his lips at the charred splotches dotting the streets. So much for the vampire's scouts. He pumped his wings, gaining altitude and his smile dropped away. Damn it. It wasn't just the docks. Fog had rolled in from the other side of the peninsula, circumventing the wards Jena had previously established and stopping abruptly at the one she'd just conjured.

How long would it hold before the Crimson Guard found a way around it? He glanced at the sun. It was still high in the sky and shadows were minimal, but they wouldn't stay that way.

A howl sounded below him, and a great wolf sprinted down the street. Chase, presumably. Others answered, joining him as he raced toward the docks. Gideon frowned and headed in the opposite direction. If they could hold that flank, he'd deal with the other.

The buffer of land between him and the sea was greater here, but the woods were dense. Gaunt forms flitted beneath the trees, too many to count, and safe from his talons. Damn it, but he wasn't going to be of any use from above and allowing them a foothold was unwise. Havers needed to eradicate as many vampires as possible before the shadows grew and they infiltrated the town. He snarled at his inability to act decisively.

If the node was going to offer any assistance, it had best do it soon.

My service for yours, you bloody pimple, and it's time to deliver, he thought at it.

Its burbling laughter tickled his mind, and Gideon dropped altitude at a sudden sharp twang to his consciousness, linking his mind with another's. It was wilder than anything he'd felt in centuries: feral and full of rage.

His mouth went dry. A soul must've stepped forward to volunteer. Gideon turned to the west, his stomach roiling at the implications, but unfortunately, a second gargoyle wouldn't be any more effective than—

His eyes widened as a massive stone dragon took to the sky.

Gideon's jaw dropped, then snapped closed, winging back as it screamed its fury, head thrashing and spitting out great globs of flame. The beast flew toward the town at an alarming speed, its sinuous form streaking through the air.

That's what he was supposed to bring to heel? He stared at it for a breath longer before recovering from his shock, snarling again at the node's thready giggle within his mind.

Gideon drew in a deep breath and roared out his challenge, focusing his will upon the consciousness leashed to his and snapped the reins. *Abide!*

The dragon pulled back as if slapped. It pumped its wings and hissed. Dear God, what the hell had the node been thinking? He shook his head, hammering the creature with his will to establishing his dominance. It was the soul inside it he needed to be worried about, not how large it was. *I, Gideon, am your general, and you will fall in!*

The great stone beast resisted, then abruptly rushed Gideon, lunging close to rake at him with its claws. Sparks flew, his skin the flint to the steel of the dragon's claws. He twisted from their grip and slammed a fist against the beast's solar plexus. It screamed, a shudder running through it as it winged backwards, its barbed tail lashing at him.

Chips of stone and a cloud of dust exploded from the impact, and he reeled back, then flew around its bulk, its slavering jaws snapping at him. Gideon punched its jaw hard, a puff of granite exploding into the air. He got behind the creature while it was dazed, and grasped one of its horns, tearing back its head, to bare its throat, his legs wrapped around the creature's neck.

"You will abide, recruit, or I will end you!" he shouted with another burst of his will, his talons pressed beneath its jaw in warning. The beast tensed, and Gideon sank his talons into its stoney flesh. "Your rage will play out," Gideon hissed through gritted teeth, "but only at my command, and your insolence delays you from your satisfaction." He jerked the beast's head down toward the forest. "The battle awaits."

The dragon's eyes rolled in their sockets, and Gideon's talons sank deeper, his fangs bared, clearly remembering the bitter moment of his own submission. His general had never let Gideon forget that he was as far above him as Gideon was to the mortals surrounding them, and that he could be destroyed just as easily.

Then be it at your command...general, a gravelly voice rumbled through his psyche, tinged with the same loathing Gideon still felt.

Thus it had always been between a general and his recruits.

"I need a name," he growled, jerking the beast's head again.

A pause, and then— *Nyxx* it hissed into his mind.

"So be it." Gideon's chest heaved as he sent out a mental image of the task he would set it to. This battle of wills he had won, but it would be the first of many. "Leave none standing."

He released his grip, and the dragon chuckled, then

screamed again. It reared back and was past him in a flash, its flames cutting a wide swath through the fog around the dome and incinerating everything in its path.

Gideon swallowed heavily, watching in awe. The dragon's primal glee at the destruction it wrought beat back at him through their bond. A dawning respect for his own general niggled at him before he turned back to the town. The dragon would protect their northern flank and the wolves, the south. He would hunt the streets in between.

Chapter Twenty-One

OPHELIA TACKED up another blanket over the long floor-to-ceiling windows spanning the front of the Witchery's third floor. She frowned at the thick black smoke that had begun to drift through the deserted streets and dim the sunlight above. That wasn't from the vampires, but she was pretty sure it didn't mean anything good. The shadows it was creating were going to be a problem.

"You've got to be fucking kidding me," Felix said, staring at his phone. He and the rest of the coven had trickled in, taking turns holding the ward over the town. Currently, that was Ms. Pao, Aggie, and Sweets. The rest of them had spread out, two to a floor, shoring up the Witchery's defenses and keeping watch.

Which left Jena, Felix, Mr. Sheffield, and Matilda to argue —sorry, *debate*—the most ethical way to read entrails. Ophelia didn't know why they bothered. She wasn't an expert, but she was pretty sure Matilda was. Granted, ethics probably didn't figure into whatever method she was describing that made the rest of them so pale. Whatever. Ophelia didn't care. She was willing to bet Chambers didn't either, and if he had, they wouldn't be in this mess to begin with. The rest of them should just let her have at it.

The sour little witch peeked over Felix's shoulder at his

phone's screen and snorted. "So much for you killing the dragon."

"What?" Jena squawked, leaning close. Her face went whiter.

Ophelia and Mr. Sheffield followed suit, all of them stared agog at the reel someone had posted of a dragon decimating the woods outside of Havers. Jesus, you could see smoking skeletal remains of vampires as it winged past, kicking up the haze its destruction had created.

"No way," Felix breathed. "It was solid stone."

"And now, I'm betting it's a gargoyle," Jena said, pinching the bridge of her nose. "Wow, I did not see that coming."

Felix cocked his head at the screen, humming. Whoever was recording had zoomed in on a vampire writhing in flames. "No. But I can't say that I'm mad about it."

"You will be when the fire spreads," Matilda muttered. "Wind's blowing it straight toward town."

"I might be able do something about that," Mr. Sheffield murmured, bending to pick up a piece of chalk. "Felix, if you'll assist me in augmenting the ward?"

He frowned, but went with him to join the circle of witches.

"I can't believe Aggie didn't see any of this. She must've," Jena muttered, looking at Ophelia like she knew something the witch didn't.

"Well, she did say she wasn't telling you anything until—"

Jena's eyes flashed. "I'm not naming my kid after her."

"Fine, but I still think she's got a reason for it, and after meeting her, I'm betting it's a good one. Probably. I mean, unless she's just fucking with you." That was also a strong possibility.

The witch glowered at Ophelia. "You're not helping."

"Yeah, I know," she huffed. "Give me something to do, I'm about to lose my mind." Her anxiety was edging on full-blown panic with Gideon out there. If she didn't have something to keep her busy, things were gonna go downhill fast.

Jena chewed her lip, glancing between the circle of witches and Matilda cackling as she set up a makeshift altar. Ophelia really didn't want to know what all those long pins were for. By the look on Jena's face, she was already well acquainted and wasn't a fan. She sighed. "Yeah, I get that, but there's not really—"

A muffled scream came from downstairs, and their attention snapped to the steps.

"Are they inside?" Ophelia's hand rose to her collar.

"I didn't feel anything breech the ward," Jena said, moving closer to Ophelia, her eyes wide. "But that sounded like Mrs. Hill."

Something thumped below them and a man shouted.

"And that was Rick Kleppet," Matilda said, joining them. She'd pulled a pouch from her pocket and loosened the drawstrings.

"S-should we go help them?" Ophelia licked her lips, hoping the answer was no.

Jena shook her head. "We need to protect the circle. If the ward goes down, whatever's outside it will roll over us."

Shuffling footsteps sounded in the hall below, then slowly began to climb the steps. Jena pressed closer to Ophelia's side, and Matilda stepped in front of them, her eyes narrowed and her lips moving soundlessly. She reached into the pouch, a ruddy glow spilling from its mouth.

A grizzled head popped into view, and Jena sighed. It was that big warlock with the bushy beard that'd been downstairs with them earlier.

"Gregory MacKey, you stop right there," Matilda shouted.

He glowered at her from beneath his grizzled brows and kept shuffling forward.

Oh, dear God— "He's been compelled," Ophelia rasped, edging back.

"Idiot," Matilda snarled, hurling a fistful of power at him and yelling something in a language Ophelia didn't understand. The cloud rolled over him, and he fell to the side like he'd been poleaxed, the floor beneath them jumping as he hit.

"Holy crap," Jena said. "What did you do to him?"

The little witch shrugged, wiping her hand on her pants. "Roofied his ass. He's a little bit bigger, but if my ex-husband's anything to go by, he'll be out for the next few hours."

Jena's brow raised. "And which ex-husband was this?"

"You mean which one it wasn't," Matilda corrected primly, tucking a curl behind her ear. "Why pretend to have a headache when you can have peace and quiet instead?"

Ophelia snorted. "And you just carry around a bag of that stuff with you?"

"Well, it's not gonna do any good in my sock drawer. I'd say check his pockets, but the only thing we're gonna find in Greg's wallet are coupons for frozen vegan burgers."

Jena pinched the bridge of her nose. "When he wakes up will he still be compelled?" she asked Ophelia.

She shook her head. "I don't know."

"Great." Jena chewed her lip, glancing at the steps. "Then I guess we better get something to tie him up with from downstairs and check on Mrs. Hill and Rick."

Okay, so she said that, but Jena wasn't moving toward the stairs.

"Oh, for the love of God, when did you turn into such a pussy?" Matilda slapped a hand against Jena's chest as she pushed past them and kicked Greg's arm aside on her way down the stairs.

"There might be some rope in the hall broom closet," Jena called after her. She buzzed her lips. "Damn it. Matilda's right, I am being a pussy, but I keep thinking that I'm going to turn around and my father's going to be there. He scares the shit out of me, Ophelia, and it's not…it's not just me I have to think about." She frowned, rubbing her abdomen.

Ophelia grimaced. Crap. Was this where she was supposed to say something reassuring? Damn it. She had nothing. "Um, yeah. Unfortunately, if Greg or whatever his name is made eye contact with a vamp, I'm going to bet they had him open the drapes downstairs in the shop. It's a public space. If they've got a shadow walker with them, we're screwed. Who was on the first floor with him?"

"Um…I can't remember. I think Otis and Mr. Rondo are in the basement." Jena went pale, and her throat bobbed. "Oh shit. Luna Birdsong was with Greg."

Ophelia vaguely remembered the tall, twenty-something witch from earlier. She hadn't said much, just kind of sat to the side hiding behind her hair and let everyone else talk.

"She's a newer member." Jena's eyes pinched shut. "We have to go down."

"What about the circle?"

Jena glanced over her shoulder and exhaled slowly. "Matilda can handle things when she gets back. We'll check on what's going on downstairs, and then make sure Luna's okay," she said it like she was convincing herself, then— "You wanted something to do right?"

"Yeah. I did…" But this sure as fuck wasn't it. Goddamn it. Ophelia followed Jena to the steps, warily eyeing Greg. Whatever that stuff had been, it'd knocked him out cold.

The second floor was creepily quiet. They tiptoed down the hall. The warlock with the long nose was on one of the couches, bent over with a cloth to his head. Matilda was by the door, crouched over the woman with the pink sweatsuit. Her neck was not at a natural angle.

Matilda looked up at them, furious. "She's dead."

The warlock let out a heaving sob. "I didn't think anything of it when Greg came upstairs. It happened so fast…

God, what are we going to tell her family? The twins are only six."

Jena wiped tears from her eyes and just shook her head, a hand over her mouth.

"We'll figure it out later," Matilda spat. "Help me get her onto the couch. Rick, take this rope and go upstairs. Greg's out, but lord only knows if he's down. Poor man's gonna be a mess when he finds out what happened, big oaf's never harmed a fly."

Jena nodded in teary agreement, and Rick sniffled his before staggering from the room. Ophelia swallowed the guilt gnawing at her. It wasn't her fault, she knew it wasn't, but she couldn't help but feel responsible. She helped Jena and Matilda carry Mrs. Hill to the couch and lay her out. They stood there for a moment, somber.

"Well, her death's not going to be a total waste," Matilda muttered darkly, karma sparking at her fingertips. She pulled a little sickle knife from her belt and sliced off a hank of Mrs. Hill's hair. "I feel a curse coming on—and it's a doozy."

"You're not going to get any argument out of me." Jena blew out another breath. "Ophelia and I are going down to check on the rest of the coven. You have a handle on things up here?"

"Oh, I've got them all right." Matilda cackled, leaving them.

"I'm guessing she's your bad witch?" Ophelia asked, more than a little afraid of the tiny woman.

Jena nodded still looking at Mrs. Hill. "She's questionable at the very least, but right about now, I'm glad the coven has her. Whoever's responsible for compelling Greg isn't going to be walking away from Havers." She wiped her eyes again and turned to the door leading down, her expression hardening. "Come on, let's get this over with."

∽

GIDEON CROUCHED ON AN ICY PARAPET, his eyes narrowed on the shadowy alley below. Smoke striated the air, rendering everything in shades of gray. The sun had been reduced to an opaque orb slipping toward the western horizon, and the temperature was dropping fast. They had maybe four more hours of daylight, and then things were going to get interesting.

Not that they weren't now.

Something skittered below, and Gideon tensed, leaning forward. A woman's form darted across the alley's mouth, backlit for a brief moment. He surged forward, diving for her, his wings tight against his back. The vampire hissed, his weight taking her to the ground. She exploded into a writhing mass of rats as they hit.

Gideon rolled, crushing as many as he could beneath him. It wouldn't kill the vamp, but it would slow her down. He was fairly certain this was the second time he'd tussled with her and based on the brief glimpse he'd gotten of her irises, it'd taken its toll. She'd need to feed soon, else risk going into a frenzy. As long as the townsfolk stayed out of the way, Gideon was fine with that. The creatures couldn't seem to access their powers when they were in the throes of madness, becoming much easier to put down.

A scuff came from behind, and another of them slammed him to the filthy asphalt, its fangs ineffectually scrabbling at his neck. Gideon reared up, tearing the creature away. His talons ripped across its throat, severing its head with a wash of gore.

Case in point. Gideon scowled, tossing the limp body of the revenant to the side and wishing they all died as easily. He'd come across several dozen of the creatures, but had only managed to reduce that number by half. To say that was frustrating would be a serious understatement. He got to his feet, listening.

He couldn't shake the feeling that something was off. The

streets were eerily quiet, distant screams and the crackle of the dragon's fire a subtle backdrop of destruction. Within his mind, he could feel the beast hunting, playing with its victims. Hopefully he'd put down the lion's share of them. Once Nyxx's rage was temporarily sated and he became bored, he'd fall into deep sleep as the soul continued to meld with its new form.

Which, considering Gideon had no idea what to do with the beast, was probably for the best. His thoughts went to the weres, wondering if that could be the source of his angst.

He launched himself back into the sky and flew to the far side of town. The main body of the Westside pack had formed a line, facing the bank of roiling fog occluding the docks. Others grouped together in reserve. Gideon landed beside one of the larger beasts, and the wolf turned its head, catching him with its bright blue stare. He huffed and gestured with his muzzle for Gideon to follow him to a covered bus stop, out of the wind.

A moment later, its form wavered, bones cracking and popping, and Chase stood before him with nary a stitch on.

"Goddamn it's cold," he shivered, cupping himself.

"Indeed," Gideon said, immune to it. "And it appears you're at a stalemate."

Chase nodded, coughing. "Yeah. It doesn't make sense to run out there, and for the most part, whenever one tries to pop over, it doesn't last long. There's another group of us hunting down the ones that got away. How about you? What the hell's up with all the smoke?"

"The node saw fit to install whatever soul volunteered into what remained of your dragon," Gideon said tersely. Although effective, dealing with the beast going forward was bound to be more than a little problematic, especially if it didn't have an alternate form.

The man blanched. "You serious?"

"I am. My apologies in advance, but Nyxx has reduced

everything on the northern side of town to scorched earth, including the twin to what's out there," Gideon said, nodding toward the bank of fog. "I imagine having him do the same here would be less than desirable?"

"Yeah, you could say that," Chase snorted, rubbing his arms. He frowned. "I don't fucking like this. There's something we're not seeing. Why the hell would they attack now?"

Gideon frowned. "I had the same thought, but don't—"

"Pst-pst-pst-pst!"

Gideon started. What the devil was that?

"Pixies," Chase said, as if Gideon had asked the question aloud.

Gideon's brow furrowed, looking around for the tiny nuisances, then scrubbed a hand across his face. He didn't have the time nor the inclination to deal with their nonsense.

"Pst-pst-hey-stupids!"

"Shhh-quiet-dummy-just-go!"

There was a bit of a scuffle, and one of the creatures zipped up from a sewer grate to hover inches in front of Gideon's face. He snarled, drawing back.

"Nah-nah-nah-thump!" the inane creature jabbered, waving his hands and pointing where he'd come from. *"Trouble-trouble-trouble!"*

"What?" Chase asked.

Another one of them appeared, shoving the first out of the way. *"In-the-Below-trouble-trouble-trouble-argh!"* She put her fingers in front of her mouth like fangs and lunged at her compatriot's neck.

Gideon went cold. "Vampires. In the sewe—ah, the Below?"

The two nodded rapidly. *"Coming-coming-coming-super-super-bad!"*

"Super-bad," the first said with some kind of a gyration Gideon was fairly certain was meant to be a dance move.

The second punched him. *"Going-to-Jena's-Jena's-Jena's!"* she shrilled, pointing in the direction of the Witchery.

Ophelia.

Gideon launched into the air in the same breath Chase resumed his wolf form, thundering through the streets toward the shop.

Chapter Twenty-Two

OPHELIA CREPT down the steps into the shop, cursing herself for offering to go first. She'd been banking on Jena putting up more of a fight, and now she was stuck leading the fucking charge. Ophelia frowned. She wasn't gonna make that mistake again.

A line of muted light came from beneath the heavy velvet curtain at the base of the steps. Ophelia nudged it aside and peeked out, Jena's rapid breath hot on her neck. Damn it. The curtains over the massive bay window in the front of the store had been ripped from their rungs, and the smoke-filled street beyond was on full display. Ophelia scanned the rest of the shop, craning her ears, but couldn't tell if there was anyone else in there.

tha-thump…tha-thump…tha-thump…

Her breath caught at a steady beat over by the windows. She turned back to Jena. "Do you hear that?"

The witch's eyes widened. "Hear what?"

tha.thump.tha.thump.tha.thump.tha.thump.

Wait, was that…? Ophelia's brow knit, and she put her hand to Jena's throat—

"Oh my God! What are you doing?!" the witch screeched, batting her hand away.

"Shh! Quiet! I'm checking your pulse. I think I hear— Just shut up a minute." Damn. Ophelia licked her lips. "I can hear your heartbeat, little Aggie's, and I'm pretty sure there's someone alive in the next room."

"Really?" Jena whispered, a hand on her abdomen, then scowled. "Her name's not Aggie."

"Sure it isn't. Come on, I think it's okay." At least, Ophelia didn't hear anyone else alive in there. Granted, that was kind of a subjective criteria, considering the virus was keeping her heart pumping, but it was more of a *sa-swish*, and she didn't hear that, either. She slipped from behind the curtain with Jena on her heels.

Other than the ruined drapes, the shop looked completely normal. They picked their way through the display tables to the storefront window. Right below it, a woman's legs stuck out from beneath a mound of velvet, and the heartbeat was definitely coming from that direction. "Stay back and let me go check it out," Ophelia said, darting over in a crouch.

She knelt and dragged away the heavy fabric. The woman beneath it was in sad shape, but she was breathing, no thanks to the long purple bruise running over her temple. If Ophelia had to guess, Greg had ripped the curtains down and bludgeoned the witch with the rod.

"This her?"

Jena put a hand to her lips and nodded, looking ill. "Yeah, that's Luna."

"Okay, well, she's alive," Ophelia said, frowning at the unconscious woman. She was thin, but tall. All that dead weight was gonna be a bitch to lift, and with Jena pregnant... yeah, that wasn't happening. "But now, what do we do? I can't carry her upstairs by myself and you're not helping."

"And those aren't going back up anytime soon," Jena said, scowling at the mangled curtains. One of the fixtures had been torn from the window's casement and the rod was bent. She chewed her lip. "Damn it. Splitting up was stupid. We all need to be upstairs with the rest of the coven. Let's get Otis and Clint from the basement. They can carry her up."

Ophelia stared at her. Was she for real?

"What?" Jena asked, clueless.

"Have you ever watched a single horror movie? Like, even one?"

"Of course I have, why?"

"Then you know how fucking stupid that is. 'Oh, let's just go into the basement, *do-do-do*." She rolled her eyes, then pulled her thumb across her throat and made a face. "I might as well kill you now and save whoever's down there the trouble."

Jena scoffed, crossing her arms over her breast. "That's not gonna happen."

"How do you know?"

"Because you're not wearing your six-inch hooker heels so you can fall dramatically when you try to run away," Jena snarked, batting her lashes. "Besides, do you have any better ideas?"

Yes, but abandoning everybody and shadow walking to Klineville to wait this out didn't seem like an appropriate answer. Ophelia glowered at her, not totally taking it off the table, but goddamn it, this friend thing sucked. "Okay, fine, but this time, you're going first."

"Fine."

"Yeah, well, it better be fine," Ophelia muttered, standing.

Jena started back across the shop. "I just said it was."

Ophelia took one more look at the woman on the floor and trailed after her. God, this was a bad idea. "You know I hate you, right?"

"It's mutual and so very, very much." Jena wet her lips and pushed the door to the storage room open. It squeaked loudly, because of course it did.

"Good. As long as that's clear." Ophelia fingered her ear, still hearing heartbeats. It was like a bizarre version of tinnitus. How the hell did she turn that off?

"Is there anyone in there?" Jena whispered.

Ophelia paused for a minute. Not in there, but... "No. I'm pretty sure there are people downstairs, though."

Jena froze. "People? Like, more than two?"

"I don't know, more than one. It's not the easiest thing to count, and yours and little Aggie's are loud as hell."

"Will you stop it? I'm not naming her Aggie!" Jena seethed.

"You are, but whatever." Ophelia pinched across her temples, trying to concentrate on what she was hearing. "Three. I think there's three."

"But there's only supposed to be two!"

"Oh my God, I know, so are we going or not?"

Jena screwed up her mouth and karma sparked purple at her fingertips. "Yes, we're going." She opened the basement door before Ophelia could protest. That, surprisingly, didn't squeak, and they blinked at the bright light coming from below.

"They must be using one of Chase's LED spots," Jena murmured, starting down. "Mr. Fynbender? Mr. Rondo?"

Ophelia winced. How fucking stupid was she? There was no way she'd ever watched a horror movie, because they were definitely about to be murdered by some dude with an ax. The way the steps creaked beneath their feet was on point, even if the light wasn't. It was bright enough to see the motes of dust they were kicking up. That shouldn't have been creepy, but it was. Ophelia shivered with more than dread. It was colder down here than she remembered.

And completely empty. What the hell?

The little rectangular windows had cardboard over them, and a big spotlight was in a corner, illuminating the rest of the room.

"I thought you said you heard heartbeats."

Ophelia shrugged, going over to retrieve her shoes from the last stupid adventure the witch had signed her up for. "I thought I did, but it's not like I'm an expert."

Jena put a hand to the wall where the secret entrance to the Below was. "Where do you think they went?"

"I dunno, but we probably shouldn't hang around—"

The door at the top of the stairs slammed shut, and the light went out. They gasped, and a low chuckle rumbled through the darkness.

The light flicked on again, and Ophelia held a hand over her eyes, squinting.

"Boo." A tall man stood with his face over the spotlight, stark shadows running up his face. He laughed again, straightening up. "Just kidding. I couldn't help but overhear you two discussing horror movies and decided to have a bit of fun."

Holy crap, that was the guy who killed Chambers—Jena's dad. What the fuck was he doing here? He stepped to the side of the spotlight wearing a tailored, black suit and bowler hat right out of the 1800s.

Jena scooted to Ophelia's side and put a hand on her arm, trembling. "W-what did you do with Mr. Fynbender and Mr. Rondo?"

"Hmm? Oh, those two." He adjusted his cuffs. "They're in the parlor upstairs, probably wondering the same. We had been having such a lovely chat before you two interrupted. But, no matter. I also brought up that young lady you left on the floor of the shop. Rather callous of you to abandon her like that, darling. Really, anything could have happened to her in that compromised state."

Jena's mouth opened like she was going to say something, then she closed it again and took a slow breath. "What do you want?"

He put a hand to his breast as if wounded. "Why, to better know my child, of course. Isn't that every parent's most fervent desire?" He moued, his bottom lip sticking out. "We parted on such poor terms. Let's make amends, shall we? Forgive and forget?"

"You're crazy." Jena stumbled back and Ophelia steadied her. "You need to leave me alone."

"Alas, I'm afraid that's not in the cards." He smiled, and it was panty-dropping charming.

"Damn," Ophelia murmured. Jena scowled, elbowing her. "What?" It wasn't like she was interested, but just…damn.

"Ah. And there's the little queen. You've been very naughty." He waggled a finger at her, and his emerald-green eyes flicked over their shoulders to the wall where the hidden door was. "But, alas, now's neither the time nor the place to become acquainted. A contingent of the Crimson Guard and several scores of vampire revenants are about to swarm out of that tricky little hole in the wall. Now, you ladies can either come with me, or, well, let's not dwell on the alternative."

Jena's throat bobbed, and she glanced at Ophelia. "I don't believe you."

"I do," Ophelia whispered hoarsely. She wasn't sure what she was hearing, but it was getting closer—fast. With that stupid LED on, there were zero shadows in the room to escape into, and even if they could get past Jena's dad, she wasn't going to be able to waddle up the stairs fast enough to outrun the Guard.

Jena's father's grin widened, like he knew Ophelia had just figured out he was the only option. "Then shall we?" he asked, holding out a hand. A pentagram tattooed over his palm writhed.

They both stared at it, then jumped as something hit the wall behind them, scrabbling. A rat's snout poked from a crack between two of the stones.

Fuck this. Ophelia might not know what his deal was, but she knew exactly what the vampires would do to them if they got in here. She grabbed Jena and shoved her toward her father. "Suck it up, buttercup," she hissed. "We're going."

"What!" Jena's eyes widened, and she dug in her heels.

Her father caught her arm and Ophelia's hand in the

process. "I knew I was going to like you," he said to her. This time, his grin made her stomach drop for an entirely different reason than it had before, but it was too late now. Before Ophelia could react, the three of them had vanished from the basement.

~

GIDEON LANDED on the Witchery's roof and raced inside. A circle of witches chanted within the chalk-drawn circle on the floor, and in the far corner, Matilda bent over an altar, her hands dark with blood. A large, unconscious man was trussed up nearby, and between the two, a group of unfamiliar warlocks stood around a prone woman, arguing. There was no sign of Jena, nor of Ophelia.

"Where is she?!" Gideon roared.

An elderly warlock with a shock of white hair raised a hand in supplication, stepping forward. "Peace gargoyle. If you interrupt the circle—"

Fuck their circle. "Where. Is. Ophelia?" Gideon slowly enunciated, the knuckles of his fist whitening as he glowered at them from beneath his brows. Below, a door crashed open, signaling Chase's arrival.

The old man's throat bobbed. "We don't know."

"But we will within the hour," Matilda spat over her shoulder, flicking gore from the blade of her knife. "Haruspicy takes a hot minute, and scrying for that sack of shit's never worked."

An hour? They didn't have an— Gideon swallowed his rage, the urge to eviscerate everyone in the room throbbing at his temples. "What sack of shit?"

"Jena's father," the white haired man said, glancing toward the stairs.

Claws skittered in the hall below, then paws pounded up the steps. Chase leaped into the room, morphing back into his human form as he landed. He took in the room with one sweeping glance and growled, stalking toward the warlock. "Tell me I didn't hear that. *He* has Jena?"

The old man held up his hands again. "That's our theory. No one saw anything, but we'd split into pairs to secure the building. Clint and I were in the basement when William—Jena's father—appeared." The beefy man beside him nodded, and the growl in Chase's chest deepened.

"He started prattling on the way he does, and then we heard the girls at the top of the steps." The old man scowled. "William got that damned look on his face like he'd hit the lottery, and the next thing we knew, we were in the parlor with Luna slumped over poor June's body, and William was gone."

Chase's eyes narrowed. "Did he kill her?"

"No." The old warlock glanced at the man who'd been tied up. "But after seeing what happened to Luna and June, *some* of us thought it best to regroup before we rushed down there blind. That was what, two, three minutes ago?" He scowled at a man with a nose that would give a raptor pause.

"And time keeps ticking," the beefy man snapped. "If he's down there with them, we need to move."

"Jena's more equipped to deal with William than any of us," the man with the nose retorted, holding a bloodied cloth to his head.

By the look on Chase's face, he didn't agree.

And neither did Gideon, these warlocks were all cowards.

"Then they could still be down there," he growled. And if the pixies were to be believed, that's where the vampires would be coming from. He pushed past the poor excuses for men. "I'll be back for answers. I suggest you have them ready."

He hurried downstairs, and Chase fell into step with him, an odd camaraderie of shared purpose forming between them. They got to the main floor, and Gideon looked around the cluttered shop, his temper spiking, and at a loss at how to get to the lower level.

"This way," Chase said, taking the lead through the merchandise and into a storage room packed with goods. "It's just over—"

A door on the far side of the room flew open, and a horde of slavering vampire revenants tore up from the basement. They caught sight of Gideon and Chase and let out unholy shrieks, long strings of saliva spattering from their decomposing maws. Gods, every last one of them had gone completely feral. Gideon slammed the door to the shop closed, hoping to stop the fiends from getting any farther. He shoved a crate against it, resolute that they hadn't enough logic left in their moldering skulls to move it.

By the time he'd turned, Chase had morphed back into a wolf and rushed the creatures. They scattered, a group charging at Gideon.

He tore through the first's neck with his talons, the others tripping over its corpse and tangling themselves in a rolling rack of heavy robes. It went down, trapping them beneath it. Gideon tore a loose board from a crate, staking the floundering creatures with its jagged end. He panted, his gaze flicking up from the carnage.

It was obvious that even in their frenzied state, the revenants had little incentive to engage with the were, attempting to keep their distance. They skirted around the big wolf, rolling their stark white eyes and foaming at the mouth. No doubt their aversion was due to the charm Chase had swallowed earlier, though the room's cramped confines gave them little recourse.

The wolf had no such qualms. He tore into them, gore spraying over the housed wares as the fiends flailed ineffectually trying to escape his teeth and claws.

Unfortunately, for each one he put down, another two appeared from the basement. Gideon rushed forward, ripping free a vamp that'd jumped on the were's back, relieving the creature of its head in the process. Gideon snarled; stupid or not, their sheer numbers were becoming a problem.

He needed to stem this at the source before they were overrun.

Gideon dove into the fray, his talons tearing out hearts and slicing through spines. He waded through the dripping corpses, kicking limbs and headless torsos out of his way, making for the steps. Behind him, Chase ended the remaining revenants and followed, limping, his fur matted and his jaws soaked with gore.

"Close the door behind me and hold the line here," Gideon growled.

Chase paused, then huffed his agreement, blood bubbling at his nostrils and his chest heaving.

Gideon kicked a revenant in the chest as it attempted to gain access to the room, sending it sprawling into the ones behind it. They fell halfway down the flight, the frenetic mass at its base buoying them back up like gruesome crowd surfers, backlit by the overturned spotlight casting manic shadows onto the ceiling.

Gideon launched himself into the morass of bodies, slaughtering all in his path. He snapped a fiend's spine over his knee and used the creature to bludgeon another, cracking their skulls together. His talons shredded through jugulars, ripping through tracheas, and beheading the foul beasts.

The mob refused to lessen. He swore, his gaze sweeping the room. Where the hell were they coming from?

Movement on the far wall caught his eye. There, in the shadows, a darker spot. A hole had been blown through the fieldstone foundation, and a tunnel lay beyond. Fiends darted from it, disappearing into the churning mass of monsters. Gideon dispatched another creature, ineffectual claws skittering across his skin. His gaze narrowed, focusing his will on the bedrock beneath him, calling upon it to heed his command.

A low rumble began, the earth shifting beneath his feet. Frenzied monsters fell to their knees, and his talons swept through their necks like a scythe. Jagged rocks exploded from the packed earth of the basement's floor, impaling the creatures, then sped toward the wall, drawn there as if by a lodestone, piling up and fusing together, cutting off the revenants' ingress.

A grim smile curved Gideon's lips, and he cracked his knuckles, attacking with renewed vigor. Without reinforcements, it took very little time to put the rest of them down. He wiped a spatter of gore from his eyes, surveying the room.

That Ophelia wasn't among their number did little to console him. Something incongruent by the steps caught his eye. He knelt, sweeping up of the snakeskin heels he'd picked out for her yesterday. She wouldn't have left them if given a choice. Certain dread filled his being.

Whatever creature Jena's father may be, he had them both.

Gideon's fist tightened around the shoe, and he strode back up the steps, leaving the carnage behind him. It was time to get answers.

Chapter Twenty-Three

OPHELIA STUMBLED against Jena as they appeared beside a roaring bonfire within a circle of standing stones. It was vaguely familiar. Had she been here before? The late afternoon sun lit the sky, and it was warmer than it had any right to be. Not that she was complaining about that, but— "Where…?"

"The ruins above the node," Jena rasped, looking just as disoriented. "This is the circle at the center of the garden where we summoned you."

Ophelia chewed her lip. Okay, that tracked, but how had Jena's dad gotten through all the wards back at the Witchery and here? Weren't they supposed to keep assholes like him out?

"How right you are, my bright little star!" Jena's father crowed. "And now for introductions." He bowed low, sweeping off his hat. "William Seymore, at your service."

"Hey! That's my mom's surname, not yours," Jena spat.

"Modern times, darling, and you must admit, it has a ring to it." He stood, replacing his hat and turned to Ophelia. "And you are…?"

She was pretty sure he knew, but— "Ophelia Diamondé."

"Mmm." He nodded, as if turning that over in his mind. "Both quite auspicious. Ophelia's Greek in origin and means 'advantage,' if I'm not mistaken, and Diamond, eh? A most rare gem, formed by extreme heat and crushing pressures."

Ophelia snorted. Diamondé was a perpetual pain in her ass—spelling and pronunciation wise—and she was pretty sure her first name had been inspired by the chick that offed herself in Hamlet, but whatever.

"I wouldn't scoff, names hold power, you know. I can't wait to discover what my granddaughter will be called."

Jena put a protective hand over her abdomen. "She's not going to be your anything."

"What's that saying? 'Men plan and the universe laughs?' Or was it God? Gods?" William bent down and swept a bag of marshmallows off a picnic blanket that'd been laid out. "Hmm. No matter. Would you like a s'more? I know it's a bit gauche to start with dessert, but your mother couldn't get enough of them when she was pregnant with you."

Jena glared at him, backing against one of the stones. "No, and you need to take us back to the Witchery now."

"Oh, I'm afraid I can't do that. Ophelia?" he drawled, his brow raised and waggling a bag of Puff-Mallows at her.

"Um. I'm good, thanks." What the fuck was going on? Gideon and Chase were going to freak when they found out she and Jena were gone.

William didn't seem concerned.

"Hmph. You two don't know what you're missing. Creating the perfect s'more is one of my many talents." He waved his hand and a long toasting fork appeared in it.

"Why are we here?" Jena gritted out, looking around like she was gauging her chances for escape. Judging by the frustration on her face, they weren't good.

"I wanna know how he got past all the wards," Ophelia added.

That damned grin slid over his face again. "It's a delightful fact that all magic is merely suggestion when approached from the right angle, and, more often than not, I prefer not to comply." Her father impaled a marshmallow and crouched down to hold it above the coals. "As far as why you're here, would you believe me if I said I wanted some bonding time with my only daughter?"

Jena narrowed her eyes at him. "No."

"Well, then I don't know what answer to give you. There we go." He slowly turned the fork. "Nice and golden. Personally, I like them crunchy, but Rebecca preferred them this way. Much less interesting, if you ask me. The char is what balances the sweetness and kicks their flavor over the edge."

"That's disgusting, and what I asked you was why we're here," Jena snapped. "God, are you always like this?"

"Fiendishly charming?" Her father grinned over his shoulder. "Yes, I'm afraid so. Hand me a honey graham would you, darling?"

She crossed her arms over her chest. "Go fuck yourself."

He chuckled and stood to retrieve them and the chocolate himself. Ophelia's stomach rumbled. Were those salted dark cocoa squares? Damn, talk about sparing no expense.

"I do love your spirit," William said to Jena as he assembled the dessert, "but I'm afraid it's rather counterproductive. You and I aren't enemies, you know."

Jena snorted. "Wow. That's news to me after you murdered my mother and tried to kidnap me."

"Technically, that was an attempted abduction. You're far too old to kidnap," he raised a finger at her huff of protest, "but I will admit mistakes were made. I never meant for things to escalate with your mother to where they did. I rather miss her. She was…exceptional." He got a dreamy look in his eye and turned away.

"What about killing one of my key witnesses?" Ophelia asked, trying to get the line of questioning back on track. "We saw you snap Chambers's neck."

"Oh, that." William waved a dismissive hand, then ran a

finger under his eye. "Totally unrelated to your case, but I'll allow the timing was poor."

"That's bullshit," Jena spat.

He glanced over his shoulder, his expression one of total agreement. "My words exactly. Can you believe that after he failed to make good on a bargain we'd struck, he had the audacity to contact me in hopes of alleviating the predicament he'd found himself in?"

"Yeah, I can." Jena pinched the bridge of her nose. "And I'm assuming you granted his request by murdering him?"

"Well, of course." Her father flashed that grin again. "I'm sure I don't have to tell you how important the fine print is, and karma's a sticky, sticky wicket." He thrust the s'more he'd finished making at Ophelia, and she took it reflexively. "There you are. Be a good girl and eat it while it's still gooey."

"Do not put that thing in your mouth," Jena snarled.

Ophelia looked between them, not sure what kind of a fucked-up family dynamic she'd stumbled into, but positive she wanted to stay out of it. Her stomach growled again, and she glanced at Jena. The witch glowered back.

"Tell me you're not tempted." He waggled the bag at Jena again.

"Not in the slightest."

"Well, if you insist on being obstinate, then no dessert for you," William said, crouching with another marshmallow on his toasting fork. This one he gleefully thrust at the coals. "See, I would have made a marvelous parent, giving boundaries and such."

"Too bad you don't have any," Jena muttered.

"And it's incredibly freeing. You should try it sometime." He chuckled as his marshmallow burned, then he extinguished it with a quick puff from his pursed lips.

Ophelia glanced at Jena, then raised hers to sniff. She didn't know what the big deal was, and it smelled really good…

"Don't," Jena growled.

Ophelia rolled her eyes and took a crumbly bite of goo. God in heaven, it was divine. "Oh, stop it," she said around her mouthful. "If he saved us from the vampires, he's not going to kill us now with poisoned s'mores. Besides, the node doesn't seem to mind he's here."

"Yeah, and like you pointed out, it didn't mind the dragon either," Jena snapped.

"True." Ophelia licked a glop of chocolate off the side of her hand. "But that kind of worked out with the whole fire-breathing-gargoyle-thing." Granted, there was still time for it to go horribly awry, but silver lining and all that.

Jena made a noise of disgust and turned back to her father. "And I wouldn't put it past him to have told the frickin' vampires exactly how to get down there in the first place."

"My, you're a clever girl." William licked a crumb from his lip. "You're right. I did tell them about it."

"Y-you what?!" she sputtered.

Ophelia glanced between them. "Jena, you literally just said—"

"I know what I just said, but I didn't think he'd admit to it!"

"Why would I deny it? How else would they have known how to circumvent your ward and get into Havers?" He raised his brow and took another bite, then sucked marshmallow from his thumb.

Jena stared at him in disbelief. "Why would you do that?"

"Now, that is the question, isn't it?" He grinned at her and popped the last of the s'more into his mouth. Ophelia had long since finished hers and was dying for another, poison notwithstanding, but she was pretty sure that if she asked, Jena would murder her.

The karma sparking at the witch's fingertips underscored the theory. "Yeah, that is the question, and you need to answer it."

"So tenacious." He shook out his pocket square and wiped his hands. "You get that from your mother, I'll have you know. I'm acutely reminded how tiresome her intensity could become at times. Of course, there were far more moments that made up for those. She was quite the firecracker." He snapped the cloth in the air salaciously before tucking it back into his pocket.

"Ugh! Just—stop talking about her!" Jena didn't quite stomp her foot, but it was close.

Ophelia scooched over to the picnic blanket and took a seat to watch the show. She had a feeling they were going to be there for a while, and, as sketchy as Jena's dad was, he was equally as entertaining. Well, unless you were Jena. She looked like she was going to blow a fuse. Ophelia paused. Shit. That couldn't be good for the baby.

"You get that he's pissing you off on purpose, right?" Ophelia asked. "Look, it's obvious he's working toward his own agenda, and if the node doesn't mind him being here, whatever it is, it's probably serving it in some way. Not for nothing, but my ill-intent charm didn't zap him when he grabbed us either."

Jena spun at her, realization dawning over her face and the karma at her fingertips fizzling. "Damn it, she's right, isn't she? What deal did you make with the node?"

William frowned at Ophelia. "Well, aren't you a little killjoy. I take back what I said about liking you."

"Why are we here?" Jena asked again.

He drew himself up to face them, tonguing his cheek. "As I said earlier, karma is a sticky wicket, and as much as I loathe the natural order of things, a certain balance must be kept. Fortunately for me, the ends often justify the means." That grin slicked across his face again. "Otherwise, I'd never have any fun at all."

Jena put a hand to her temple. "That makes absolutely no sense."

"Doesn't it, though? Order through chaos, chaos born of order. My specialty's the latter, though I have been known to dabble in both, and I can assure you, I've quite the work ethic." He flicked out his pocket square again, offering it to Ophelia. "Do clean yourself up, darling, we need to meet up with my associates shortly."

Ophelia's mouth went dry. "A-associates?"

"Why yes, of course. You didn't think this was our final destination, did you?" He grinned with a low chuckle. "Oh no, my little queen, as eager as I am to become reacquainted with my daughter, there's someone still waiting who's equally keen to be reunited with you."

Oh, hell no.

Ophelia dove for the nearest shadow and landed hard on the flagstones. What the fuck? Why wasn't it working? She screwed her lids shut, praying that when she opened them, she'd be in the bathroom of the sushi restaurant back in Klineville.

William chuckled and Ophelia opened her eyes to glare at him. Had she thought he was charming? He wasn't, and Jena's attitude toward him was making more sense than Ophelia wanted it to.

"What did you do?" she snarled at him.

"Me?" he asked, a hand to his chest like he was affronted. "Oh, no, not this time. I'm afraid blocking your little shifty shadow skills is entirely the node. It's quite invested in the outcome to this little soirée, and we can't have you wandering about when there's places you need to be, now can we? Do get up, you look incredibly undignified rolling around on the ground like that. What would people say?"

"The node wouldn't do that," Jena spat, helping Ophelia to her feet. "And there's no way it would let you just hand her over to a bunch of vampires!"

He buffed his nails against his jacket. "Are you sure, darling? As Ms. Diamondé so helpfully pointed out, it doesn't seem to object to my person. Why would it quibble over my intent to deliver her to a few undead if that assured its safety? Well, I shouldn't say 'few,' it's to be two, precisely."

Sweat broke out over Ophelia's brow, and she dug her fingers into Jena's arm. "I-I can't go back to that, I can't." Her gaze swept around the circle, looking for anything she could use to stake herself, and landed on the bonfire. Her throat bobbed. It would be over quick. Visions of that burned marshmallow went through her mind, and she whimpered.

"Huh, you'd think you'd be more pleased about satisfying your contract," William said, cocking his head as he planted himself squarely in her path. "And they were so happy at the prospect of being reunited with you."

"Look, you asshole, I don't know why you're doing this or what you did to the node, but it stops now," Jena growled, pushing Ophelia behind her. Karma sparked purple at her fingertips, and her hair stirred around her in an ethereal wind.

A sly smile spread over his face. "Oh, no. Not this time, darling. You're just going to have to trust that Daddy knows best and sit this one out." Her father made a gesture, and shadows sped from the edges of the circle, cocooning around Jena and snuffing her power. He caught her as she fell and lowered her against a pillar with a gentle pat to the head. Her eyes fluttered and closed. "There we go, sleepy time for you."

Ophelia stared at him, agape, trembling. "What are you going to do to her?"

"Hmm?" He straightened up and turned to her. "Why, absolutely nothing. Not yet, anyway. It's all about timing, and certain bargains must be kept. If nothing else, I am a man of my word." Ophelia cringed back as he stepped toward her and brushed a lock of her hair behind her ear.

"There, there, little queen. You have no reason to fear for her safety. I can feel that diabolical witch's spell to locate me pricking across my skin as we speak. How irresponsible of me to leave Chambers's corpse behind." He smiled, and there wasn't a shadow of a doubt that it hadn't been an accident. "That brawny beau of my daughter's is probably already on his way to collect her with your gargoyle in tow, which means it's time for us to leave."

Tears stung her eyes. "Please, don't do this," she whispered raggedly.

William dabbed her cheek with his pocket square. "If I were you, I'd be less concerned about what I'm about to do and more focused on what's already been set in motion."

He glanced past her, his gaze catching on something. She went to turn, and his grin was the last thing she saw as the stones around them winked from view.

GIDEON TORE up from the basement, back toward the third floor with Chase limping after him. He'd found a pair of sweatpants somewhere, and his body was gouged and bruised from the revenants. Gideon was honestly surprised the were was still standing.

"She wasn't there?" Chase panted, trying to keep pace.

"No," Gideon spat. "That creature has her, and I'll be damned if he left any indication as to where they'd gone." And as much as he wished to rage, flying off half-cocked wasn't going to do anyone any good. He needed more bloody information. A direction, a clue, something to go on.

Matilda had best have answers.

Gideon sprinted up the last flight of stairs, to the main room. That group of warlocks was still arguing. They stopped abruptly as Gideon strode into the space, stripped and stippled with gore. He ignored the lot of them and headed for Matilda. She frowned, polishing the blade of her sickle knife, the weasel's corpse splayed open behind her on the altar.

"Well?" he demanded without prelude. "Did your spell work?"

"Oh, it worked." The little witch's frown deepened. "But I don't like it."

Gideon raked back his hair, struggling to keep from throttling the woman. "I care very little for your preferences at the moment," Gideon growled as Chase joined them. "Where are they?"

Matilda let out a heavy breath. "At the ruins. I saw the three of them amid the standing stones, then I swear to God, that son of a bitch looked directly at me, smiled like this was a game, and disappeared with Ophelia.

Chase came to full attention. "Jena's still there?"

Matilda nodded. "It's a safe bet."

"Let me grab my coat and I'll meet you at your truck," Gideon seethed, not waiting for Chase's response. He needed to check his damned phone to see if Renard had gotten some information on the creature by now. None of this was making sense. The node should never have let him cross its wards, never mind get that close. And why would the fiend take Ophelia and leave Jena behind?

What the hell are you thinking? he bellowed at the node.

The cursed thing didn't reply, its childish whispers oddly absent from his psyche. Gideon flung the door to the roof open and swept up his coat, digging for his phone.

One message flashed across his screen, but it wasn't from Renard.

It was a photo of Ophelia, and she was aboard a ship.

Chapter Twenty-Four

OPHELIA STUMBLED as she appeared with William beneath a bright blue sky, his hand a vise around her upper arm. He pursed his lips, texting with his free hand. Before she could see what it was, the ground beneath her listed, and he pocketed the phone. She staggered to keep her balance, the smell of the ocean thick in her nose. Her stomach roiled. Oh God, they were out to sea. They had to be.

She blinked at the late afternoon sun, while high over head, seabirds cried to one another high overhead, confirming her fears. Tears pricked her eyes. Ophelia took in the deck of the ship and the vampires scurrying around them. There had to be at least a hundred of the Crimson Guard aboard, and by the size of the vessel, they were over deep water.

Bile stung the back of her throat. God, what had she done, what had she done? This was a death trap, and Ophelia was certain she was here and not at the Citadel solely to lure Gideon to his doom.

Anger twined with her anxiety. What in the actual fuck? The node was supposed to protect them both! That was the whole fucking point of the covenant Ophelia had made with it, why Gideon had pledged—

Oh God, Gideon.

Her anger paled at what his would be. When he came back and found her missing, he'd tear the town apart, and if he discovered she was out here, he'd come for her, consequences be damned.

And the deep water would kill him. She had to get out of—

"Ah! Kremlyn!" William cried, jerking her around. "There you are. How goes culling Havers's herd?"

The vampire prince stood at the ship's rail in the full black tactical regalia of the Crimson Guard, only a long scarlet sash around his waist to indicate his rank as their leader. Sunlight glittered in his close-cropped salt-and-pepper hair, and he ran a hand over his stubbled chin, malevolence glinting in his remaining eye.

Her stomach rebelled, and she dry heaved as Jena's dad dragged her forward. *No. This isn't happening, it isn't.*

"Far more slowly than we were led to believe it would," Kremlyn said, stepping away from the steel rail. Beyond it, a dense fog churned, doing nothing to mute the sounds of battle and thrashing water. Kremlyn didn't seem to notice, his gaze intent on Ophelia. Her insides turned to ice. He snapped his fingers and pointed to the ground at his feet. "Come."

Ophelia started forward before William's grip on her arm stopped her. She glanced at him, then raised her chin. "No."

"Say it again." A malicious grin bloomed across Kremlyn's face, and he tongued a fang, slowly crossing the deck toward her.

"N-no." She trembled, shrinking back.

"We can take it from here, sidhe." Kremlyn's eye flicked to William.

"I'm sure you can."

Her legs went weak as he released her. She fell to her hands and knees, her vision tunneling. No. This wasn't happening. He wasn't really going to leave her here...was he?

"However, there's still the matter of payment," William said, his voice as cold as the vampire's.

Oh God, he was.

Kremlyn snorted, then motioned to one of his guards. "Bring her inside."

Behind her, heavy boot falls sounded. They were oddly attenuated, like she was caught in a nightmare. She curled up into a ball, retreating into herself. *This isn't happening. You're not really here, you're not—*

Rough hands closed around her shoulders, and a jolt of power surged from the charm around her throat. A vampire screamed, and steaming ribbons of offal sprayed across the deck. Ophelia gagged at the overpowering reek of ozone and burning flesh. She skittered back through the carnage and pressed herself against a coil of rope, gripping her charm and blinking a spatter of blood from her lashes.

Kremlyn stood just beyond the smoking remains of his guard, his cheeks sucked in and something far too close to amusement in his eye. "There's my little bird. I told you, this one has talons," he chuckled to the rest of his men that'd borne witness, then crouched down so that his gaze met hers. He swept a crimson smear from his cheek and popped the gore into his mouth. "Hungry, Ophelia? Your irises are awfully pale."

The guards around him laughed, and Ophelia looked away.

"I told you once," Kremlyn crooned. "Fly as far as you might, I will find you. Now, it's time to come back to the nest and take your punishment for defying my will."

Ophelia shook her head, trembling as she clutched the ill-intent charm. "N-no."

"No? Then tell me, do you have more tricks up your sleeve?" Kremlyn asked, eyeing her charm with a sly grin, like he knew it was spent. "Will that little trinket save your gargoyle when he comes? Oh yes, I know all about Gideon Sperry, including what will kill him, and we're miles from the shore."

She went still, and his smile spread to slick across his face like rancid oil. He nodded to another of his guards, and the vampire hauled her up, snapping the chain from around her neck and flinging the charm into the ocean. The guard pinned her arms behind her back.

She cried out, and Kremlyn laughed as he closed the distance between them. "Now that we have that out of the way..." He grasped her jaw, fingers cruelly pinching her cheeks. His eyes narrowed, and he scraped a thumb beneath her eye. "What witchery is this?" he murmured.

Oh God. Her tatuaj. She'd forgotten they weren't there anymore. Ophelia pinched her lips closed and looked away. His fingers tightened, and she bit back a whimper.

He smiled fondly at her. "No matter, little bird. We have all the time in the world. I'll enjoy making you sing for me."

"Perhaps you do, but my time's limited," William said, squaring his lapels. "Might we move this along?"

Kremlyn's jaw tensed, but he grunted his assent, striding across the deck to the hatchway leading down. William followed, and the guard dragged Ophelia after them. She bit back a sob, her heart bleeding. No. This wasn't right. She didn't understand. How was this happening? She'd done everything she was supposed to. How could everything have gone so wrong?

The guard cursed as her legs gave out again, and he picked her up, throwing her over his shoulder like a sack as they descended into the bowels of the ship. Ophelia's head swam, corridors twisting, harsh metal grating becoming solid planking, then worn carpet. The smell of the sea distant, replaced by a dank thread of mildew beneath too-sweet chemicals, presumably meant to eradicate it.

Kremlyn stopped at a door midway down a long, paneled hallway and knocked.

"Enter," a velvety voice answered.

Vesper. Ophelia's vision tunneled again, her head light and her body going lax. No. This was too much. The guard grunted, hefting her higher onto his shoulder as Kremlyn opened the door. Cloying perfume and the scent of old blood rolled over her. Ophelia's stomach lurched, the combination sending her into a spiral. Not again. She couldn't face her again.

"Ah, you have her," the vampire queen purred when they entered the posh stateroom.

Ophelia went limp, her mind shutting down.

She stared blankly at the plush, crimson carpet, silent tears tracking down the sides of her nose. Absently registering them as they fell, vanishing into the sea of thick pile. Retreating into herself. This wasn't real. She wasn't here.

"Was there ever any doubt?" Kremlyn asked, lifting a decanter from a cocktail cart.

The guard flipped Ophelia off his shoulder, onto the floor at the vampire queen's feet. Ophelia lay there, cheek pressed into the pile, inches from Vesper's diamond-studded shoes. If she didn't resist, they would get bored and go away. Soon. It would be over soon.

"Mmm," the vampire queen hummed. "And what is the status of our incursion?"

"Dicey," Kremlyn sourly admitted, pouring himself a glass of ruddy liquid. "As expected, the sea fae have been problematic. The sirens in particular. We're going to have to rethink deploying the rest of the troops by LCVPs. The smaller boats are a liability. It's too easy for the sirens to lure our men into the water. What they're not already chumming the ocean with, the sharks are finishing. I've never seen so many in one place."

Vesper's jaw tightened. "How many have we lost?"

"At sea? Four score and three patrol boats. The bastards are going after the through-hull fittings to swamp us. It's clever, I'll give them that, but it shouldn't be long now." He raised his glass and eyed Ophelia over the rim. "Once the gargoyle comes for her and we're rid of him, the invasion can start in earnest."

"You've neutralized the guardian?" Vesper asked William.

"As promised." He swept up the decanter from the cart. "She won't be an impediment to your plans, and the gargoyle should be en route. I'd suggest moving closer to shore, you're a bit too far out for him to convince himself rescuing her is possible. Would you care for a glass?" he asked her, pouring one for himself.

"The only thing I have interest in drinking runs through Havers's veins," Vesper hissed, her fists clenched around the arms of her chair. "We've already wasted enough time and manpower alike. Kremlyn tells me our land troops are in shambles. You've some explaining to do, sidhe."

William sighed, swirling the liquid in his glass. "Perpetually, it seems. However, in my defense, no one had any way of knowing that the gargoyle would be able to rouse the dragon's corpse. It simply isn't something that's done." That sly grin slicked over his lips, and he licked them. "Are you sure you don't want a drink?"

Vesper scowled, and Kremlyn slammed his glass down onto a table.

"Yet it was, and your weak excuses don't mitigate the fact that my entire northern flank is gone," Kremlyn growled, his heated gaze flicking from Ophelia to William. "Along with the revenants from the Inchisoare we sent below ground—both dispatched at your suggestion."

Jena's father tsked. "Again, with all due respect, that would be directly attributable to Gideon Sperry, which whom I'm afraid you're responsible for involving in this venture. And pardon me for saying so, but it was a rather glaring lack of foresight on your part recruiting a gargoyle in the first place, especially one without ties to a node."

He held up a hand forestalling whatever Vesper was about to say. "But be that as it may, I've managed to salvage the situation. The node's guardian won't give you issues, and here's your runaway, as promised. Now, that, along with getting your troops into the town proper, upholds my end of the bargain. I believe I'm owed some quid pro quo before we are at quits?"

The two vampires glowered at him before Vesper pulled a small pouch from her waistband and tossed it at him. "Then we are at quits."

"Marvelous." William grinned, fingering whatever was inside through the fabric. His grin widened, and he tipped his hat, then was gone.

"I don't trust him," Vesper muttered, staring at the empty space where William had just stood.

"No, but whatever he's planning on doing with those centipede eggs, it can only be to our benefit," Kremlyn muttered, back to staring at Ophelia. "And as I said, it won't be long now. Prepare her. I want the gargoyle to see her as mine before he dies."

Vesper's lips tightened. "As you wish." She clapped her hands and silk rustled, her attendants descending on Ophelia. Pairs of smaller, smooth hands grasped her limbs, scoring her with their sharp nails and carrying her away, deeper into the bowels of the ship.

GIDEON'S FIST tightened around his phone, resisting the urge to wing it out over the rooftops. He had little doubt Ophelia was aboard one of the ships making up the vampire's fleet, but to attempt to get her on his own was a death wish. There was no way he could survive flying out over the ocean to search for the right one.

He roared his frustrations into the heavens, but it was as useless as he.

Damn it, he needed more intel, and the only person that

might have that was Jena. He grabbed his coat and glided to the street below, Chase's truck already running in front of the shop. Gideon landed, his wings shimmered from existence. He pulled his coat around himself and climbed in the passenger seat. The door was barely closed before Chase peeled away from the curb.

"There's clothes in the back," he said.

"Thoughtful of you."

"Not really, just prepared. It's a shifter thing."

Indeed. Gideon pulled on a pair of sweats and a horrendously stained Henley. The truck flew through the abandoned streets, toward the shimmering curtain of light bubbling around the town.

Chase swore, crouched over the steering wheel. "You think getting through the ward is gonna be a problem?"

"Only if the node makes it one." Gideon's jaw tensed. And if it did, things were going to escalate quickly. "In either event, I would suggest slowing down when you get there."

Chase grunted, the speedometer dipping as they squealed around a corner, and the ward cut across the road ahead of them.

"Here goes." He drove straight for it, the vehicle slowing to a crawl as they passed through and came out on the other side. "I guess the node doesn't mind us leaving."

He floored it again, and Gideon frowned, not sure that was the case. Despite the coven channeling its power, the node's presence had been distant and distracted. It seemed almost...disconsolate. What the hell was going on with it?

"Issue?" Chase asked, glancing over.

Gideon shook his head. "I don't know. Ever since the Jena and Ophelia were taken, the node's been strangely preoccupied, like it's unhappy about something." His phone pinged, and he scrambled for it.

"That your guy?"

"No," Gideon frowned. "Judge Carey. He forwarded my

recommendations with the evidence and allegations I sent him earlier to the Department of Justice. It looks like they're going to take up the case against Fayet and the tribes, which would make Havers a witness in the case."

"That's good news, right?"

"Theoretically. If I have any say in the matter, there won't be anything left of the tribes to prosecute."

Chase snorted. "From your lips to God's ears."

He took a sharp corner, and the node's power riffled over Gideon's skin as sharply as it had earlier, the wards leading to the ruins still in place. He frowned. Despite Matilda's assertion that she'd seen all three of them here, the barriers held no taint from being breeched. His frown deepened. That meant that whoever had been here, the node had let in.

What the devil are you playing at?

The node didn't answer, just that faint sense of remorse prickling through him. Chase skidded to a stop at the end of the drive and threw the truck into four-wheel drive. They humped along the path they'd taken only yesterday leading to the back of the tor. Once parked, the two rushed up the slippery snow-covered hill to a walled garden behind a rambling mound of stones.

Gideon clenched his teeth, the sorrow and anger still radiating from the ruins setting him on edge. Dark doings had happened here, and the land still wept. He followed Chase through the thick drifts and along the garden's spiral path, tripping over canted pavers and detritus hidden by the snow. Sweat stippled Gideon's brow as they crossed a small bridge and skirted around a tall stone wall to an opening at its end.

"Jena!" Chase cried, darting through the break and into a large circular patio ringed with seven standing stones. A large bonfire crackled at its center. He ran to his wife, crumpled against an upright pillar and swept her into his arms. "Baby, baby! Wake up!"

Gideon scanned the area, his heart in his throat. After what Matilda had said, he hadn't expected Ophelia to be here, but her absence still cut him to the core. He slowly crossed the wide stone pavers, the power of the node thrumming uneasily beneath his feet.

What did you do?

What we had to... came a faint reply laden with apology.

Gideon growled, resolute. *Then I shall do the same.*

He stopped at Chase's side. Jena was wan, but appeared unharmed. Her brows furrowed, and she slowly opened her eyes.

"Chase? Gideon?" She started, trying to push up, then winced, a hand at her abdomen. "Where's Ophelia and my dad—oh God." She clutched her head as if it pained her, then looked at Gideon. "He took her to Kremlyn."

Gideon's guts wrenched, and he clenched his fists. Of course, the fiend had. "Tell me what happened," he gritted out, completely bereft of patience. His anger rolled off him in waves, and the two of them cringed back from him as if it were tangible.

Jena's throat bobbed. "We were in the basement and my dad appeared. He said the vampires were coming through the Below. I-I didn't believe him, but Ophelia did and pushed me at him, then we were here."

"She was right," Chase murmured against the crown of her head. "And you're gonna be pissed when you see the stockroom."

"The basement isn't any better, but no one will be getting through that entrance again," Gideon added, with no intention of cleaning either up.

Jena bit her lips and looked like she was about to cry. "I asked him why we were here, and he spouted some line about having a bargain with the node, and chaos maintaining karma's balance, the ends justifying the means—"

Gideon drew back, hissing in a breath.

"Do you know what he was talking about?" she asked.

He ignored the question. "Was that when he took Ophelia?"

"Yeah, pretty much." She nodded, wiping her eyes. "He said she had someplace to be, and that someone was waiting for her."

Gideon's phone pinged, and he raked it out of his pocket. It was another text from that unknown number, this time with coordinates. They tagged a location a mile, mile and a half from the shore. Gideon's jaw tightened. It would be close, but… He pinched the bridge of his nose, trying to talk himself out of flying out there on a suicide mission and knowing it was already done.

"Was that information on my dad?" Jena asked.

"No. That was coordinates of where I'm assuming Ophelia is. If they're legitimate, she's on a ship just off the coast." He blew out a breath. "And I'm going to get her back."

Chapter Twenty-Five

OPHELIA EXISTED IN A HAZE. There but not, her mind recoiled from her reality. Around her, Vesper's attendants whispered, their voices sharp and sibilant. Cruel nails and harsh cloths scraped and rubbed at her face. The skin around her eyes burned, raw from their attentions, their questions becoming more frenzied.

"Where are your tatuaj?"

"How did you get rid of them?"

"Look at her eyes—what does it mean?"

Her lip was raked up as they checked for her fangs, tsking and hissing with impatience, demanding answers in hushed tones with frantic glances toward the doorway leading back to Vesper's chambers. Slapping and pinching. Her body rocked with their abuse. Her clothes rent from her. Scalding water flowed over her skin, then the sting of lye scrubbed into her flesh by coarse, horsehair brushes.

Ophelia stayed silent, her mind very far away. Watching as if everything were happening to someone else. This. This is what Thaddeus had been afraid of. The vampires finding out. Rumor was already flying wide, the door cracking and strange faces peering in at her. She quailed, shoulders slumping. Her stupidly trusting William had put Havers in even more danger than it had been. Nothing she could say would make that better, no explanation would suffice.

... "If I were you, I'd be less concerned about what I'm about to do, and more focused on what's already been set in motion..."

Set in motion. Ophelia bit back a sob. The only thing that'd been set in motion was the destruction of everything she'd begun to care about. *Way to go, Phe.*

One of the attendants slapped her upside the head, and she was made to stand, her skin crawling at the rasp of the rough towel drying her off. Tears rolled down her cheeks. This wasn't the end. Oh, no. This was only the beginning.

Bile rose into her throat as a horrific, jagged weight settled onto her shoulders, encasing her in agony. Ophelia kept her eyes closed, her breath shallow as she was sewn into the tight robe, the blinding pressure around her intense. To move, to exist, was torment.

She wasn't there.

Practiced hands set the last stitch. Her arms were lifted over her head, and a corset lowered around her torso. The ground glass lining the robe tore into her. Hot rivulets of blood trickled down her raised arms, along her ribcage, to her hips and thighs. She bit back a gasp at the sudden, cruel yank on the corset's ties. Her skin scoured away by the millions of tiny, jagged shards embedded against her flesh, her body an open wound.

The hood of the crimson robe was raised, then lowered, darkness falling over her closed eyes. Only her fingertips, the tips of her toes, her lips, and her chin remained visible beneath the horrific regalia of the Damă.

The attendants led her back into the other room, her skin slick with blood, the carpet sticky beneath her bare feet, to stand before Vesper.

"Leave us," the vampire queen intoned.

Ophelia waited as the room cleared, head bowed, willing herself not to cry. For her lips not to tremble. Knowing what was coming. This was nothing. This, she could endure. She had countless times before.

And for what? a little voice from the Ophelia that was before whispered. *You're as much a queen as she is. More so, because if you're here, her time is done...*

"Kneel," Vesper spat, leaning back in her chair and crossing her long legs with a look of supreme satisfaction on her face. The tip of her diamond-studded shoe bobbed beneath her silks with impatience. Anticipation. Whatever the vampire queen was feeling, it would translate to the lash for Ophelia.

She slowly lowered herself down, and Vesper kicked the robe beneath her, forcing Ophelia to kneel upon it. Jagged shards dug into her flesh, and her eyelids fluttered, her mind far away from the pain, back with Thaddeus and Gideon in the garden. A strange feeling stirred in her breast.

... *"You and the rest of the Damă are all the little queen bees the virus has spawned to fly far, far away and perpetuate our kind..."*

Except they didn't. Vesper hoarded them away and tore off their wings like a sadistic child.

"My. Just look at you, back at my feet, where you belong," she crowed, standing as if to better inspect her. "I hope your little sojourn was worth it."

Ophelia stayed silent, images playing through her mind. Waking up to Gideon. Walking at his side through town. Him pointing at their little house up on the hill. She'd never get to see the inside. Never get to find out if Jena caved and named her kid Agatha. That hurt more than she thought it would. All of it did. Her psyche bled freer and faster than her body beneath the robe, and that strange feeling in her breast redoubled. William's words about what had been set in motion echoed through her mind, then Thaddeus's voice.

... *"At first, the lines darken, then they become blurred. Once that occurs, it allows one to incrementally access the other tribes' abilities..."*

Shadow walking. Hearing heartbeats. What else did she

have access to? Her breath hitched, and Vesper tsked, pacing behind Ophelia to whisper at her ear.

"Tell me, does the blood of Havers taste as sweet as I've dreamed it to be? I imagine my poor deluded husband let you sip from his cup. Thaddeus always did have a soft spot for orphans and mongrels."

And Vesper would murder him as assuredly as she'd murder Gideon by luring him from the shore. Even after exile, she wouldn't let the Thaddeus rest. No. She needed to steal away his chance of redemption and grind it beneath her diamond-studded shoe like everything else. She'd take the blood of Havers and turn it into a weapon against any who opposed her. Ophelia's fingers twitched into a fist.

Vesper laughed softly. "I bet he adopted you with open arms, wanting to share the bounty he's kept from me." She raked back Ophelia's hood and raised her chin, scowling. "Such a little whore. Did you seduce him like you seduced my son? Kremlyn's obsession with you is irksome, but one way or another, it won't last." Her eyes narrowed. "I promise you that."

Ophelia met her gaze. Once the threat would've given her comfort. An end. A way out. Now, it sparked something deep inside of her. A certainty came over her, that feeling in her breast growing to consume her. This wouldn't be her end. Not by Vesper's hands. Nor by Kremlyn's.

Vesper pursed her thin lips, as if gauging Ophelia's silence. "But first I'll have your secrets and my errant husband's. Tell me, have you discovered how he continues to defy my will? I know the answer lies in Havers's blood. Is that what erased your tatuaj?"

… *"Focus on what's been set in motion…"*

Ophelia stared into Vesper's calculating ebony eyes, the tatuaj surrounding them turning them into sucking pits, a monster in their depths. This woman. This *queen*. She was the embodiment of hate, set to destroy anything and everything around her.

Yet, Ophelia's tatuaj were gone, that stain removed from her being…but her abilities remained.

The slow thump of the vampire queen's heart beat in Ophelia's ears. She looked away from Vesper's diseased gaze and embraced the emotion smoldering within, slowly breathing out as Ophelia put a name to it.

Rage.

Yes, it was rage, but not the kind Ophelia had survived on for all those years at the Citadel, impotent and poisonous. No. This was the righteous rage of oppression. Of the need to set things right. Ophelia's fingertips twitched, gore spattering to the carpet.

And this rage, like her name, had power. An advantage borne of every last crushing pressure she'd been subjected to by the Vampire Court.

She was not a Damă. She was Ophelia Diamondé, and she'd use this power—the power of a queen—to take back her own.

"You know something." Vesper's eyes narrowed. "What have you discovered?"

Ophelia raised her gaze to meet the vampire queen's, overcome by a strange calm, all that righteous fury tightening in her core. It was time for her and all the rest of them to reap what they'd sown. It ended now.

"That all you've done has made me stronger."

She focused on Vesper, sending out her rage in a concentrated burst of power, erupting flesh.

The vampire queen's head exploded, her body torn asunder. It was thrown back onto her chair, tattered ribbons of entrails spattering down around her twisted ribcage, her blackened organs glistening in the cabin's amber light.

Ophelia slowly stood and plucked out Vesper's heart, crushing it in her fist before dropping it to her feet and grinding it into the floor. She looked up at the gasps in the doorway to the other chamber, glowering at the three attendants cowering there.

"Die," she growled, her voice thick with compulsion.

They dropped to the ground, lifeless. Their corpses withered, aging in an instant and desiccating into brown husks.

Ophelia stood there for a moment longer, then raised the hood of her robe, and calmly walked from the room.

It was time for Kremlyn and the rest of the Crimson Guard to meet their new queen.

GIDEON PACED before the dying bonfire, his chest heaving. He could do this. He could get to the ship Ophelia was on. His reactions would be slowed, but the Court would be trapped aboard, and he could hunt them at his leisure. Unless they escaped via the shadows, but—gha! He tore at his hair, he had to do something!

Jena's brows furrowed. "But I thought gargoyles couldn't cross saltwater."

"We can't," he said succinctly. "But if I can make it to the ship…" He trailed off, not liking the uncertain desperation in his voice.

"Magic doesn't work out there, Gideon."

"I'm aware," he snapped back at her.

"Look," Chase said, frowning, "all the boats in the harbor have already been put out to sea, but maybe we radio one to check it out? This is shady as fuck. Who the hell would send you coordinates? It's gotta be the vampires trying to lure you out there. We don't even know if she's on one of the ships."

"The photo I received earlier from the same number says otherwise." And Gideon had a very bad feeling Jena's father was at the top of the list of possible senders. "It doesn't matter if it's a trap. I have to try." He had to go to her. He stripped out of his great coat and borrowed sweats.

He was airborne before they could argue, his mind in a tumult and Jena's father at the center of the storm. Chase's recounting of the fiend's offhand comment saving him. Jena's of how her father had encouraged her to take the node in hand. Him saving her and Ophelia from the revenants in the basement. And that comment about balance.

Gideon's jaw tightened at the implications, but it made too much sense to dismiss out of hand, no matter how improbable. It would also explain Renard's silence. There were rumors of creatures acting as karma's agents, recruited to do its bidding after epic breeches of propriety. Distributors of fortune, neither good nor bad, they sowed chaos, and in doing so, balanced karma's scales in their wake.

Whatever Jena's father had been, Gideon was positive he'd become a Nemesis.

Though what it was about Havers that had drawn one of his kind here…it didn't matter. Gideon had little doubt William had been the one who sent the photo and the coordinates as part of his task, but be that for the good or otherwise… Damn it. A part of Gideon screamed that trusting intel from such creature could only lead to folly.

The rest of him didn't care, as long as it also led to Ophelia, and in his heart of hearts he knew it would.

Gideon winged higher into the atmosphere, circling over the node. He paused to glance at the sleeping dragon curled up in the smoking desolation outside of town. A frown ghosted over Gideon's lips. If he should perish, so would Havers when that leash snapped.

The node plucked at him, as if to hold him back. He ignored it, his wings beating closer to the ocean, gaining more altitude. Gideon snarled. If the node was so damned concerned, it should have stopped Kremlyn from taking

Ophelia in the first place. The dragon could raze the entire peninsula for all he cared.

A speck resolved on the horizon, and his eyes narrowed, the dense fog covering the rest of the ocean conveniently pushed back from a single vessel. Too conveniently. That it was a trap wasn't in question, but if there was any chance he could save Ophelia, he had to take it.

The effects of the ocean were immediate as he left the shore. He dropped altitude, his body weight increasing, his wings not as responsive, hardening as he flew. *A mile Gideon. You crossed the damned ocean once, you can make it a bloody mile.*

Unfortunately, that hadn't been under his own power. He knew what to expect, but the rigor in his limbs this early on wasn't a good sign. Gideon struggled to hit an updraft, his reactions too slow and sweat stippling his brow. He dipped lower towards the sea.

Gideon struggled to gain altitude, his wings flailing as he searched for Ophelia. She had to be there. Visions of how he'd found her in the bathroom crowded his mind's eye. The thought of that son of a bitch laying his hands on her fueled Gideon's rage, and he pumped his wings harder. His jaw tightened, tendons straining at his neck. He would make it, or die trying.

Chapter Twenty-Six

OPHELIA GHOSTED through the ship's corridors, a cacophony of heartbeats from above bleeding into each other. They fluttered and jumped, erratic amidst the battle at sea.

Save one.

Memories of the massacre at the Citadel tripped through her mind. Of the single man standing at the center of the carnage, dispassionately disemboweling those that had risen against him. Severing their heads. The slow thud of his pulse against her afterwards. The emptiness in his eyes.

Kremlyn.

A grim smile tipped her lips as she locked onto it, letting it guide her steps. Worn carpet becoming solid planking, then harsh metal grating; the smell of the sea sharpening.

She passed few moving through the stark hallways. Those she did pressed themselves to the walls and averted their gazes, her crimson robes marking her as Kremlyn's property. The doctor all those years ago had been right. The vampire prince suffered no rivals for his concubine's attentions, and at the Citadel, to look upon them uninvited meant a death far more final than vampirism had "gifted" them with.

Here, it meant the same, but their ends came at Ophelia's hands.

Shadows writhed at her command and flesh ruptured. They slumped to the ground, eyes unseeing pits within their tatuaj and their corpses desiccated. Eviscerated. Gore spattered against long rows of piping and dripped through harsh metal grates as a warning to those cowering from her like rats below.

She slowed only to swipe a dagger from one of her victim's belts, tucking it into her wide sleeve. Blood trickled from her ravaged flesh, the robe's horrific rasp grounding her in her body, her mind fixated on the task ahead, and her fury buoying her.

This ended now.

Ophelia turned from the splayed remains, the dagger's hilt sticky against her palm. Ahead was the door leading to the main deck.

And to Kremlyn.

A flutter of fear-tinged anticipation coursed through her and was silenced by her rage.

She pushed open the metal slab and stepped onto the ship's deck. A breeze lifted the stiffened edge of her hood shading her eyes from the bright sunlight. The fog had blown back from the rails, leaving the boat in an eerie pocket of open water. Battle raged around them, the sea faes' screams and thrashing waves, seabirds shrilling, diving for spoils.

None of it registered, her attention fixed on the man standing in the center of it all, his heartbeat a siren's call, luring her footsteps closer.

The vampire prince turned at the low scrape of her trailing robe against the deck. His brows furrowed as she neared, darkness glinting in his eyes, warning off his guards. They turned their backs, and for all intents, the two of them were alone.

"Little bird." Kremlyn faced her, displeasure creasing his face. "Have you been gone so long you've forgotten the rules? You know better than to leave your cage."

She wet her lips, the tang of copper teasing her tongue. "Vesper sent me."

He frowned. "Did she now?"

Ophelia dipped her head, her fist tightening around the dagger hidden in her sleeve. His aura was tangible, beating against her. A malaise, snuffing out her light. Fear crept back in, and she trembled. Kremlyn's hand snaked out, gripping her throat and pulling her closer. She gasped, her hood falling back enough for his eyes to meet hers. His gaze roamed over her face, calculating.

"No, I don't think she did," he murmured, running his nose along her cheek and breathing her in. She froze beneath his predatory stare, and his fingers around her throat tightened. "You reek of blood not your own. Did I say you could feed?"

"I didn't," Ophelia rasped, fighting for air.

"Lies." He licked a spatter of gore from her jaw and chuckled darkly. Her stomach roiled, sweat beading at her brow. "Ah, I've missed you. Do you know why?"

Ophelia shook her head, eyes closed, rooted as his other hand slid around her, cruelly cupping her backside and pulling her against him. Glass ground into her flesh, and she bit back a whimper, everything he'd ever done to her crashing through her psyche and beating her down as surely as his fists had.

"Your continued defiance," he gritted out. "I long to see that fire dim in your eyes and know that I'm the one who broke you. And I will, Ophelia. I promise you that."

Her rage flickered. He already had. In so very many ways, but Gideon had put her back together, and she'd be damned before she let Kremlyn take anything from her ever again.

A low whistle sounded, and he dropped his hand from her throat. "Ah. Right on schedule." A wicked smile slicked over his face, and his attention moved from her to the sky. Ophelia's gaze darted to where he was looking.

Gideon. A fist clenched around her heart. Oh God, he'd come for her.

Vampires skittered around them, rushing to the gunwale, shouting and pointing. The fist in Ophelia's chest tightened. Gideon was struggling. He fought to gain altitude, but the beat of his wings was jerky and uncoordinated. He dipped lower toward the sea.

Oh, Deo… Please God, no. Not him…

"Do you think he'll make it?" Kremlyn crooned in her ear. "He could. I wonder how much damage he'd do before the ocean renders him completely impotent. I thought about it. Letting him land, then leaving him to suffer as a statue. Would you like him to watch you take your punishment?"

She bit back a sob, tears tracking down her cheeks. Gideon seeing her like that wouldn't just break her—it would destroy them both.

"But I've a sneaking suspicion that would end our game far too quickly, and I haven't even begun to get my fill of you." Kremlyn pulled her against him again and chuckled at her whimper. "Thank me, Ophelia. I've decided to show your gargoyle mercy instead."

He raised a hand, signaling, and a massive blast came from the ship, rocking the vessel as several projectiles sped toward Gideon. He fought to change his trajectory, but was too slow, the ocean siphoning his strength. Ophelia watched in horror as they slammed into him, grit and stone exploding into the air, and Gideon plummeted from the sky, the icy waves below swallowing him whole.

A harrowing scream ripped from her throat. "*Noooo!*"

Kremlyn chuckled malevolently, his hardening member pressing against her abdomen. "There's my little bird's song. Sing it again for me, darling. Give me all that pain from knowing you'll never see your gargoyle again."

Ophelia panted, then she wet her lips and swallowed, that strange calm descending over her like a shroud. Her rage flared anew, fear leaving her.

Her gaze slid from the waves back to the vampire prince's. He was wrong.

She would see Gideon again, and she would see Kremlyn in hell. She clutched the dagger in her hand and thrust it into his gut. He gave a strangled grunt, his eye flying wide in surprise.

"You want all my pain?" she gritted out, her voice thick with compulsion. "Then take it."

His face twitched, rage blossoming across his countenance, and his body trembling beneath her command, fighting to regain control.

"Shh…" Ophelia twisted the knife, keeping him close, his guard oblivious to what was going on. "What's the matter, Kremlyn, does it hurt?" she murmured, sawing at him. He coughed, a bloody mist speckling her face and a long line of gore erupting from his mouth, painting his chin.

Several guards glanced over at the sound, their hands going to their weapons.

Too late.

Long, writhing shadows shot from her, spearing into the troops. Vampires exploded into steaming piles of gore, their dark entrails heaped in mounds where they'd stood, bones blasted over the deck and embedded in the cabin walls, their weapons scattered across the deck.

Fear flickered in the depths of Kremlyn's eyes, and beyond it, where his soul should've been, something turned its attention toward her.

"I'm not your little bird, and tell your master Havers is mine," she hissed, another shadow rising to rope itself around his throat. Ophelia stepped back, her rage condensing into a tight ball of fury. She sent it out, her entire being willing him to suffer everything he'd ever visited upon her. Kremlyn screamed, flailing as his skin was stripped from his body, muscles erupting into gelatinous globs, and his innards exploding into steaming trails of viscera across the blood-soaked deck.

The sound of waves against the ship's hull was the first sound to register in the silence. Then the cry of birds. Their wings flapping. Landing to gorge themselves on the macabre bounty.

Ophelia staggered, the rapid the heartbeats of those cowering below the last to reach her ears. Let them stew in their fear. She wanted them to see what could happen when they finally emerged. What would happen if any of the filth dared to show their faces to her again. She was a queen, but she'd be damned again before she claimed the Citadel as her kingdom.

She knelt and plucked up a dagger by her feet, slicing through the corset and robe, then shucking it off. Her flesh a ruin of red, rubbed raw and sliced deep, and a pool of gore at her feet, she stood naked and shivering amid the massacre.

Born anew.

Her gaze found the point off the stern where Gideon had disappeared. She ran toward it and dove into the icy water.

The shock of it disoriented her, the frigid salt searing agony over her open wounds, she seized, then flailed, unable to tell which way was up, everything a murky gray green. A serpentine tail flashed past her, and then again, circling her. A merwoman floated before her, brown hair streaked with emerald billowed out around her lithe form. Her eyes were as black as the abyss, yet kind.

Ophelia pressed her hands together making wings, then pointed frantically in the direction she hoped Gideon was in, air bubbling from her lips, her gaze beseeching the woman to help her.

The merwoman cocked her head, then took Ophelia's hand, dragging her into the deep.

Long minutes passed with nothing but the murky expanse before them and circling sharks above. A group of shapes flitted by, then something long and sinuous. The merwoman gave it a wide berth, swimming faster as it neared, and heading steadily downward.

Ophelia's lungs burned, her body crying out for air. Damn it, this was going to hurt, but she inhaled, seawater searing into her lungs and burning her from the inside, her entire body throbbing. She blinked her stinging eyes, fighting back her tunneling vision. Around her, it grew darker, and the pressure changed.

Her ears popped. Shapes began to resolve from the murk, then large pillars of stone. The pointed bow of ship. Tall outcroppings of kelp swayed with the tide, and tiny fish and snails hid amongst the green-black and burgundy leaves.

The ocean floor was sandy, scattered with stones and shells. Crustaceans picked at dead things, white flesh feathering from needle-fine bones. The merwoman stopped, her hair clouding around her and her tail drawing up. She pointed ahead.

Gideon.

He'd landed with arm outstretched, and his wings unfurled. One had embedded in the ocean floor, keeping him upright. Long rays of muted light cut down around him from the surface, scintillating with the water's flow. His frozen expression was that of pure anguish.

Ophelia swam to him and wrapped herself around his torso, sobbing. No. She wouldn't let it end like this. There had to be some way to make this right!

The merwoman swam around them, circling. Her shadow fell over Ophelia.

Her shadow.

Ophelia turned, gesturing wildly for her to swim around again. The merwoman pulled back for a long moment, then seemed to understand. She hesitantly began another circuit, and Ophelia tensed, her mind going blank. Shit. Where to bring him?

Jena. Jena would know what to do. She could fix this. Ophelia focused on the third floor of the Witchery, praying to God that this would work like it had before. *Please, please, please—*

The merwoman's shadow fell over them, and Ophelia willed herself through it with Gideon, everything going black.

GIDEON RAGED INSIDE of his prison of stone. As soon as the saltwater had hit him, his form had solidified, his eyes clouding over, and his consciousness trapped. Distantly, he felt his bond to the dragon tatter and fray. Thank the Gods the beast still slept. If it hadn't, it would have already snapped its leash and gone on a rampage.

The town. The node. Ophelia. He'd failed them all. It didn't register when he settled into the seabed, already numb to everything around him. The insidious saltwater slowly saturated his stone form, pushing him deeper within. Soon, he'd cease to exist. What that looked like, he hadn't a clue. No grotesque had ever come back from the ocean's grasp. Would his soul find its way back to the node or drift eternally in this dark grave?

Time passed. Hours. Days. A millennia. He had no gauge, only the deepening sense of aloneness. Of the inevitability of his demise.

And the lingering bitterness of regret.

It made the abrupt halt of this consciousness shrinking that much worse. He raged anew. Was this it then? To be held in limbo, neither alive nor dead for the rest of his days—

No. Something…something was happening.

A spark and then a prickle, subtly growing stronger. The node's consciousness tickled his, laughing and flitting about. He growled at it, and it retreated, then returned, its power sweeping through him, pushing the ocean from his being. His consciousness expanded, filling his chest and spreading through his limbs. His fingers twitched, lungs expanding as he drew a rattling breath.

His eyes fluttered and opened.

The coven stood around him chanting, and behind them—Ophelia.

He tried to rise and fell back, his head pounding. His skin softened, wings and horns reabsorbing into his body, a thick crust of salt over his skin. Gideon spat it from his mouth as the coven ended their spell, and Ophelia rushed forward, throwing herself on him and beating his chest.

Her eyes were red and cheeks tear-streaked. "I told you to stay away from the ocean, you asshole!"

"You did. I should have listened," he grunted, woozy. He blinked, the room lit by the rising sun. "How long?"

"Almost two weeks." Ophelia burst into tears and collapsed against him.

"Mmm hmm," Sweets hummed. "You're lucky she dove in after your dumb ass and that cantrip of mine finally dried you out. We've been at it morning, noon, and night trying different ways to augment that spell. Saltwater and a damned gargoyle." She snorted. "You're lucky she could hear your heartbeat, otherwise you would've been left for dead after day one."

Gideon grunted, gratitude stinging his eyes and his heart fuller than it had any right to be. "Indeed," he managed, his thoughts still fractured and muzzy, but one thing was crystal clear.

The witch had no idea how right she was. Immersion in saltwater had always meant certain death for a grotesque. On the rare occasion one of his kind had been retrieved from the sea, reviving them had been impossible. He stroked Ophelia's hair, wondering if any of those remained trapped as he had been. He'd have to speak with the witch later. That spell would need to be relayed to Renard and the rest of his brethren.

"What about the vampires?" Gideon asked, his lids heavy. "Your father, the node?" Gods, he still felt adrift.

The coven exchanged glances.

"No one's seen my dad since he left Ophelia on the ship." Jena frowned. "From what I can piece together, he somehow convinced the node that it would save Havers if it let him take Ophelia. I mean, I guess he wasn't wrong, but…God, I hate him. I have no idea why he does any of what he does."

"I may be able to offer some enlightenment, but it's a discussion for later," Gideon said. "And the Vampire Court?"

Chase cleared his throat. "It doesn't exist anymore. After Ophelia managed to bring you here, Thaddeus claimed his place as the vampire king. He took what's left of the Crimson Guard back to the Citadel. He's promised that they won't be back, and I'm pretty sure the feds' investigation will guarantee it. Things are not looking good for the vampires or Fayet."

"No, but even if it didn't, what happened on the vampire's flagship would," Jena said, glancing at Ophelia. "Enough of them saw the aftermath to steer clear. All I gotta say is don't piss her off."

Gideon's brow quirked at Ophelia, and she shrugged.

"Female rage is a thing. We can talk about it later. Let's get you cleaned up. Right now, all you really need to know is that Havers and the node are safe."

"They were never my concern," he murmured, struggling to sit up.

A smile teased her lips. "Maybe not, but since I'm now Havers's resident *dhampir*, I'm pretty sure that it's one of mine."

After
Two Months Later

OPHELIA SAT on a stone bench outside her house, the garden around her teeming with flowers. She hummed, dipping her brush in water before dabbing it in a bit of pink to finish off the watercolor. Though it was growing late, the sprays of white tulips wavering in the breeze had been too tempting not to paint.

She bit her bottom lip, smiling at the stupid hobby and setting her brush aside. She held up the painting. Not totally crappy. God, if anyone had told her this time last year that she'd be living in a frickin' vicarage and painting flowers in her garden she would've punched them.

Actually, she still might punch them, but that was beside the point.

She sat back and fished a cigarette out of the pack at her side. Below, the town was peaceful. Surprisingly, instead of being bored, she was grateful things had calmed down. The weeks after the vampire invasion had sucked. She'd almost felt bad for Felix having to deal with the media frenzy. And Havers's residents had not been pleased about all the destruction the dragon had wrought, though you wouldn't know it now.

Especially after Chase had bought up the majority of the destroyed property. He'd used a bunch of it to expand his business, but the rest was being turned into a park and would have some kind of a kid's camp eventually. The way he talked about it, Ophelia was pretty certain he had grand plans to populate it with his and Jena's kids.

Ophelia snorted, lighting her smoke. Good luck with that. Jena still hadn't had the first one, though it was supposed to be any day now, and they still hadn't decided on a name. Aggie was so bitchy about it that the two of them were staying with Felix while the manor house was being built. Ophelia looked in that direction. Gideon had gone out there earlier to help set the foundation with Nyxx and to help the new grotesque figure out his abilities.

Him assimilating to his new form was going smoother than any of them had predicted. It probably helped that the dragon did have a human version he could morph into, and you'd never know he was a zillion pound fire breathing monster. The dude was downright scraggly. He'd moved into Thaddeus's old digs and took up right where the ancient vampire had left off as the town weirdo.

Ophelia shook her head, taking another drag, and the lights flicked on behind her. Soku must be getting ready for dinner. When Thaddeus had left to rule what was left of the vampires, Ophelia had gladly hired the brownie to keep house for her and Gideon.

Soku had jumped at the chance. From what Ophelia could glean, the revenants had really fucked the Below up, and a lot of the lesser fae had moved topside. Not that any of them would give details. Whatever was happening down there, even the pixies were staying mum. They'd collected their ungodly amount of coconuts and had been weirdly absent from the streets thereafter. Jena was kind of freaking out about it, but what kind of trouble could they get into with coconuts?

Whatever. Ophelia didn't care. She was just glad the king thing was going pretty well for Thaddeus. He'd made a bunch of sweeping changes, and the tribes weren't taking volunteers anymore. She wasn't entirely sure that was voluntary, but with the investigation the feds had opened into their involvement with the turbine conspiracy, he really didn't have a choice.

Fayet wasn't doing so hot either. The neighboring town's mayor had been ousted, and the last Ophelia had heard, the pack over there had replaced any semblance of government. That wasn't exactly a boon, considering the Fayet pack hated the one in Havers, but it was what it was.

Which also summed up the whole situation with Jena's dad. No one had seen him since that night, though Jena swore she could still feel him hanging around. Gideon had been working on tracking down every whisper and rumor of Nemeses, but whether that was really what he was, or what he really wanted, was anyone's guess. The repository in the City of Light hadn't been able to come up with anything, and whenever William's name was mentioned around the gargoyle, it put him in a foul mood.

Headlights bobbed over the hill, and Ophelia dropped her cigarette, snuffing it beneath her stiletto. A moment later, the car pulled up to the gate outside the garden, and Gideon got out, frowning.

Ophelia stood and sauntered up to the gate. "Hey, honey, how was work?" she simpered.

He snorted, walking toward her with a slight limp. Despite the witch's spell, he still suffered from his stint below the waves, but the hitch in his stride was improving. "Nyxx might have a human form, but his dexterity remains that of a lizard."

"That good, huh?"

"Mmm." Gideon pulled her into his arms. "You've been smoking," he said, nuzzling against her neck.

Her fingers tangled in his hair. "Would I do that?"

"You would," he sighed, "and now I'm not going to give you your gift."

Ophelia pulled back to glare at him. "What gift?"

"I suppose you'll never know," he deadpanned.

"Gideon!"

"Oh, very well, just wait one moment," he chuckled and kneeled down to tie his shoe. Ophelia huffed, looking up and rolling her eyes. He knew she hated it when he made her—

"Phe?"

She looked down and her breath caught as he held up the diamond engagement ring she'd left by the sink all those years ago. Her hand rose to her lips. "I-I thought it was lost?"

His intense turquoise gaze caught hers. "For a time, as you were. As I was. But now, here, in this place, Ophelia Diamondé, would you once again permit me the eminent honor of becoming my wife? I vow that I will love and cherish you for eternity."

She nodded, unable to speak, and he slipped the ring over her finger, grinning.

"I'm assuming that's a yes?" he asked, standing.

"Yes, yes, of course it's a yes!" she cried, throwing her arms around his neck and kissing him.

"I knew you'd been smoking," he murmured after a long moment, a twinkle in his eye.

Ophelia sighed. "It's a grievous crime, I know."

Gideon grinned again, wetting his lips. "And what are we going to do about that, counselor?"

"Might I suggest reeducation? I obviously have no idea what belongs in my mouth and what doesn't." She squealed as he lunged for her and raced back into the house with him hot on her heels.

Dinner would have to wait.

THE END

Special Thanks to:

Thank you first to all of my readers who have been clamoring for more Havers-by-the-Sea. Although this series was originally meant to be a standalone, my brain really doesn't work that way. Every new installment has been like opening a door to a different part of the Star-Crossed world, and it's one of my favorite things to step inside and see what's waiting for me.

Because, spoiler, I have no clue until I start writing it, and I wouldn't have it any other way. Discovering what happens is as much fun for me as it is for you.

And this is really a fun series to write. I hope that you get as much of a kick out of my sense of humor as I do. This one I giggled more than once while writing the frenemy situation between Jena and Ophelia, and the pixies somehow end up stealing the show whenever they're on the page. I promise that someday we're gonna figure out what the hell they're doing with all those coconuts.

Thank you also to my beta readers who kick my ass when it needs kicking and let me know when they're laughing at my jokes. Especially my mom, who does more of the former than the latter with that stupid pointer in hand.

Big props to my editor, Lori Walker, on this one. She co-signs my ridiculous pub dates and argues with me over legal precedent and the correct usage of "sac" as only an ex-lawyer can.

Also, so much gratitude to Jena, my PA over at Book Mojo, who designs my covers and gets done all the crap I have no idea how to do. My books would be lost in the Kindle sea if it weren't for her.

And, last but not least, there is another installment of the Star-Crossed Chronicles coming. Aside from what the pixies are doing with those coconuts, I need to figure out what William's deal is and what the heck Jena names her baby.

Until then, stay safe and don't make any bargains with stupidly charming men.

THE DAE DIARIES - URBAN FANTASY WITH SPICE

One Night in Bliss — Flame & Shadow — Air & Darkness — Playing with Fire

THE PRICE OF TALENT - SPICY DYSTOPIAN ROMANCE

Breeder — Breaker — Destroyer — Binder — Conspirator — Split Overlord — Exile — Dyad *

THE MAW OF MAYHEM - PRN MC EROTIC ROMANCE

Bites of Mayhem — The Maw of Mayhem — Grimdarke Darker — Kit-Kat — Katherine — Deuce *

STAR-CROSSED CHRONICLES

Weres and Witchery — Wards and Warlocks — Vampires and Vendettas

ANTHOLOGIES & STANDALONES

Secrets We Keep — Sense, Sensibility, & Shifters — Fairytale

*Forthcoming

ABOUT THE AUTHOR

AK Nevermore is a bestselling author of paranormal, dystopian science fiction, and urban fantasy romance. She enjoys operating heavy machinery, freebases coffee, and gives up sarcasm for Lent every year.

A Jane-of-all-trades, she's a certified chef, restores antiques, and dabbles in beekeeping when she's not reading voraciously or running down the dream in her beat-up camo Chucks.

Unable to ignore the voices in her head, and unwilling to become medicated, she writes full time. Her books explore dark worlds, perversely irreverent and profound, and always entertaining.

Want more Nevermore?
Sign up for her newsletter and never miss a release!

aknevermore.com

www.ingramcontent.com/pod-product-compliance
Lightning Source LLC
LaVergne TN
LVHW040040080526
838202LV00045B/3422